The Lan

Jane Welch was born at
centre of rural England,
sand years ago the Vik ... for the
winter, their forces led by ... Ragnar Lothbrok's sons,
including Ivar the Boneless.

Jane spent much of her childhood in a remote coastal wilderness in the Scottish Highlands. With no electricity, TV, and before internet, Jane immersed herself in reading the world's best fantasy novels and scribbling her first short stories on any paper she could find. School and work competed with her writing and it was not until taking a part time job teaching skiing in the Pyrenean mountains that she finally had the space and time to write. Surrounded by the magic of those ancient mountains, she embarked on the first of the nine books that make up the Runes of War Saga.

Jane has continued her travels and research and is now working on a new series, inspired by the beauty of the Mediterranean Sea and its remote islands. In particular, her imagination was caught by a climb to a lighthouse, ruined since antiquity, standing sentinel above twin harbours.

Jane lives and writes in beautiful Devon on the south-west coast of England with her family and noble dog, Odin.

Also by Jane Welch

The Runes of War Saga

PART ONE: *The Book of Torra Alta*
Vol 1. *The Runes of War*
Vol 2. *The Lost Runes*
Vol 3. *The Runes of Sorcery*

PART TWO: *The Book of Önd*
Vol 4. *The Lament of Abalone*
Vol 5. *The Bard of Castaguard*
Vol 6. *The Lord of Necrönd*

PART THREE: *The Book of Man*
Vol 7. *Dawn of A Dark Age*
Vol 8. *The Broken Chalice*
Vol 9. *The Allegiance of Man*

The Runes of War Saga

PART TWO:
The Book of Önd
Vol 4. The Lament of Abalone

JANE WELCH

HARPER
Voyager

Harper*Voyager*
An imprint of
HarperCollins*Publishers* Ltd
1 London Bridge Street,
London SE1 9GF
www.harpercollins.co.uk

HarperCollins*Publishers*
Macken House, 39/40 Mayor Street Upper,
Dublin 1, D01 C9W8, Ireland

This paperback edition 2024
1

First published in Great Britain by Earthlight,
an imprint of Simon & Schuster Ltd 1998

A catalogue record for this book is available from the British Library

ISBN: 978-0-00-860901-6

Typeset in Goudy by Palimpsest Book Production Ltd, Falkirk, Stirlingshire

Printed and bound in the UK using 100% renewable
electricity by CPI Group (UK) Ltd

For George, with boundless love.
Thank you for being so perfect.

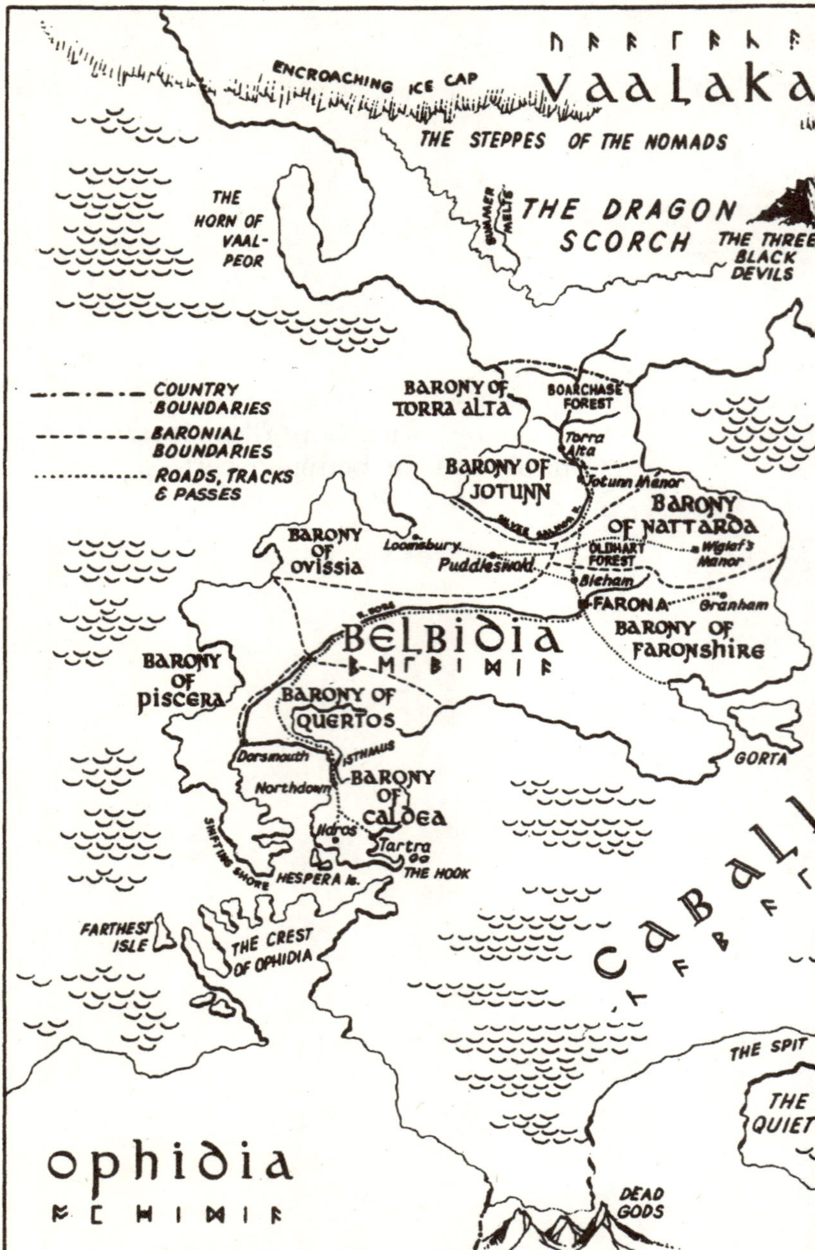
ENCROACHING ICE CAP
VAALAKA
THE STEPPES OF THE NOMADS
THE DRAGON SCORCH
SUMMER MELTS
THE THREE BLACK DEVILS
THE HORN OF VAAL-PEOR
COUNTRY BOUNDARIES
BARONIAL BOUNDARIES
ROADS, TRACKS & PASSES
BARONY OF TORRA ALTA
BOARCHASE FOREST
Torra Alta
BARONY OF JOTUNN
Jotunn Manor
BARONY OF NATTARDA
OLDHART FOREST
Wiglaf's Manor
BARONY OF OVISSIA
Loamsbury
Puddlesvold
Bleham
FARONA
Granham
BARONY OF FARONSHIRE
BELBIDIA
BARONY OF PISCERA
BARONY OF QUERTOS
Dorsmouth
ISTHMUS
Northdown
BARONY OF CALDEA
Ildros
Tartra
THE HOOK
SHIFTING SHORE
HESPERA Is.
GORTA
FARTHEST ISLE
THE CREST OF OPHIDIA
CABALL
THE SPIT
THE QUIET
DEAD GODS
OPHIDIA

ENCROACHING ICE CAP
CAIRN
CEOLOTHIA
THE TONGUE
THREE SISTERS
CAMALLIA
LAKE OF TEARS
FROSTED PEAKS
THE SERPENT
THE SMOKIES
SEA
DESERTS OF GLAN

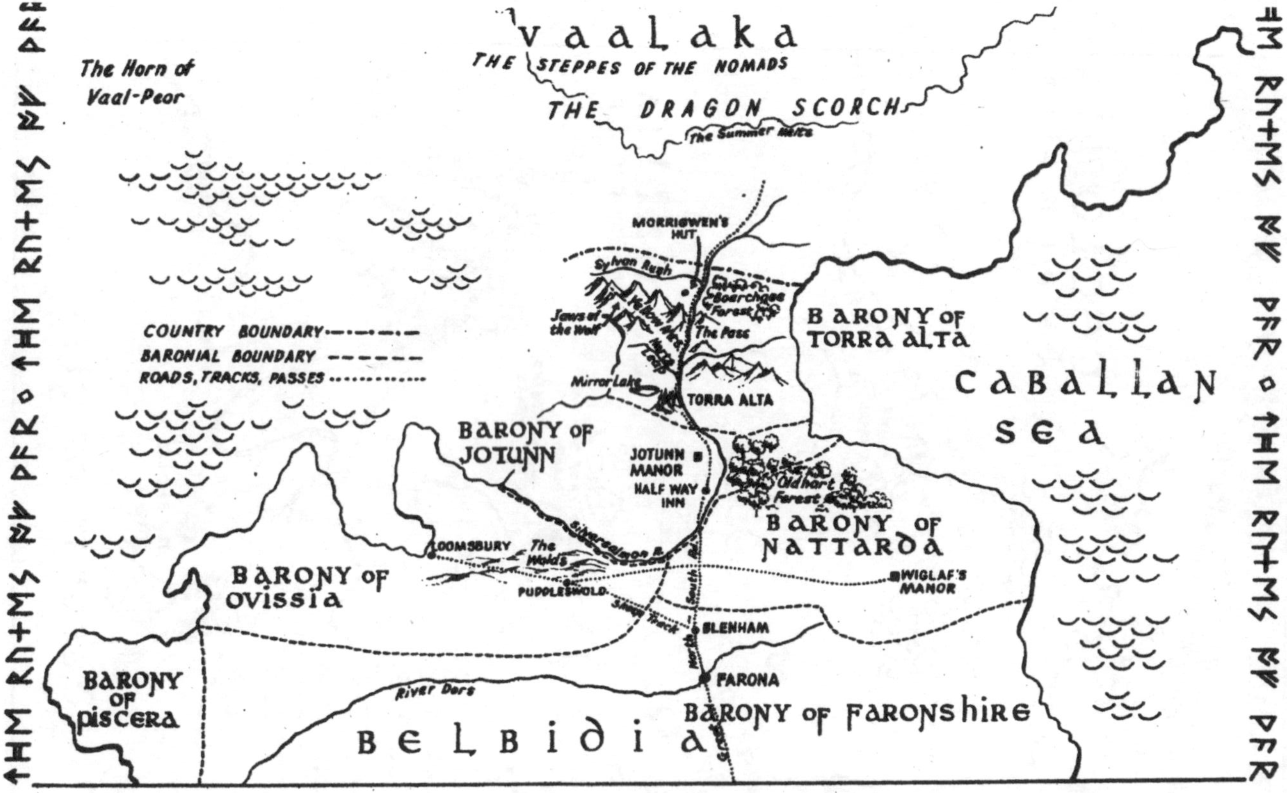

VAALAKA
THE STEPPES OF THE NOMADS
THE DRAGON SCORCH
The Summer Melts
The Horn of Vaal-Peor
COUNTRY BOUNDARY
BARONIAL BOUNDARY
ROADS, TRACKS, PASSES
MORRIGWEN'S HUT
Sylvan Rush
Boarchase Forest
Jaws of the Wolf
The Pass
Mirror Lake
TORRA ALTA
BARONY OF TORRA ALTA
CABALLAN SEA
BARONY OF JOTUNN
JOTUNN MANOR
HALF WAY INN
Oldhart Forest
BARONY OF NATTARDA
LOOMSBURY
The Wolds
Silversalmon R.
PUDDLESHOLD
South Rd.
Sheep Track
WIGLAF'S MANOR
BARONY OF OVISSIA
BLENHAM
North Rd.
FARONA
River Dore
BARONY OF PISCERA
BARONY OF FARONSHIRE
BELBIDIA

PROLOGUE

The rusted iron jaws snapped shut. Jagged points of splintered bone burst through her torn hide as the rusted teeth bit deep. Wapeka jerked back her long neck, screaming as the wrenching pain in her shattered hindleg racked through her body.

She kicked frantically to rip herself free but the iron jaws held fast. In panic, she scrabbled and tore at the metal teeth, chewing at her leg and shredding flesh. Thick dark blood smothered her blue-grey muzzle.

It was hopeless. After the frenzy of pain came seeping numbness. She knew it was over. The sadness swept through her, cutting more cruelly than the iron jaws. Only then did she turn to acknowledge the staring eyes of her three cubs. The two he-cubs, one grey, the other tawny, padded closer and started to suckle but for a moment the third, a she-cub, held back. Pure white, like the tumbling waters of the Silversalmon River, she had eyes the like of which Wapeka had never seen before in a wolf. They were beautiful but frightening in their intensity; dark blue-green, shiny like a holly leaf glistening after a frost. Her snow-fresh coat was bespattered with spots of her mother's blood, like winter ground stained by fallen ripe berries.

Wapeka's little cub began nuzzling her, urging her to get up.

The mother wolf looked at her through a deepening haze that glazed her eyes. There was nothing she could do for them now. Winter in the Yellow Mountains was harsh; they would starve without her – and if they did not, the men would get them, just as they had finally trapped her.

She thought she had outsmarted them, even the most cunning. Yes, the one with the long beard, who wore a grey-blue pelt, but he had found her den. She had been so careful to leave tracks heading towards the Chase before picking her way north again, and she had thought herself so clever when she avoided leaving tracks in the snowfields by painstakingly carrying her cubs one by one over the scree slopes. She thought she had outwitted him: the one who wore the blue-grey pelt.

She knew that pelt; her grandmother, too, had failed to outwit this trapper. How could she have been so arrogant to think she might?

She had lost. She accepted it, embraced it, hoped she would die here in the trap before the man came to torment her further. She accepted death for herself; it was part of the cycle. But not now, not yet. For the sake of her cubs not yet.

Wapeka slumped back onto her side so that her cubs could take their fill of her milk before she made them go. There was a sweet pain as they suckled: the sweet comfort of giving all that she could to them; and the agony of knowing this was the very last time. She knew their chances of survival were minimal. She closed her eyes against the pain, barely able to raise her head now. She had lost so much blood. The ravens were already gathered in the trees, waiting for her, signalling to the trapper that his snare was full. He would come soon.

The pups were whimpering. Her smallest, the little

tawny wolfling, was falling asleep after his feed but they must leave now. She snarled angrily at them to go. Swallowing back her pain, she turned to the biggest of her litter. With nudges of her wet nose, she urged him to head north towards the high mountains and the pass where the snows would still be thick. Man dared not tread those snow-clad peaks in the winter months and her sister would be there. She would protect them.

Wapeka warned her cubs that the man would come soon.

Their eyes were startled, disbelieving.

She snuffled at them, wanting to appear calmly at ease, and hoped they would understand that her time had come, as it comes to all, and that they must leave her.

The largest pup, his grey hair still fluffy, his eyes round and his tail bristling, staggered up onto his oversized feet and nuzzled at the side of her head. He made no attempt to go. The white she-cub cracked a high-pitched yowl and crept closer, her eyes imploring her mother to rise.

Wapeka desperately fought to mask her pain . . . and her sorrow. The terrible knowledge that she would not see her beautiful litter grow to adulthood, that she must die knowing they had but little chance of living through the winter, overwhelmed her. She looked from her cubs to the ragged white peaks crowning the northern horizon. She must impress on them the importance of getting to those snowbound crags. But they were so young . . .

The snow-white she-cub whined and snuggled closer to her mother's thick warm coat.

Wapeka snapped at her daughter and sharply nudged her away with her nose. Maybe her cubs would be strong enough to survive the savage cold and grim hunger that they faced without her. They had to reach the high hunting grounds where her sister would protect them.

She implored them to keep to the shadows, warning them of the eagles harrying the crags.

Eagles and more! She thought of her grandmother's warning earlier that year about the gathering of beasts in the sky. The rest of the pack had mocked the old wolf's words, saying she had grown blind with age and mistook thunderclouds for demons. But Wapeka had believed her.

She twisted her head to watch through a darkening haze as her cubs stumbled pathetically over the scree and dragged their floppy little bodies through the snow. The little white she-cub faltered, turning uncertainly back and Wapeka snarled her disapproval. With a whimper the white cub scampered after her brothers, tripping over her paws as she went.

Wapeka watched until they were lost from sight. She closed her eyes against the insufferable grief, almost welcoming the crushing pain in her hindleg. When she was too weak to raise her head, the first of the ravens dropped out of the trees and began to peck at the bloodied mess of her leg. The man would come soon, the man with the blue-grey pelt. She could smell his scent clinging to the rusty iron jaws.

Too weak to even kick at the carrion birds with her free legs, she could do no more than moan as she suffered the slow long hours of her death. Her bloated tongue lolled from her open jaws. She blinked open her eyes and watched as the ravens warily approached her muzzle. She was too weak to care. She wished the ravens would peck more voraciously and finish her off quickly, but instead they abruptly took to the wing in a startled cloud.

He was close. His odour was strong; the sour scent of man.

Great Mother, protect my cubs, she prayed. Embrace me into the bliss of Annwyn, into the one consciousness. Mother, above all else, protect my wolflings.

He stood over her, his boot level with her muzzle. She felt a stab of pain as he kicked her ribs, testing for response. She was not dead yet but it made little difference. Something glinted in the man's hand as it caught the sun – a flash of brilliant white intensity. It swelled to encompass her, like the sun engulfing a dwindling flame.

She kicked once as her body fought the pain of the knife.

Mother, I am coming home, she thought with welcome as the sweet embrace of merciful death enveloped her.

In crone's cauldron and runic stave,
In ancient henge and sorcerer's cave,
I am the power of the mage.

I am the necromancer's song;
Druid and wizard call on me;
I am the runelord's mastery;
In Earthbound magic I am strong.

In chasm deep and sacred well
In rocky steep and briny swell
And sunbright gemstone, there I dwell.

In bryony and celandine,
Oak, hazel, ash and mistletoe,
Through forest bear and sparrowhawk,
Through every man and beast I flow.

I am within: I am without
For I am Önd, the breath of life.

CHAPTER ONE

Caspar checked over his shoulder. No one was watching. In his haste he slipped and grazed his hand on the rough stone as he scurried down the slime-coated steps.

Coiling down to the forbidden underworld, the whisper of his padding footfall echoed loud in the narrow confines of the stairwell. He winced at the noise and slowed as he neared a side door that led to the disused back entrance of the wellroom. He could hear the sound of clanking chains and squealing pulleys that dredged up the sulphurous water from the roots of the Yellow Mountains to be purified by raging furnaces. Heat and golden light poured around the edges of the heavily reinforced door.

He crept on tentatively. Perhaps he should go back rather than risk displeasing all three high priestesses?

He thought how his furtive behaviour would upset his mother and disappoint Brid, and was about to turn back when a prickling sense of foreboding urged him on. Something had changed in the unlit chambers. An uncertain frown wrinkled his brow and his nostrils flared as he breathed in the stale hot air. Beyond the whiffs of sulphur from the wellroom was a smell he hadn't noticed before. And he didn't like it.

Once below the side entrance to the wellroom, he took a firebrand, that he always left in a bracket on the wall, and struck a flint. The firebrand sputtered reluctantly into flame and, in its wavering light, he hurried down the last of the steps to the outer dungeon door. Here at the bottom of the steps, the stairwell was dank and smelt of long disuse.

He reached for the ring of keys at his belt and cursed as they jangled in the stultified air. His fingers quickly felt out the familiar texture and shape of a crudely fashioned key the length of his outstretched hand. With a guilt-laden sense of intimacy, he inserted it into the steel door before him and listened as the mechanism creaked and clacked. The lock released. He shouldered his weight against the reluctant bulk of the vast doors, bruising the point of his shoulder, and forced them just wide enough for his slender frame to slip through.

Though he had thickened a little in the three years since the Vaalakan siege and his boyish muscles now had the sinewy strength of an athletic youth, he had not grown as much as he had hoped. A hazy red stubble spiked his chin but it was not dark enough to be obvious. The most noticeable changes were in his expression and mannerisms. Though his mother's return had given him a sense of worth that he had lacked through his childhood, many had commented how his honest, open manner was becoming withdrawn and moody. Caspar denied it though he knew the weight of his responsibility preoccupied his mind.

The flame of the firebrand guttered and smoked, failing to a red point that glowed for a moment before dying. Caspar swore. With nervous fingers, he trimmed the torch and hastily struck the flint of his tinderbox.

The dungeons smelt. Not of flesh nor decay. No man nor woman had been imprisoned here below the levels of the wellroom for many generations, not since his ancestor, Baron Pellinore, had spies incarcerated here during the Ceolothian wars four hundred years ago. Still the dank air held the smell of death. Caspar struck the flint again but still the fluff refused to catch. The hairs on the back of his neck prickled. He struck the flint again.

From the brief flash of light, shapes and images sprang up, sharply defined against the blackness. A body-shaped cage, hanging on rusted chains, was given eerie form and substance by an intricate weave of cobwebs that bulked its core. Again, he struck the flint. It illuminated the sinister shapes of what he knew to be shin-breaking ankle stocks. Coils of rusted chain lay like nests of sleeping snakes on the dust-choked floor. With the light gone the smell seemed stronger and his nostrils flared. He couldn't place it; sickly sweet like fouled straw from the mews yet rancid and fishy. His hand shook as he repeatedly struck the flint.

He needed the reassurance of light to calm his feral imagination. He knew there was nothing down here besides the rusted chains, a few spiders, the occasional rat and, of course, the heavy oak casket containing the Druid's Egg. He'd crept down to visit the casket countless times during the past three years. During that period the garrison had been brought back to strength and the frontier castle repaired. It seemed so much more than three years since they had driven back the Vaalakan hordes and even longer since he and Hal had first met Brid. He missed that innocent period of his youth. Too much had changed.

But the dungeons, this chamber of misery, had not changed in all that time – until now. Today he felt a twinge of fear.

At last, the tinder caught and he held it against the firebrand. It crackled back into life, the flame flickering reluctantly and the black oil giving off a dark trill of smoke that dispersed into the dungeon's gloom. He steadied his hand and took a deep breath.

The smell was gone. The dungeons seemed normal again and his overpowering fascination for the Druid's Egg quickly chased away all fears from his mind. He licked his lips with anticipation as he picked his way across the floor towards an insignificant-looking low oak door in the far corner. He unlocked it and opened it slowly, almost reverently, his mouth dry with nervous anticipation.

The door opened on a small pit hewn out of the solid rock, barely big enough to hold a cramped and stooping man. An ancient oak casket, banded by ribs of steel, its wood darkened by much polishing with linseed oil, sat inconsequentially at the back of the rocky cell. A plain but large padlock secured the hasp.

Caspar's hand itched to release the lock. He yearned to touch the Egg. His mother, Keridwen, had impressed on him that it was a fearful thing of terrible powers, too easy to misuse, and had with ominous tone called it by its ancient name, Necrönd. All three high priestesses had warned him against handling it and had even forbidden him to come down here at all; but he had responsibilities over Necrönd that they clearly did not understand and he was old enough now not to be so cowed by their disapproval. Naturally it was right to be cautious but, even though he sensed the disturbing power of the Egg, he was not afraid.

Necrönd could bring back life, could call the spirits of the ancient beasts of legend from the Otherworld and give them form. Trapped within its shell was the breath of life, the essential Önd of those beasts banished from this world by the First Druid. Their wanton savagery and brooding hatred of other life made coeval existence with man impossible and so the ancient thaumaturge had bound their life force within the Egg. Now they were no longer free to walk the Earth but were trapped in the parallel world of spirit. Only the one who held Necrönd could summon the beasts of power. And Caspar was that one. How then could he be afraid?

He checked the lock on the casket and, just to satisfy himself that he would know if anybody disturbed it in his absence, he plucked a hair from his fringe and placed it over the hasp. As he was about to squat down by the casket, the door groaned behind him. A cold sweat sprang up on his palms and forehead and the torchlight wavered in the blast of air. He steadied his breathing and told himself that it was just a sudden backdraught created by the wellroom furnaces.

His concentration had been broken but he was reluctant to leave the Druid's Egg. Rather than hurry away, as he knew he should, he thoughtfully began tracing out the runes carved deep into the wooden surface of the casket. Under Brid's tuition he had learnt much of runespells and, even if he didn't already know by heart what these sigils meant, he would have had little problem deciphering them.

After the lifting of the Vaalakan siege, Lady Keridwen had removed Necrönd from her son's possession and placed it in the casket. Together with the other two high priestesses, Morrigwen and Brid, she had inscribed the runes on the arched lid and, with the aid of Caspar's father, had it removed to the security of the dungeons.

It had taken Caspar months to find the three keys needed to reach the Necrönd but he had achieved it and, one by one, had a smith copy them before the high priestesses noticed any were missing. Later, he had felt compelled to steal the original three. With each passing year he had been more troubled by his guardianship of the Egg and decided he could not allow even his mother to have access to it but he could never find the keys again.

He feared he had risked being down here too long. What if his father, Baron Branwolf, heard of his disobedience? That was another matter altogether. He dragged himself to his feet, locked the cell door behind him and picked his way through the dungeons. Snagging his foot in a chain, he tripped, falling against the iron maiden, which swung and creaked alarmingly. The touch of the metal felt rough and cold as he steadied it. He pulled away with distaste and took hurried strides towards the dungeons' outer steel doors. Hesitating, he put his hand to the door, fearing that someone was watching. Though he could hear nothing, the uncomfortable feeling wouldn't leave him. Perhaps Morrigwen had sent someone to spy on him. Of late, she always wanted to know what he was doing. Today he felt particularly anxious and thought it prudent to extinguish his torch before he opened the door just in case anyone was looking down the stairwell for him.

He twisted his torch into the dirt of the dungeon floor to snuff the flame. The oily acrid smoke smarted his eyes and he coughed. Then, as darkness swelled into the tall chamber, he could smell the stagnant aroma again. Even through the smoke he could smell it, though it was faint as if carried from afar on a breeze. Hurriedly, he heaved open the heavy steel door. A whispered breath caressed his cheek and something lightly brushed the skin at the nape of his neck. He rushed through the door, slammed it shut with a resounding clang and fumbled for his keys. With an echoing clatter, they dropped to the floor. He stooped to retrieve them and, with sweating fingers, at last managed to lock the doors.

Trembling, he took the spiralling steps two at a time, dropped his firebrand back into its bracket and steadied himself for the last few paces before returning to the bustle of castle life. Outside the thin crisp light of early morning filled Torra Alta's inner courtyard. He inhaled the sharp air and smiled. It was mid Horning, a month he loved for its sharp freshness and silvery landscape. His breath billowed out in a cloud of warm white vapour.

"Oh, Spar," a soft voice despaired. "I thought I'd warned you."

Caspar spun round guiltily and nudged at his crooked nose with his hand before raising his eyes to meet his mother's reproving look. Her level stare pierced through to his soul. He could not hold her gaze and turned away from the deep concern welling out of her startling blue eyes.

"It does no harm. I am its master; the rules are not meant for me," Caspar protested surlily.

"You do not understand the power. Do not meddle with it; I won't be able to protect you if you do."

Keridwen did not continue to chide her son but left her warning hanging as she turned towards the keep. Her sharp departure made Caspar feel all the more guilty. Perhaps he shouldn't visit the Druid's Egg – well, not every day anyway. He knew she was expecting him to run after her to apologise and he was determined that he would not. He turned sulkily away from her just to prove that he could not be so intimidated and glimpsed Branwolf's solid figure at the arched entrance to the keep.

He decided he would take his horse out for a gallop up into the mountains and check that the trappers were obeying his father's command.

Caspar's eyes turned back to linger on Keridwen for just a second longer and he changed his mind. He didn't want to hurt her and decided that storming off like that only made him look guilty. He ran after her.

"How's Morrigwen?" he asked a little too casually, trying to divert the conversation away from himself.

"I think you should see for yourself before . . ." The high priestess faltered and turned away, gazing westward to the snow-capped mountains that glistened in the brilliant sunshine. "Time is passing. She is older now than any other person I've ever heard of." She raised her sad eyes to the blue and gold of Torra Alta's standard fluttering above the brightly coloured stone of the new west tower. The rebuilt tower stretched up even higher than before, a great lance above the blocky keep, the Dragon Standard snapping and cracking as its rich cloth caught in the sharp breeze.

The old Crone had insisted on the top turret room of the rebuilt west tower, maintaining that it gave her the best view of the Yellow Mountains. The whinstone walls of the buttressed castle, with its sheer foreboding towers were perched on a narrow pillar of rock that jutted out of the canyon. The Tor climbed to a height level with the surrounding jagged mountains, affording an advantageous view over the Pass. But, in truth, Morrigwen was rapidly losing her eyesight and Caspar doubted she could see the length of her room let alone across the canyon to the snowbound peaks.

He began the spiralling climb to the turret room. Born to the steep terrain and hard life of the mountains, his muscles hardly noticed the effort but he didn't wonder that Morrigwen barely left her rooms; the arduous climb would be too fatiguing for her frail body. If she wished to go elsewhere, a soldier was summoned to carry her – something she suffered with ill-grace.

The door to the turret room was slightly ajar and he crept in almost soundlessly on his soft-soled leather boots. Except for a humble bed, the chamber was devoid of homely attire and instead was filled with fascinating and macabre artefacts of divination. But today Caspar took in little of the details; he was too shocked to see how fragile the old Crone had become. Her wispy veil of silver hair hanging in gossamer-like tatters about her shoulders, she sat with her back to the door, gazing west towards the Yellow Mountains that Caspar could see through the narrow crack of an arrow slit window. Sitting neatly on a low stool at her feet was a young girl stroking a scaly red salamander that basked and blinked in the warmth of a crackling fire. Her luxuriant chestnut curls were swept back off her innocent, wide-eyed face and caught in a gold clasp at the back of her head. She was reading aloud from a dark leather-bound tome that rested in her lap, the coarse yellow leaves rustling as she turned them.

The sound of the girl's mellow voice, full of the soft northern accent of the Boarchase, distracted Caspar. He stopped in his tracks, contemplating her privately for a moment before she was aware of his presence. Wistfully, he noticed how the early morning sun slanting through the window spangled the burnished colours of her hair. May was not so attractive as Brid but she still made his heart flutter. Brid was long since lost to Hal and plans for their wedding were to be made on his young uncle's return.

The old Crone raised a thin, hideously twisted hand to silence the girl's reading. "So, Spar, you have managed to drag yourself away from Necrönd and deigned to visit me."

Caspar started, his freckled complexion blushing a deep crimson as May turned in alarm at his unannounced presence. "How did you know?" he stammered, losing his cultivated composure and feeling foolish.

"I always know. My eyes may be failing me but I've not lost my senses. You've grown so darkly brooding this past year that you make the air turn cold about you. Come, sit by the fire. Here at my feet. You seem in need of warmth and contemplation. Merrymoon, read on." The ancient high priestess always insisted on calling May by her given name.

May rose, offering a polite curtsey to the son of her liege-lord. "Lord Caspar," she stammered.

"Don't. Please," he hissed as he settled himself at the old Crone's feet. Try as he might he had failed to make the girl feel comfortable with him. She seemed afraid of his friendship and, even after three years of politely trying to court her, she still kept him aloofly at arm's length. "Please call me Spar," he begged.

May drew her legs closer towards her chest, tucking her woollen skirt neatly around her ankles in retreat, and flitted him one brief enigmatic look before returning to the tome in her lap.

"Oh, May, please—" the Baron's son started to protest but stopped when Morrigwen turned her frosted white eyes on him, searching helplessly for his features.

"Leave her be, Spar, and sit," she commanded imperiously.

Caspar could not disobey. Though he was the son of one of the most powerful barons in Belbidia, the old Crone still intimidated him though he liked to pretend she did not.

"Read on, Merrymoon." Morrigwen slumped back into her creaking rocking-chair while the girl fumbled for her place.

"'*And before the old Crone should die, the Maiden must seek throughout the world to find her successor.*'" May stopped in her tracks. "Must I read this, Morrigwen? It speaks of things that should remain unspoken . . . It is not yet time . . ."

"Child, I despair of you. It is well beyond time. Would you have me suffer in this decrepit, aching body forever? Brid is shortly to be married – that is, if ever that arrogant young man returns from doing the King's bidding in Farona. When that happens, she cannot be the Maiden anymore. And, besides, do you honestly believe I will see it through another winter? We must find the child who will, in turn, take on the responsibilities of the Maiden, the Mother and the Crone and we must find her quickly. The Trinity of high priestesses must survive."

Her swollen fingers clawed impassionedly at the arm of her chair. She took short wheezing breaths before bursting out angrily, "Who will continue the work to guide the people in the ways of the Great Mother? There will be pestilence and more plagues. There is so much more work to be done. Two years ago, when half the spring lambs in Ovissia died of a failing sickness, I thought the landlord farmers would listen to us and turn to our ways, just as the common folk were doing. Didn't you?" she demanded of Caspar.

He nodded compliantly, wishing only to quiet her outrage for fear that her anger might suddenly be too much for her frail body.

"After the loss of the lambs," she continued, "I thought they would see that the sicknesses were due to the excessive numbers of sheep they farmed but instead the farmers only made things worse. To counter their losses, they have done nothing but increase their stock numbers. I know the common folk, who daily feel the soil beneath their feet, understand but the powerful and the rich want more power and more riches and in the end, there will be nothing for any of us. The sickness will get worse. They disturb the balance of Nature and now, even here in Torra Alta, we are forced to cull the wolves. They blame the wolves on us because we preach that they should live to maintain the balance, but of course the wolves are moving south when there are so many sick lambs to be had there. I have not enough years left in me to make them understand!" Her voice rose with anguish and, again, she beat the arms of her rocking-chair with clenched fists. "What will become of the Yellow Mountain wolf if we do not soon find a new Maiden? Those that hate the old ways will triumph and all will be lost."

"But there is no one now who actively opposes the ways of the Old Faith," the auburn-haired youth protested. "Even King Rewik has permitted us to worship as we wish."

"Dear, dear Spar, how ever could you have been born so innocent? There are always enemies. Your own uncle, Gwion, lived alongside you, his evil intent festering for twelve years, and not once did you smell it." She shuddered. "And to think I brought him up as my own son. You killed him, Spar, but you cannot free me from the haunting memory of his evil. It's like he's still in this room, trying to poison me with his foul breath where he failed with the fang-nettle. I wish you had brought his body home or at least found it. Often, I fear he did not really die."

She fell silent for a while, sorrowfully lost in regretful contemplation before returning to the point. "Of course, there are many who still oppose the Old Faith. The greed

of the wealthy stops them from hearing our quiet voice of reason and their recent losses turn them further away from the path."

Caspar rubbed at his nose, resentful that the priestess had made him seem foolish in front of May. Though the girl's hazel eyes remained lowered to the page, he still felt that she was assessing him. But she showed no sign of heeding their exchange and softly continued to read aloud from the ancient text.

"'*Heed that the Maiden be of innocent age when she is ordained into the Trinity for only then will she fully learn the secrets of the ancient ways. Without father and without mother must she be to avoid prejudice and favour. With the wild gleaming eyes of the old ways this child, blessed by the Great Goddess, will be found under a favourable moon. Love her dearly for she is the future, the spring of all hopes, the vessel of our ancient words, bearing them to the never-ending generations of tomorrow.*'"

Morrigwen sighed and raised her hand for the girl to stop. "I have twice performed the search. Once for Keridwen and once for Brid. In both instances the search took many years. Would that I had started this quest long since but the signs were not favourable. Now each new dawn for three years without fail, I have cast the rune stones and each day they have been unfavourable – until this morning. Today I cast the runes and they told me that somewhere on the face of the Mother Earth, a new chapter in history has begun. The search must commence. She must be found." The ancient Crone paused in her croaking speech, her breath coming in hoarse gasps. "Then will I die at peace. For I have waited long enough for this release. The cycle of life, death and rebirth must be completed. My body pains me." She moaned and let her head droop onto her chest.

Caspar presumed she had fallen asleep and began to

rise but as he did so, she snapped her head up and croaked angrily at him, "Build the fire up, boy."

May blushed at the abrupt tone used towards the Baron's son.

Caspar smiled, untroubled by the form of address. Once, perhaps, he would have been wounded by such demeaning treatment, but he didn't care now; his confidence had grown in the years since his mother's return and he would come of age by the end of the summer. He knew he was nearly a man and that was all that mattered. He collected wood from a willow basket at the far side of the room and brought it to the hearth.

"No, boy, no," Morrigwen scolded. "Not ash, not Nuin. Burn the hazelwood, burn Coll. It is my only strength now. The smoke enhances my inner senses and hones my intuition. Such is all that is left to me now."

As Caspar sought through the log basket, carefully selecting the slender brown-grey branches of hazel, Morrigwen let her head slump against the fur-covered back of her rocking-chair. Her fingers, the joints swollen and crooked, worried over the shards of smooth bone in her cupped palm, each time-worn piece engraved with a single sigil. "I trust you have paid heed to your lessons in the use of runes," she croaked at the youth.

He nodded and, remembering that the old woman could no longer see through the opaque white layer that glazed her once vivid blue eyes, coughed and muttered, "Yes, Morrigwen, of course."

She grunted sceptically. "Then carve ᚲ, Kano the rune of fire on that hazel log."

Caspar felt for the small knife that he kept in his belt. "The rune of fire carved on hazel should bring a flash of insight," he said brightly, keen to demonstrate his knowledge.

Morrigwen's eyebrows rose in brief surprise and a faint smile stretched smooth the crinkled lips of her toothless mouth. "Mind you carve it neatly and with the love of the Great Mother in your heart. I must divine what the fates have prepared for us."

Painstakingly, he etched the rune into the grain of the wood. "Great Mother, open our eyes and lend us the sight," he murmured and tossed it into the fire.

Again, a rare smile flickered across the old Crone's face. "We'll make a true runelord of you yet, Spar."

Caspar grinned at the unexpected and uncustomary warmness in the old woman's tone and, as he raised his face to study her expression, he was surprised to see that the crepey folds around her mouth and eyes had already sagged into the relaxation of sleep. Her mouth lolled open and a gentle snore escaped in uneven snuffles from her throat. May rose and pressed her palms around the woman's blue-white hands, her eyebrows slanting as she drew them together in concern.

Though the Crone slept, Caspar was loath to leave the chamber: the air was too charged with sorcery. He sensed the hazelwood smoke opening up the channels of magic. He crossed to a low stool and sat breathing in the sweet, homely smell, letting his imagination dance with the flames, surging and fading with the wild energies of the fire. He wondered briefly how his young uncle Hal fared on his journey to the court of King Rewik. No doubt he would be riding with Ceowulf as planned. The youngest son of the Baron of Caldea, Ceowulf, had spent the winter with their neighbour, Baron Bullback of Jotunn, after marrying his daughter, Cybillia.

On the day of his departure Hal had loudly announced that he would set the date for his own wedding on his return. Caspar gulped back his torn emotions, remembering how Brid had laughed delightedly, though there had been a hint of reservation in her smile.

He had overheard her whispering to Hal, "You don't know what you're saying. I am one of the Three." He had noted her quick glance towards the older priestesses.

Caspar's mind embraced the vivid image of Brid's lithe form.

"Brid!" The Crone lurched forward in her chair, dropping the runes as she woke abruptly from her sleep. The sigil-carved bones clattered across the floor, sending the scarlet salamander scurrying to cower beneath May's stool.

"Whatever's the matter?" May demanded, glancing between Morrigwen and Caspar who had already leapt to his feet.

The Crone waved a dismissive hand, while placing the other across her chest to still her fluttering heart. "Just a dream. I dreamt of Brid." She squinted at Caspar. "You want to know where she is, Spar?" May wrinkled her nose uncomfortably. "You'll find her down by the inner portcullis." Morrigwen looked distractedly around the room before finally craning forward and squinting at the runes scattered on the floor. "What do they say?" she demanded.

"It's Brid's signature rune; the rune of the Maiden," May told her plainly and without warmth.

Caspar scooped up the fallen bones and placed them in Morrigwen's open palm. As he did, the sound of shouting from the courtyard below drifted up to the high turret room.

With unnatural haste and firmness for one so old, the woman grasped his wrist. "Spar, find out what the problem is and see to it," she ordered, releasing him and sitting back in her rocker. "Merrymoon, read on," she added and shut her eyes.

Caspar was only halfway down the stairs of the west tower when he heard Brid's voice rising above the commotion. Normally soft and melodious, today it was steely cold with anger. Though her voice was hardly raised, the chill in it cut colder even than the crisp Horning air. Anxiously Caspar quickened his pace.

"You evil man!" Brid snarled. "That wolf was nursing. Look at the pelt! The teats are swollen. Did you murder her cubs too?"

"It was not murder." The trapper looked uncertainly from his shaggy long-maned horse with its grisly burden to the young lady who stood before him in riding leathers, breeches and a thick bearskin cloak about her shoulders. A white, squat terrier with black slit-eyes glinting in an ugly heavy-boned skull, bristled at her heels. The dog's ears were laid flat against its bulbous short-muzzled skull. The trapper's long-legged wiry-haired hound retreated with its tail between its legs and growled nervously. "It's the tax, you know, the Wolf Tax, lass." He seemed uncertain of Brid's station. "It's good King Rewik's way of ridding the country of these beasts. It's me duty . . . um, miss, my lady, um, miss."

His eyes flitted between the girl's plain clothes, the silver torcs adorning her arms and the simple circlet that graced her high forehead, pinning back the coppery brown hair from her face.

"So were there cubs or not?" Brid demanded furiously. "King Rewik is a fool. It's all so cruel and unnecessary. The Yellow Mountain wolf is already scarce and seldom troubles man. If I had true power in this land, I would stop this barbarism. The tax should apply only to the hooded wolf. All you trappers care about is the money. One hundred wolf pelts is far too high a toll. They cannot survive it."

The man shrugged. "I thought that was very much the idea, but I'm not here to philosophize, miss. I've simply brought their pelts to the castle so I can collect what's due to me." The trapper sounded almost sure of himself but the flicker of confidence faded from his eyes as Caspar's mother swept across the courtyard towards them. Her fine cloths and glittering jewellery made it quite clear that she was of notable status. The trapper turned and bowed awkwardly.

Caspar quickened his pace to join his mother. A crowd was quickly gathering around the tall trapper, who hunched his shoulders defensively, his dark scratchy beard mingling into the stained hairs of his wolf-skin cloak. His sullen eyes looked guardedly around him. "Madam, I've done no harm," he addressed Keridwen. "The young lady accuses me of murder though I do only as is right and lawful."

The crowd pressed forward and Caspar knew he should be doing something to defuse the situation.

"He's not from these parts," an archer ventured, "otherwise he would know better than to come here with a nursing wolf, a mother wolf."

Caspar raised his right hand high above his head and cleared his throat to speak. "Men, please—"

"Stand aside!" Baron Branwolf's booming tones filled the courtyard. "What commotion disturbs the ease of my castle?"

Silence clamped its hand over the men and the crowd respectfully parted at the approach of Baron Branwolf. Thick-set and greying, the Baron swept back his heavy bearskin cloak from his shoulders, revealing a blackened hauberk. Though patched and repaired and long past its prime, it was obviously an old faithful friend, too valued to be cast out. The only mark of his baronial status was a blocky ring upon the little finger of his left hand and the confident glint of authority in his olive-green eyes. With a flick of his hand, he gestured for all to stand back while he dealt with the disturbance.

The archers hastily retreated and Caspar dutifully moved aside though both Keridwen and Brid remained firmly put. Small statured women with vivid eyes and neat elven features, both were too furiously intent on the trapper to withdraw.

"What's the problem here?" the Baron asked.

"He's taken a nursing wolf! A mother wolf!" Brid accused, pointing at the long blood-drenched skin that hung limply from the buckles of the trapper's saddle. The man was clad in padded skins, dingy and stained from the snows. His wolf pelt cloak, fair hair and long lean body immediately set him apart from those around him. Torra Altans were, for the most part, dark and heavily built, save for those like Brid, Caspar and his mother who had the delicate features, reddish-toned hair and bright eyes of the old tribes.

As Branwolf looked the skins over, the trapper began to fidget uncomfortably. "I didn't see no cubs, sir. I get paid the same price for a wolf whether she's with cubs or not so I didn't think to look, sir." He withdrew from the Baron's glare and sidled to the far side of his horse while the nobleman studied the skins.

Impatient with anger, Brid moved to draw the Baron's attention to the grey-blue pelt but Keridwen caught the young priestess's hand and pulled her back. "My lord Branwolf, have this man paid and dismissed. What's done is done." Her voice was cool and dispassionate.

"I've not done yet!" Brid would not be silenced. "Where did you murder this wolf?" She stabbed her finger at the tall trapper. "At least we can save her cubs."

"Save, my lady? Save wolflings?" He looked helplessly towards the Baron. "Sir?" The man's confusion had evidently made him forget his situation.

The Baron's presence pervaded the castle and there was rarely call for him to raise his voice. "You're not from this barony, are you, trapper?" he stated calmly as if talking to a child. "The slaying of a mother wolf in these parts is regarded as an affront to the Great Mother. The mother wolf is a sacred beast. And these are all Yellow Mountain wolves. You and your fellow trappers should put your skills to culling the hooded wolves that are causing all the problems." He nodded sagely, giving the man time to absorb his words. "So, trapper, where are you from? I would know whose men are in my barony."

The trapper took a pace back from the nobleman's intimidating presence. "Ovissia, sir," he replied succinctly, looking sideways at Brid before turning his attention to the lead-rein that he fumbled between his fingers.

Caspar might have guessed. Not only did the barony of Ovissia refuse to embrace the Old Faith, but also its livelihood was based on sheep farming. The hatred of the wolf was bound to run deep there.

"A sacred mother wolf! He's slain a sacred mother wolf; the animal that gives more to its offspring than any other. What will befall us now? What evil has he brought on us?" Brid was incensed.

"One hundred wolves a year," Keridwen bemoaned the toll. "Branwolf, you must do something. The Yellow Mountain wolf faces extinction yet the numbers of hooded wolves increase monthly. What does King Rewik hope to achieve?"

The Baron managed to ignore his wife and said with finality, "Trapper, take your pelts to the tanner. He'll pay you your dues. This business is finished," he declared loudly, turning on his heels and sending his men scurrying back to their posts. Keridwen swirled round, her loose skirts ruffling belatedly like a mist disturbed by the breeze, and hurried after him.

Caspar didn't know what to think. Branwolf could hardly defy Rewik in this matter. After the huge costs of the Vaalakan war, the country was weak and vulnerable; the baronies had to remain united. Torra Alta had suffered most, its garrison all but annihilated. Nowadays the fortress seemed to ring with the high-pitched voices of the new recruits. They were youths and boys enlisted from the outlying countryside, sons of woodcutters and huntsmen mainly. Caspar knew it would be many years before even half those wishing to be archers would be strong or skilled enough to draw a full-sized Torra Altan war bow. The fields far below in the canyon were permanently laid out for practice.

Still flecked with sweat from the arduous climb up the spiralling road to the castle, the trapper's horse plodded across the slippery cobbles towards the tannery. Brid paced after him in defiance of the Baron's wishes and Caspar fell in alongside.

"How could he? A she-wolf with cubs." Brid glowered at Caspar as if it were *his* fault. "We must find the cubs. We must do everything we can to save them and lessen the evil that will befall us for allowing the slaughter of a mother wolf. You will make him say where he killed her."

Caspar nodded. Whatever his father had commanded he could not deny Brid. Together they watched as the trapper tied his horse to a ring in the stone wall outside the tannery.

The tannery was tucked behind a wall downwind of the kitchens and was entered through a low arched door.

Inside a wizened old man with hands wrinkled like the shell of a walnut stirred and prodded at the contents of one of several large vats filled with rusty brown liquid in which sheets of skin bobbed and glugged. The trapper had already taken his skins inside. Caspar recoiled at the smell. He was unaccustomed to having a tannery within the fortress walls since the work had previously been carried out in local villages but with the introduction of the Wolf Tax the tannery had been moved to the castle. Under the king's edict, the Baron was responsible for paying the trappers the required amounts for each dead wolf and the delivery of the cured pelts to Farona, the wealthy capital of Belbidia.

The tanner bowed his head politely as Caspar and Brid marched into the tannery. "Good morning, Master Spar, my Lady Brid. You look troubled."

"The wolf." Caspar pointed at the blue-grey pelt.

The tanner nodded in immediate recognition and sadly stroked the downy hide. "Aye, this one had cubs." He glowered at the trapper whilst sorting through the rest of the skins. "They're all Yellow Mountain wolves so you'll only get the lower payment. I've had just the one hooded wolf this year as yet." He nodded towards the large skin pulled taut on stretchers at the end of the room. It was a big pelt, at least half as big again as the other skins around it, the hairs of its dark granite-coloured hide short and coarse. It had a black face and a thick black shaggy mane that rose to a tuft between its ears, giving it its name. The curved eye-teeth looked as long and as lethal as those of a large mountain cat.

The trapper shrugged. "If you don't mind, I'll have me money and be gone."

"First you'll tell us where you killed the she-wolf," Caspar said, struggling to keep his voice calm.

"To the west. I've not been long in these mountains and I'm not so sure of the local names for each peak and valley."

Caspar was piqued that the man seemed unintimidated by his displeasure but reasoned that by his very nature a trapper would have to be a hardened and self-reliant man to survive out in the harsh mountains alone. "Beyond Mirror Lake? The high tarn whose still waters reflect vividly the ring of peaks around it."

"Oh aye, if that's its name, way beyond. And beyond that high pass with the jagged white peaks."

"The Jaws of the Wolf."

"Yeah, near there. I got this one on the lower slopes towards the Chase. I saw several of them big, hooded beasts up there in the pass. Teeth like daggers in the moonlight. But I didn't trap any – more's the shame."

Brid snorted indignantly. "Traps! Couldn't you have used a bow?"

"Begging your pardon, my lady, I don't think you'd bear such a liking to these beasts if you had first-hand knowledge of them. They're not like the Yellow Mountain wolf at all and will even attack without the support of the pack. There's a cruel intelligence about them that fair chills the soul of a man."

Brid raised her eyebrows and looked disdainfully at the man as if he were half-witted. "You shouldn't use traps. It's barbaric and indiscriminate. All you're doing is slaughtering the native Yellow Mountain wolves who cause no trouble to anyone. It's the hooded wolves that attack the livestock of the lowlands."

Brid's dragon-green eyes fixed him for a long hard moment before she spun on her heel and hurried to consult Lady Keridwen about what was to be done about the death of the sacred mother wolf.

Having nothing more to say to the trapper, Caspar walked quickly to the watch-house where he was overdue to meet May's younger brother, Pip. Branwolf had ordered him to see to the day's training sessions and Caspar wanted the boy to lay out a range of targets. He had hoped that May would be pleased if he gave her younger brother some responsibility. He pursed his lips and exhaled sharply through his crooked nose. Pip was not there. He waited for a moment but then caught the tantalizing aroma of freshly baked oatcakes and sizzling venison. Tempted himself, he set off for the kitchens. He knew where he would find Pip.

"May!" he said in surprise as he turned the corner and nearly flattened her.

"Master Caspar," she said without smiling, "Morrigwen wants you again. I've been looking all over. Where have you been?"

"With Brid," he said innocently.

The girl's slanted eyebrows rose almost imperceptibly and, to Caspar, her smile seemed sad in response to his grin of warm welcome.

"Of course," she said simply, her tone becoming more aloof. "Morrigwen wishes to see you." She turned abruptly and walked away, leaving Caspar wondering how he had offended her.

CHAPTER TWO

The dark well of worn and uneven steps beckoned. Caspar could have reached Morrigwen's rooms by a different route without crossing the inner courtyard, where the black stairwell drank the sunlight falling into the courtyard, but he couldn't resist the lure of Necrönd. Besides, he could hear his father's deep booming voice echoing from near the stables and he knew he would instantly be sent to organize the younger recruits with their archery practice. Branwolf would take no excuses; not even a summons from Morrigwen over-ruled the word of the great warlord so Caspar thought it best to avoid him.

He intended only to look down into the darkness on his way past but his skin prickled and he hesitated, itching to slip down just for one little peek. He hadn't actually opened the casket in over a month now and he needed to feast his eyes on the delicate shell. He found it fascinating that something as fragile and simple as an egg could contain such dark necromantic power.

He needed to look.

No, he should look, he corrected himself. It was his responsibility and, though much of his fear earlier that morning might have been imaginary, there had been that smell. He wouldn't keep Morrigwen waiting long.

As always, he looked hastily over his shoulder before

slipping down into the blackness. Grunting, he heaved open the steel dungeon door.

He caught his breath. The light from the smoking torch cast ghostly patterns across the dungeon's floor, making the iron maiden appear to swing silently on its rusted chain above him. He shuddered and, fumbling through his keys, picked his way across the dusty floor to the cell in the far corner. He unlocked the wooden door and squeezed into the pit to kneel before the oak casket, his eyes skimming first over the runes and then the lock.

The hair was gone!

His mind raced back over the morning and he racked his brain to remember his precise movements. He had placed a hair there, hadn't he? He was sure he had but then began to feel doubtful. So much else had happened that morning. He had been disturbed by the unusual aroma, distracting him from his usual routine, and perhaps he had failed to put the strand in place? Maybe the movement of air when he slammed the door closed on his hurried exit had dislodged it? But that had never happened before.

His heart thumped in his throat and his sweating fingers fumbled awkwardly on the hasp. He barely dared look inside for fear that Necrönd might be damaged or missing.

He exhaled his held breath. It was safely intact! Relief and pleasure flooded through him as he beheld Necrönd. Its surface was smooth, pearly white veined with threads of blue, and it was quite astonishingly magical to look at. So small, so delicate, so powerful! Slowly he inched his eager fingers forwards to caress it. He could solve all their problems so easily if only he were allowed to use it. But the high priestesses, the mortal embodiment of the Great Mother, had forbidden it and he must obey.

If only they would let him once more wield its power,

he could force King Rewik to see the error of his Wolf Tax. All he need do was summon something appropriate. Not a dragon, he told himself – he would never be so foolish – but perhaps a few giants to march on the capital. He smiled. Surely that would please Brid.

Without once taking his eyes from the Egg, he continued to think on the subject and the idea seemed more and more tempting. And if he could force King Rewik to cancel the tax, why stop there? Why not remove the king entirely? His policies were harmful to Belbidia. King Rewik was a devout follower of the New Faith, was an enemy of the Great Mother; he passed laws that distressed the land. Too much grain and too many over-fat cows gnawed at the soil, weakening Her, maiming Her. Surely it would be of benefit to remove King Rewik and place someone more suitable on the throne, someone devout in their following of the Great Mother.

Someone like Hal, he thought with a laugh. The absurdity of the idea!

His thoughts darkened. And if he could make Hal king, then why not himself? Surely that would be the right thing to do since he was the one who wielded Necrönd. He blinked and swallowed hard, his mind creeping into the heart of the Egg, aware of the massive presence of life held within that fragile shell. With a start he realized that he was already holding it. His lips were dry and his heart thumped guiltily, his pulse pounding in his ears. Consciously he set it back onto its cushion of moss and wiped his hands on his breeches, his shoulders rasping against the stone walls to either side. He sat back on his haunches to think and gather his will.

The Druid's Egg looked so harmless on its nest of moss. Anyone might have argued that it should be placed on a velvet cushion edged with ermine but Keridwen had laughed at the absurdity of the suggestion. "It's an egg and a nest is best lined with moss. There is nothing more right nor more reverent than the natural substances grown of the earth," she had said.

He jumped back with a start, his skin afire. Already his hand was back on the Egg. He was disgusted with himself. How could he be so weak? He was heir to Torra Alta; no baron of a frontier castle could be weak. He should prove his control by summoning a power and demonstrating his mastery over it. A little voice at the back of his mind, quietly reproving like his mother's, told him that this was exactly what the creatures on the other side wanted; he was giving in to them. Stubbornly, he ignored it. He would summon something, something not too dangerous; a centaur, that would do. Holding Necrönd, he withdrew from the cramped pit into the wider dungeon and concentrated on the image of the beast in his mind.

But other beings flashed through his mind. The flared nostrils of a dragon, gushing bursts of fire, made him hug Necrönd to his chest. The image blurred into the broad-headed, squat form of an ogre that he could so easily use to subdue King Rewik. Then more vividly came the image of a creature he had often seen on heraldic insignia. It had the rear end of a horse and the forequarters and head of a lion with vast bat-like wings sprouting from its back. He had no name for the beast but he was intrigued by so complicated a being. How beautiful, he thought and concentrated on the image.

He felt the blast of wind as vast wings beat the air. Eyes glistened in mid-air before him, surrounded only by a hazy outline. Red: he sensed red. Again, they buffeted the still air of the chamber. The torchlight wafted to almost nothing, plunging the chamber into darkness. A slow smile spread across his face as he relished his power.

Caspar sprang to his feet, clutching the Druid's Egg. "No!" he commanded, suddenly grasping what he had done. "No, I forbid you to take form!"

The air shimmered and stilled, and the manifestation blended back into the dark crevices of the dungeon stonework until it was finally gone. He sensed the energy seeping out of him and released his held breath. His nostrils twitched. He could smell that stale stench again and wondered if it had come from the ghostly beast. Feet astride, he steadied himself, blinking until the torchlight gained in strength.

The shadowy beast was gone, though the iron maiden swung and creaked on its rusted chain. Caspar felt sickened. He had used the energy of Necrönd and for no good cause but just for childish curiosity. He was a fool.

Determinedly, he replaced the Druid's Egg, snapped the hasp closed and hastily locked it, his hands shaking. He snapped off a strand of hair, licked it to give it stick, and carefully used it to span the lock before retreating from the dungeons.

Remembering Morrigwen's summons, he urgently began to run. She would be furious that he had taken so long. He must think of an excuse; but what to say? No, it was no use; he couldn't lie to her. Ashamedly, he recognized that Necrönd was turning him into a fugitive. He would not lie yet nor could he admit to tampering with the Egg. He was the Baron's son after all; he would, with dignity and purpose, simply inform the priestesses that he had been busy.

He stopped before he reached the wellroom door to steady his panting. Inhaling deeply through his nose, he was troubled by that faint aroma again. It was clearly distinct from the sulphurous smell from the wellroom; not nearly so pungent but stale and dank. He put his hand on the whinstone wall to steady himself. A feathering of air breathed over it. He marvelled at so soft a touch, like the caress of fine fur, but the breeze was cold and his fingers felt stiff where they touched the wall. He remembered the soft feel of the wolf pelt brought in by the trapper and swallowed back the bile in his throat. Was it all his fault? Was the plague of hooded wolves caused by his meddling? He had only occasionally allowed himself the thrill of handling the Druid's Egg and, just like today, he had always sent the beasts back. Surely, he had done no harm.

Screwing up his eyes against the brightness of the sun, he emerged into the courtyard and hurried for the keep, thinking to reach the west tower via the long corridors and cloisters rather than heading straight across the open ground of the courtyard. His mother might be watching and he didn't want her to see him coming from the direction of the dungeons.

The lower hall of the keep was still empty after the Vaalakan siege; its roof timbers, charred black after the fires, still unprepared. Pale rectangles on the darkened walls marked where tapestries had once hung and brightened the chamber with vivid scenes of battles, dragons and hunting parties. Only one tapestry now brightened the lower hall. It was still vividly coloured though light from a high window slanted down on it and its newness was plain to the eye. Baron Bullback of Jotunn had sent it as a victory present after the war and though Branwolf was pleased with the gift he had expressed his wish that their neighbour had sent something more practical; a couple of oxen perhaps to help drag the weighty loads of stone up the Tor needed for the rebuilding of the battlements. The tapestry depicted the Baron himself replanting the Dragon Standard above the keep, bodies of the Vaalakan dead heaped in rotting piles on the canyon floor far below. Triumph blazed from the Baron's eyes, his fist thrust up in victory. Caspar hurried past. He had the sense that those eyes followed him.

As he reached the door, which took him to a further corridor running to the base of the west tower, he paused. He well remembered the vast, colourful tapestry depicting the Ceolothian attack on the castle over four hundred years ago that had once hung here.

The figure of his great ancestor Baron Pellidore, standing tall above the crenellations and firing arrows alongside his bowmen, was etched firmly in Caspar's mind. It had been a bloody battle and the Ceolothians slaughtered in vast numbers. With that battle, the war had been won. Then as now, the Ceolothians had no fleet capable of taking on the great ships of Belbidia that were the undoubted masters of the Caballan Sea. Their only route into Belbidia was from the North across the Dragon Scorch of Vaalaka and down through the Pass of Torra Alta. Caspar had particularly liked the tapestry; he was proud of his noble ancestor and Pellinore's bravery against such numbers.

Despite Pellinore's blood in his veins, he was not so brave that he could face the thought of Morrigwen's displeasure and her probing questions without some trepidation. He ran the rest of the way, his leather soles slapping on the cool dark stones of the cloistered corridors. He swung through a door and tackled the spiralling steps of the west tower two at a time, arriving at the top turret room breathless and somewhat giddy.

The chamber was darkened by shutters though the fire was lit and four candles fluttered as he burst open the door. He had seen the strange objects in Morrigwen's chamber many times before but in the gloom they seemed more awful and sinister, the artefacts of augury and divination brooding in dark shadows around the chamber. A pot bubbled gently over the embers of the fire; a dragon's claw, curved and vicious like a sabre, hung over the mantel beside the skull of a horse; candles, chalices and daggers caught the red glow where they lay in deliberate patterns on a circular table in the centre of the room. Caspar's eyes flitted over the hares' feet, the minute bodies of wrens and rows of ermine tails, before he raised his eyes to greet the ancient priestess.

He was prepared to make his statement to Morrigwen but not to his mother who stood there in her robes of office. Soft, white silken veils, cinched tightly at her waist by a golden girdle, draped to her ankles. Her flame hair, loose about her shoulders, was held back from her face by a circlet bearing the symbol of the full moon centrally on her forehead. Though her hair was alive in the firelight he could not see her eyes in the darkness, but he knew they were fixed on him: he felt their glare cut through to his soul.

"Mother, I—" he started.

"I know," she cut him short, her voice soft with the mountain accent of her birth. "I knew you would ignore my wishes. Necrönd grows too strong for you, Spar. That is one reason why we had you summoned. You must leave for a while to learn to be without it."

"But, Mother, I cannot," he protested. She made him feel like a small boy, rather than a youth nearly of age. He avoided looking at her and fixed his eyes on the tapestry behind her. In the amber light from the fire, he could just pick out the design showing the thirteen trees of the sacred grove. He ran through their names in his head: holly, hazel, alder, ash, hawthorn, oak, honeysuckle, willow, furze, rowan, blackthorn, birch, and beech. Brid had taught him the sacred names of their spirits: Tinne, Coll, Fearn, Nuin, Huathe, Duir, Uilleand, Saille, Ohn, Luis, Straif, Beith and Phagos. It had taken him an age to learn the runes that represented each tree and even longer to comprehend their magical properties. The runes were stitched on the tapestry in silver thread that caught the firelight and he recited the properties of each tree in his mind to avoid listening to his mother.

"The very fact that you say you cannot leave Necrönd behind means that you must," she said mildly but with authority.

Caspar began reciting the properties of the trees in his head even more firmly. He watched his mother's mouth move but the words became silent as he concentrated on the trees. *Tinne brings you strength in fight; Coll for intuition and insight . . .*

In this manner Caspar managed to ignore Keridwen's words for a time but something she had just said instantly penetrated his defences.

"Morrigwen and I have been discussing you," she was saying.

Discussing him? This was all wrong! "You can't discuss me as if I were some object! Nor tell me what I can or cannot do," he objected petulantly, marching into the centre of the room. He faltered, suddenly aware that Brid was sitting behind the door. He flushed with embarrassment.

"You have been meddling, boy, and each time you meddle your will lessens," Morrigwen said bluntly. "You must leave the castle and Necrönd for some time to recover your self-control. The death of the mother wolf will bring evil on us all and we cannot allow you at such a vulnerable time to meddle with the powers of Necrönd."

"But— I—" Caspar stammered and then remembered

who he was. The old Crone still managed to make him feel helplessly young. "Only my father can give such orders," he bravely objected, "I am needed—"

His mother cut him short. "This morning Morrigwen's runes warned of an event, a happening of significance. And then that trapper arrives with the murdered body of a sacred wolf. I shall cast the runes now to see what more we can learn and how we can begin to repair such a heinous wrong. And you are here to help, Spar."

"I don't need to cast the runes to know that the cubs of this mother wolf must be found," Morrigwen growled.

"It is always wise to cast the runes, you know that," Keridwen said mildly, placing a steadying hand on the old Crone's shoulder.

Morrigwen relaxed a little and patted Keridwen's hand. "You are right. I am too vexed by this. Brid, place the candles and draw the circle. We shall see what must be done."

Brid arranged the four huge white candles that stood nearly to her waist. She placed them according to the four winds and Caspar was ushered alongside the one to the west: the west representing the future. The two older high priestesses stood by the candles at either side of him, watching him intently. He felt utterly naked beneath their glare, and was acutely aware of their displeasure and disappointment.

The Maiden paced around the perimeter of the circular room, strategically casting twigs of rowan to the floor to protect them from evil spirits as they made their spells. As she came to the completion of her circle, Caspar felt a tingling sensation welling up, as though the energy of life were intensified within their circle.

The area beyond the rowan twigs grew alive with delusive beings that whispered cruel words and tormented him, laughing at his thoughts. "You stand in the consecrated circle with Brid. Here you are joined. Reach out to her; you know you want her," they teased.

Caspar blushed with humiliation as the disembodied voices cackled like hobgoblins over his tortured response. The voices were confusing and he didn't know whether they came from spirits of the air or a part of his subconscious.

Morrigwen reached within her blue gown, which looked vast and baggy on her frail body, and withdrew a pouch made from the skin of the sacred crane, the bird of divination. From this scrip she pulled out a fistful of small white objects. They ground together in her clawed fist.

"These bones, Spar, were taken from the skulls of the women who held my office before me. And with the blessing of the Great Mother, I too will soon become a part of these runes."

Morrigwen picked three bones at random and cast them into the air, letting them fall within the circle as the Gods decided. The circle had three sectors, one representing the present, one the future and one the past. The bones clattered to the ground and Morrigwen sat back, still fumbling with the others in her hand.

"Brid, tell me of the runes," she demanded, her eyes now closed with exhaustion.

"They have fallen in a clear pattern. ᛠ, Ear, the rune of endings and death has fallen in the sector representing the past. The rune of ᚣ, Yr, the rune of regeneration has fallen in the present. And in the future lies the ᛒ, Beorc, the rune of new beginnings, the signature rune of the Maiden. It is rare for the runes to fall into such a clear pattern and their meaning seems so simple in the light of the events," Brid said authoritatively without waiting for either of the two senior high priestesses to interpret the casting. "The rune, Ear, represents the death of the wolf; the rune, Yr, the life of her new-born wolflings; and these two events lead to the rune, Beorc, and the future Maiden."

"It's all beyond me," Caspar protested. "And if we found any stray wolflings, which would be hard enough, how would we know whether they were the right wolflings?"

Morrigwen pouted and stared blankly into space for a moment, her breathing light and rapid. Keridwen rushed to her side and gripped her hand.

"Spar!" she scolded. "Mind your words! You must trust more in the design of the Great Mother. If the wolflings are to help us in the search for the Maiden, you will know it the moment you see them. The Great Mother will find some way to enlighten you. She will give you a sign."

Morrigwen's breathing was deeper now and she wagged a finger at the youth. "Many things in life would be meaningless without the wisdom of hindsight. And things that seemed meaningful often become meaningless with hindsight," the Crone continued enigmatically. "All will be revealed when you bring the wolflings to me, Spar. Brid will go with you. The runes have told me that the wolflings, if they still live, have a part to play in our search. You must find them."

"But it's midwinter. The trapper said he killed the mother near the Jaws of the Wolf. It's not a good time to be up near the high pass," Caspar objected, though most of his mind was still on the Druid's Egg as he schemed to avoid being separated from it.

The old Crone turned her sightless eyes on the youth. "All the more reason to go now. The wolflings will not last long without your help. You must find them and maybe this short separation from Necrönd will break your obsessive need to handle it. Who knows what mischief you have caused already?" Her crackling voice hardened and her fists hooked into claws as she kneaded the scrip of rune-carved bones. "How many times do you have to be warned before you take heed?" she asked coldly.

Though the old woman was so frail that her arm shook as she pointed at him, she had great presence. Her glazed eyes somehow pierced clean through to his soul though he knew she was nearly blind. His emotions balked. How could he let himself be spoken to like that by an old woman? Hal would never tolerate such treatment. But Morrigwen was the Crone and represented the most fearful part of the Great Mother and he doubted that Hal was sensitive enough to be aware of the Goddess behind the Trinity of high priestesses. The realization of their power frightened Caspar. He saw Her in all of them and loved and worshipped them for it.

Trembling, the wraithlike woman clutched the arms of her chair and painfully pushed herself to her feet. Caspar held out his hand to help her but she brushed him away.

"I don't want your help. Not the help of a youth who will not listen to the voices of sense and reason. I have told you before to leave Necrönd be. Your soul is at risk; you are already part consumed by it. Will you never hear what we are saying?" She stumbled to the thin crack of light creeping around the edge of the shutter jammed into the arrow slit window.

Contrite and humbled, Caspar shuffled after her. Once out of earshot of the two other priestesses, Morrigwen sucked in breath to speak but it racked her lungs and she coughed and spluttered, falling against Caspar for support. Her lips were blue as she struggled for breath. The chips of bone slipped from her hand. He caught two, the rest rattling to the floorboards. Morrigwen tugged at his shoulder.

"Give those to me," she demanded.

He handed her the chips of bone. Rather than look at them, she caressed the carvings with her cracked fingertips. Her face was fixed on the chink of light slicing around the edge of the shutter. The light fell on her wrinkled face and shone straight through her whispery hair to her wrinkled scalp.

"The runes were cast by the Gods. I did not mean to drop them and you caught two without thought," she said feeling around the rough-hewn edges of the chips. "This one is Straif the rune of ill-fate but the other you will not know yet." She fingered the white bone reverently. "I know this bone well. This rune was carved from the skull of my mother. Not my real mother, of course, but as I am to Keridwen, the mother that brought me up from a baby and loved and cared for me and taught me the old ways. I still feel lost without her and yearn for her comfort. I took on a heavy burden when she died. Whenever I was lost in my way, she would take my hand and give me comfort and strength. But she is gone and I must follow after. Without her I had no one to turn to but still must comfort and counsel those that follow me. And I will soon be gone and must place that burden of lonely responsibility onto your mother's shoulders." The old Crone mumbled on quietly for a while as if lost in thought as she fingered the chip of bone. "Yet my old mother helps me now."

She gave the rune to Caspar. "Keep this. The Gods meant you to choose it and it may guide you in your search. Find the wolflings. The world is unstable and, with the death of the sacred mother wolf, we must hasten our search for the new Maiden. Let us pray that these wolflings will lead us quickly to her. I am no longer strong enough to cast the spells of magic that are required of my office."

The Crone fell silent and Caspar sensed the presence of his mother at his shoulder. "Find the wolflings. Forget Necrönd for a time and try and break your obsession with it, otherwise you will destroy us and yourself, Spar."

"Open the shutters wide," Morrigwen ordered, her voice rising so that it was easily audible to all in the room. "I have more that I will say to you, foolish child, in the light of day that I hope will give clarity to your unguided thoughts."

Still clutching the chip of bone, Caspar eased out the plank of wood that filled the arrow slit, welcoming in light and fresh air to fill the circular room. The candles fluttered and danced and one to the West snuffed out, leaving a trill of lazy smoke winding to the ceiling. Caspar turned away from the window and inwards on the room. He started. His face reddened and his hand sprang up to his crooked nose. Sitting where Brid had been earlier, stroking the little red fire-drake, was May. She had heard every word.

Humiliated beyond tolerance Caspar fled the room, banging the low arched door behind him.

CHAPTER THREE

Caspar pulled the bearskin cloak tightly about his shoulders and smiled. If he had to go up to the Jaws of the Wolf, he couldn't think of a better companion than Brid.

He grinned at her worn and stained hunting leathers – quite inappropriate for a young maiden – and laughed at how they would irritate Hal if he were here to see them. His uncle liked to see his betrothed dressed in loose silky gowns but in three years had never once managed to dissuade her from wearing what she chose. He let his gaze linger on her large, startlingly green eyes, the bow of her red lips and the clear, bronzed complexion of her heart-shaped elven face.

Her busy eyes flitted quickly about her, assessing and noting all that passed, while she talked to May who stood quietly beside her. Brid's eyes momentarily fell on Caspar and he snatched his gaze away. Self-consciously he hurried across the courtyard to take the reins of his red roan stallion, Firecracker, from the two harassed-looking stable lads who were struggling to hold him. They stiffened and brushed off wisps of straw as the Baron's heavy footfall beat the cobbled courtyard.

"It'll do you good to get out into the Barony," Branwolf told his son. "The snows are packed down hard and frosted over and the farrier's worked hard fitting studs to the horses' shoes. Enjoy the ride. But look after Brid well," he lowered his voice, "or else Hal will never forgive you."

Though his father was teasing Caspar found the remark insulting. "I would never forgive myself. I would die rather than let any harm come to her," he replied sternly.

"Of course." Branwolf straightened up a little at the seriousness of his son's reply. "Still, taking a young lady out hunting in midwinter is a great responsibility."

"I'm not taking her," Caspar muttered. "She's taking herself; she insisted on coming right from the start." He looked darkly at his father. He loved him dearly but right now he was resentful of his domineering manner. Couldn't he see that at seventeen he was no longer a foolish boy? Did he have to question his every decision? He wondered that people wouldn't have more faith in him if he were a little taller. He resented his fine-boned frame. He was still more than a hand's length shorter than Hal, who had grown into a handsomely proportioned young man with enigmatic saturnine features. In his opinion it hardly befitted the heir to the great northern barony of Torra Alta to be so slight. He had none of his father's nor Hal's presence.

He shrugged. Clearly his father didn't understand what it was like to be young, and explained with exaggerated patience, "I told her that Pip and I could find the wolflings but she insisted, saying that it would take the skills of a high priestess to recognize them. Besides, with old Brock along as an extra precaution we should be perfectly safe. I'm quite capable of leading a hunting party."

Branwolf had recommended that he chose old Brock to come with them. He was one of the few men to survive the siege and one of only a handful of experienced and fully trained men in the garrison. He was also showing his irritability towards the new recruits, whose ineptness and unruly behaviour had sapped so much of his good humour that the Baron thought it expedient for the old man to take a short break from his usual duties.

Caspar swung up easily into his saddle and felt glad of the springy step of his hot-blooded horse as Firecracker skittered beneath him. His three companions, Brid, old Brock and May's younger brother, Pip, were mounted on deep-chested, heavy-boned Torra Altan mountain horses, which were sure-footed in the harsh terrain of the northern Barony. He had at first rejected the idea of taking Pip, who was still not quite fourteen, but Keridwen had persuaded him that it would be a kindly gesture as the boy was of an age when he needed some recognition and responsibility. Besides, fourteen was quite old enough for a young lad to ride out into the Chase even during Horning. Pip had proved troublesome when not given enough to do in the dark winter months of castle life. His energies clearly needed channelling towards something more constructive than using the chickens for archery practice. Fortunately, Pip's aim had not yet improved otherwise he might have found himself in a great deal more trouble.

"Where've you been hiding away this morning? We've been ready and waiting for ages," Brid complained, as Caspar's stallion swung its quarters into her mount.

Ignoring her comment, he urged his horse past her so that he could bid farewell to his mother and May.

Keridwen looked at him reproachfully. "Spar," she whispered as he leant down to kiss her forehead, "you've been down to Necrönd." Reaching up she gently pushed his hair back from forehead. "Give it up. Its powers are not for you and will overcome us all if they are misused. Let this expedition put it from your mind. You must learn to live without it. You are my son, Spar; I know you have the strength. I pray you will not fail me."

Caspar smiled self-consciously at May and wondered if she would ever be able to respect him after witnessing so much of the high priestesses' discourse with him. He nudged at his crooked nose and decided to ignore the matter entirely. He gave her a smile, though it was more nervous than he had intended. "I wish you could come with us. Perhaps in the spring . . ." He didn't know how to say it. To May it must seem unfair that Brid could join their hunting party when she could not, but the priestess was an accomplished horsewoman whereas May would have had difficulty keeping up, especially in the icy conditions.

"No matter, my Lord," May replied dismissively. Her hazel eyes would not meet his. "It's not the place of a wood-cutter's daughter to go on such expeditions."

Caspar sighed. A year ago, she would have yearned to ride gleefully alongside him, chattering happily, but not anymore. Since her sixteenth birthday she had become increasingly aloof towards him.

Trying to brush away his self-doubts about May's feelings and the constant nagging call of Necrönd, he kicked on and led the small party out through the portcullis. The narrow road that spiralled the Tor was precariously steep and mostly shaded from the sun. They picked their way carefully, sliding and clattering on the slippery track. From here the Silversalmon looked like a steel-grey ribbon woven through a white blanket. Its sinuous body meandered through the flat bottom of the snow-covered rift valley that scythed north-south through the Yellow Mountains, forming the Pass between Vaalaka and Belbidia. At the foot of the Tor Caspar stopped briefly to look up at his home.

The castle of Torra Alta stood alone in the Pass, perched on a great pillar of rock whose summit had once housed a nest of dragons. Over a millennium ago Caspar's forefathers had slaughtered the dragons and built the mighty fortress over their lair, creating what they hoped to be an impregnable stronghold to protect Belbidia from all northern attack. For a thousand years Torra Alta had enforced its rule over the pass through the Yellow Mountains, lashing out from high on its rocky throne at those foolhardy enough to challenge its might. Caspar was fiercely proud of his heritage.

But the castle, as it once had been, had fallen to the Vaalakans. Only their renewed faith in the Great Mother and the reuniting of the Trinity of the three high priestesses had won it back from the barbarians' clutches. He thought of Morrigwen's words warning him that she must shortly die and how the trapper's actions would bring evil on them all. They must find the wolflings.

Here at the root of the Tor they were caught in its needle-like shadow. Swirling mist feathered the contours of the frozen ground, swallowing the horses' legs. Pip sat clumsily on his horse, a short-legged dun gelding. He was still heavy with his hands despite Caspar's diligent training.

"Shall we cut through the mountains, Master Spar?" Pip asked brightly.

"No," Brid interjected before Caspar had a chance to reply. "The snows will be too thick. We'll cut north along the Silversalmon and then west through the shelter of the Boarchase Forest then turn south towards the Jaws of the Wolf."

"Yes," Caspar agreed, feeling a little foolish that he had not been quick enough to reply before Brid, though he was at least gratified that Pip looked to him for confirmation.

"With the snow so thick, how are these wolflings meant to survive?" Pip bluntly voiced the question that Caspar had been itching to ask. He had hesitated from raising it for fear of upsetting Brid and dashing her hopes.

"The rest of the pack will look after them as best they can. Wolves care for one another," Brid replied matter-of-factly and Caspar hoped she was right.

"But if they're part of a pack, we'll never know them," the younger boy argued.

Brid sighed patiently at him. "Of course, we'll know them. The Great Mother will mark them out for us."

Caspar glanced sidelong at Brid and bit his lip. He guessed that she was making too light of the problems. Like Pip, he doubted they would survive and if they were part of a pack, they would find it difficult to get close enough to see any markings let alone capture the animals. Still, it was wonderful to lead his first party out into the Boarchase and, at those moments when he managed to put his problems and the thought of Necrönd to the back of his mind, he was thoroughly enjoying the ride.

"Just what do you think you're doing questioning the lady and Master Spar like that?" Old Brock's grumbled words floated forward through the still air as Pip fell back alongside the old soldier. "Your job is to know your place and listen for orders, not waggling your tongue about at those better than yourself."

"Trouble with you, Brock," Pip replied, his voice fluctuating from low to high in over-excited haste, "is you have nothing better to do than fuss on like an old lady-in-waiting. My protocol was perfect."

"Protocol? That's a long word for a little scallywag like yourself. And you've no business using words like that. What you need to learn is that a man should know his place."

Pip smiled that smug carefree smile of his. He knew it infuriated all adults who were misguided enough to think they could tell him what was what. "Protocol's not such a difficult word. *I* can read," he boasted impressively. "But you're right, a man should know his place. But that doesn't mean he has to like it or stay there. Perhaps some of us aren't as accepting as you, old man."

"You're a whippersnapper and should be flogged till you learn some respect, lad," Brock grumbled though his weathered old face showed no signs of harshness.

"Huh! And just who's going to do that? You, old man?" Pip's taunt fell on deaf ears. Brock was no longer listening. Like Brid and Caspar, he was taking in the silvery river valley and marvelling at its rugged beauty.

Once clear of the long thin shadow of the Tor, they reached a section of beaten track that had thawed out in the crisp sunshine. To free the fresh horses of their energy, they pushed into a steady rolling canter. As they pounded the hard ground, Brid drew her cream mare alongside Caspar's feisty stallion.

"What was Morrigwen saying to you yesterday so quietly before you stormed from the room?" she shouted quickly as if she had been saving the question, waiting for the right opportunity to ask. "Apart from warning you, yet again, to leave Necrönd alone, of course."

The tone in her voice made the youth bite at his lip and pull his horse to a walk. He tried to regain some composure by loosening his hold on the reins and allowing Firecracker to toss his head without jerking his arms from their sockets. "I won't tell you if you're going to be like that."

Brid laughed, the sound as warm as the caress of the summer sun. For a moment Caspar thought the mist had cleared, allowing the sun to kiss the ground in a sudden burst of golden brilliance. "Oh, Spar, tell me, please."

Caspar looked at her more happily. "She gave me this."

He reached beneath the thick folds of his cloak and into his leather jacket, bringing forth the flat chip of bone.

Brid held out her palm for it, her fingers white in the cold northern air. She looked at it gravely. "Was it just this one?" she asked.

Caspar shook his head. "No, there was another: blackthorn, the rune of strife," he solemnly answered, fully aware of the impact of Straif's nature.

Brid raised her eyebrows knowingly and nodded in resignation. "Things that are worthwhile and never easily won. It is the same with love or fortune and even plain happiness. Nothing good comes easily but is always struggled for, even life itself."

Caspar sensed the heart-felt emotion behind these words and considered Brid's tempestuous relationship with his uncle. If only Brid had chosen him over Hal, she would have been spared so much heartache.

The Maiden looked back at the rune in her palm. "I've not taught you about this one yet. Did Morrigwen tell you its meaning?"

Caspar shook his head.

Brid turned the chip of bone over in her hand. "Of course, you stormed off before she had the chance. It is not a rune used for writing but a sacred and rarely used rune for divination only. It is the rune of the wolf: it represents the wild and savage side of life."

"Morrigwen merely said it might guide me in our search."

"She could have said more. In conjunction with the rune Straif, she might have warned you to fear anything wild or savage – the wild beasts of the Otherworld controlled by Necrönd perhaps. But then you didn't stop to hear more, did you? You saw May and fled."

"I didn't flee," Caspar retorted sharply and was glad that

Pip was too engrossed in argument with Brock to overhear Brid's words.

He glanced over his shoulder, noting how uncomfortable the lad looked on the dun. He had become awkward and clumsy of late, the result of a sudden growth spurt. Apparently, the woodcutter's son had inherited much of his father's characteristics, being large and solid. His sister, May, was small and light like her mother had been while Pip was already taller than Caspar. He had a dark head of straight brown hair and suspicious eyes that he was never afraid to level at any man.

Like old Brock, Pip and May had been amongst the few survivors of the final Vaalakan onslaught and, though the orphan of a poor woodcutter's family, Pip had quickly taken to castle life. When not stirring up mischief, he had made himself surprisingly useful, eagerly helping with the horses and the weaponry, though he was loath to work in the wellroom. He had spent most of the siege labouring in the swelter of the furnace rooms and even now, after three years, his hands were still stained yellow from the long months of service scraping sulphur from the vats after the mineral had been extracted from the water. When the new recruits were drafted, he had quickly discovered the usefulness of being one of the few with previous experience of garrison life. He had taken every opportunity to be at Caspar's side, particularly if it meant helping to organize the archery practice – though he was no more handy with the bow than any of the other lads fresh from the villages.

His bow was slung across his back now, not the long Torra Altan war bow, which he was still much too young to draw, but a short hunting bow lavishly decorated with ivory inlays. It was an expensive weapon for a commoner to bear but Caspar had given it to him since he had no more use for it himself. Caspar preferred a bow of plain design made from stagbone and holly, the treasured gift of an ancient shamaness.

Somewhere behind them a dog howled. Pip drew his bow and was waving it threateningly in the direction of the noise. "What was that?" he exclaimed. "There aren't any of those big wolves so close to the castle, are there?"

Brid laughed and, with just the touch of her calves and a slight shift in posture, turned her cream mare expectantly back to face the castle. "No, of course not."

The howl turned to a piercing yip and Caspar groaned. "Trog! He's got out."

The dog came galloping into view, his white, thick-set body pulsing with short jerky strides as he leapt in and out of the mist in his efforts to catch them. When he saw them all halted and waiting, he dropped to a bumbling walk, his tongue lolling from side to side.

"Oh, Trog, how on earth did you escape from the guardroom? You were meant to stay behind," Brid scolded the dog but with a wide smile on her face. "You always slow us up, don't you, boy?"

"And you're a rotten hunting dog," Caspar added.

"Don't be rude about my dog," Brid admonished with a laugh.

"Well, he is. He barks and yips during stalks, scatters stags like skittles and tries to tackle boar all by himself. He doesn't know his own match. The number of times I've had to save him! You're a wretched animal, Trog."

The dog twisted his ugly bulbous head up at the sound of his name and appeared to grin self-appreciatively.

Three miles further on Caspar had the white terrier, an Ophidian snake-catcher by breed, strapped to the back of his saddle. Trog's paws were already sore from the frozen ground and the dog was too tired to walk further.

"You should have stayed by the fire where you know you really want to be," he told the dog as he snuffled contentedly, his muzzle rested on Firecracker's rolling quarters, his head lolling from side to side. The track was now cutting through wooded areas and his voice sent clouds of birds cawing into the sky.

"I don't remember there being so many crows and rooks," Pip muttered as they rode steadily northward towards the Boarchase. "We've always had eagles and merlins. Even from the Chase we could see them above the Yellow Mountains crags but I don't remember there being so many crows."

"Nor ravens," Brid agreed. "There must be more carrion about." A vast hooded raven was circling slowly above a valley cupped out of sight beyond the canyon walls. Gradually the great black bird drew more of its kind, darkening the sky with their mocking flight as they waited for some poor beast to die before diving down to clean up the carcass.

Caspar felt guilty. He knew it was the hooded wolves that encouraged the carrion and he feared it was his fault. He didn't know how but he feared that he helped them across the divide, creating the flesh to clothe the miasma of their spirit as he imagined how the beasts must once have been, ranging the wild mountains.

For three years now his nights were haunted by sickening dreams of creatures squirming out of the Egg, reborn incomplete, the wounds of their death still visible on their flesh. Slain by man, he sensed their wretched hatred. They were his to control but he feared them. Could it be that he unwittingly released them through his dreams? He shrank from the thought.

Soon they approached the fringes of the Boarchase. Brid and Caspar admired the silvery glint of the dozing river as it emerged from the dark green shadows of the red-trunked pines. Here the Silversalmon was a smoky green, quiet and mysterious in its journey as if preparing itself for the storm when it crashed angrily through the rocky terrain of the canyon.

Pip was now riding ahead of the others, eager to reacquaint himself with the woodlands of his birthplace. Caspar had noted, half with irritation and half with amusement, how like Hal that was. Pip somehow always contrived to take the lead though he was certainly not born to it. It appeared that Pip had an ambition to rise to command and, though the lad was but a woodcutter's son, Caspar believed he would.

The road ahead diverged into two tracks and Pip halted to wait for the others and see which route they wished to take. He wheeled his horse more with effort than with expertise and the animal, a well-natured beast, clomped round. The movement had none of the glorious grace of Caspar's stallion but it had all the obedience that his feisty red roan lacked.

As they drew nearer to Pip, Firecracker suddenly reared and danced sideways, forcing Caspar to press himself forwards onto the horse's mane to prevent himself from being scalped on an overhanging branch.

"Steady, boy." He soothed Firecracker's russet neck and slapped the thick rack of muscle ridging the stallion's crest. "What is it, boy?"

The erratic movements of his mount never once unsettled the horseman. He sat easily, his supple body flowing with the animal's movements. The highly strung stallion shook at his bit and the curb chains jangled, the sound loud and harsh in the eerie hush of the wood.

"What's startled Cracker, Master Spar?" Pip asked softly, using the familiar form of address that the garrison of

Torra Alta used towards all their seniors apart from the Baron himself.

"I don't know. I didn't see anything." Caspar looked about him, peering into the shadows while keeping a firm grip on Firecracker's reins. His horse shied again, shrieking and snorting a challenge into the half-light of the forest.

Caspar was unsettled by Firecracker's nervous excitement and immediately thought of Necrönd and the shadowy beasts it summoned. He should not have left it behind. It wasn't safe, whatever Morrigwen and Keridwen thought. Too many strange things were happening of late.

He looped his reins over the raised pommel at the front of his saddle and strung his bow, his eyes darting into the shadows. The woods were close around them. The air smelt different; dry, dusty and sweet with resin. It would have had a lulling effect on Caspar's mind but for the unnatural silence. He loosened his cloak. The trees protected them from the sharp winter breeze and now in the still of the forest he felt uncomfortably warm wrapped in the heavy folds of his bearskin cloak.

Trog was growling low in his throat, though whether from a suspicious sense of unease or because he was becoming uncomfortably sick from the horse's jolting gait, Caspar didn't know. As he looked round to check that the dog was secure, a movement caught his eye. Something dark streaked around the bole of a tree and sped off through the undergrowth.

"A pine marten," Caspar suggested lightly.

Old Brock nodded in agreement but the other two, both brought up in the woods and more familiar with their surroundings, shook their heads.

"Too big," Pip said firmly. "Definitely too big, and the fur's too long."

There was a sudden shriek, which sent Firecracker dipping back on his haunches, his nostrils flaring angrily.

"A jay?" Caspar asked uncertainly. "Or a magpie . . . ?"

Brid looked doubtful. "It could be a magpie but I don't think so. They have more of a rattle in their song."

Caspar felt some relief as the ground ahead rose and the trees thinned to a bare humped area of ground, which climbed above the forest like the back of a whale cresting out of a green sea. He preferred open spaces where he could more easily see approaching danger. He didn't know why he felt so insecure but the easily recognizable sounds of a woodpecker's hollow hammering, the piercing indignant song of a wren and the beautiful tones of a wood-lark went some way to soothing his fears. Whatever creature had slunk through the woods had passed them by.

Brid was looking sadly about her at the desolation. Until recently, the ridge must have been wooded like the rest of the Chase. All that was left was a circular crown of uprooted trees about the top of the hill, the earthy mounds of their roots lying like tombstones. Fringing the ring of fallen trees were acres of neatly rowed saplings, none more than hip high. The layout of the whole area was clearly man's work.

There was something terribly forlorn about the uprooted trees. To Caspar they seemed like slain warriors that had been abandoned to hold an impossible outpost alone; the surrounding saplings in their marshalled columns like a triumphant invading army. Brid wheeled her cream mare and looked round in disgust.

"At least they've replanted much of this," she conceded. "But how could they have stripped bare so large a tract?" The whippy saplings covered possibly two hundred acres though the very crest of the hill was naked except for the ring of torn-down trees. The bare, rounded earth rose barrowlike, a monument to the death of the old trees. Caspar wondered why the foresters had shunned the crown of the hill and left the bodies of the old trees to rot.

"It might be three years ago that they stopped felling the trees but the legacy lives on," Brid said sadly. "I came through here last year while visiting the woodcutters' villages and that ring of trees up there was still standing. It was once an ancient circle, a sacred grove."

Pip nodded. "Even though he was a man of the New Faith, Pa warned us never to touch the trees of the sacred groves for fear of curses."

"Then what brought the grove down?" Caspar asked.

"With roots upturned like that, only the wind, Master Spar," Pip explained, knowledgeable in his native environment.

"But we haven't had any especially high winds, not in the last three years," Caspar argued. "If they were susceptible, they would have blown down years ago, surely?"

Brid smiled indulgently at him. "The grove would have been protected by the dense forest around it. But so many trees were felled before the Vaalakan invasion that no surrounding trees were left to protect the grove. Exposed high on the dome of the hill, they would have been susceptible to even the mildest storm," she explained as she picked her way through the birch saplings towards the fallen trees. "Though the Barony of Torra Alta has now fully re-embraced the ways of the Mother, there are some things that it is too late to save. Many things are lost, never to be found again."

The vertical walls of the upturned roots were clogged with mud and pebbles, and plated with scales of honey-coloured fungi. Vast white puffed toadstools grew in the soggy roots and old man's beard, the winter coat of travellers' joy, sprawled across the felled bodies of the ancient kings of the forest. Brid slithered from her horse and ran to the centre of the decimated grove. Scorch marks blackened the earth where a fire had been lit in the confines of a crude stone circle. Strange, thought Caspar. It was an unlikely place to camp on such exposed ground.

Brid clearly thought it odd too. She was stooped to the ground, raking through the fallen branches and leaves until she was down to bare earth.

"Here, let me do that," Brock anxiously offered, only to be rebuffed by a dismissive wave from the priestess's earthy hand. He stepped back warily and shrugged.

Caspar knew better than to interfere with Brid when she was bent on a purpose and he noted that Pip clearly was not about to offer. The boy's eyes flitted from her back to the roots of the trees behind them and at a blackthorn in particular. Caspar caught the barest glimpse of what the youth had seen; a scurrying animal shying away from sight. Black fur and long thin legs like a pheasant, he decided, though he thought the combination unlikely.

While old Brock made a show of standing guard over his young companions, Pip turned back to Brid and knelt to examine her find. Both were frowning.

"They look like the spoor of some large bird," Brid mused.

"None that I know of," Pip added.

Caspar was irritated by the way the youth always talked to the Maiden as if she were his equal and not One of the Three. It irritated him, too, that here in the woods, the two of them were so naturally at ease with one another while he felt excluded and clumsy. He had spent many adventurous days hunting in the Boarchase for stag and boar but that clearly did not give the same feeling for the woods as the careless days of childhood, left to roam idly and explore the world alone.

While Pip and Brid argued over the nature of the tracks, Caspar released Trog from the back of his saddle and let the dog scrabble amongst the tree roots. The snake-catcher was instantly alert, his head down snuffling amongst the dirt. His blunt white nose was quickly a muddy brown. He snorted to clear his nostrils before plunging his nose back into the ground, whimpering excitedly and digging furiously. Soil sprayed out from between his back legs.

"A badger set," Caspar suggested.

Pip looked as if he were about to nod in agreement but Brid shook her head and turned towards the fallen rowan tree that had attracted Trog. "No, I don't think so. Take a look at this." She beckoned him to the fallen tree as Trog snuffled his way towards the roots of a blackthorn.

A strip of decayed sodden bark had been peeled away, revealing the fibrous trunk beneath, crawling with woodlouse. A patch of the pale wood was scraped smooth and bore several notches. They appeared purposefully carved.

"Tree runes?" Caspar asked, thinking about the time in Caldea when they had come across similar scratches.

Brid nodded and looked back with enlightenment at the strange scratchy footprints. "Kobolds," she announced.

"Kobolds?" Pip's peppercorn eyes looked blank. "Never heard of them. And I've seen every creature there is to be seen in the Chase."

"They're little tree men," Caspar started to explain.

"Elves, Master Spar? I'm not a kid anymore. I know there's no such thing."

Brid looked at the youth impatiently. "Kobolds are little half-sized men with twiggy limbs that live amongst trees.

But I agree, there's not been any in these parts since Morrigwen was a girl, or so she says. Funny half-witted creatures with no malice in their hearts but little sense of right or wrong, so the *Book of Names* tells us."

"What do the runes say?" Caspar asked, peering closely at the vertical scratches and unable to make head nor tail of them.

He was surprised, however, to see that Brid looked only a little more enlightened than he did.

"Father Forest save Hobs Slack in Trows Forest." She scanned them over again, frowning as if she must have made a mistake before giving out a deprecatory laugh. "I must be losing my senses; isn't Trows Forest in Ceolothia?"

"Why have the kobolds come here and how do Ceolothian kobolds speak Belbidian and isn't Father Forest just a story?" Pip asked in one long breath. "Pa said it was just a story."

Brid threw up her arms as if to defend herself from the barrage of questions while Brock grunted in disapproval and frowned at the woodcutter's son for his impertinence.

"Most of the old peoples, the goblins, sprites and pixies can use Belbidian because it is the root language of all the tongues of the Caballan. Kobolds' mouths can't form human speech though. They have their own language, which is unintelligible to man but they use Belbidian when they write in tree runes." Brid paused in her hurried explanation to draw breath and Caspar took the opportunity to interrupt her.

"So, who is this Father Forest?"

"Whether he exists or not I can't say but in legend he's

an old white stag who roams across the world, protecting the forests. Evidently the kobolds believe he exists. I imagine they've come here, to what was once a sacred grove, because this would be a likely place for him to visit; a spiritual watering hole if you like."

Brid spun round, raising her arm sharply, and pointed. Caspar followed her line of sight just in time to catch a glimpse of a black hairy shape running on fragile spindly legs as it hurried for the cover of the dense undergrowth lower down the ridge.

"How could we have mistaken that for a pine marten?" Caspar felt like laughing.

"I didn't mistake it," Brid said firmly. "I was right; it's definitely a kobold. And that's a good sign. It shows that Belbidia is becoming a safer place for the old creatures that were hounded out during the era of the New Faith."

"It's not been so safe for the mountain wolves," Pip remarked dryly.

Brid ignored him and looked towards the horses. "Well, we'll never find these wolflings if we don't get moving."

Caspar brightened at Pip's impish expression. It was something he particular liked about Pip. Being able to dismiss the boy's practical jokes as youthful high spirits made Caspar feel much more mature and magnanimous. Still Pip had upset many of the castle staff by his arrogant behaviour. The older women particularly disapproved of him for "getting all above his station" as they would say. Caspar laughed at their indignation. At least Pip wasn't obsequious like many of the newly recruited soldiers. He called him Master Spar but beyond that he treated him very much as a normal person. With Hal gone, it gave him someone else to talk to and relieved the isolation of his privileged position.

Caspar unhooked Firecracker's reins from the upturned

root where he had been tethered and was about to mount when he had the vague feeling that something was missing. He felt around his person, checked his bow and the dagger he kept in his belt and then looked about blankly. He must be mistaken.

Brid was also looking about her but she seemed very much more concerned.

"Where's Trog?" she demanded.

All four of them looked around anxiously.

"Trog!" Brid called into the still air. She put her fingers to her mouth and produced a surprisingly piercing whistle from her feminine lips, sending a host of rooks scattering into the air.

There was no reply.

CHAPTER FOUR

Above his head the overhanging eaves glistened with dripping icicles. Hal's chainmail chinked as he trotted briskly along the narrow streets; he was determined to put a good distance between himself and Ceowulf.

He put the man from his mind for a moment and gave Secret an appreciative slap on her thick neck, delighting in the way the morning sunlight glinted on her rich liver chestnut coat. It was like highly polished wood, alive with texture. He squeezed his spurs lightly against her sides and gathered her up with the reins, encouraging an energetic but dignified gait as they approached the palace.

All he lacked was the suit of armour Branwolf had refused him. No doubt if Spar had asked for one he'd have been given it right away, no matter the expense. But Branwolf had muttered on so much about the cost of masons, carpenters and materials to rebuild the walls of Torra Alta that he had not pushed the issue further. He pouted. He needed that coat of armour. How would anyone take him seriously as a knight if he didn't have full armour for himself and a shinning bard for his horse? Now that would impress! Secret would look magnificent beneath the skilfully fashioned sheets of burnished steel. If he presented himself like that the king would surely give him a prestigious position in his army immediately. He might even ask him to lead it!

The air was chill. Farona had probably not seen such a cold winter in years, he thought, noting the city folk muffled in layers of woollens. None of them enjoyed the cosy warmth of his bearskin cloak. Many of the children had their feet bandaged in rags to protect their skin from the biting cold of the paved streets. Rewik should do something for them, he thought bitterly, knowing that his brother would never allow such suffering in Torra Alta.

His moody thoughts returned to his companion. He was cross with Ceowulf. For most of the day he had deliberately distanced himself from the big Caldean, but as he fell under the shadow of the grey palace walls, he considered that they would have to come to some form of compromise. He wheeled Secret to wait for the knight.

"So," Ceowulf grinned calmly, "you've decided to apologize."

"I most certainly have not," Hal said stiffly as their mounts drew level. "You were in the wrong and you know it." Though he held a great respect for the experienced knight, he was glad that he had thickened out and grown taller lately so that the big Caldean no longer overshadowed him quite so much. Even as a youth he was aware that he cut a fine figure but now at twenty he was happy to consider himself handsome. "I am my own master and will do as I please."

The dark knight raised one of his distinguished flat eyebrows, his deeply tanned face creasing up into a supercilious smile. "Don't be a fool, Hal. There is no man born who is his own master. Every one of us is beholden to someone."

"You're full of sanctimonious tripe," Hal replied tartly, snapping up his reins and drawing Secret to an abrupt halt. "I have no wish to present myself to the king in your company. I am ashamed to be associated with you. Call yourself a knight! You're a slave to your woman." Hal knew he was being overly ardent but he couldn't help himself. He was furious with Ceowulf for laughing at him and even more furious that the man seemed totally unperturbed by his displeasure.

"That I freely admit. I am Cybillia's devoted slave as much as she is mine. And that, I fear, is why you are so angry. You're afraid you don't have quite the same hold on Brid as she does on you."

"That's a lie!" Hal found his hand flying to the ornate hilt of his rune-engraved broadsword. "How dare you insult me? I demand satisfaction!"

Ceowulf laughed. "What? A duel here before the king's threshold? What fools we'd look. I've known you a good three years now, Hal, and I'm still waiting for you to grow up."

"Are you too cowardly to accept?" Hal challenged his friend.

"No, but I am too weak with laughter. Just because the lady we passed on the road was not immediately overwhelmed by your famous charm and was offended when—"

"I said nothing unchivalrous," Hal protested. "I'll run you through if you dare say otherwise."

Ceowulf threw up his arms in mock defence. "In truth, noble lord, you said nothing but your eyes said it all; they lusted for her. You could see she was a merchant's wife and you know how they hate to be patronized by noblemen. Hardly surprising that she rapped your wrist with her riding crop."

"I merely said how fine a figure she cut riding side-saddle and expressed a wish that we would see more of her in Farona. It was perfectly innocent."

"It was not, Hal. That wink you gave her didn't even have a double meaning; it was absolutely blatant."

"Still, you had no right to laugh at me in front of her and preach on about what Brid would think."

"I rather felt you needed reminding since your eyes were already wandering to her maid. She seemed a little keener to take up your offer."

"How dare you presume to tell me what I can or cannot do?" Hal felt his skin prickle with anger.

Ceowulf shrugged. "Dear friend, I was merely trying to spare you a rounded flaying from your conscience. Let me tell you, it's far better to avoid such situations."

Hal was dismayed to find that he was now approaching the palace at a lacklustre gait. This would not do. He wanted to approach with style, the sun gleaming on his chainmail. He wanted to be noted as a knight of substance not as a bickering, inexperienced, half-forgotten second son of a baron. He was his own man, not yet his nephew's subject, nor Brid's puppet and he wasn't going to have Ceowulf suggest that he should behave as such.

He twisted round in his saddle to face the big Caldean knight. "I haven't married her yet, you know. And until I mumble through my wedding vows, I'm still a free man."

"Oh, if only I were so strong that I could so lightly throw off the shackles of conscience," Ceowulf mocked.

Hal growled though he was forced to turn his scowl to a rather feeble smile as they were greeted by the palace guards.

"We come at the king's behest," Ceowulf boomed grandly. "Lord Ceowulf, son of Baron Cadros of Caldea. I accompany Lord Hal, brother to Baron Branwolf of Torra Alta, summoned from the most northerly Barony of his highness's realm. We are eager to be presented."

"Welcome, knights!" The senior guard dressed in red,

yellow and gold livery signalled for a groom to take their horses before leading the noblemen forward on foot.

Hal had little liking for the king's palace. Of course, there was much to be admired. The halls were stuffed with all manner of treasures bought from the provender of the golden wheat fields that grew in Belbidia's heartland. Garish tapestries and antlers the size of oak branches, row upon row, decorated its long, arched corridors. Polished marbled floors echoed with the sound of smart efficient feet as pages, servants and lesser vassals fussed about their business. But the palace itself was like a broken man stripped of his soul, dull and lifeless. Hal thought the place needed some gossip, some frightful scandal to give it a bit of sparkle.

On the heels of the guard, they swept, shoulder to shoulder, through the tapestried corridors in silence until they came to the arched and studded double doors that barred the way to the throne-room. Hal tapped his feet irritably as they waited for an official to knock before they were permitted to enter. Ceowulf was still smirking at him. Hal ground his teeth, trying to control his temper.

He didn't like to be reminded of his relationship with Brid. She was as beautiful as the stars on a frosted night or the first blossoms of springtime before they were faded by the brightness of full summer. The world came alive around her. She was so full of energy and ideas. She had so much spirit, so much presence – he had to admit almost too much. But what galled him was that she held a higher office than he would ever attain and Ceowulf was happy to point that out.

He forgot all about the king's men and grimaced at the Caldean's calm face. Ceowulf was annoyingly unflappable but Hal had to admit the man was right. He shouldn't have behaved towards the merchant's wife in such a manner. He had been too brash with her. Still, it wasn't Ceowulf's place to castigate him.

On reflection, however, Hal considered that his friend hadn't actually rebuked him. Ceowulf wasn't one for passing judgements; he knew that. It had been more of an amused observation than pronounced disapproval and Hal had taken umbrage only because he knew Ceowulf was right.

Just as quickly as his black temper had overcome him, the cloud lifted from his mercurial mind. If he had no other grace, he did at least know his own faults. He flashed the Caldean a beaming smile just as they strode into the throne-room to meet their king.

King Rewik was a thin man with sharp hawkish features. He sat stiffly erect, braced in starched clothes of an austere cut, though his hair in contrast was wayward. Wispy and greying, it straggled around his neck while his tall gold crown encircled a shiny bald pate. He was attended by grave lines of bishops and churchmen and, beyond them, an assemblage of nobles. His eyes flicked towards Hal and Ceowulf, while he continued to address the gathered courtiers. After a drawn-out soliloquy, he inclined his head in the direction of the latecomers, indicating that they should take their positions nearer to the throne and await his pleasure.

Hal was immediately annoyed. The king's summons had been imperative and here he was, forced to listen to his Royal Highness discussing the marbling for his private chapel. Hal tried to imagine what Brid would say if she were here but found it impossible. He smiled warmly at the thought of her. He was surprised that, though he had been gone from Torra Alta little more than a week, he was already missing her. He wondered if she were missing him and had a sudden stab of doubt. She was alone with Spar.

He didn't have many doubts about Brid's affections but he was always suspicious of Spar's. Oh sure, for the last three years Spar had been courting May, a delightful girl; kind, generous and pleasantly pretty, a lesser version of Brid in many ways. But, concurring with the castle gossip, Hal suspected that Caspar only chased after May as a substitute for Brid, whom everyone knew he worshipped. He wondered how May tolerated it.

Even Branwolf had tried to break his son's infatuation over Brid, constantly inviting merchants and noblemen with eligible young daughters and employing the prettiest of girls to work in the keep. But with both Brid and May too close for comfort, Caspar had managed to ignore them all. Only when he and Caspar went off to the capital to participate in tournaments or to enjoy festivities at other noblemen's castles did the youth become swept up in the revelries and satisfy his lusts with a couple of the many girls eager for the company of young noblemen.

Still, he had every faith in Brid and was proud to be chosen by Branwolf when Rewik asked for a representative from each barony to meet at the palace on this day in mid Horning.

Rewik drew a deep breath and looked sternly at the latest arrivals to his assembly. "You are late. I asked for you to be here on this date and expected you after breakfast. It is now near noon. Every other representative was here as requested. Do you have anything to say?"

"Your Majesty, only that we have long breakfasts in Torra Alta," Hal quipped.

A titter of stifled laughter ran round the vaulted throne-room though Rewik glared coldly at the young raven-haired Torra Altan. Ceowulf stood carefully on Hal's toe and pressed his boot firmly downwards, warning him to hold his tongue.

At last, the king jerked his head away. Stretching his narrow mouth to uncomfortable limits, he graced his court with a rare smile. "I have decided to take a wife."

Hal found his eyebrows involuntarily rising in surprise. It had long been understood amongst the noblemen and merchant-classes of Belbidia that the crown would pass to Rewik's brother, Prince Renaud. After all, the king was already into his fifties and had never before shown any inclination to choose a wife. Hal wondered what could possibly have brought about this abrupt decision. He glanced around the assembly, curious to find Prince Renaud's face and judge his reaction. Like his brother, he was tall and thin though he moved with more grace. He had the usual Belbidian dark brown hair and greenish hazel eyes but there was something regal and defiantly self-assured in his distinguished jutting chin, sharp nose and dignified but relaxed stance.

Hal knew him to be many years younger than his brother, still being in his early forties, and was judged by all to be considerably more handsome. Their mother had suffered from a weakening ailment and lost many children between her two sons, which accounted for the gap in their ages.

If Renaud was galled by Rewik's sudden decision to marry, he didn't show it. No doubt the announcement had not come as a surprise as it had to the rest of the murmuring throng who looked from the king to his brother, gossip welling and stirring in their minds. The prince returned their curious stares with a flat smile but Hal could guess at the churning emotions behind it.

To Hal, Renaud's one quick glance at his feet and then towards his king had said it all. His own suppressed emotions surged up from a deep pit in his belly. He knew what it was like to be second in line.

No one, however, had ever suggested or even hinted that he would succeed above Caspar. Renaud, on the other hand, had believed for many years that he was his brother's heir. What a galling shock it must have been to learn of the king's intentions. Hal half-smiled. At least he no longer coveted Torra Alta. No, he had Brid and as her husband he would have considerable standing. At the back of his mind, however, there nagged the realization that it would only be reflected status and he knew he yearned for glory in his own right. He consoled himself with the thought that there were seven barons of Belbidia but only one Trinity of high priestesses in all the countries of the Caballan Sea. When he married Brid, surely his status would exceed Caspar's. Then it would no longer matter that he was not a baron.

Rewik was speaking again. Hal missed the first part of the announcement, something boring about state protocol and that they were all here as representatives of their baronies to sign a treaty approving the marriage – a formality only.

"Who's he marrying?" Hal whispered to Ceowulf.

The sombre knight shook his head in mock despair. "You're as feather-brained as Spar sometimes," he groaned.

Hal grimaced in protest at the insult.

"Princess Cymbeline," Ceowulf whispered.

"Of Ceolothia?" Hal asked in disbelief.

"The very same. Is there another we should know about?"

"But surely she's barely twenty," Hal protested, counting on his fingers. He had met the princess's brothers at the famous Camaalian tournament and knew that the princess was younger than both Prince Tudwal and the Prince Turquin. He looked sideways up at the throne, his silky black hair dangling over his dark olive eyes. It wasn't much of a love match. Still Belbidia was a powerful country and, no doubt, Ceolothia looked to make a useful ally. Hal wondered if the princess had ever seen Rewik or his likeness.

The king tilted his head back as he drew breath to speak. "The wedding is to take place here in Farona after a seemly engagement. Princess Cymbeline will be escorted here where she can become accustomed to her new home. My brother, Prince Renaud is to lead the escort party as it would be unbecoming for a king to fetch his own bride."

"Oh yeah," Ceowulf murmured sceptically under his breath. "It's only because he gets seasick and doesn't wish to bow to the King of Ceolothia, which he would have to do if he visited his court."

"I feel that to give my envoy sufficient pageantry I would like Prince Renaud to be accompanied by a number of eminent peers and would welcome one or two volunteers."

Rewik could say no more before Ceowulf grabbed Hal's wrist and pulled him forward, saying loudly that they would be honoured to form part of the escort.

"We would?" Hal was taken aback. "Who gave you leave to speak for me?" he grumbled under his breath.

The Caldean shrugged nonchalantly.

"What about Brid? I promised I would arrange our wedding as soon as I returned from Farona, and . . ." He swallowed his words; he knew he wanted to go with Ceowulf. Brid would wait and besides the separation might make her less inclined to take him for granted. He loved Brid with all his heart but she was after all only a woman and he shouldn't be entirely at her beck and call. A trip into foreign lands was really quite appealing and he wouldn't be breaking his promise because he would leave straight from here and so wouldn't be returning from Farona just yet.

Rewik pursed his lips and stared hard at them for several seconds before looking hopefully around the throne-room for more favourable volunteers but the other barons and their representatives were already voicing their concerns about other issues.

Baron Wiglaf's eldest son from Nattarda complained of border disputes with Jotunn. The Baron Godafrid of Ovissia spoke so loudly about wolves that nobody could distinctly hear why the Baron of Piscera was so concerned to return home, especially amidst the general shaking of heads and shuffling of feet as the other nobles dodged Rewik's eyes.

One of the king's wizened advisors nodded towards Hal and Ceowulf, "A perfect escort if I may suggest, your highness. These men have both seen action, which is something rare nowadays amongst Belbidian nobles."

King Rewik seemed unconvinced. "Princess Cymbeline is a cultured lady and, like myself, worships the civilized god of the New Faith. To send her an escort comprising my brother and two nobles known for their close affinity with the pagan worship seems at the least a trifle indelicate."

"Sire!" Hal exclaimed loudly. "I must protest—"

Rewik waved him down. "I am convinced by my bishops that no harm can come of allowing men to worship these gods of the earth though my sense of logic laughs at such a ridiculous notion. However, I will not wrong the delightful Princess Cymbeline by providing her with an escort of pagans."

"Perhaps I might redress the balance." A young man, Hal judged about three years older than himself, with a small, pointed nose, arched eyebrows and flappy ears, stepped forward. Though he was of lighter frame, paler hair and lacked the long whiskers, the family resemblance to his father, Baron of Ovissia, was unmistakable. The cloudy light falling through the stained-glass windows played on his busy hands that fidgeted anxiously; otherwise, he seemed composed, his voice well-oiled with pleasantries. "For such an important cause as the safe journey of the king's future bride, I am willing to leave the problem of the wolves to my father and younger brother. Let me assure his highness that we in Ovissia will always remain faithful to the one-true God and he can trust in our proper conduct regarding his future bride."

"That is good, Lord Tupwell. This is better." Rewik looked much cheered as he nodded vigorously at the eldest son of Baron Godafrid.

Hal wasn't so pleased about the choice. Though the man seemed personable enough, he outranked both himself and Ceowulf. The young Torra Altan had no care to be ordered around by a man who, he was certain, would know little of life beyond sheep farming. That, after all, was all they ever did in Ovissia. Inadvertently he sniffed his disapproval and Ceowulf glowered at him, reminding him to keep his manners.

"And I, Your Majesty!" Another nobleman, whom Hal didn't immediately recognize, stepped forward. Dressed in a fine emerald doublet over silken leggings, he undoubtedly felt he was quite the picture of courtly fashion though the attire was unflattering on the man's stocky legs. He did, however, have a likeable smile.

Great Mother! It suddenly dawned on Hal that this was the Baron of Piscera's youngest son, Hardwin. The man had gained a couple of stone since he had last seen him only last year in Caldea and the athletic Torra Altan hadn't immediately recognized him. Hardwin, he remembered, had not participated in the tournament training that summer, which Ceowulf had organized, but had come only for the courtly entertainment.

"Good! The five of you will leave at once." Rewik snapped his fingers and a page came running forward with scrolls of petitions. Affronted, Hal realized they had been unceremoniously dismissed.

The noblemen dispersed and he nodded polite greetings to those who caught his eye as he made his way over to greet Prince Renaud. Ceowulf, with his impeccable courtly manners, was shaking hands with his father's nearest neighbour, the Baron of Quertos, and tenderly kissing the hand of his youngest daughter. Quite pretty, Hal mused to himself, but not a candle to Brid. He marched purposefully across the room to shake hands with the prince.

"Well, young Lord Hal from Torra Alta. So nice to have you for company," Renaud said in an all too perfunctory manner.

"Are we taking many men?" Hal asked, eager to strike up a conversation, his voice deep and self-assured like his brother's. He raised his chin and stared Renaud levelly in the eye to prove that he would not tolerate being patronized.

"What?" The prince seemed distracted as if lost in his thoughts. "Oh, men? A dozen, no perhaps a score. No need to make too big a fuss but Ceolothia is large and lawlessness is common in the uncivilised areas, I am warned." He was looking beyond Hal and towards the throne, which Hal found immensely peeving. "You can ride, I take it? We'll do the first part of the journey by sea but we'll have to take to the wretched saddle for over a hundred leagues through Ceolothia's miserable interior in order to reach the king's court at Castabrice. Can't have you saddle sore and looking foolish in front of the men."

Hal was frowning. Clearly the prince had been paying

little attention earlier. "I can ride, sir. Nobody has ever doubted my abilities."

Renaud didn't seem to notice that he had caused affront. "Just be ready by morning." He turned and swept away just as Ceowulf was approaching to greet him.

The knight raised his eyebrows. "Pleasantly mannered," he commented wryly.

Hal smiled at the sarcasm. "I hope you can ride, Lord Ceowulf. We don't want you shaming the royal escort. If I were . . ." The words and smile died on his face as he overheard a loudly whispered remark.

". . . and, I'm surprised the king has chosen a Torra Altan to go to Ceolothia for his bride. Seems a wry choice to me. They can't even keep their own women in order and I wouldn't trust such rough characters to escort a bride."

Hal spun on his heels, his hand automatically flying to the ornate hilt of his sword. In one graceful sweep the blade sprang into the air, the coloured light from the stained-glass windows dancing across the bright metal. His eyes narrowed to slits as he caught the expression on Baron Wiglaf's sneering face. As one, the line of bishops stepped back in horror, murmuring their disapproval – not so much because the nobleman had drawn his sword but at the pagan runes engraved along the length of it. They were clear, angular blood-red letters cut deep into the cold hard steel. The king, however, looked on dispassionately as if vaguely amused to see how his subjects would resolve their quarrel, though after a moment's pause, he snapped his fingers at the guards who lined the throne-room.

"You insult the name of Torra Alta, you insult my kinsmen and you insult my future bride!" Hal's voice bellowed deep and rich at Wiglaf, Baron of Nattarda. He looked contemptuously at the lord of the region grown wealthy on its creamy cheeses and rich butters.

Ceowulf groaned. "Hal, this just isn't the place to sort a quarrel."

"Listen here, you udder of a man, you baron of bloated cows, the name of Torra Alta is too good to be befouled by passing from your cud-filled mouth," Hal insulted him, only to find himself surrounded by Rewik's guards. Each man brandished a pike. He looked at them disdainfully. "Do you think your feeble wands will deter me from defending the honour of my barony?"

"How can you talk of honour when Torra Alta allows fiendish wolves to run free within its borders?" Wiglaf, somewhat bolstered by the support of the king's guard, stabbed his fat finger at Hal. "Is it not well known that Branwolf opposes the Wolf Tax and lets the beasts spawn in the Yellow Mountains and so spread throughout the rest of the realm? Belbidia would be a better place if both were removed."

"Here, here," the general cry went up.

Baron Wiglaf continued, "If Branwolf allowed my men into his barony we'd see the last of these wolves in a matter of weeks. Three score men accustomed to the work would get every last little pup and we'd be rid of the pestilence for good. But instead, as soon as the quota is met, he forbids, *forbids*, I tell you, any more killing. I say he's set on driving the wolves south to ruin the rest of Belbidia. That's what I say he's doing."

There was a murmur of agreement.

"It's because he has no sheep," the long-whiskered Baron Godafrid of Ovissia complained, though in the mildest of tones. "He'd change his tune a lot quicker if his horses or boars were suffering. Very different businesses horses and sheep." His son, Lord Tupwell, looked at his father as if he were a fool.

"He's doing it to disrupt the civil peace in Belbidia,"

Wiglaf roared. "He's set this plague of wolves on us and he'll follow with his men and his witches to force their stinking paganism on the rest of us. The man's a traitor!"

Hal looked at the pikestaffs around him. He knew he shouldn't do it, not here in the king's throne-room. It was tantamount to treason to strike at the king's guard but he knew he could wield the great runesword without causing injury and he couldn't let the Baron of Nattarda get away with calling his brother a traitor.

He tensed his sword arm, meaning only to threaten and cow the bloated man into an apology but then caught a glimpse of Ceowulf shaking his head at him, warning him not to use the weapon.

That was it! That was enough! Ceowulf had told him too many times today what he could or could not do. Hal spun round, the great sword sweeping in a whistling arc around him. A cacophony of metallic chimes rang through the hall, jarring all ears with its echoing steel song.

Hal grinned.

Four guards were staring in disbelief at their shattered weapons. Sparkling dust choked the air where the great runesword, blessed with the power of the Goddess, had shattered the weapons. The king's men held only broken stubs in their trembling hands.

Hal's grin broadened. "Thank you, Mother," he whispered. "Thank you for the expression on their faces."

He turned to gloat at the Baron of Nattarda whose lower jaw was struggling to rise from his chest, his eyes blinking furiously in disbelief. The raven-haired Torra Altan sauntered casually forward and stared the man in the eye.

"You will retract your slander," Hal said lightly with an arrogant smile on his bronzed face and threat in his eyes.

The baron stuttered uncertainly. "Your Majesty," he called weakly for assistance.

The king snapped his fingers and Hal was vaguely aware of scurrying feet and doors being flung open as a further squad of foot soldiers hurried to the throne-room. He knew he would be forced to apologize to the king for this outburst but he wasn't about to lower his sword until Baron Wiglaf had publicly declared that his brother was at least the greatest and most noble of all Belbidia's barons.

"Say it," Hal snarled, pressing the tip of the sword into the centre of the man's doublet just where the buttons strained to retain his bulging gut. "Say that you retract your slander and declare that Baron Branwolf of Torra Alta is a most fine and upstanding nobleman. Say it!" He used the sharp tip of the runesword to prod a little harder.

The Baron of Nattarda looked vainly towards the king but failed to catch his eye. Finally, he threw up his hands. "I retract. I retract. Baron Branwolf is the most honourable of noblemen."

"Good." Hal instantly relaxed and sheathed his sword.

The moment Hal was once more surrounded by the king's guard, Wiglaf began protesting, his fat face swollen with indignant shame as he began puffing like an enraged child. "Sire, Your Majesty, this maniac should be put in chains and thrown into a pit."

Hal looked down his nose, satisfied that he had humiliated the man and shown him to be a coward. Disdainfully, he turned his back on the guards and bowed low to the king who approached, his face smouldering with repressed anger at Hal's attack on his guard. "Your Majesty, forgive me for this unseemly outburst but I found myself forced to defend the honour of my kinsman whom I am here to represent. I am ever your servant and pray I have not offended you," he said with aplomb, his self-confidence having only grown stronger in the last few years.

Hal hoped he was saying more or less the right sort of thing though Rewik looked unimpressed. The tension was broken by a laugh from Prince Renaud. "My brother, don't you think this hot-headed young man has proved himself to be a perfect escort for Princess Cymbeline through Ceolothia's treacherous interior? Look at his ability with the sword!"

Rewik's scowl turned to a faint smile and he nodded appreciatively. "You are right. Indeed, you are right. Let the incident be forgotten." He waved his soldiers aside. "Just so soon as young Lord Hal has apologized of course."

Hal found Ceowulf's eyes hammering into his forehead, willing him to behave. For a moment he thought he would obstinately refuse to back down but, just as suddenly, he changed his mind. Since Ceowulf was expecting him to continue with the quarrel, he would surprise the knight. He bowed gracefully towards the king. "Forgive my outburst. The heat of the moment. All the excitement and the thought of such an honourable trip brought the blood to my head," he excused himself smoothly if not sincerely.

The king nodded and, to Hal's satisfaction, he saw the faint hint of consternation flurry across the Caldean's face. Ceowulf wasn't one for being caught off guard but he had certainly surprised him this time.

The affair was over.

Prince Renaud was signalling from the far end of the throne-room, summoning them to join him, Tupwell and Hardwin in an antechamber. Tupwell's eyes sneered at him from his pale cheeks. Hal smiled smoothly back, ignoring the squinted look of haughty disapproval before taking his leave of the king and making purposeful steps towards the marbled archway. When he was nearly beyond earshot from the general company in the throne-room, he caught the middle part of a hushed conversation.

". . . too powerful by half. Since the resurgence of the Old Faith many of the simple folk of the land would rather look to Branwolf than their own lords, or even the king, simply because he is the husband of the high priestess Keridwen. Now we hear that his young half-brother here is betrothed to another one of the coven. After the wheat blight and the outbreaks of disease in the animals these past two years it's too much. Now with this plague of wolves pouring south from his barony and the concentration of pagan power in Torra Alta with its unnatural hold over the common people, I am becoming uncomfortable, very uncomfortable. And if something isn't . . ."

Hal had turned on his heel but, through the stirring crowd, he couldn't make out who had spoken with such hostility.

CHAPTER FIVE

"He couldn't have gone far." Caspar tried to sound reassuring.

"Unless he's after a bitch," Pip chipped in brightly.

"Oh, shut up," Brid snapped at the youth. "Just shut up and keep looking."

"Sorry!" Pip answered back, evidently hurt. "I was only pointing out—"

Caspar waved a warning hand to silence him.

"Trog just doesn't wander off. He's too lazy for a start. And I'm worried!" Brid added with feeling. "Trog!" she shouted again. There was no answer and she began looking at the ground for any tracks he might have left.

"My lady, in these frozen conditions the snake-catcher wouldn't leave any tracks. The ground's bone hard," old Brock pointed out. "He's probably picked up a scent."

Caspar crossed to take another look at the fallen rowan tree and scrutinize the tree-runes carved by the kobolds. He still couldn't make sense of them and after a while he shrugged and turned back to the spot where he had last seen Trog digging under the root-ball of the blackthorn. They had been so intent on the kobolds that Trog could have run off at any moment without them noticing – but it was unlike the dog. The scent of a stag or boar had never excited him that much in the past.

"We're deep in the Chase," Pip murmured, his voice cracking upwards. "It's a place of mysterious things." He grinned, his eyes wide and sparkling with a sense of adventure, but his face dropped as he caught the priestess's expression. "Oh, Brid, please don't worry so. The dog's got sharp enough teeth to look after himself even if he were surrounded by trolls."

Brock took Pip by the arm and drew him aside, clucking and fussing like a speckled hen. "Don't speak to the young lady like that," the old soldier scolded. "Your sister might speak to Morrigwen without regard for her office but she's training to become a servant to the Great Mother so that's different. Now you're old enough to know better and you'll set a bad example in the garrison if you carry on like this. Just because your sister—"

"Don't you judge me by my sister!" Pip suddenly reddened, not bothering to lower his voice as Brock had done. "My position is not won through her. I'm my own man. She doesn't look after me."

Caspar was taken aback by Pip's sudden outburst and the furtive glance that he cast in his direction.

Pip continued excitedly, "I know what the soldiers say. I have ears and—"

"Pip, what are you talking about?" Caspar stopped his words. "You've evidently misunderstood some innocent remark. What could May's relationship with Morrigwen possibly have to do with you? Nobody holds it against you."

Pip rudely threw his head back and sighed. "Never mind, Master Spar. Let's just find the dog." He moved away from the uprooted grove and pushed his way moodily through the saplings.

Too aghast to speak for several moments, Brock spluttered and puffed in indignation. "Sir, I'll fetch him back.

The whippersnapper! The insolent pup! Speaking to the Baron's son like that. I'll . . . I'll . . ."

Caspar waved Brock's blusterings aside. He watched Pip's back as the boy weaved through the saplings. He knew he should call the lad back and reprimand him for his insolence but he truly didn't want to. It was just Pip's way and he was worried for the boy and wondered what might have upset him. Thirteen was such an awkward, confusing age, he reasoned, feeling that at seventeen his experience of life was both balanced and mature.

Caspar wondered what talk the boy had overheard. The only gossip he had heard about Pip was that several of the younger castle maidens had tried to win his attentions and been roundly rejected. This had increased his popularity amongst those not yet spurned but had also made one or two bitter against him.

Before Hal had left for Farona, he had laughingly remarked that Pip thought himself too good for them. "He's waiting for a girl with a title," he had told them. "Position and good fortune."

Brid had overheard this remark and scoffed at her betrothed. "Oh Hal, you do miss the point."

Something had distracted them from the conversation at the time and Caspar now thought to ask Brid what she had meant but the timing was bad. The priestess was down on her knees, using a root broken from the foot of the holly tree to delve beneath the dark fungus-covered roots of the blackthorn. A twist of honeysuckle embraced the rotted trunk. She paused for breath and took a moment to look at the rambling plant.

"Uilleand, the tree of hidden secrets," she murmured, combing her fingers thoughtfully through the twines of honeysuckle before recommencing her work. She then began muttering at the dog's scrape marks, "Oh Trog, whatever were you doing digging down here amongst the blackthorn? I've told you a thousand times not to go near blackthorn." Her voice was beginning to catch in her throat. "There's quite a big hole down here. Maybe he's dug down under the roots and got stuck," she suggested anxiously, holding her breath to listen for any sounds of scratching or whimpering; but there were none. "Well, aren't you going to help me dig for him?" she demanded, angrily looking up, her fingers clogged with damp soil and her face smeared with earth where she had wiped aside a stray lock of hair.

Caspar jumped down beside her, a stout length of wood in his hands, and started to dig furiously into the wide scrape beneath the upturned roots of the blackthorn. "He couldn't be here," Caspar argued as he dug. The hole narrowed as they went deeper. "It's only a small burrow not big enough for a badger let alone Trog."

"I know that," Brid replied impatiently, sitting aside so that Caspar could dig more freely.

"So why am I burning up energy here?" he asked, though he continued to do Brid's bidding.

"Because Trog was digging here," she replied laconically and to Caspar's mind illogically.

He looked at her sideways and dug a little less determinedly.

Brid threw her eyes heavenward before explaining, "I want to know what he thought was down here. Something drew his attention and it wasn't kobolds. Kobolds live in trees not burrows. If we find what interested him maybe we'll have a better chance of finding him. And if you're not going to dig properly you can move out of the way and let me do it."

"My lady, let me," Brock offered but the two young Torra Altans ignored him. Caspar redoubled his efforts, breaking away sodden roots and stabbing at the ground with his stick. He was vigorously worrying at a few supple stems that refused to be parted when suddenly he stopped and sat back on his haunches.

"What is it?" Brid demanded.

"A carcass. It looks like the ribcage of a deer."

"A deer? Don't be daft, Spar. Why would anyone bury a deer deep beneath the roots of a blackthorn?"

"Perhaps it was some form of sacrifice. After all this is an ancient grove."

"If it were a sacrifice, they would have burnt the deer, killed it and burnt it, but more likely eaten it. Let me look."

Without any hint of squeamishness, Brid plunged her hands into the earth, working with her makeshift trowel to clear away the loose soil.

Caspar could see clearly now that it wasn't the carcass of a deer but a wolf. The maggot-ridden ribcage was still firmly strung together with sinews and muscle, and it had been stripped of its viscera.

Secured to the inside of the ribcage was a small, rolled bundle, tied with leather thongs. For a moment the two Torra Altans stared at the bundle speechlessly before Caspar cut the threads of leather that held it to the backbone.

Without thinking, he handed the roll to Brid for her to examine though he immediately regretted it. He wondered why he didn't take things more on himself rather than always deferring to someone else, be it his father, any of the three high priestesses or, worst of all, Hal.

"Why would anyone hide a package inside a wolf's ribcage?" Brid wondered as her nimble fingers untied the leather tresses and rolled open the pelt. A jagged pebble the size of a walnut slid out onto the ground. Brid stooped to pick it up before it could get lost amongst the roots. Most of the stone's surface was rough and grey in colour but a portion had been chipped away to reveal a section of deeply coloured gemstone within.

"Look," Brid said in amazement, holding up the stone-encrusted gem to the winter sun. "It's beautiful. Such a deep gold shot through with bursts of red. I've never seen one so big."

"A sunburst ruby!" Caspar exclaimed as she handed it to him. She didn't, however, relinquish the rolled strip of hide from which it had fallen. Caspar watched as she unfurled it.

"A strange message," she mused to herself.

"Well, what's it say?" Caspar demanded as Brid's silence lengthened.

"'*Rich finds around Mirror Lake and Dragons Claw Valley.*'"

"Rich finds of what?" Caspar asked, holding out his hand to take the pelt.

Brid pointed to the raw gemstone in his other hand. "More of those I imagine."

Caspar frowned thoughtfully and looked from the wolf's carcass to the gemstone and then to the message. "But—" he started and then thought more deeply. "But why the secrecy? Why hide the message in a wolf's carcass? It all seems so dramatic. If there are sunburst rubies to be found in the Yellow Mountains why is someone being so secretive about it? Why haven't they gone straight to my father with the news?"

Brid gave him the same sort of despairing look that Hal was apt to. "Obviously because they don't want him to know about it. Any gemstones found in the Yellow Mountains are rightfully his. All this secrecy can only mean that someone wants the gems for themselves without paying him tribute like the iron workers in the far west and the sulphur miners on the Ovissian border."

"That's daft though," Caspar protested. "Of course, they could steal *some* but no one could get away with a full-scale mining operation without my father knowing."

Brid raised her eyebrows thoughtfully. "No, you're quite right. It doesn't make much sense. There's not much point trying to mine without first gaining your father's permission. But someone's hidden this message here so they must have a purpose. Someone thinks it's worthwhile to take the minerals."

"Thieves!" Caspar exclaimed indignantly.

Brid slipped the uncut jewel and the roll of wolfskin into her scrip before rising and looking thoughtfully around. Although she appeared to be focusing on the far distance, Caspar knew she was really looking deep into her mind, puzzling through the import of their extraordinary find.

"Put the carcass back as we found it," she instructed and Brock jumped to her order. "No, wait." She turned back to her scrip, pulled out a hare's foot and, with her knife, carefully cut a small patch from her bearskin cloak. She screwed her brow into a thoughtful knot before quickly nicking the inside of her arm with her knife and using the bloodied blade to stain characters onto the parchment.

"What are you writing?" Caspar asked, wincing at the cut on her arm.

Brid smiled. "Wait where the Sylvanrush and Whitehart meet," she read out loud with a degree of satisfaction. "We could, of course hide out here and see if anyone turns up but there's nowhere to hide with all the trees stripped away and we must find these wolflings first."

Caspar nodded in eager agreement. "Where the two

rivers meet is an obvious place and it's on our way. We'll deal with this on our return from the pass. If someone's waiting there, we'll know they're suspicious," he concluded.

Brid rolled the hare's foot up in the strip of bearskin and stuffed it inside the ribcage, leaving Brock to finish burying the bones. Caspar strode eagerly towards his horse. "Right, we'd better be moving on quickly. We'll get the wolf cubs first and then set up vigil where the rivers meet. Now where's Pip? Hasn't he come back yet? Did you see him again, Brock?"

The old retainer looked vaguely around him and shook his head. "His horse is gone too, Master Spar. Silly lad must have come back for it and then rode off alone."

Caspar groaned. "Well, we can't very well go on without him – nor Trog for that matter. Maybe he's picked up the dog's trail," he added optimistically.

It didn't take them long to find the steadily paced tracks that the gelding's studded shoes had left in the crisp ground. Caspar reflected that he had made a poor leader so far. He'd lost a dog and one of his party already.

"Oh Mother, he's a stupid fool," Brid cursed as they slid into the dark shadows beneath the tall evergreen pines. The ground crackled and snapped as the horses' hooves crunched over fallen cones and dead wood littering the forest floor. It took a moment for Caspar's eyes to adapt to the gloom and he was too late to avoid a branch that whipped into his face and scratched his cheeks.

"I'm sorry about the lad, sir. Please, it's my fault: I should have kept a better eye on him," Brock repeatedly apologized despite Caspar's best efforts to silence him. "I don't know what's gotten into his head, strutting off like that. He knew we'd already lost the dog. I feel responsible, Master Spar."

"It's certainly not your fault," Caspar said reasonably.

"Perhaps Pip caught sight of Trog," he added, surprised to find himself defending the impudent youth.

Brid looked at him sideways as if to tell him to be less gullible. When Brock dropped back a little distance she discreetly murmured, "It's because of you and May. He must have sloped off in a sulk after Brock mentioned how the garrison mocked him."

"What about me and May?" Caspar pouted. "He must know something I don't. She's not paid the slightest interest in me in ages."

"Is that right?" Brid retorted sceptically, slowing to scan the forest floor.

Brid always seemed to know so much more about what went on than he did. She was quite quick-witted, bubbling with life and goodwill at one moment then the next minute wise and coolly serene. It made her aloof but all the more alluring for it. In the last three years the boyish lines of her athletic figure had filled into more feminine curves but without losing any of her graceful energy. Her extraordinary eyes were captivating too. They seemed to laugh impishly and yet had the wisdom of an ancient. She was so full of contradictions and Caspar felt his chest tighten as his eyes embraced her.

What was he thinking?! Though there was no one to see him, Caspar felt his skin flush crimson. How could he still think such things about Brid when he had promised May a hundred times that she was the only one in his heart.

Caspar sighed at the thought of the gentle-souled girl who thought so little about herself and cared so much for others. She, too, was unusually small and light boned in stature like the three high priestesses and himself. Though she lacked Brid's colouring and fiery energy, there was a strong resemblance between the two.

It was soon growing dark. The northern winter sun had been creeping behind the trees for some while now, setting their straight trunks aflame in the rich evening light. Caspar had no idea where they were. What was Pip thinking, riding off like that? The noble youth found himself facing the familiar dilemma of how he could reasonably discipline the younger brother of the girl he wished to marry. It was an awkward situation and he didn't like awkward situations. They were embarrassing.

He had been wrong allowing the boy to have so little respect for him that he could just strut off like this. It was unthinkable . . . and yet not in the circumstances. There had been so few left. Just a handful had survived the Vaalakan siege and they shared a bond of comradeship born from the hardship, grief and final triumph. Now for three years they had worked shoulder to shoulder to restore the castle to its former glory and, naturally, those survivors, like May and Pip, the Captain and Cook, had been drawn close to the Baron's family.

Pip had always been impish but the trait had been encouraged by Cook, and even Keridwen, of all people, took pleasure in it. They had laughed indulgently at him rather than scolding him when he stole cakes or mimicked the sergeants by rudely strutting up and down beside them. The women had all felt so sorry for the newly orphaned boy. But Caspar knew he had let it go too far. One day he would inherit Torra Alta and if Pip were ever to hold a position in Caspar's castle, he would need to learn the sort of respect that the Captain showed to his father. Nobody gainsaid Branwolf. There again nobody gainsaid Hal either, Caspar thought gloomily. No, it probably wasn't Pip's fault after all. Ultimately it was his own. He shook away his thoughts and peered at the darkening ground.

Judging by the tracks, Pip had kept up a good pace and seemed to have a direct purpose. After stooping low over Firecracker's shoulders for some while, Caspar sat up and finally broke the silence. "He clearly couldn't be lost so what's he doing?"

No one could give him a sensible reply.

The sun's rays cut horizontally through the thinner regions of the forest, casting long leggy shadows. They had been following Pip's trail for a long while and a mist had begun to seep up from the ground. It would be dark soon. At last Brid turned her shadow-cloaked face towards Caspar. "I just can't see his tracks anymore. We'll need to find somewhere to rest for the night."

"Pip will have to stop too," Caspar argued. "If we can keep going just a little longer perhaps, we'll catch him up."

Brid's dark shape shrugged. "I doubt that we'll find him before tomorrow now but we can try. Pip!" she called hopefully out into the gloom and then after a moment's pause, she shouted more insistently, "Trog!"

The silence of the forest seemed to swell as they vainly waited for a reply.

"I can't understand it," Brid despaired. "Trog would never abandon me and he'd certainly be able to follow our trail. How could we lose both of them?" she groaned and then whistled a shrill boyish whistle that cut through the twilight. The sound was swallowed by a long, low mournful howl that rose to a screech. The hairs on the back of Caspar's back prickled and his hands tensed on the reins, steadying Firecracker who plunged against his bit.

"That wasn't a Yellow Mountain wolf," Brid murmured, slowing alongside Caspar. "We must find somewhere to shelter right now!"

Caspar didn't argue. He had never seen a hooded wolf alive but he had seen their skins. They had been nearer the size of a pony than a wolf with teeth that jutted two inches below their lower lips. "Where do you suggest we stop? We've long since passed the village where we normally stop at the Tusk and Antlers and its some way to the next."

"We're also a long way from the main track," Brid reflected, "but when I lived here, there used to be a charcoal-burner out this way. If we can find him, he'll give us shelter but they do tend to move around quite a bit."

She urged her horse off the track onto a small undulating path that dipped in and out of the mist. In the growing darkness the roots of the trees were like the black gnarled faces of hanged murderers against the white shroud. The stillness was oppressive. But at least the moon was up and with Brock bringing up the rear, Caspar took the lead and pushed Firecracker to a faster pace.

Though a wolf's howl could travel a long distance, Caspar was certain the animal had been close. He cast back over his shoulder. He had not heard the snap of twigs nor the rustle of branches but he had already convinced himself that he could hear an animal close by. His stallion's ears were flattened against his skull and he threw out anxious kicks with his heels.

"We'd better find this place quickly," Caspar warned, his fingers twitching nervously at his bow.

Brid's face gleamed white in a stray beam of moonlight that spilt down through the trees. There was another howl and Caspar's ears rang with the noise. His heart thumped. Closer now, much closer, the sound of breathing and rustling leaves was gaining on them. Brid's horse plunged wildly off the track, bucking into the tangled undergrowth.

Padding footfalls were suddenly audible as the animal raced forward with a yowl, teeth gnashing. All three horses panicked, laying back their ears and fleeing at breakneck speed through the dark of the forest.

Caspar hunched low over Firecracker's stretched neck, wincing as the branches whipped past his head. He thought of nothing except Brid's safety. To either side, he caught glimpses of glowing eyes and the flash of white teeth as a moonbeam glanced off the keen points of fangs. There was a stifled cry from Brid as they broke out into a clearing.

Two pairs of red eyes glowed ahead where the rest of the pack was waiting to spring. A wolf, the size of a small pony, launched itself at Brid's horse and latched onto its flailing hock, its teeth, white daggers against the dark of the horse's hide. Raising his bow, Caspar twisted awkwardly to make the shot over Firecracker's ears. There was a stifled howl and then a thud as the hooded wolf fell away but he had been too slow to save Brid's horse, which was dragging its leg and staggering forward.

Firecracker side-stepped the body of the wolf and for the briefest moment Caspar thought with detachment that he had earned the extra twelve guineas for felling the beast. There were two more wolves closing on Brid, the pack honing its attack on the wounded animal. Breathing heavily at Caspar's side, Brock loosed several arrows but felled only one beast. Caspar reached over his shoulder to the quiver on his back, snatched up an arrow and aimed again, just as he heard the sound of snapping jaws at his heels.

There were too many of them. Caspar turned all his thoughts to saving Brid who had nothing but a hunting knife and her sacramental sickle with which to defend herself. He expertly loosed arrow after arrow without pause, barely aware of the screams of pain from the wolves. To get a better aim he wheeled Firecracker into the tangle of undergrowth at the edge of the clearing. He loosed one more arrow and found himself hurtling towards the leaf mould as Firecracker lashed out at an attacking wolf only to get his hoof snared by the undergrowth. Caspar stifled a scream as his unprotected head glanced the root of a tree and then Firecracker's body rolled on his foot, twisting his knee joint.

It took him a moment to gather his senses as he gazed up into the moonlight. He could hear the wolves scattering through the forest, a few whimpers and the heavy grunts of distressed horses. Dazed, he heaved his head up from the forest bed and blinked into the gloom.

"Brid," he murmured before he could quite see clearly. "Brid!"

He twisted to look for her. Earth and leaves were caught in his fringe and smeared across his face, obscuring his vision. As he brushed them aside an abrupt movement caught his attention. A stag, yes, surely it was a stag tossing its vast, branching antlers. It was standing over a dark mound lying at the foot of an old yew. Caspar pushed himself up onto his elbows; the effort sent his head reeling. The stag swung its head towards him, and for the briefest moment moonlight fell across its face. The face of a man, Caspar thought in disbelief.

Their eyes met and then the beast, whatever it was, vanished into the forest. Caspar staggered towards the heap that was Brid's body. "Brid," he called urgently. "Brid."

He rolled her over and to his relief she groaned. Hugging her to him, he closed his eyes in thankfulness. Shortly he became aware of someone standing over them.

"Whatever were you thinking of? Whatever possessed you to be out in the forest after dark? The forest ain't safe at the best of times. We'd best be hurrying to my home." The voice was deep, soothing and calm, as reassuring as a father's voice to a troubled child. The man had huge round dark eyes and straggling long grey hair. In the moonlight it looked like ivy hanging from the tall stump of a broken tree. As tall and broad as the strongest bowman, the man's presence gave Caspar overwhelming comfort.

"I saw a stag, with the face of a man," he stammered, still gathering his senses.

The man chuckled. "There are many stags in the forest. Must just have been a young buck in the moonlight; nothing to worry about. You do what you can to gather the horses while I carry the young lad."

"She's a maiden," Caspar automatically corrected, whilst thinking that the stag could not have been young; he had seen the twelve points of its magnificent antlers.

"I'll carry her," Brock spoke from the darkness. He swept Brid up as if she were no more than a baby.

"A maiden, eh? So, what exactly are these youngsters doing out so deep in the Chase a' night?" the forester asked Brock. "Eloping, eh?"

Brock stammered for an answer while Caspar laughed at the absurdity of the idea. "No, no, we're looking for wolves."

Caspar watched the man stiffen. "Trappers then, are you?"

"Never!" Caspar was affronted. "Though I wouldn't be sorry to see the back of these hooded wolves."

He limped towards Firecracker who was pawing and snorting at the ground nearby. Brid's cream mare hung her head low between her knees, blowing hard and, as Caspar put a hand lightly on her neck, he found she was trembling. He soothed her muzzle, purring soft nonsensical words to calm her.

"Steady there, now girl, the wolves have gone. Now, let's

see what damage is done." The mare plodded obediently forward as he tugged at her reins though she favoured her near hindleg. "Poor lady," Caspar sympathized. "But not to worry; Brid will see you put back to rights." With a horse in each hand, he plodded after the tall man who led Brock's horse, noticing with surprise and admiration the length of the man's bow. He must have driven off the last of the wolves, he thought with gratitude.

They wound their way deeper and deeper into the forest and Caspar found himself leaning against Firecracker to take the stress off his knee. At last, they could see a small glowing circle of light ahead and as they approached he saw it was firelight shining through the round window of a long, low forest dwelling.

It was more a byre than a house and when they halted outside, he saw that, although it was well thatched with faggots of twigs and rushes and clad with sods of mossy turf, it was little more than a covered hollow in the ground. A small round window near ground level let out the light of the welcoming fire into the night. A circular central section of the roof rose to a conical peak, the very tip left uncovered, allowing the mellow wood smoke to escape and slide down the thatch to mingle with the night mist.

A hide flap covered an entrance wide enough for livestock. It was approached by a ditch dug deep into the ground. The stranger descended into the dugout, calling out for him to follow with the other horses. Once down in the hollowed-out channel, Caspar saw how it divided ahead. The stranger gave him Brock's horse to hold before slipping away beneath the hide curtain to his left and opening it wide so that Brock could more easily carry Brid within. The forester returned moments later to help Caspar with the horses.

Caspar hesitated. "We lost one of our party earlier in

the day: a young boy named Pip. I must go after him," he explained. He was loath to abandon Brid but on the other hand Pip was alone in the forest.

"You won't get anywhere looking for someone in the dark. You'd best rest and then I'll help you in the morning."

Caspar was eased by the man's solid confidence. He was right. Visibility was dropping rapidly as the mist thickened and, besides, the forest was Pip's home. He would likely have friends that would give him shelter or at worst he would be able to climb a tree for the night. It would be cold but he had his bearskin.

Grunting, the tangle-haired stranger heaved aside a grid of logs lashed together with ropes that sufficed for a door. Carrying a smoking torch, he led Caspar forward into a deep underground chamber.

"The old barn was useless against the wolves," the man explained shortly. "I had to dig this out instead. So very much easier to protect. Now let's see to this mare." The forester began washing the cut on the horse's hock. "Just a flesh wound," he announced presently. "Sore no doubt but the tendons and muscles ain't torn. Rest will be the best thing for her. Like yourself."

Caspar never thought to question the man. Somehow, he trusted him and followed him out of the horse pen and through the hide curtain into his thatched home. Brid was lying on a deerskin by the fire, her head resting on a pillow of blankets. Her eyes were open and she was tentatively prodding the back of her head. Brock had retired to a discreet distance, warming himself in the shadows at the edge of the hearth.

"It's all my fault," he said as Caspar approached. "The boy wandering off like that. I might have known the rascal would run off to see his old friends. I should have looked out for him. Oh, Master Spar, I'm sorry."

Caspar did his best to assure the man that he was not to blame, while feeling guilty himself.

"I must have fallen from my horse," the priestess muttered, slowly beginning to look around her. She smiled faintly on seeing Caspar and then looked curiously around the room. A strange-looking, old woman fussed at her pillows before shuffling away to stir the contents of a black pot. It swung from a tripod standing astride the flames, a comforting slurp and bubble mumbling away within. Caspar ran his tongue across his lips as he caught the smell of meaty broth. Brid stirred and looked round at the woman.

"Who are you?" Brid asked, frowning at the woman and then the forester who was standing by the doorway. "Do I know you?" She sounded suspicious.

The man shrugged and drew nearer to the fire, lowering his solid weight onto a stubby, three-legged stool. "You may do but I doubt it. I haven't been here in years. It must be over sixteen years now and you don't look old enough to remember me." The skin of his weathered face crinkled into a smile. "But I know you, Brid." He looked at her eyes. "You might have only been little more than a baby but there could be none other alive with eyes like that."

Brid barely returned his smile. "I'm at a disadvantage, huntsman," she addressed him as she quickly scanned the long bow that was now hanging by the entrance.

After a moment's heavy pause, he said simply, "Harle. Call me Harle. And this is my mother."

The woman smiled a beaming smile full of healthy white teeth. Caspar was surprised. She seemed too old to still have such good teeth. Like her son, her hair was ragged but lighter, weeping like willow fronds over her shoulders. The firelight gave a greenish-grey hue to her face, though she seemed more unwashed and earthy rather than sickly.

"Come sit by the fire, son of Keridwen. Join your man here," she whispered, nodding at Brock, who looked uncomfortably perched on a tiny stool. "And, Brid, some food will help you. Taste my broth and in return tell us your story." Her voice creaked, groaned and sighed like the wind disturbing the boughs of a tree.

Brid sat up though she still looked pale after her fall. Reticently, she eyed the two strange forest dwellers. "I have no story to tell," she replied guardedly.

"No?" The old woman shook her head sceptically. "Well, eat up all the same. I'll not have good broth go to waste."

Keeping his head down to avoid conversation, Caspar slurped hungrily. The strange woman and musty-smelling man unsettled him and he had no wish to make conversation. He concentrated on the soup but couldn't quite recognize the flavours. Boar meat, yes, surely that was boar meat but the mushrooms . . . A strange earthy flavour, he thought, gradually beginning to feel more relaxed. Harle stood, his matted hair brushing against the twigs of the roof above, and plodded towards a crudely fashioned table set with many jugs and jars. He reached for a stitched leather jug and five horn goblets. After splashing amber fluid from the jug, he handed the first to Caspar.

It was tangy and sweet with honey. Caspar rolled it around his mouth, enjoying the richly sweet flavours that reminded him of the ripeness of summer. He swallowed and wasn't prepared for the sting at the back of his throat and stifled a cough as he realized the brew was far stronger than he had anticipated.

Brid wasn't drinking. She was looking over the brim of her raised goblet, studying the old woman. She was an odd shape with extraordinarily long fingers and arms sprouting from a thick body. Caspar decided she looked like a coppiced willow. Brid kept silent until the old woman enquired after Morrigwen.

"I'm afraid she's not been so well of late," Brid said sadly.

"She's old! It never ceases to amaze me that Morrigwen is still alive," the gnarled old woman said, her voice sighing. "She's long lived for one of her kind. So very long lived. Though not for much longer. The body of the human endures so few years. Such a shame for she's a wise woman." She looked disapprovingly at Brid as if to imply she were not so wise.

The woman bent awkwardly, her bones creaking as she poured Brid more broth. The high priestess, sitting cross-legged on the rug by the fire, appeared to have warmed to the woman because she held out her bowl gratefully. Caspar was surprised. Brid rarely ate much and could only assume she was trying to please their host.

Brid pouted quizzically at Harle's mother. "I'm sure I should know you," she repeated.

"You should," the woman replied. "You used to lie cradled in my arms long enough but you wouldn't remember that. Now, little maiden, you are full grown and it is nearly your time to take a husband. You must soon release Morrigwen from the torment of her old bones. Still, you cannot do that till you have found the child who can take up your office, is that not right?" The woman raised her bushy eyebrows. "Morrigwen has sent you to search for her?"

"What makes you think so?" Brid asked, rubbing at the back of her head.

"Oh, I know many things. And there have been signs to draw us back this way. Now tell me if I'm right or not."

"Morrigwen has sent me to look for some abandoned wolflings," Brid admitted. "One of the trappers killed a mother wolf."

The old woman sucked in a sharp breath and dropped the goblet from her hand. It crashed to the floor but she didn't so much as look at the spilt liquid. She stared at Brid for a long hard moment. "A mother wolf! Yes, you must find her cubs. But with all these trappers about it won't be easy. The wolves are wary."

"It seemed straightforward enough at the time. We thought to travel through the Boarchase before turning south towards the Jaws of the Wolf where we hoped to find the wolflings. But we lost our dog and then Pip went missing and finally—"

"Ah yes, finally the hooded wolves," the woman muttered, lowering herself stiffly onto a stool and leaning forward to mutter conspiratorially to Brid. "The young man's very quiet, eh? His eyes speak volumes, as they say, but his mouth is silent."

Brock retreated politely to a corner of the dugout, cradling the warm bowl of broth in his callused hands when Harle made to sit beside Caspar. At first the youth found himself only grunting small words in response to the man's questions but, despite himself, he was soon talking comfortably to Harle. The man was so at ease with himself, which gave Caspar confidence, helping him to forget his problems. He couldn't help mentioning their find in the forest. He noticed how the tall earthy stranger was sweating slightly. There was an unusual animal smell about him. Musty, Caspar thought, a bit like horse.

Brid fingered inside her scrip and produced the uncut sunburst ruby and the wolf pelt. "What sort of person would hide this inside the ribcage of a wolf and then bury it?" she asked Harle.

"That's easy. Someone who wants it found by a trapper. It would be the best place to hide a message intended for one of those rogues. Their dogs smell out wolf a mile off and no one else would be likely to find it, not buried."

As their talk dwindled, Harle's mother brought them blankets to sleep on and Caspar stretched out by the fire since there was nowhere else to bed down. The sweet liquid had gone to his head, taking away the pain from his knee, and he had no difficulty drifting off though his slumber was troubled by nightmares.

He tossed and turned as bared teeth snatched at him out of the dark. Suddenly he was back in Torra Alta, creeping down to the dungeons where rotting prisoners moaned in the stocks, tortured by men with hot irons. A stinking corpse stood upright, enclosed in the box of the iron maiden, its hands still gripping the bars of the cage.

Caspar tried to stop the men torturing the prisoners but, as he turned on them, their laughing faces elongated into the snarling jaws of wolves. There were wolves everywhere. He ran deeper into the dungeons to protect Necrönd but he couldn't get to it for the wolves barring his way. Hundreds of them packed the dark chamber, squirming and coiling over and around each other. Behind him the men cried for his help.

The sound startled him from his sleep. Brid was calling his name urgently and he shook himself fully awake. A breath of cool dawn air slid into the dwelling where Harle stood holding the hide curtain aside, looking out into the forest.

"Brock's gone," Brid said worriedly.

CHAPTER SIX

Pip chewed at his lip, wondering what excuse he could possibly give for his long absence and turned his pony back in the direction of the distant grove of fallen trees. Of course, he should have shouted to Master Spar the moment he had first seen Trog's footprints but he had been too busy sulking about Brock's words. That must have been well over an hour ago now.

He'd only been trying to prove his worth by finding the dog alone, but tracking wasn't as easy as Brid and Master Spar made it seem and he had quickly lost all trace of the paw prints. Trog had left no more than a dozen marks in the hard ground, and he had undoubtedly obliterated them himself by now. Though he had increased the area of his search, he had been unable to find any more. After being gone so long and travelling so far, he couldn't face going back empty handed. Maybe if he looked just a little longer . . .

He knew the forest better than most. He wanted to prove that in his own native environment he could succeed where Brock would fail. He needed to prove his worth as a man. He knew many in the castle thought him an ambitious little upstart riding on the back of his sister's good fortune. If she were to one day marry Lord Caspar then naturally her brother would be given position but Pip wanted to win that position for himself. He needed to be at least a sergeant by the time he came of age.

No one, however, would promote someone who could desert the Baron's son for so long without very good reason. He'd been a fool. He should have turned back hours ago and apologized for his wayward behaviour. He despaired. Master Spar would now think him entirely irresponsible. He certainly couldn't go back without first finding Trog. The dog had to be out there somewhere.

Master Spar had always been so good to him and had never treated him as a common woodcutter's son. No, he had no call to be upset with his overlord – except for his relationship with May.

Pip gave up the dilemma over whether to turn back empty handed or continue his solitary search for Trog as he fell to brooding over his sister's relationship with the nobleman. Thinking made him hungry and he twisted around to delve into his pack for some food. He ignored the dried venison, thinking he'd have to be really hungry before he ate that and pulled out a thick hunk of bread and a small egg pie. He rummaged further down to find the spiced apple cake that he knew Cook had provided.

"Sumptuous!" he said out loud as he held a piece of cake reverently up before him. To save himself from digging through the pack again, he put the dried venison and some oatcakes into his pockets for later. He then fell back to brooding about May and her prospects with Master Spar.

Really, he should be nothing but happy about the opportunity provided by the situation. He was pleased for May, of course, that she might marry well – assuming Caspar's intentions were honourable – but he didn't want to be favoured because of his sister. He knew he had won a great deal of respect from the younger recruits who found it easier to come to him for information or directions rather than approach the older men, but now . . . Pip groaned. He'd shown himself to be entirely irresponsible and the only thing he could do was to quickly get back to Master Spar and apologize. Perhaps on the way back he might think of a good reason why he had taken his leave for so long. He could say he had seen suspicious poachers or even a repeated sight of Trog and that was why he had not immediately returned to report his findings of Trog's footprints.

He shrugged. No, it wouldn't work and Brid would immediately see straight through the lie. The very thought chilled him. Those eyes cutting straight to his soul; he would never get away with it. He pouted. With his mother he had been able to get away with the odd white lie and Cook never questioned him but the three high priestesses always knew. Pip grinned to himself, wondering how Master Hal managed to keep his relationship with Brid. The merest flutter of his eyes towards another girl and Brid knew about it even if she hadn't been there to see. Hal, it seemed, still enjoyed perusing other maidens. Some people didn't know when they held a perfect emerald in their hands, the castle gossips would say. Pip was only glad that he wasn't the only one to win their censure.

He was still chortling away to himself when he heard a sharp high-pitched bark not far to his right. He snatched round his head to peer into the undergrowth, which was thick with dead bramble.

Surely that was Trog, he thought with great relief, not because he had been worried for the dog but because he would now be vindicated for his disappearance and forgiven for the trouble he was undoubtedly causing. The thought of what old Brock would be saying about him turned his blood cold.

"Trog," he called and whistled as he turned his heavy mount towards the sound of the dog.

The yip became a frenzied bark, and the undergrowth was disturbed by wild thrashings. Pip urged his horse through the thorny brambles and was soon kneeling by the stricken dog.

Trog ceased struggling, lay back and looked into Pip's eyes. The trusting terrier seemed certain that Pip would free him from his torment. The youth looked in horror at the steel jaws clamped around the dog's front paw, a bracelet of crimson circling the limb, and swallowed hard.

"Poor Trog," he murmured, trying to sound as soothing and reassuring as he could and then yelled urgently into the air, "Brid! Master Spar! Help, help!" He knew they would be nowhere within earshot but he couldn't help himself. "Brock!" he shouted in desperation.

Trog began whimpering, his stubby tail thudding pathetically on the ground. No one could hear them. He'd just have to get the dog out on his own.

"Bloody bastards doing this," he told the dog. "Bloody, murdering, barbaric bastards!" He put his hand on the dog's shoulder and felt him tremble. "Brave boy," he praised. "Brave, brave dog."

Trog thumped his tail faster but gave out a low warning snarl and nipped gently at Pip's hand as the boy slid his arm down towards the rusty jaws. Pip quickly retracted his hand, realizing that he was increasing the dog's torment. He didn't know what to do. Panic scattered his thoughts and he took deep even breaths to steady himself. He couldn't get near Trog's leg and couldn't see how to open the trap. Could it be levered open?

He gritted his teeth and drew a deep breath, preparing himself for what he had to do. Weaving his fingers between the iron jaws, he determinedly ignored the dog as Trog chewed at the back of his hands.

The grim jaws were stiff and Pip feared for his fingers, certain that if his grip slipped, the trap would slice straight through the slender bones. For a moment he worried that he didn't have quite the strength to wrench the jaws apart and that they would snap closed on Trog again, causing agonizing damage. He arched his back, bracing himself to give his arms something to lever against and strained down and apart with all his might. His neck muscles bulged. The jaws gave fractionally, just enough for him to pull his leg up underneath his coiled body and press his foot down on one arm of the trap. This allowed him to release one hand so that he could work the pin that he hoped would hold the jaws open. He pushed down with all his strength. At first nothing gave and then suddenly the trap sprang open and he lurched forwards.

He never saw the look of relief in Trog's slitted black eyes as something solid hit his temple and he swam into blackness.

Numbly aware of a swinging motion, his lolling head dragged and bounced on the leaf-mould. He blinked his eyes, trying to gather his senses. There was a pole above him and his wrists and legs were lashed to it, in the manner of a slain deer. Feeling queasy, he gritted his teeth against the rising nausea, and tensed his muscles against the rolling sway. He could make no sense of the situation.

Trog, he remembered with a rush. He struggled frantically. An extraordinary chattering noise, like the sound of agitated magpies, filled his ears. He gazed at twiglike feet, and bodies clad in thick fur to their knees. Kobolds! Brid had said they were harmless. Harmless! His head was throbbing. He twisted his neck sideways, looking for the dog. Despite his bleeding paw, he was cruelly tied to a similar pole. His muzzle was tightly wrapped in cloth and his head lolled lifelessly to the rhythm of the uneven march.

Pip was relieved for the dog, reasoning that, at least if the poor animal were senseless, he was no longer suffering – though he prayed he wasn't dead. Everyone at the castle adored the cheeky little rascal, however much trouble he caused chasing chickens and stealing from the kitchens. Pip understood that! Cakes, always cakes. The dog would ignore hunks of meat and rounds of strong-smelling cheese in favour of cakes. Cook had tried hitting him with the rolling pin but nothing had deterred him, not even a cake baked with mustard, an entire pot of mustard, left out deliberately on the table. Trog had simply ignored it as if he had known it for a trick. The latest theft had been some lemon tartlets tucked at the back of the pantry. Nobody had yet worked out how the dog got in. Pip grinned to himself. He wasn't going to let on and spoil the fun. It amused him, the amount of puzzlement and confusion he caused.

Trog was so much part of castle life, avidly watching the archery and trying to join in the sword play. He paced past the soldiers, nose arrogantly in the air, as if inspecting them, though he always wagged his tail at Baron Branwolf with great respect. The dog knew how to look after himself. Cook had begged the Baron to have the dog banished from the castle or at least restrained but Trog treated the Baron with such a show of deference, and growled so effectively at anyone who caused Branwolf displeasure that the amused nobleman wouldn't hear of it. Far from restraining the dog, he even allowed the terrier to sit up to the high table on his own special chair. Pip could only admire such cheek. Trog was a dog after his own heart; he knew how to get on in the world.

Pip's head swam and his wrists hurt where the ropes chafed him. His fingers were a horrible sickly white colour. Though sore, he wasn't at all afraid; Master Spar would find him and sort these half-sized twigs out. He scowled to himself. How could he let himself be captured by these little scraps of creatures? He'd be a laughingstock, lose his status amongst the new recruits and the trust of his overlords.

It was only after a long period of self-retribution that the first pang of unease crept into his mind. They were travelling east, away from his old childhood haunts. He was troubled since he didn't know the lay of these woods. He could hear the gush of a river somewhere to the north. Groggily he reasoned it was the Sylvanrush, the river that ran from west to east through the centre of the Boarchase before joining up with the Silversalmon. They must be nearing its upper reaches. He groaned, wondering whether Master Spar would ever find him and groaned further, remembering how he had slunk off without a word. Master Spar might just assume that he had deserted them and returned to his native forest. He didn't dare imagine what Master Spar must be thinking of him.

Pip was mortified. He had brought disgrace on his family name. With a pang of guilt, he wondered what May would do. She was his elder sister and since their mother died, May had fussed and clucked over him irritatingly, but he loved her and now he had shamed her. Would Master Spar think less of May now for having such a foolish brother?

"Ow!" he yelled involuntarily as his head scuffed the bark of a fallen log.

Long fingers with nodulous knuckles reached out and

grabbed at his hair to raise his head and stare into his eyes. A warty face, with big wide eyes and narrow slits for nostrils, thrust up against him. Greyish brown skin, like the soft bark of an ancient yew, rasped against his as the creature exhaled stale, earthy breath into his face. Scratchy fingers probed his flesh and pinched the skin on his flushed cheeks as if testing for plumpness. Pip had the horrible feeling that these creatures wanted to eat him and he admitted to himself that he was just beginning to feel a little disconcerted.

Without warning the kobolds halted and Pip was dropped to the ground. Shrivelled bracken scratched against his face. Trussed up to the pole, he felt humiliated. He flexed his fingers, trying to get some blood to them.

"Set me loose, you bastards. Set me free. I am the Baron's man. You'll hang for this. If you don't let me go . . ." Trog jerked on the ground next to him and Pip kicked frantically in a vain effort to free himself. "What have you done to the dog? Cut him free. Can't you see he's injured? He's suffering."

Trog was still lashed to the pole though at least the tight thongs had inadvertently stemmed the bleeding. Pip hoped the dog's leg wasn't broken. He was a very stocky animal and he had little doubt that his bones were at least twice as thick as the longer leaner legs of a Yellow Mountain wolf.

"Trog!" he called out.

The dog feebly raised his head.

"You bloody bastards!" Pip screamed again. "Cut him free. He's Baron Branwolf's dog, you idiots. He'll skin you alive for this when I tell him. You stupid spawn of the devil."

The kobolds scattered, chattering raucously. Pip became aware of a large pair of furry boots standing over him.

"What the hell have you brought this boy here for?" The voice was gruff and coarse – Belbidian certainly but not a Torra Altan, Pip was sure.

Another deeper voice came from between the boughs of the big old beeches. "What's that horrible row about, Fingers? Silence those vile goblins, otherwise I'll—" The voice abruptly stopped. Pip heard dogs snarling and yipping and twisted his head to see a man leading a string of ponies. The packs on their backs jangled with black iron traps and all manner of chains, knives, cleavers and ironmongery. "Fools! I'll burn the lot of you."

There was a terrified shriek from the kobolds and then silence. They bristled and twitched like brushwood in the wind, their little fur coats looking entirely ridiculous on their thin bodies. Poor foolish creatures, Pip thought. They've no idea what they're doing.

"I told you we'd burn Hobs Slack if you messed up," the trapper threatened. He was short but squarely built with straight blond hair that hung in ragged tangles. Moss and burrs clung to his unkempt beard where he had pushed himself through the undergrowth. "Think of your little koblings still rooted to their mothers and unable to flee, crackling and snapping in the flames." He laughed gruffly.

The man spoke Belbidian well, but his accent was dull and monotonous. Though at home with the words, his mouth moved uncomfortably over the vowels and, certainly, he was a foreigner. Master Spar, when he told of his journeys abroad, explained how all the countries bordering the Caballan Sea used Belbidian as a common language. Belbidia had the earliest and largest trading traditions and so was the most widely spoken language.

Pip struggled to sit upright, but the pole meant he could only roll awkwardly from side to side. Straining to raise his head from the earthy forest floor he looked from the man to his lead pony. A carcass was slumped across its back. Frosted grey and slightly built, it was a Yellow Mountain wolf. Living in the high mountains so far from civilization, feeding off ibex and hares, it could never have done any harm to man and had probably never even seen a sheep in its dreams.

Snapping and growling round the ponies' heels were four large dogs, liver in colour and of indeterminate breed, their tufty hair coiling in disorderly rosettes. Well, that was the scent that Trog had so eagerly picked up, Pip decided, seeing that two of them were bitches.

"Who are you?" the Belbidian trapper demanded. He had dull dark hair, wide-spaced eyes and a slack jaw. Pip wondered that he hadn't been nicknamed Fisheyes rather than Fingers until he noticed the man's right hand; three middle fingers were missing. "Are you a spy? What are you doing messing about with my traps?"

"Trying to free the Baron's dog," Pip replied sternly, wondering suspiciously why wolf trappers would be worrying about spies.

His answer had the desired effect. The fish-eyed Belbidian stiffened and shifted his weight uncertainly from one leg to the other. There was a long heavy silence before he accused, "You're lying."

"Why would I lie?"

"To get yourself out of trouble."

"I'm not in any trouble," Pip replied, trying to keep his head. "These little creatures have just made a mistake, that's all."

"What are we going to do with him, Ryder?" the Belbidian addressed his rougher companion.

"We can't very well set him free. He might only be a boy but he could still be a spy. We'll have to kill him or take him with us."

Pip couldn't understand why the trappers couldn't let him go.

"Couldn't we just tie him to a tree?" Fingers suggested. "The forest is dense enough in these parts and it'll be ages before someone finds him – if the wolves don't get to him first, of course."

Pip shuddered.

"Was he alone?" The blond trapper turned to the cowering kobolds who instantly leapt up and down, vainly trying to hide behind each other, some vigorously nodding their heads while others earnestly shook theirs. "Foolish, worthless creatures," the man growled. "We can't risk it. We'll have to take him with us – at least till we get out of Belbidia," he added ominously. "The boy's body might raise a search. It would be safer to bring him. But why the hell did you bring this animal along? A dog's worth nothing to us," he shouted at the little creatures.

One kobold, a little braver than the rest, pointed repeatedly and defiantly at Trog, whilst attempting a howling noise.

"Wretched creature thinks the dog's a wolf," the fish-eyed trapper concluded. "Well, you've got to admit he's a rum looking dog. Never seen the like myself. Perhaps we could skin him and get our money for the hide. Perhaps the Baron wouldn't notice."

"Wouldn't notice the skin of his own dog! You can put your own head in the noose but you're not putting mine there, after all the boy might be telling the truth about being in the Baron's service. Look at his bow." The sturdy foreigner held it in his fist and waggled it at his companion. "I'll tell you what we're going to do," he informed his comrade, making it quite plain which one of them made the decisions. "We're going to take them both with us and get rid of the boy once we're through Belbidia. Or perhaps . . ." He looked thoughtful for a moment and patted at his breast pocket which chinked with money. "Well, let's just say I might have other plans. Yeah, and now I think about it you're right; that's a rare looking dog and I might have something in mind for him too." The man suddenly looked surprisingly regretful. "But there again I doubt he'll live that long."

"Let me at least see to his leg," Pip begged.

"I won't have anyone say I'm a man to let an animal suffer unnecessarily." The fair-haired trapper laughed at his joke. "Yeah, sure you can see to the dog." The cold blade of his knife slid between Pip's fingers and his hands were suddenly free though his legs were still tied to the pole. The trapper then deftly cut the bonds on Trog's legs. "He won't be going anywhere. He'll have lost too much blood from the trap. They never normally last this long."

"You bastards," Pip swore under his breath and dragged himself and his pole awkwardly across the earth to reach Trog. His hands were throbbing with the return of blood. Clumsily, he fumbled to unwind the cloth from the dog's muzzle and tenderly ran his hand down the injured foreleg. The trap had sliced through the flesh to the bone but the leg wasn't broken. The dog didn't so much as twitch when he touched him. "Brave dog," he reassured him. "Brave boy." He used the cloth that had muzzled Trog's jaw to wrap around the wound. Not knowing what else he could do, he crept up close to the dog to keep him warm.

He scowled at the two men who were busying themselves around one of the shaggy ponies. Ryder, the coarse-bearded squat foreigner, with his ash white skin, sagging eyes and prominent forehead, was pulling a sack from behind the saddle. It wriggled and squealed.

"Just give me a moment," he muttered through his grubby beard, fumbling in his pockets to produce a thick leather glove. His comrade scowled as he opened the sack.

"Can't stand to see the blighters alive. It makes my flesh creep. What the hell did you leave them alive for?"

Ryder grinned, put the glove on his hand and plunged his arm into the squirming sack. There was a brief, sudden silence followed by an outburst of high-pitched snarls and squeals of protest. Finally, he dragged out a tiny wolfling that hung limp and helpless from its scruff, which he pinched in his fingers. After a second the pup began to struggle. "Prize white coat this little one's got. Not a mark on it. I thought we'd buy ourselves a little grace with his personage and make a present of them."

"What would he want with a live wolf?"

"Who are we to question what he wants? He said he'd pay me most handsomely for a live wolf cub and I'd say these ones aren't even weaned. So, we'll take this lad and his dog and the cubs right the way back home. If he's the baron's man as he says he is, he might just have been sent to spy on us. Perhaps they've got wind of us."

"Why would I be spying on you?" Pip protested. "I was with a hunting party." He looked at the wriggling cub and decided not to mention what they had been hunting for. The trappers wouldn't believe him anyway. What on earth Brid wanted with wolf cubs he couldn't fathom either. All she had told him was that they were looking for some wolflings marked out for them by the Goddess. Still, there was never any use guessing at the reasoning of the three high priestesses; they were apt to demand any number of extraordinary things. Morrigwen's chamber, May had told him, was full of all manner of macabre objects.

"What's your name, boy?" Ryder dropped the pup back

into the sack, tied the knot firmly and dumped it heavily to the ground.

Pip closed his ears against the animals' crying. He told himself he wasn't sentimental and that they were, after all, merely wolflings. Only they cried! They cried just like a baby crying for its mother. They were lost, afraid and helpless, and needed food, warmth and comfort.

"Here, boy, answer me." Ryder's boot thumped into his shin.

"What's it to you? You don't need my name," Pip retorted sullenly, taking great pains not to wince. The man's brutality made him feel stubborn and he casually ignored him, soothing Trog's coat instead.

The trapper's eyes narrowed as he drew back his foot ready to kick harder but he was distracted by a small movement from the dog. "The bloody brute's still alive! I'm impressed! Good-sized brute too . . . not too tall but powerful. Might be promising . . .We'll have to see if he's strong enough to make it all the way across the Scarp, through Trows Forest and back home."

At the mention of Trows Forest, the kobolds, who had slunk away and were clumped together around the roots of an ash, began to chatter nervously. Several shrieked like birds warding off a predator from their nest.

Ryder kicked dirt at them and they were instantly silenced. He turned back to the dog. "You got some of that witch's medicine left, Fingers?"

The Belbidian slapped his pockets until his hand fell against a bulge in his jacket. "Yeah," he replied uncertainly, "But you're not going to waste it on a dog?"

"I've been thinking that we could make good use of this dog. His personage might really like him. I've never seen the breed before but he looks like he'd make a fine fighting dog to me. Look at them teeth. Nastiest set of gnashers I've seen on a dog. Aye, perhaps he'd be real pleased with this brute and the three wolf cubs. What's the Baron of Torra Alta doing with a dog like this if it's not for fighting? Can't serve no other useful purpose. He's certainly not a hunting dog."

Pip was about to protest that Baron Branwolf would never allow dogfighting but he bit his tongue, realizing that the assumption that Trog was a fighter was probably all that was keeping him alive.

"Here." Ryder snatched the cloth bundle from Fingers's good hand and flung it at Pip. "You mix this powder up with water and slap it on the dog's leg. We carry it in case we get our fingers caught in a trap." He pointed vaguely at his partner's left hand. "It happens sometimes."

Pip shuddered. "God knows what's in it," Fingers muttered. "It's witch-brew but the stuff works."

Pip looked at the yellow paste. Sulphur and something, he thought. He couldn't mistake the sight nor smell of sulphur, not after spending so much time working in the wellroom. After the Vaalakan siege, Branwolf had teasingly jested that one day Pip should become the new wellmaster since he probably knew more about the well mechanisms than anyone else alive now. Although Pip was eager for praise and grasped hungrily at the idea of promotion, he had that day seriously considered running away. The wellroom was the last place on earth he would like to work. The stench still haunted him. Despite Hal's mocking condemnation of his first attempts with a sword, he wanted to be with the men, learning to fight like a soldier. He would be a soldier like the Captain, a great soldier and have ballads written about him. No one had ever written a ballad about a wellmaster, that was for sure.

He'd need a new name, of course. All the heroes of ancient folklore had far more respectable names than he had. Now someone could write a ballad about Ceowulf; that would sound fine. Names like Abelard or Brunghar and Beotric, Atterton and Halgard. They all sounded like heroes. But Pip! If he had been Peppin, maybe. There had been a king called Peppin once and many people had asked him if Pip was short for Peppin but it wasn't; it was plain Pip. Hal said that was good since he was just plain Hal, though many people thought it short for Halbert or Halgard.

"Yes, but Hal sounds noble and Pip doesn't," he had protested.

"That's because it is, my lad." The raven-haired young noble had smiled at him wryly.

Pip swore that one day he would change his name and become captain of the guard.

He tended Trog's leg, gently closing the jagged lips of the torn flesh and pressing the paste in and around the deep wound. The dog stirred, raising his head and straining his neck round, weakly trying to nudge him away with his nose.

"I know it hurts," he sympathized. "I know. But this way it'll heal fast."

"I don't know how it didn't break his leg." Fingers stared casually at the dog. "It nearly always breaks their legs – excepting the hooded wolves, of course. I've only ever trapped two of them, mind, but their legs weren't broken by the trap neither. No, they'd chewed their leg fully off to escape before I ever got back to the trap. I'd never have believed it possible if I hadn't seen it for myself. Terrible sight, the stump of a leg left in a trap. The bones were still intact where the steel jaws closed on them but the animals had gnawed right through higher up. Devilish creatures. There's a maddened desperation in them." Fingers told this tale quite matter-of-factly and it turned Pip's stomach.

"Can't you kill these animals decently with a bow? Do you have to do it with traps?"

The man scowled and his foreign-sounding comrade laughed dryly. "No good saying such things to him, boy. He's got more respect for these creatures than to face up to them like that. Take a man down soon as blink at you if you get too close. Look what they did to him."

The Belbidian trapper pulled aside a kerchief that was knotted at his throat. Old wounds striped his skin, the healed flesh puckered and scarlet. He gave the boy a crooked smile. "I got that at home in Ovissia," he muttered. "Some say I was lucky but I don't. I didn't save my little boy. He was tending the sheep when the wolves slunk down from the hills. Just like any good shepherd, he tried to protect his flock but they killed him and took off his body. Bloody Torra Altan wolves! What's the Baron think he's doing letting them breed like they do here? I tried to save my boy but I couldn't and one of the devils did this to me. Think I could go back to tending sheep after that? I left the farm to my eldest and I've been killing them ever since. Makes me sick to see these three cubs squirming and alive."

He looked down at the ground and scuffed at it accusingly with his toe. "Demons and devils is always what comes out of this barony. Ruled by demon witches this place is. Baron Branwolf's no more than a pawn of the pagan witches. No decent man worships the Earth Goddess."

"No decent man kills animals with traps," Pip retorted, his blood boiling with indignation. How dare he speak about the Great Mother in such a way? The Great Mother has nothing to do with devilry. "She keeps the balance of nature. She makes the natural laws," he quoted Brid.

"Yeah? You telling me that these great wolves are

natural?" The fish-eyed Ovissian snarled at him. "Seems to me your precious Goddess has put demons in them."

Pip didn't know what to say. He turned back to tending Trog.

"How are we going to get this boy all the way to Ceolothia?" Fingers asked.

Ceolothia! Pip thought. So that's where the other trapper was from; a professional hunter from the vast northern forests of Ceolothia. King Rewik's Wolf Tax was evidently more lucrative than he had thought.

The Ceolothian looked at Fingers as if he were an idiot. "How do you think we're going to get him there? He'll walk. A trapper's never short of ironmongery and it won't take me long to make some shackles that he'll not escape from."

"Don't you feel a bit bad doing something like that to your fellow countryman?" Pip turned to the Ovissian, thinking him the softer touch out of the two.

"Fellow countryman! No lowland Belbidian considers Torra Alta part of Belbidia anymore," he snarled. "Not since your baron's let us suffer all these wolves. Putting beast before man just ain't right. I don't feel no loyalty towards any Torra Altan."

Pip turned towards Ryder. "You might be able to shackle me but the dog still won't be able to walk. Not with a leg like that."

"Oh, he will in a couple of days. I can put him on a pack until then. Besides he's got three good legs left. Amazing what an animal can cope with when he has to."

"Bastard," Pip mumbled under his breath.

Ryder rummaged through his saddle-bags and Pip heard the disconcerting chink of metal as the man produced a trap with a length of chain attached. He grinned at it.

"This will do just fine," he said, measuring out the length of chain with his arm. With a bit of work, he soon had a shackle that he snapped shut around Pip's neck. He took the chain and worked it around the base of a tree, securing it with a twist of metal that he hammered closed. Pip immediately tested it, trying to work the metal free with his fingers. It didn't give a fraction.

The Ceolothian laughed at him. "You can keep yourself busy with that as long as you like but you won't get it free."

Gloomily, Pip decided the man was right and was grateful that he hadn't bothered to tie his arms or legs.

"A few of those varmint kobolds to guard you will leave me and Fingers free to clear the last of our traps in the area," the Ceolothian laughed. "I'll feed these wretched wolflings when I get back. Starve them a little and they won't be so much trouble, I reckon." With that he flung a gourd full of water at Pip and turned towards his ponies.

Pip slumped back against the tree and took a long swig from the gourd. He glared at the ring of kobolds while the two trappers set off to finish their business. Standing, he kicked dirt up at the kobolds, venting his frustration. To his satisfaction they scattered behind the trees and it was some while before they tentatively returned to keep their vigil. He managed to get Trog to drink a few gulps of water before he sat back again, gloomily wondering what he could do. Master Spar and Brid would think that he had deserted them. He was horrified at the thought. It was the end of his career for certain. He wondered whether they would find him. He didn't even know precisely where he was. These wretched creatures had carried him too far.

It was some moments before he remembered the sack. It wriggled and squirmed just beyond his reach. He crawled to the end of his chain until it cut into his throat and then lay down in the dirt, stretching his feet forward towards the sack. Pressing his heel over the sack and into the earth, he was able to drag it little by little towards him until, at last, he could get his fingers to it.

"Poor little things," he found himself saying as he opened the sack and looked down into their blinking eyes. They mewed pathetically. Instinctively he slid his hand into the darkness to comfort them but withdrew it sharply with a yelp.

Pinpricks of blood oozed from his forefinger where one of the pups had bitten him. Teeth like needles, he thought more warily and pulled his sleeve over his hand for protection. He opened the sack a little wider. "You need feeding," he told them and finally managed to grab one by its scruff and lift it out. It was reddish-brown in colour and hung limply without stirring. He stroked its head but it barely reacted. It looked sick.

"I don't think you're going to last long," he told the creature sadly and put it down into his lap while he prepared to look at the other two. The next was grey. Definitely the biggest of the three with greenish yellow eyes, it had the makings of a snarl gurgling in its throat. It struggled frantically. Pip wisely dropped it back into the sack and, using the cloth to protect his hand, he separated out the last pup. This one was pure white with deep blue-green eyes. It hung placidly from his grip and ceased its mewing. Pip had the uncomfortable sense that the wolf cub was studying him. Then quite suddenly it began to struggle and twisted round to hook its thin needle fangs into the flesh of his thumb.

"Mother, you're worse than a ferret," he swore and dropped it back into the sack. "Ungrateful creature. I was trying to help you."

He sat back, sucking at his thumb. What was he doing with these creatures anyway? They were just wolves and hundreds of wolves were being killed every year now. There was nothing special about these cubs. Brid had said that the ones they were looking for would be distinctive in some way. He couldn't allow himself to get all sentimental over some wolflings; he and Trog were in enough trouble already. A garrison soldier wouldn't be sentimental over them, not at a time like this when he had brutal men to contend with.

But poor things, they needed feeding. He couldn't stop himself wanting to help them. Unstoppering the gourd, which Ryder had flung at him, he poured a small quantity of water onto his hand and offered it to the weak little tawny cub in his lap. It raised its head momentarily to sniff at it but then apathetically slumped down again. Pip picked the animal up and turned it over, holding it in one hand and then dribbling water into its mouth with the other. He had a degree of success. Though much of the water splashed to the ground, the little creature definitely drank some of it.

Pip was so absorbed in the procedure that he found his spirits rising. Now that the trappers were gone and he was only guarded by the kobolds, much of his earlier trepidation evaporated. Master Spar would come for him. Of course, he would. Master Spar was a Torra Altan and a Torra Altan never forsook one of their own.

He glared up at the kobolds, surprised to see them creeping forward, watching curiously his behaviour towards the wolfling. One or two tilted their heads, looking almost sympathetically at the little animal. Pip couldn't understand them. He turned back to his dilemma with the pups and how to help them. If they grew strong enough, perhaps he could set them free but he knew that was the worst thing he could do for them. Better to kill them quickly and mercifully than let them die of starvation.

He felt a wet nose against his hand and looked to see Trog struggling to sit up, evidently curious about the pups. Pip offered him some water in his palm before summoning the courage to draw out the grey pup. This one was strong enough to lap from his hand and he sensed it relax as it accepted his comfort. He slipped it back into the sack and quickly scooped out the white pup. She was far more wary of him and it took several minutes of gentle coaxing before the cub would drink. When she did, Pip felt an immense sense of triumph.

"Look, Trog, look; she's drinking!" he exclaimed but then grimaced at finding himself talking so excitedly.

Trog lazily opened an eye and Pip decided he would try putting the she-cub down alongside its tawny brother. The white pup curled around the weaker one and fell asleep momentarily but was soon mewing again, no doubt with hunger.

Pip felt a sense of despair. He felt responsible for these animals now and they were suffering. He felt through his pockets for his emergency supply of food. Dried venison, he thought in disgust. It had been their staple diet during the siege and he couldn't eat it now without thinking of his mother. He offered it to the big grey wolfling first but the animal didn't seem to know what it was. Finally, Pip put some into his mouth and chewed it into a fine paste. He spat it out into his hand and offered the tiniest amount on the end of his finger. The wolf sniffed at it but still wouldn't take it. As a last resort Pip turned the grey wolfling upside down, waited for it to cry again and then dribbled the slimy paste into its pink open mouth. The pup coughed and spluttered but finally swallowed.

It took all Pip's patience to feed all three pups in this way though the tawny one took very little. By the end they were used to him and he no longer had to put the grey one back into the sack. He sat back against the tree, content that all three pups were fast asleep, cuddled against Trog who nudged at them affectionately with his nose before sighing and falling asleep himself.

Ruefully realizing that he had fed most of what food he had to the wolves and Trog, Pip wondered how long he would have to wait for the trappers to return. He took the last few mouthfuls of water from the gourd and stared up into the darkening sky, looking for the moon. He hoped the magic of the moon would lead Master Spar and Brid to him soon. He was hungry.

CHAPTER SEVEN

It was cold, the dawn sun just a pale ghost behind the white shroud of mist that clamped down over the forest. Caspar kept close to Brid, fearful of losing her too as they searched the woods around the dwelling for any sign of Brock. The woods rang with their worried voices but there was no answer to their calls.

"The sun'll burn through soon," Harle said knowledgeably. "We should go back for breakfast and horses before searching further."

They nodded.

"He's gone after Pip," Brid concluded as they reached the hide entrance to Harle's sunken dwelling. "Late last night he kept saying it was his fault that Pip had taken himself off."

Caspar groaned. "First, I lose Trog, then Pip and now Brock. I told Father I was capable of leading a party on my own. You realize this is the very first time I've led a party into the Chase without Hal along to look after me? And everything has gone wrong. Everything! What was Brock thinking of? He's normally so sensible."

"Perhaps he thought he could bring the young lad back and save the lady from traipsing through the woods with all these dangerous wolves abroad," Harle suggested. "Like as not he'll be back before you've finished breakfast."

Breakfast was an impatient affair. Caspar's pricking

conscience made it difficult for him to eat the plate of sorrel and fried mushrooms, and when Brock still hadn't reappeared by the end of the meal, they decided to set out and search further afield.

Caspar was only too glad to have Harle with him. Though apparently a simple commoner, he had a natural authority about him and clearly knew the interlacing tracks of the forest well. Happily, he let the tall forester guide them, though he was surprised that the man opted to do so on foot. He paced out on long legs, covering the ground effortlessly and Caspar couldn't quite work out how he kept up with them as Firecracker jogged restlessly alongside Brid's new mount. They had left her cream mare in Harle's barn to rest her leg and she had taken one of his deer ponies instead.

As a general rule foresters kept no saddle horses, only draught horses for drawing logs and ponies for carrying home slain deer. The Boarchase was an ancient forest and historically the game had been reserved solely for the Baron but the deer had become so numerous that Caspar's grandfather had altered the rights and declared the game open to all those that lived in the forest. Branwolf had explained that the move was essential, not only to make sure that the people of the Boarchase had enough food, but to also stop the deer from destroying the forest.

Brid frowned lightly at the tall man who had barely raised a sweat as he jogged through the rustling carpet of leaves. She turned to Caspar, her elven face alive with thought, and raised her eyebrows, communicating her surprise at Harle's speed. Caspar shrugged and turned to look at the hunter, but he was gone.

The youth reined to a halt. "How did he do that? He was right there beside us just one second ago."

Brid was smiling strangely. "Now I do know how he

does that. With his wispy grey beard and hair, earthy skin and greenish-grey hide garments the colour of beech bark, he need only stand against a tree to blend into the background. It's how he keeps up with the horses that beats me."

"Well, I don't like it." Caspar wheeled Firecracker around. "It's not natural."

"Now that's where you're wrong. It's altogether too natural. He does it better than I do. I never saw him leave either. Whoever he is, he has a profound understanding of the old ways." She wound her plait about her fingers. "I wish he hadn't left us." She quickly raised her hand to quiet his reply. "Listen; the birds have stopped singing," she whispered.

Caspar felt a cold shiver tremble up and down his spine.

Brid nodded her head forward, indicating that they should keep moving. "There's a smell about these hooded wolves," she continued after a moment's thought. "A Yellow Mountain wolf could pass within ten feet of you without you knowing but not a hooded wolf. They have a stale odour about them, a mustiness like barn animals that have wintered too long in a closed shed, though not quite so pungent."

Caspar nodded, remembering the smell.

"They don't smell natural," she continued. "Where do you suppose these wolves have come from? Vaalaka's northern tundra, Ceolothia's forests?"

Caspar prodded at his crooked nose. In his heart he felt it was his fault. He wished he had brought Necrönd with him. He felt insecure leaving it unguarded at Torra Alta.

Unguarded? That was a ridiculous notion, he corrected himself. It was in the fortress's deepest dungeons, locked behind a steel door. Nowhere in the country could it be safer. Still, he felt it was vulnerable.

Brid stopped and sniffed the air.

Caspar stiffened in the saddle. "I can smell something too." He snatched up his bow and nocked an arrow to the string, his body tense and alert, anticipating a snarl of attack. Where was Harle? He had felt safe with the man marching beside them and now he was unnerved without him. A twig snapped to his right and Firecracker danced up in alarm, though Caspar relaxed as he recognized the snuffle and grunt of a boar foraging through the undergrowth for acorns.

Where had Pip and Brock got to? He couldn't understand it. Half of him was furious, thinking that Pip must have left them deliberately but he was also horribly worried for the boy. And now Brock was missing too and all because Pip was churlish and irresponsible enough to wander off alone.

"I'm sure Pip would have headed towards his old home as it got dark," Brid said, ducking to avoid the overhanging ivy-strangled boughs of a rotted elm.

"I hope nothing's happened to him," Caspar said flatly. "What could have possessed him to wander off?"

"He's young and hot-headed," Brid commented. "And he was very angry."

"I don't see why," Caspar objected.

"No?" Brid sounded sceptical. "He didn't think he had your respect. He wanted to be appreciated for himself rather than earn position through his sister."

Caspar bit his tongue. "What will May think? He's her only kin. She'll hate me forever and lately she's grown more and more cold towards me."

He had known Brid for nearly four years now and in that time, she had become his closest confidante. He could tell her anything and she always seemed to understand. He knew Hal didn't like him talking so personally to his betrothed but Caspar couldn't see the harm in it. Hal had always been a jealous person. Uncomfortably he realized that he was missing Hal. Pip would never have wandered off if Hal had been in charge; he wouldn't have dared. And if he had gone missing Hal would have found him. Hal was good at sorting out problems.

He drew abruptly to a halt. There in front of him, leaning patiently against a chestnut tree, was Harle.

"How did you get ahead of us?" Brid asked suspiciously.

Harle stared back at her, his grey eyes unfathomable. He didn't seem to hear Brid's question because he ignored her without showing the least hint of evading her scrutiny. No man, thought Caspar, could so ignore Brid without some expression of trepidation. The older Brid grew, the more respect she commanded. She wasn't quite the child she used to be, he thought with a twinge of regret.

"I've found a dun gelding," Harle said coldly.

"Pip's horse!" Caspar exclaimed, brightening.

"I'm sorry, it's not good news and I advise you not to look at him," Harle warned.

Caspar knew all too well why. He could hear the mocking caw of carrion birds. "Wolves?"

Harle nodded. "Hooded wolves, judging by the damage. They tend to worry the carcass more than eat it."

"Any sign of Pip or Brock?" Brid asked hurriedly.

"I'm not sure," the hunter replied, though Caspar had an inkling that he probably was.

"Show us," he ordered.

"The young lady won't want to see it," he reminded Caspar.

The Baron's son looked at Brid and was annoyed with

Harle for presuming that he was being inconsiderate towards her. But he knew Brid well. She was better able than he to look upon death and he knew it would upset her no more to see the animal dead than to hear that it had died. "Do you want to see Pip's horse?" he asked to prove his point.

Brid nodded. "Yes, of course."

Caspar looked back at Harle triumphantly. "Lead on," he ordered, trying to inflect his voice with the sort of confident tone that befitted a baron's son.

A cold sweat sprang out on his hands and neck at the sight of the carcass. He imagined what work the wolves would have made of Brid, Brock and himself if it hadn't been for Harle. Furrowed fang marks lacerated the hide across the horse's quarters and the gut had been torn open and dragged out into long coils. The stench was terrible.

He swallowed hard and dismounted, treading carefully to avoid the bloody remains that were scattered over a large area. "There's no sign of any human footprints or of anything being dragged away. It doesn't look like Pip was here." He tried to sound authoritative.

Brid looked at the animal and then at the tracks where its hooves had cut into the hard earth. The studded hoofprints were easy to see despite the severe ground frost. "This way!" she called as she tracked back along the horse's trail.

Again, Harle left them but after a mile or so following the hoofprints, Caspar saw him ahead, stooping over a tangle of crisp dried bramble.

"There's blood on the ground," Harle told them as they hurriedly approached. "Be careful," he warned suddenly, taking up a loose branch and jabbing it at the ground.

Caspar started at the sound of snapping wood and

jarring metal. He watched as Harle flung aside the branch and wrenched up a black metal contraption from the ground. The branch had been cleanly bitten in two.

"A trap, a wolf trap," Brid exclaimed, her voice sharp with anger. She leapt down from her deer pony to examine the ground.

"And here's Pip's footprint! Or at least I think it is," Caspar triumphantly declared as he searched amongst whiplike strands of bramble that criss-crossed the ground around the trap. "At least we've found some trace of him."

"And Trog," Brid added solemnly. She held the trap in one hand and carefully ran her fingers over its clamped teeth. She pinched something between her thumb and forefinger. Caspar tripped in his haste to look at her find but hardly noticed the brambles that scratched his face.

"It might be wolf's hair," he suggested as he examined the clump of coarse white hairs in the Maiden's grasp.

Brid gave him a dubious look. "True, true it might, but it's not, is it, Spar?" She gave the hairs to him to hold and then brushed her hands over her thighs and plucked at the leathers, retrieving several of Trog's hairs that had embedded in her clothing. She held them up for comparison with the ones retrieved from the trap.

"They're the same," Harle pronounced solemnly over Caspar's shoulder.

Brid's face was white, her eyes darkening with alarm. "Trog," she whispered tenderly, "if anyone's harmed you . . ."

Harle examined the ground, carefully pushing aside the brambles and clambering over the fallen tree-trunk until he reached a patch of earth scattered with fallen pinecones.

"Kobolds," he announced looking at the three-pronged

prints that looked like they'd been left by a large bird. "A great many of them heading deeper into the Chase."

After much argument they concluded that the kobolds must have carried Trog and Pip away since there was no sign that either of them had walked away from the area. They found another set of large prints, fresher and overlying the others.

"Brock's by the size of them," Harle decided. "With luck he's just a little way ahead of us."

They tracked the scratchy kobold footprints for most of the day and Caspar began to despair that they would ever catch up with them.

"Mad creatures," he complained as the birdlike prints doubled back on themselves for the third time. The larger plodding prints of the man were confused but generally cut a straighter path, which at least saved them time compared to tracking the kobolds. "What could they want with Pip?" Caspar asked as the tracks converged on a forest pool.

Brid wasn't listening. "Where's Harle?" she asked, scanning the surrounding forest.

"He's gone off again." Caspar was unperturbed by this latest disappearance.

"No, he hasn't, not this time." She sniffed the air. Caspar smelt nothing unusual but then, just for a moment, he caught the faintest hint of something like dried herbs, musty but sweet. Brid seemed mystified by it. "I was watching him very, very carefully. Normally he just stands still and then creeps around the far side of a tree, angling himself to blend in with the vegetation but this time he didn't. I was watching him. One minute he was there—" She stopped mid-sentence and put one finger to her lips. "Look, there, ahead."

It was drawing towards dusk and the light played tricks

with Caspar's eyes. One minute he thought he was looking at a thatch of shrub and the next minute he saw antlers, very long antlers with many points. A very old stag.

"There at the other side of the clearing by the water," Brid insisted.

Caspar caught his breath. A great white stag stood by the pool, dipping its head towards the dark waters to drink. Its ears pricked and then flattened before it swept away, elegant, powerful legs carrying it over a fallen beech as easily as if it had wings, and then it was gone. There was a moment's hush and then a sudden snarl. Wolves! Caspar drew his bow but they were clearly after the stag.

Great black shapes darted between the trees. Caspar frowned. It must have been a trick of the half light but it looked as if something rode on the back of the leading wolf. He grimaced at the sudden stale smell, then his expression faltered as he remembered where he had smelt that odour before. It was the smell from Torra Alta's dank dark dungeons.

As quickly as they had come, the wolves were gone. The horses trembled beneath their stunned riders.

"Did you smell it?" Brid asked.

Caspar nodded.

They stood watching for several more minutes before Brid said worriedly, "Harle's been gone a long time. Do you think he's all right?"

Caspar thought that Harle was better able to look after himself than most and said as much. "We'll have to find shelter for the night. We can't stay out in the open with those wolves running loose."

Brid looked around her thoughtfully. "We're a little north of the Sylvanrush river. If I'm right, there's a village on its north bank about a mile and a half from here. We'll just have to come back at first light to pick up the trail."

Caspar nodded, accepting her advice without question.

After a short ride Brid was proved right. Ahead, in the crook of the river, nestled a small cluster of huts surrounded by weeping willow trees lit up in the bright light of lanterns strung amid their boughs.

The village, as Brid had called it, was no more than six wattle and daub huts, their roofs clad with turf. They had no chimneys as such but curls of smoke puffed from a central vent in each conical roof.

"Hello!" Caspar called out, not wanting to startle anybody. "We seek shelter for the night."

There was no answer even though the fires were burning high and people were clearly at home. Brid slid down from her horse and knocked lightly at the nearest door. Again, there was no answer and she knocked harder.

"In the name of the Great Mother, answer us. You cannot leave fellow Belbidians out in the forest with these wolves. We beg shelter for the night," she called out.

The door creaked tentatively open and a man with a shaven face and eyes that blazed red in the reflection of the lanterns peered through the narrow crack. He frowned at the girl for a long minute before he spoke. "What's your name?"

"Brid," she replied softly.

"Brid!" he repeated and held the door half open, still barring their entry and yet not quite excluding them. "Wife," he called without turning his face from them. "Come see if I should let this lady in. She calls herself Brid though she looks like some sprite all dressed up in forest hunting leathers, she does."

The door was suddenly flung wide and a tall middle-aged woman, her hair tied up in a tight bun, thrust her face out into the lantern-lit night. She took Brid's hand and drew her inside while saying to Caspar, "Quick, quick, now put your horses in the barn round the back and make the door fast. Then come in straight away. Quickly! It's fully dark and them wolves will be out in number."

Caspar made no objection to the way the woman addressed him. In the circumstances it was natural that she should take him to be Brid's servant so without complaint he led the horses away. It didn't take him a moment to settle them in the barn and give them hay and water. As he hurried back to the dwelling, the men of the village were stoking up crackling bonfires around the village.

"It's the only thing that keeps them wolves at bay," the forester said as he ushered him into his home. Brid was still waiting for him in the cramped porch and the forester warmly invited them in.

The cottage was crowded with women, children and five young men eating at a long table. The men carried knives and hatchets on their belts and they all fell silent, staring at Brid and Caspar as they entered.

"My lady," the eldest woman in their number scuttled forward and bobbed an awkward curtsey. "Welcome to our home. We are honoured to have One of the Three here with us. Please forgive the simplicity of our hospitality. And your page."

Brid laughed and looked at Caspar with a twinkle in her eye. "Thank you for your welcome," she said graciously. "But this young man is not my page. This is Lord Caspar of Torra Alta."

There was a stunned silence followed by a dismayed babbling, much straightening of clothes and hurried wiping of grubby mouths while those at the table lowered their food back to their plates and ceased eating as they rose to their feet. Caspar felt awkward. He wasn't used to causing so much of a stir and he preferred to remain anonymous.

"Please, please," he begged, "don't make a fuss. I don't ask for any special ceremony."

Brid seemed to be enjoying his discomfort. Her laughter rippled through the cosy dwelling, soft and light like elven music. The villagers turned towards her, the look of dismay easing from their expressions. "Sit! Sit down and get back to your meal," she told them with confidence.

Caspar felt foolishly lost for words. Too many eyes were fixed on him and he felt himself nudging at his crooked nose to hide his flushed expression. He thought he had grown out of this habit and was annoyed to find himself behaving so ill at ease. The table was being rapidly cleared and the most comfortable stool brought forward for him.

He groaned. The people had seemed so relaxed before he had entered and he was mortified at how much commotion he was causing. "Please, please stop," he begged. There was instant silence and they all turned to hang on his words. This was not the reaction he had wanted at all. Consumed with self-consciousness, he rounded on Brid and mouthed, "Why did you tell them?"

"Oh Spar," she murmured in his ear, "I couldn't resist the look on your face." Her eyes were sparkling with laughter as she teased him. Caspar struggled to regather his sense of humour. "Just sit down and behave naturally," she told him. "You can't go around your barony pretending to be someone else. Do you imagine your father does that?"

"No, of course he doesn't." Caspar couldn't imagine anything more unlikely than Branwolf feeling embarrassed in front of his people. He took a deep breath. It was up to him to set the tone. Everyone was looking at him. He coughed to clear his throat. "My lady Brid, I would be honoured if you would take the most prominent place since you represent the Great Mother." At least his show of chivalry allowed him to shift some of the focus from himself.

Brid turned back towards the foresters and settled amongst them. She always made herself feel at home wherever she was and it took her no time to put the common folk at their ease where the noble youth had failed. She was one of them after all. She picked up a small child and smiled warmly, striking up an animated conversation about the child's doll made from twigs and an old rag. The girl's mother quickly responded to this gesture and laughed along with Brid as the small daughter chattered away about her doll. Soon the household returned to their seats and were quietly munching on oatcakes spread with creamy white mountain honey. Caspar's eyes widened at the sight; he hadn't eaten in ages.

"Those look good," he exclaimed involuntarily and the woman of the house smiled.

"My own recipe," she said with a pleased smile, holding the plate out towards him.

Caspar took one and bit into it. "Sumptuous!" He glowed at her and the woman grinned broadly, offering him another.

"We've got no meat," she apologized. "Game's been scarce since the wolves came."

At the mention of the word wolves there was sudden silence and the young girl on Brid's knee began to cry. Her mother swept her up into her arms while the man who had let them in leant forward towards Caspar. "We beg of you, sir, you must do something about these creatures."

"There's the Wolf Tax," Caspar lamely muttered.

"Of course, sir, we know. It's true the tax is right rapidly thinning out the Yellow Mountain wolves but we've lived with them for generations and they've never caused much harm. I've known more men gaunched by boar's tusks than savaged by wolves in these parts until of late. It's the hooded wolf that does the damage, circling the huts when the fires burn down. And they grow braver daily."

"Hush! Don't speak so in front of the childer," an older woman warned.

Caspar lowered his voice to a whisper. "I know. We were attacked in the forest and it was only the timely intervention of your neighbour, Harle, that saved us."

The man frowned quizzically. "There ain't nobody that goes by that name in these parts." He looked to his wife for confirmation and she shook her head.

Caspar was certain that they had Harle's name right but he was distracted from puzzling over it by the thought of more food. "I could still eat another of your honey oatcakes," he said brightly. "They're better than our cook's though I wouldn't dare tell her." He was enjoying these people's company and the heaviness he had felt at Torra Alta was lifting.

The woman beamed from ear to ear, obviously thrilled with the praise, and came forward eagerly with a piled plate. "My lad goes high into the mountains for the honey." She nodded at a tall youth sat by the fire. "You noblemen must have a taste for sweet things because the other gentleman paid me to bake an entire batch for him to take with him. When was that now? It must have been just before the winter set in. He said he had a long journey to make and nothing would sustain him better." She was evidently very proud of her cakes.

"Another nobleman?" Caspar asked in surprise.

The woman nodded. "Oh aye, he came up from the south over the mountains. A brave man! That was where my son found him. He'd lost his way it seemed and was meant to meet someone who would guide him on his journey but, somehow, he had missed him. He paid for shelter and guidance through to the northern edge of the forest."

Caspar felt troubled by this news and thought of the message they had found with the sunburst ruby. It all seemed very odd indeed. He had thought that ruffians might be plotting to steal Torra Alta's minerals but not noblemen. That was quite a different matter. "Did he say who he was or where he was going?" he asked casually, trying to disguise his concern.

"Well, we didn't like to ask but we all rather guessed he wasn't from the Barony. He had no bow nor brown bearskin." The woman nodded at Caspar's that was draped over a bench by the door. "There's few Torra Altans that don't wear bearskins. My son took him to the edge of the forest, where he waited until one of them foreign trappers turned up. Still the nobleman paid me handsomely for the cakes."

Fidgeting with a length of wood in his hand that he had been whittling into a staff, her son spoke for the first time. He was a tall lad with a self-conscious hunch to his shoulders. "He wasn't quite alone. There was another fellow with them and even now the thought of him makes me shudder."

"It was only the forest shadows playing tricks with your eyes," his mother interrupted. "You know how they do."

He shook his head. "It weren't. Just for a moment he turned full towards me. Hooded, he was, in a black cloak but the face behind was obscured in a mist that clung only to him and his eyes glinted red like a wolf's. It weren't natural."

An involuntary shudder ran through Caspar's spine and he rebuked himself for being taken in by the boy's imagination. No doubt the woman was right about her son seeing things awry in the deep shade of the forest.

That night they slept around the fire and awoke early. Eager to resume their search, Brid and Caspar bade their farewells and set off back along the Sylvanrush river. Overnight, the kobold trail had been criss-crossed by several small rodents, a few deer, one or two boar and a badger. Caspar hoped they were heading in the right direction as the kobold tracks spiralled round and round an ash tree before continuing west again. Brid was frustrated.

"Stupid creatures, what on earth could they want with Pip? Kobolds don't interfere with humans, not out of their own free will anyway. Something is driving them." She looked thoughtful for a moment. "You know, we first picked up their trail where we found the sunburst ruby. You don't think the kobolds could have something to do with that?"

Caspar wasn't listening. "What's that?" He waved for her to be silent while he listened. "I can hear someone singing."

"That's not singing, that's crying," Brid corrected him.

They were following a track of sorts, probably worn by deer, which linked one forest glade to another. The bedraggled winter undergrowth was low to the ground, more a tangle of dry twigs than anything else, which snapped and crackled under the horses' hooves. It at least made winding through the forest easier. Caspar followed Brid as she turned and headed for the source of the noise.

"It can't be Pip; he'd never cry," Caspar told the priestess but she didn't respond.

She pointed through the forest towards a large log covered in plate-like fungus. For a second Caspar thought he saw a large goat but then he got the distinct impression that it had arms.

"It's a kobold," he said bitterly and drew his bow. "It had better tell us where Pip is."

"It's not a kobold," Brid contradicted him.

"No, it looks more—" Caspar started. The creature had gone, entirely vanished. They both stared at the fallen log for a full minute.

"I was looking straight at it." Brid's voice was a low murmur. "I was looking straight at it and then it just vanished."

"Perhaps it was something in the woman's honey cakes," Caspar suggested as lightly as he could. But he couldn't calm his tingling nerves. He had seen the creature as clearly as he now saw the log it had been sitting on, and then it had simply vanished. He nudged his horse forward to examine the log. Firecracker stamped and pawed the ground, moving forward reluctantly as if disturbed by something ahead.

"It was here, sitting in the shade of that tree. The light touched it and it just vanished." Brid slipped down from her horse and stirred aside some dry shrivelled leaves and prodded at the log with the toe of her boot. Flakes of soggy bark peeled away, exposing the crawling woodlice that inhabited the layers beneath.

"Was it a goblin?" Caspar asked. "If it wasn't a kobold, it must have been a goblin."

Brid stooped and plunged her hand into the deep pile of leaves to retrieve something bright and shiny. "Look, a pipe," she exclaimed. It was made of polished wood, the fingerhole surrounds inlaid with mother-of-pearl. She held it to her lips and blew softly. The sound was deeply mournful.

It came as no surprise to Caspar that she could play the pipe. Brid could do anything she put her mind to. No, it was the tune that surprised him, mysteriously beautiful but without happiness, the sighing notes of a lullaby. Caspar found himself swaying to the sound but, as a thick musty aroma began to permeate the air, Brid dropped the pipe in dismay. The smell was stale and unwelcoming, quite discordant to the sound of the pipe that conjured images of a lazy summer mist creeping out of dawn mountains.

Caspar looked at Brid in alarm and instinctively clutched her to him. Though she had stopped playing, the song of the pipe continued though seemingly from far away, the sound echoing as if it were funnelled through some ravine. Brid clung to him.

He'd never known Brid to be afraid before but now she was trembling. He didn't know what was so terrifying and for a moment he felt gratified that she clung to him for comfort. It made him feel strong. All those old, suppressed feelings of wanting to love and protect her welled up and he braced his arms around her, stiffening to envelop her like a suit of armour.

But if Brid was afraid . . . His confidence shrivelled.

The forest seemed to fade, becoming a dim haze around him. He could hear that sobbing again, the merciless crying of ultimate despair, like a lost or abandoned child. It reminded Caspar of May after the siege. At night he had heard her crying softly for her dead mother. It was a heart-rending noise. Now he found himself clutching hold of Brid for comfort.

The sharp outline of the trees returned and the sound of crying was whisked away in a gust of wind. Caspar's head cleared. He came out of this dazed state into one of instant alarm. "The horses!" Firecracker was rearing and plunging against his reins where he had been tied to the branch of a tree and Brid's deer pony was shrieking wildly. Caspar ran to grab the stallion's reins and instantly froze.

Beyond the horse, creeping low to the ground was a hooded wolf, its narrow yellow eyes fixed on Firecracker. Its black lips were pulled taut over long yellow teeth. Caspar's skin felt suddenly cold with fear.

"Brid," he whispered in warning, trying to keep his voice steady whilst fixing his eyes on the wolf, hoping that his stare would root the animal to the spot. "Brid," he managed to say matter-of-factly so as not to startle her into panic, "there's a wolf here. Just walk back slowly." He inched his hand up for his bow that was strapped to his saddle whilst keeping his eyes firmly glued on the crouched animal before him. "Steady, Cracker," he soothed his horse as he crept around the animal's flank.

Brid's pony shrieked in shrill panic, the noise goading the wolf to attack. Caspar loosed his arrow, the released bowstring thwacking against his wrist as the quarrel spat towards its mark. The wolf screamed in pain and rolled over with the arrow pierced clean through its neck. Caspar felt the relief ease through his taut body.

"Another!" Brid yelled.

He spun round but couldn't see it. Automatically his hand reached back for his quiver and, in response to a lifetime's training, he had an arrow slotted to his bow without pause in his movements. But he still couldn't see the wolf.

"And another! To your right!" Brid yelled.

Suddenly Caspar saw the beasts tearing towards them through the dark undergrowth, the thin light of the winter sun reflecting in their eyes. The first was heading straight for Firecracker. He loosed his arrow, knowing already that he didn't have time to stop the rest.

"No!" Brid was shouting.

Caspar's ears were filled with the mad medley of her voice, the squeals from the horses and the salivating snarls of the wolves. He felt neither panic nor fear as he let his training take over. The wolf was in the air, coming straight at him as he reached for another arrow. He didn't have time, he knew he didn't have time, but all the same he reacted. His fingers brushed over the quill; he had the forked tail of the flights in his fingertips now and was swinging the arrow up and forward like a dagger. He could smell the wolf's hot breath, could see into the dark wine-red depths of its gaping throat.

Brid was screaming, though not with panic but with ferocious fury at the attacking wolves. Then he heard it again, the mournful song of the pipe and the sound of crying. The sound swelled in Caspar's head and the world span and wavered before him.

The wolf was fading and shrinking as if the very air were devouring it. Caspar found himself falling. Stumbling backwards, he clutched onto Brid. She held the pipe in both her hands.

Together they tumbled to the ground.

The wolves were gone. Caspar looked around in disbelief. The log with its plate-like fungus was just as it had been though the dun little creature with its plaintive crying had returned. The wolf he had shot through the neck was there, somehow crawling away into the undergrowth, blood bubbling from its wound, but the others were gone, simply vanished.

"Brid?" he stuttered but she waved his questions aside as she stood and slowly looked around in bewilderment. He was shaking with adrenaline from the shock of the attack. Where were the other wolves? Where were the horses? He gulped back his panic and looked towards the Maiden. "Brid, are you hurt? Are you all right?" he asked urgently.

"Yes, Spar," she said distractedly and then smiled.

"Whatever the danger, whatever has happened, you never fail to worry about my safety."

Caspar was taken aback. It was such a strange thing to say right then just after they had been attacked by wolves. But then the whole place seemed strange, dreamlike even. He couldn't explain. Somehow, he felt distanced, detached from his surroundings and conversely more aware of himself. He couldn't quite explain the feeling. It was as if his emotions were suddenly more real, more intense, as if thought were the reality and the tangible physical being had become abstract. He blinked and shook himself. Had he been injured and was now delirious with wounds? Had the wolves simply chased off after the horses?

Sitting on the log and seemingly oblivious to their presence, the strange little dun creature was still crying softly. Brid was walking towards it.

"It might be dangerous," Caspar warned.

"How could anything so unhappy be dangerous?" she retorted, stooping down to the level of the pathetic creature. "Hello," she said, settling onto her knees and gently raising a hand towards the creature's bowed head.

Big round eyes, veined red with weeping, looked from Brid to Caspar. They were set in a strange face, which he would have described as human but for the short fawn-like horns that protruded from the top of its head.

CHAPTER EIGHT

Hal longed for a hot bath and a cake of soap. Each night he had removed most of the mud from Secret's coat but the salt-laden grime collected on her caparison was impossible to rinse out and the once rich blues and golds were now faded and tide-marked. His horse was a mess and he knew he looked little better.

He felt dirty. His skin itched from the grime collected off the huge mudflats inshore from Ceolothia's only sizeable port of Narwhal Ria. The weather had been atrocious. High winds had swept briny spray inland for miles, and even the constant Ceolothian rain of the following weeks had not yet managed to rinse it from his bearskin cloak and leather hose. The rains and spray had turned the low-lying road, which led north-west to the capital, into a brackish quagmire and for the last hundred leagues they had spent much of their time coaxing the horses through knee-deep mud. He really needed that soapy hot bath. Even some soapwort and a clear stream would do but there was none forthcoming in this godforsaken land.

The rest of the company was an equally miserable sight, especially poor Hardwin. The short-legged Pisceran, who had been so proud of his fashionable clothes when they left Farona, had not stood up at all well to the journey. He was plucking at his soiled silk leggings in dismay, disgustedly working his fingers over a hole that had appeared at his fleshy knee. Prince Renaud was in much the same state. Only Lord Tupwell, heir to the barony of Ovissia, looked relatively clean. He seemed to have an endless supply of fresh doublets.

By the time the Ceolothian capital of Castabrice came into view, Hal was beginning to feel very uncharitable towards the bulky Caldean who rode at his side. After all it was all Ceowulf's fault that he was drenched through to the skin.

Hal peered through the rain at the terraces of stone houses that rose in tiers up towards the crowning central palace. "Have you ever been there?" he asked, though he had already guessed the reply. Ceowulf had been a mercenary, plying his trade widely amongst the countries of the Caballan Sea, and had been almost everywhere, or so it seemed by his tales.

The big man nodded. "It's a strange place with too many walls and restricted quarters. The yeomen, the servants and the merchant classes all have to keep to separate areas. The Ceolothians love their hierarchies and take protocol very seriously."

Hal groaned. "How boring!" His thoughts quickly flitted to King Dagonet's household. He had met the king's eldest sons, Prince Turquin and Prince Tudwal, before and had not enjoyed the experience. He really didn't want to turn up at King Dagonet's grand court looking as he did. What would the young ladies of the court think of him? He knew he was physically a very presentable young man; he had been told so many times by many ladies – not that Brid ever said anything like that to him – and he liked to maintain that impression.

He felt guilty. His wandering thoughts of Brid and other ladies had reminded him of last summer when Branwolf had sent him to the Caldean court. Ceowulf had set up a specialized training ground at his father's castle in the hope of rivalling the knights' school in Camaalia and it was an ideal opportunity for Hal to practise his jousting. Hal had thoroughly enjoyed himself but had perhaps spent too much time with the young ladies. They had been so eager for his company! Though young, he was skilled with a lance and such displays never went unnoticed.

Brid had been entirely icy on his return, despite having spent much of her time apart from him in the sole company of his nephew, Spar, who, in turn, had forsaken his attentions towards May. Everyone else had felt sorry for May in all this, standing as she was in Brid's shadow; but he didn't. She was the orphaned daughter of a woodcutter and it was understood that Caspar would one day marry her. It was a fairy tale.

Caspar had spent months trying to make it up to May, but both Hal and Brid had refused to apologize to one another. The two of them had sulked for well over a week, causing much amusement and wagging of tongues amongst the castle gossips. In the end they had independently decided to ignore the whole matter. He did love her so very much; but if only she weren't so infuriatingly right the whole time.

She was born and raised in the wilds of the Boarchase forest, encouraged to roam the savage terrain of the bordering Yellow Mountains and Hal had thought that life in the castle of Torra Alta would tame her. He had hoped that, once she witnessed his ability to motivate and organize and saw how highly he was regarded by the men, she would be more heedful of him. But as it turned out, she commanded so much respect herself that he had begun to feel entirely overshadowed by her.

Hal sighed. Though Brid undermined his self-confidence,

he couldn't help loving her. He was himself with her, freed from all pretences because she saw straight through them. He scowled and found Ceowulf laughing at him.

"What's so damn funny?" the raven-haired Torra Altan snapped.

"You are. You look so serious."

"I just want a bath, that's all. Is that too much to ask? We're approaching Dagonet's court and I don't want to become an object of ridicule for Prince Tudwal." Hal remembered the young man with great dislike from the time he had spent at the Camaalian training arena. "Look at us! We all look like vagabonds!"

"A man is not judged by looks alone." Prince Renaud joined their conversation. "His worth is in his soul not his appearance, or do you pagans hold a different view?"

"No, Sir," Hal replied politely though he hoped there was no hint of obsequiousness in his tone. "As they say, a man should not be judged by his looks any more than a war-horse should be judged by his caparison but in my experience he often is. And if I am to be judged I would prefer people to gain a favourable impression of me rather than take me for the mudlark that I might appear right now."

"He's worried that his very fine features are obscured beneath a mask of clay," Ceowulf teased.

Hal glared at his friend through slitted eyes, making Ceowulf grin all the more.

"You take yourself too seriously, Lord Hal. No one at King Dagonet's court is going to think either one thing or the other of you," the Prince told Hal smoothly. "After all, you are here merely as an escort."

"I still think we should stop to bathe at the first public house we see," Hal suggested.

The prince drew himself up on his horse and peered

down his thin nose. "I am of royal blood and I'm not bathing in some common public house. The disease, man! Think what manner of disease I might catch."

Hal thought Prince Renaud unwise in this matter. King Dagonet might see it as an affront if they arrived dripping with mud, even if it was Ceolothian mud. Then the thought suddenly struck him that this might be a deliberate ploy. Everyone knew that Prince Renaud coveted Belbidia's throne for himself and perhaps he wanted to insult King Dagonet in order to deter him from giving away his daughter to his brother.

Ceowulf was diplomatically covering up Hal's disgruntled noises by talking loudly about the city ahead. "Of course, you've heard about Castabrice. It's built over one of Ceolothia's first mineral mines though they say that the sunburst rubies are mined out here now and King Dagonet has to rely on the mines in the inaccessible northern reaches of his realm."

"Sunburst ruby mines, eh?" The prince began to look interested in Ceowulf's lecture but Hal hung back until the troops behind drew level. The men nodded politely as he fell in alongside them.

"Makes you glad to be a Belbidian, doesn't it?" Hal joked and held out his hands to catch the rain.

The men laughed. "Always been proud to be Belbidian," an old fellow with smiling eyes and round red cheeks agreed. He wore a sergeant's badge on his sodden cloak.

"Where do you come from, Ogden?" Hal asked the sergeant. He had long since taken the trouble to learn all the men's names and was happy to make conversation. He was aware of Prince Renaud casting annoyed looks over his shoulder and, no doubt, he would be dressed down for this later. The prince disliked any fraternizing with the troops but Hal didn't care what his seniors thought. Prince Renaud was only his cousin, after all, and he wasn't intimidated by him.

"Bleham, Faronshire, sir. A miller's son, naturally, but I thought I'd break the family mould and join the king's service."

Hal smiled at him. "Do you enjoy working for the king?"

The man shrugged dismissively. "We all work for the king, don't we, sir, be we soldier, ploughman or merchant? Near half our pay seems to go straight back in taxes – to rid the country of wolves they tell us. I can't see that hiring a few men to slay wolves costs all that much." The man paused and suddenly looked concerned. "But I shouldn't be saying things like this to you, sir, being such a fine man of Belbidia. You'll forget my words I hope," he blustered. "I meant no offence."

"No offence taken, my man," Hal replied with a laugh. "None taken at all. I'm a Torra Altan and I like to hear a man speak his mind."

Castabrice was large before them, the great structure rising out of the plain like a mountain. A dun haze surrounded the city from the thousands of fires that made their pathetic attempts to keep the winter dampness at bay. Hal longed for the clean crisp cold of Torra Alta. Though it could be bitter and the snows treacherous, it was infinitely better than this insipid, pervasive dampness that made even his young bones ache.

Secret's hooves beat out a firm ringing tone on paved road for the last upward mile before Castabrice and they were soon at the city wall. Their way was barred by the gates that filled a vast arch twenty feet high. They were tall solid wooden gates studded with black bullets and reinforced with steel bars. King Dagonet's emblem of a standing bear was carved into the two stone pillars at either side and a pattern of scrollwork linked by circles formed a border around the edge of the design. A guard of six mounted soldiers was waiting to greet them.

One moved forward and bowed in the saddle. "Prince Renaud of Belbidia, King Dagonet sends his greetings," he announced in careful Belbidian full of the dull flat tones that were characteristic of the Ceolothian language. He eyed their weaponry, in particular the paraphernalia of long swords, light lances and javelins carried by Hal and Ceowulf. Much to Hal's satisfaction the Ceolothian guard led them directly to a private house where they were courteously offered food, wine and a bath to prepare themselves before being presented to the royal court.

Unlike the prince or the other noblemen, Hal and Ceowulf saw to their horses themselves. It was a lesson Hal had learnt from his nephew though he knew they had wholly different motives. Spar's horse was entirely unmanageable and easily upset by rough hands. Hal would never dream of having such a silly beast but all the same he had often noted how impressed people were by Spar's determination to deal with his own animal. It created an air of mystique and unpredictability about the creature, which Hal liked to cultivate about Secret.

To this end he had also added three rows of curb chains to her bridle, which jangled impressively, though he never actually tightened them enough to have any effect on the horse. In fact, Secret had a very gentle bit in her soft mouth. That was why she was called Secret. She was totally biddable and well-mannered but he had taught her to lash out backwards if he tapped her shoulder, and bite on command.

As he vigorously brushed her liver chestnut coat, working himself up into a sweat with the effort of combing through the thick layers of mud, he found himself smiling and thinking of Brid. She had chosen the horse for him and done much of the training, which Hal was grateful for, since Brid had a light touch with horses and he hadn't wanted Caspar involved. She had laughed at him for adding the curb-chains to Secret's bridle. He missed her.

The honeyed mead was strong and invigorating as it burnt down his throat and fired his stomach. The walls of King Dagonet's hospitality house were hung with the vast snarling heads of black bears that had once been prolific throughout northern Ceolothia. Hal looked at them and wondered what Brid would have said about them but the mead was strong and the thought soon drifted hazily out of his head. After several more goblets had lubricated his throat, he stood on a chair and raised his cup, spilling the treacly brew down his sleeve. He still hadn't bathed yet so he didn't care. In fact, he wasn't sure that he would have cared even then. "Here's to King Rewik's new bride," he toasted boisterously.

Renaud flashed him a black look from the doorway. Hal hadn't meant to be so riotous and had only joined in the jollities because Renaud had been absent and still in his bath. But the man *would* enter just when he was toppling from his chair to be caught by Ogden.

Hal sat down sulkily and reflected that of course Renaud didn't want anyone to toast Princess Cymbeline. After all, she ended his immediate claim to the throne.

Several hours later, after Hal had doused his head in sobering, chilled water, bathed and changed into somewhat fresher clothes, they were ready to make their approach to the palace. Hal found the intricate system of roads, alleys and plazas entirely confusing. Ceowulf explained that the city was divided into four concentric circles: the poorest areas around the outside, the shopkeepers within that, the merchants' houses near the core of the city and the king's palaces at the heart. The road didn't cut directly through these quarters to the palace but climbed through a mazelike, spiralling route that passed through each section of the entire city before reaching the golden gates guarding the palace.

Faces stared out from behind windows and half-opened doors at their solemn procession and Hal felt quite ridiculous taking so long to reach the central quarter. He decided it was a ruse by Dagonet to make any approaching visitor feel ill at ease and said as much to Ceowulf.

"I'm sure you're right. I believe he has a passageway beneath the streets for his own use."

"So, he never meets his people?" Hal asked rhetorically.

"Well, who would want to walk through these streets if they could possibly help it?" Prince Renaud interrupted. He had evidently been listening to their conversation, his head held high as he studiously ignored the blond-haired Ceolothian crowds that waved, cheered or merely stared with cold disinterest. Washing lines strung high above their heads were the only things that brightened the dark, overshadowed streets. Hal wondered how their clothes ever dried in the rain.

Typical of Prince Renaud, he thought. Even if he did find it distasteful to march through the gloomy streets, he should know that the only way to rule a people well was to understand their needs. Hal sniffed in disgust and Ceowulf flashed him a look of warning. Once Renaud had pulled ahead the knight breathed, "Don't be so obvious, Hal. Can't you conceal your thoughts just a tiny little bit? Your attitude towards Renaud might one day go against you."

Hal looked at him suspiciously. "What do you mean?"

The big knight shrugged, his dark eyes looking straight

ahead beneath flat, black brows. He was not entirely attractive but there was something in his self-possessed and yet humble expression that the ladies clearly found appealing. Hal had noticed it on many occasions. "It depends if you want to stay at Torra Alta under your nephew or try for a position with the king perhaps."

"I'd stay at Torra Alta," Hal replied without needing to think. It wasn't just that he loved the mountains, the fresh crisp air and the wild hunts. And it wasn't just that he would miss Spar, however annoying the boy might be, but he knew he could never take Brid away from Torra Alta. She would feel trapped in the city and it wouldn't be fair. He didn't, however, explain his reasoning to Ceowulf for fear of being thought sentimental. A man should not base his life around the whims and wants of his woman, he told himself, or at least he shouldn't be *seen* to do so.

"Well, I wouldn't burn any bridges," Ceowulf said sagely. "You don't want to make enemies of your cousins."

"I'm not intimidated by Renaud."

"Clearly!" Ceowulf retorted as if he had made his point for him. "But I think you ought to be. He's the king's brother, and perhaps you should remember that."

Hal sniffed in disgust. He didn't like the prince; he seemed to see himself only as a prince and never as a man, which Hal considered most unprincely. Most of the men laughed at him behind his back though there were just one or two, Hardwin's men in particular, Hal noted, who seemed more in favour of the prince. Prince Renaud didn't know the sergeant's names even. Imagine! He conjured a picture of Renaud on the battlefield having to shout, hey, you, do this or, you there, do that and half a dozen soldiers turning round not understanding what he had wanted. Though Hal disliked King

Rewik he decided he was a better king than Renaud could ever make.

"You want to stay under your nephew at Torra Alta? Have you no ambitions then?" Tupwell, the heir to Ovissia goaded, butting in on their conversation.

The man almost made Hal wish they hadn't stopped to take a bath. Whereas he liked to look healthily smart as befitted a confident knight, both Tupwell and Hardwin were fastidious to the extreme over their appearances. Tupwell, though he possessed a well-formed body and broad shoulders, was overly fussy and garish with his dress.

For the royal occasion, he had donned a purple hat decorated with a long peacock feather. He spent long tedious minutes trying to arrange his flappy ears beneath the hat but they persisted in sticking out. The feather was unsoiled and Hal wondered where he had stowed it throughout the journey to prevent it becoming damp. Everything of Hal's was damp. Tupwell wore a green doublet and a lightweight cloak woven from the finest wool interlaced with threads of gold and silver that formed an expensive border. Hal considered the rich clothes to be highly impractical and most unknightly.

"Just look at the way he rides," Hal muttered to himself, glowering at Tupwell's exaggerated hand movements and the way he joggled in his seat. What added to Hal's dislike of him was that he was the eldest son of a baron. Who was he to talk about ambition when everything in life had fallen into his lap? He would never have to struggle for riches or position; he merely had to wait and Ovissia would be his. Hal urged Secret up behind Tupwell's dappled mare and considered encouraging her to take a bite at the animal's swaying rump but finally restrained himself as he heard the bustle of commerce ahead.

The noise swelled as they passed beneath another gated arch in the city's inner walls and negotiated wide steps in the road to ascend to the trading quarter. Silversmiths, ironmongers, candlestick makers, weavers, jewellers, cartographers, all busied themselves along the thoroughfares. The terraced streets were narrow, overshadowed by tiered stories that virtually met above their heads, letting only a slither of sunlight edge down to the cobbles. The Ceolothians were a pallid people and no wonder, Hal thought. As they trotted through this sector, Tupwell began to take more interest in things around, no longer pretending that the people didn't exist. He halted alongside a silversmith and turned on Hal.

"Look, perhaps you would like to stop to buy your little woman a trinket here. They say that pagans like trinkets." There was a sneer to his voice. "What do you think, Hardwin? Would it not be strange to be like Hal and betrothed to a heathen? I mean, all the world knows that pagan women rule their men."

Hal's hand was already on his sword but Ceowulf was pushing his horse between Hal and Tupwell. He laughed lightly. "Listen, friend," he said to Tupwell. "I've not met a man yet that has the say-so over his wife and I'm sure neither you nor Hardwin will change that, so let's hear an end of this."

Ceowulf's remark did little to pacify Hal. He was stung. Did everyone really laugh at him for being Brid's puppet? But he wasn't! He would show Tupwell, show the world and he would show Brid too.

Blazing with anger, he controlled his temper only by grinding his teeth. A few years ago, he would simply have punched the man but now he had more self-restraint.

He hardly noticed his surroundings until they passed from the steep, narrow streets into a wide market square;

only then was he coaxed from his self-indulgent thoughts. Beyond the furrier stalls, which were laden with wolf pelts, and alongside the stinking cattle pens were the sad and weary faces of men and women chained up for sale. Huddled together, they were kept out in the rain, ready to be brought by the slave merchants to labour in the frozen north of Ceolothia's deepest mines. The sight made Hal sick to his stomach.

They hurried across the square to climb a series of terraces to the next quarter. Here the impressive and brightly coloured facades of merchants' houses were overshadowed by the king's palace that was set like a tall white rose amongst a bed of pansies. The palace's white marble walls gleamed even in the overcast light. An open pointed archway led them into the complex of cloisters and stables.

Hal forgot his sulk as he found himself staring at the bejewelled inner gates glinting with sunburst rubies. King Dagonet was rich. Very rich indeed! He was disgusted, though, by the great black bear chained like a guard dog beside the gate. It lashed out viciously as they passed. With a maddened look to its eyes and streaked with white scars across its muzzle, there was no doubt that its trainer had been over vigorous with a whip – or more likely a length of chain, he decided, judging by the depth of the scars.

The Belbidian nobles trotted under the arch in smart formation with Prince Renaud first followed by Tupwell as the next in rank then Ceowulf and Hal and lastly Hardwin. The troops on their uniform chestnut horses briskly followed. Clearly unsettled by the long journey through the streets, Prince Renaud stiffened as a blast of trumpets sounded to their right. Grooms sallied forth from the stables and Hal warned them to be wary of

Secret's heels as she was led away. The Belbidian noblemen were ushered into a long entrance hall.

Set high above the rest of the city, the atmosphere within the palace was bright and airy. Huge intricately carved ivory screens feathered the sunlight as it fell from tall windows onto polished pale limestone floors inlaid with seams of silver. Fine furniture, so lavish and delicate that to Hal it looked like it could blow away in the wind, lined the length of the hall. The pages led them forward, throwing open door after door as they were guided through a maze of corridors and halls all lavishly decorated. In many, arms and trophies were ostentatiously displayed but looked entirely out of place above the refined and delicate furnishings. Hal caught his foot against an upright elephant's tusk that formed part of an arch and the delicate structure toppled to the ground with a resounding crash. He hurried on without looking round, pretending that it he knew nothing about it.

Ceowulf stifled his chuckles. "King Dagonet would have a fine kingdom if his wealth were better spent," he muttered more soberly just as they halted outside the throne-room.

Hal's reply was drowned in an ear-splitting fanfare of trumpets as they were bustled forward into the circular chamber. Pillars lined the throne-room and sashes and garlands were looped between each of the many capitals. Before them, across the expanse of white marble floor, was a high throne, the scrolled woodwork decorated with rows of bear teeth. The high throne was surrounded by lesser thrones, which in turn peered down on rows of cushioned chairs that lined the walls. Prince Renaud marched forward unbidden and stooped his head in a perfunctory bow. Hal cast his eyes from side to side, quickly taking in the faces of the court before raising his head to meet King Dagonet's gaze.

He was a fat man with round red checks. It was difficult to say whether his hair was blond or grey but it was certainly very pale and hung in thick flaxen lines to his shoulders. He smiled a warm welcome that Hal had not expected from the father of Prince Tudwal. His crown of gold, set with a fist-sized ruby nugget, evidently troubled him because he had taken it off and was fiddling with it in his lap, tracing over the faces of the brilliant stone set in the front. Two of his sons stood to either side of him and glowered at the crown in annoyance. Prince Turquin and Prince Tudwal had hardly changed in the three years since Hal had met them.

Prince Turquin hadn't even bothered to look up as they entered. His younger brother, by contrast, the straight harsh lines of his hair emphasizing the blockiness of his muscular face and body, had raised his eyebrows at Hal and snorted in amusement. He was sweating slightly and since he was still wearing a fashioned hauberk, thick with studs, and gauntlets of fluted steel, Hal judged he had come straight from the practice fields without bothering to prepare himself for the arrival of the royal Belbidian party.

Hal set his jaw and confronted the over-bearing arrogance that stabbed out of Tudwal's pale blue eyes. The Torra Altan finally broke his cold stare and looked beyond Tudwal's wide shoulders to a third son that he hadn't met before. He sat near the queen, a broad happy smile filling his vacant features. He was briefly introduced as Prince Tullis and his happy disposition undoubtedly shamed his stern brothers.

Hal was instantly reminded of a dark smear blotting the long illustrious history of Ceolothia's royal family. King Dardonus, one of King Dagonet's distant forefathers, had married the daughter of the King of Lonis, a beautiful dark-haired woman, but after many years they had failed to produce an heir. Then one day, quite mysteriously, King Dardonus presented his court with a baby son and daughter, neither of whom looked one bit like his wife but every bit like his fair sister. The son grew well but suffered so many fits and moments of simplicity that he was deemed unfit to rule and the crown passed straight to his sister's son – no woman had ever ruled in Ceolothia; the very idea was considered laughable. Ever since then each generation of the royal family had produced at least one son suffering from the same sorry affliction, just like Prince Tullis.

Dagonet's family all had extraordinary blond hair. It was straight and thick and shone like polished silver yet with none of them was it more beautiful than with a lovely young woman who sat upon a delicate throne cushioned with ermine. A white-gold circlet crowned her head and her straight silver-blonde hair swirled around her shoulders. Like all Ceolothian jewellery the circlet was encrusted with sunburst rubies. Hal found himself forgetting that there was anyone else in the room other than this dazzling jewel of King Dagonet's only daughter.

Why me? He sighed. Why did I have to come all this way to be so tempted? He thought of Brid and tried very hard not to look at Rewik's future bride but she was so fascinating, far too distracting for an honest man like himself.

Aware that Tudwal was observing him coldly, Hal smiled politely, and he hoped dismissively, before falling back to admiring Princess Cymbeline.

Her gown of tailored satin hugged her bosom and waist before flaring out in the widest skirt he had ever seen. Sashes and bows decorated the hem and the whole dress sparkled with countless sapphires and diamonds. Her clothes alone would be worth a king's ransom.

King Dagonet was bumbling his way through introductions, quickly running through the names of his tall, well-muscled sons without much ceremony before taking a deep breath to introduce his daughter.

"And this is my daughter Princess Cymbeline, without question the loveliest maiden in all the world and the utter joy of my heart." He coughed and dabbed at his eye as if suddenly remembering that he was about to lose his daughter to the King of Belbidia.

"Oh, don't be so ridiculous," the queen muttered stiffly. Though Prince Turquin looked embarrassed, Prince Tudwal glanced towards his sister and held her gaze for a brief moment without showing any emotion. Hal had no siblings so he wasn't sure how he would have reacted if he had a sister and she were so favoured.

King Dagonet ignored his wife and continued to gaze lovingly on his daughter. She returned the look with equal devotion. Unlike the queen, her features were softly rounded, which enhanced her feminine curves. When she looked up, it was with a sweet smile that utterly contrasted with the flat half-smiles of Turquin, Tudwal and her mother. She was her father's daughter, there was no doubt about it. The king seemed to know this, because he constantly looked at her, beaming with pride.

Hal shook himself alert. Someone had mentioned Torra Alta and he looked up brightly, trying to appear as if he knew exactly what had been said. He relaxed. It was only Prince Renaud introducing him and irritatingly calling him Halgard, as people sometimes mistakenly assumed Hal was short for. He puffed up his chest indignantly. Hal was short for nothing and was a fine name in its own right.

"Hal," he corrected. "Not Halgard but Hal."

Renaud looked at him archly. "How dare you interrupt?"

The king smiled at Hal. "No, no. A man should be known by his rightful name. Who are we after all if we have our names taken from us?"

Hal grinned back, noting with pleasure how this exchange further annoyed Tudwal and Turquin. Princess Cymbeline looked pleased and he was quite convinced that her eyes lingered on him before she fluttered her eyelashes and lowered her gaze. He sighed to himself. It could do no harm to look, could it? That wouldn't hurt Brid since she would never know.

Someone nudged him in the ribs. "You're staring," Ceowulf hissed.

Hal growled in his throat. Ceowulf had to stop telling him what to do. He pursed his lips and obstinately continued to study the beautiful princess. Was this lovely maiden really meant to marry an ancient scraggy hawk like King Rewik? The very idea was appalling.

CHAPTER NINE

Brid knelt down in front of the sobbing creature and gently held out her hand. "What's the matter, little woodwose?" she asked.

"Be careful," Caspar warned.

Several loose tendrils of Brid's coppery brown hair had worked free from her braid. She swept them back behind her neat ears and turned to look at Caspar. "What do you mean be careful? Don't be ridiculous, Spar. The poor thing's crying."

She tugged gently at its little furry hands, trying to pull them away from its face, but the woodwose only cried louder. How Brid could be so calm after being attacked by wolves was beyond Caspar's understanding.

The little horned creature sobbed on and on so Brid sat down beside him and put her arm around his juddering shoulders. She patiently soothed him until, at last, the poor woodwose curled up and flung himself against her bosom. She hugged him close and rocked back and forth as if cradling a child.

Caspar was slowly becoming calm enough to take in his surroundings. He frowned in puzzlement at bluebells. But it was too early for bluebells. Snowdrops possibly but not bluebells. And there were buds on the chestnut trees, little sticky buds; and furry yellow balls feathering the pussy willow trees. The month was Horning, not quite even spring, yet this was more like Ostara or Merrymoon. The air was fragrant and he could hear singing.

He was dreaming; he must be dreaming. He must have been hurt by the wolf and was now suffering the hallucinations of a high fever. The voices must be those of the foresters. They must have saved him and now he was in their hut again – at least he hoped he was, wrapped up warm by the fire, hearing their voices. They were singing. The voices were getting louder, the sound haunting like the piercing notes of a distant piper.

Caspar suddenly remembered the pipe. Brid had been holding it when all this strangeness happened.

The sobbing ceased. The little horned woodwose was breathing in fits and gasps, his head still buried in Brid's shoulder but at least he had stopped crying. Finally, he pulled himself away to look up into Brid's face.

"She's gone," he whispered. "I can't get back to her."

"It's part of the cycle," Brid soothed as if she understood what he was talking about, though Caspar most certainly did not.

The creature had a long narrow face with a broad flat nose and dark brown eyes. The skin of his face was covered in a fine sandy down that lengthened to a pointed beard at his chin. His hair was short and curly, making a nest for his two velvety horns like those of a young roe deer. Caspar agreed with Brid that he did indeed appear to be a woodwose, a half deer, half man that he had read about in fairy tales.

"My Primrose, she's gone on without me," the woodwose announced.

"If you truly love her, you'll meet her again."

"But will I?" The creature looked at his hands in dismay. The fingers were short and fat, the nails over-large and grotesquely thickened. "It seems the Great Mother has yet to decide what I will be. Look at me. Just what am I?" He looked imploringly at Brid. "Tell me what I am. You speak to Her. You know Her. Beg for me, I pray you. Plead my cause. I must return. With Primrose dead, who else will look after my Sorrel? Who else will care for her with these beasts abroad?"

"What beasts?" Caspar asked, completely at a loss as to what the creature was talking about.

"Wolves, fool. Big, bad wolves. Are you telling me you didn't notice them? Who ate you anyway? And you shouldn't speak out of turn. It's not very nice talking to a fellow without first saying who you are." His head jerked away and his ears, Caspar swore, almost seemed to prick up as he turned towards the sound of the singing. "They're getting closer," the furry little man said anxiously. "Quick, we must go. Quick! Quick! Follow me," he ordered excitedly, but he didn't go and instead looked urgently around, leaping up and kicking about in the undergrowth. "Where's it gone? I need it! I need it!"

Caspar thought the creature quite mad. This was quite the most absurd dream he had ever had.

"Oh, you've got it." The woodwose turned back towards Brid and relaxed somewhat as he saw the polished oak pipe in her hands. "Well now, what are we waiting for?" He beckoned them on before darting away over the log and appearing only a second later on the far side of the glade, standing on a mound of earth and waving frantically at them to follow. Brid rushed after him and, in complete bewilderment, Caspar followed her lead as she ducked and weaved through the forest to keep up with the little woodwose. When at last they could barely hear the singing, the creature stopped, plucked a piece of grass and nibbled at it thoughtfully, his mouth moving in quick nervous twitches.

"Give me the Pipe." He held out one short-fingered hand to Brid. "I need it."

Brid was out of breath. "You know you shouldn't have it. There'll only be trouble." She kept the pipe behind her back.

"Give it to me!" The little woodwose stamped a cloven hoof.

Caspar felt some intervention was needed. "Now steady on, little fellow. What's this all about? If Brid says you shouldn't have it—"

"I told you it was rude to talk without us first being introduced," the short furry man petulantly interrupted and chewed a little faster in irritation.

"You talk to Brid without knowing her, so why take exception to me?"

"But I do know her." The creature pouted. "Everybody knows her. She's the Maiden. The birds know her, the hares know her, we all know her." He looked down uncertainly at his slender body. "Even the smaller wolves know her."

"But not the hooded wolves," Brid interjected.

"No, not the bad wolves," the little woodwose agreed. "But everyone else does. And we know her, of course. The Maiden, One of the Three." He looked at her and cocked his head to one side.

Brid laughed and Caspar frowned. "Who's we?" he demanded, feeling more and more confused.

The little woodwose's face fell. "We're not we anymore. We used to be the herd, but not me, not now. Sorrel has a coat as shiny as a polished chestnut, such dark rich colours and her eyes are as dark as a deep forest pool. And am I never to return to her?" His shoulders began to shudder. "Will she never know me again?" He looked imploringly at Brid. "Please give me the Pipe. Before it's too late."

"It's already too late," Brid told him firmly but gently. "It's much too late. You have to accept it. There's nothing you can do – and nor should you. It's against Nature."

"But I have to get back to my little Sorrel. The wolves!" he exclaimed. "Give me the Pipe."

"Now steady on." Caspar put a restraining hand on the woodwose's arm but the creature snatched it free and leapt up away. "Don't you talk to me till I know you," the creature objected.

"Spar," he told him, offering his outstretched hand.

The little creature looked at him sideways. "Of what herd? Spar means nothing to me."

"He's from Torra Alta," Brid explained, "and my dearest friend."

Caspar's heart leapt to his throat. Brid had never said anything like that about him before. From the very moment he had met her, he had loved her with all his body and soul. Now she described him as her dearest friend. More dear than Hal, her betrothed?

"Any friend of yours . . ." the creature began, stepping closer. "Fern," he nodded at Caspar in greeting, "from the Sylvanrush herd. Oldest herd in the forest. Pleased to make your acquaintance." He turned abruptly back to Brid. "Now can I have the Pipe?"

"No," Brid replied firmly. "It's not yours. You've taken it from them and you're meddling with things that should never be interfered with. They'll come looking for it."

"Please," begged Caspar, holding up his hands to silence them. "Please, can someone tell me what's going on. Brid, what has happened to the wolves?"

The little woodwose paled at the mention of wolves. His chewing stopped and a piece of grass fell from his sagging mouth. He looked around him hurriedly.

"They're not here," Brid told him gently.

"Brid, please," Caspar implored, his frustration rising. "I need to know what's going on."

It was pleasantly warm and the air was fresh with the scent of bluebells that grew in great swaths like a rippling sea beneath the delicate shade of the trees. The oaks were covered in bursting buds and the beeches were dappled with fresh lime green leaves that fluttered in the light spring breeze.

Caspar could only believe he was dreaming. He must be dreaming. Brid sat down amongst the bluebells, carefully keeping the pipe away from the troubled little creature. She took a deep breath and looked at Caspar.

"Now sit down and I'll explain."

"We haven't got time to sit down. We need to find Pip and Brock. It's the first time I've been in charge of a hunting party and I've lost two of my men," Caspar complained. "What will Father think of me?"

"There's no point hurrying. It's the nature of the place. Time doesn't run in quite the same way here."

"Brid!" Caspar threw his hands up in despair, feeling that he was going quite mad.

"It's *the* Pipe, I think," she started to explain. "Now sit down, Spar, and stop looking like a startled hare. It's not so complicated if you just give me a chance to explain. The Pipe must have powers a bit like Necrönd, able to open up channels between life and the Otherworld. When Fern played it, he must have briefly opened up a gateway that took us to the Otherworld."

"And I need to get back before I'm fully changed," Fern tried to explain but Caspar was still at a loss.

"You mean we're in the Otherworld?"

Brid nodded.

"Doesn't that mean we're dead?"

"Fern is," Brid said lightly. "But we're here because the

music in the Pipe surrounded us and carried us between worlds."

"We must get back!" Caspar's mind was filled with urgency.

He felt clammy all over. They were in the world of the dead! And yet it seemed totally wholesome and peaceful and Fern was neither in a state of decay nor spirit, though he did have a blood-soaked kerchief knotted around his neck. Caspar finally sat down heavily beside Brid and resigned himself to hearing her explanation. He trusted her. If she said there was no urgency, then he believed her.

"So," he said, "we're in the Otherworld."

"Rye Errish," the woodwose corrected. "The singers call it Rye Errish."

Brid nodded. "This is a place of truth where we all have our deceits stripped from us, a place of cleansing before we pass into the bliss of Annwyn where all is forgetfulness when we join with the Great Mother."

"And how does anyone know this?" Caspar asked sceptically. Normally he would hold his tongue but here he felt a compulsion to speak his mind.

"Because just once in every thousand years or so someone is reborn who remembers."

Caspar blinked as he tried to absorb Brid's words.

She continued, "And occasionally spirits are seen walking the earth, ghosts if you will, the image of those dead. They are the souls of the dead that are so desperate to return to their lives that they fight the transition and slip back as shadows into the world. Sometimes they tell of this place."

Caspar was still trying to make sense of it. He looked hard at his hands to make sure they were still solid. He turned them over, flexing his palms, and in doing so caught the back of his hand on a bramble. He watched the beads of blood well up from the torn skin.

"And Fern needs to get back, only it's too late," Brid concluded.

"It can't be too late. I haven't fully changed. I need to get back. The wolves attacked us and I tried to draw them off while Primrose stayed with her. But the wolves . . . they got Primrose and, while she lay dying, I promised her I'd look after Sorrel but the wolves came back. I led them away from my fawn but they caught me in the end. Who's going to protect Sorrel now? It doesn't matter that I'm changing. I can still look after her. I promised her mother. I must protect our fawn. I must go back. Give me the Pipe."

"No, Fern. It is wrong to try and work against the wheel of life that turns only one way for us mortals. We must take the Pipe back to them."

"Them?" Caspar asked.

"The singers of magic," Fern replied heavily. "But, Brid, I promised."

The Maiden shrugged. "You have already passed through death to the Otherworld – to Rye Errish. Death releases you from the promises of your last life."

"But Sorrel is suffering. I must help her."

"Brid," Caspar urgently interrupted, "if the wheel of life turns only one way, how are *we* going to get back?"

Brid didn't reply; her attention was still fixed on the horned woodwose. "You cannot go back, Fern. The Great Mother has already decided that you are no longer a deer. Look at you. Soon you will be a man."

"I don't want to be a man," Fern argued, plucking at the moulting down on the back of his hands. "I must go back and look after her. Give me the Pipe; I need to try again."

"But can you really get back? You only appeared for a moment."

"I know." Fern hung his head. "I must have the tune wrong. I've been trying all morning. I tried to get through Nuin's door but I couldn't get past the High Circle. When they tried to stop me, I snatched Duir's Pipe."

Brid pushed a wisp of hair away from her ear and froze. "Listen. The singing is growing louder. We must take the Pipe back to them."

"No. Do you know what they'll do to me?" Fern objected, grabbing hold of Brid's hand as if he were a small child. "It's so slow being a man. I don't want to be a man; I want to be a deer."

"At the time of your death you must have wished it," Brid said thoughtfully.

"I did," Fern agreed. "I wanted to be a man because he is the only creature that can kill the bad wolves. Man can kill anything."

"Yes," Brid said heavily. "Yes, and it's a great burden for us."

"But why? The freedom! Think of it, living a life free from fear."

Brid raised an eyebrow at the creature. "But we have responsibility instead. True freedom is a life without responsibility. The more powerful the human, the less freedom they have. Now, Fern, we must give the Pipe back and you must accept that."

"I can't. Not now. I've been practising. I've nearly got the notes right, I'm sure."

"But you only succeeded in sending the Pipe across the divide and when I picked it up, it brought us here."

It was beginning to dawn on Caspar what had happened. Because of this funny little creature, half man, half deer, they had avoided being torn apart by the wolves by slipping across the divide into the parallel universe of the Otherworld, the world of spirit. "It's like we're dead," he murmured in horror.

"Oh no," Brid said calmly but with great solemnity. "We shouldn't be here at all. It's all a mistake. The wolves might not have killed us. Harle might have saved us. We will explain ourselves, return the Pipe and ask to be sent back. It's all a mistake, you'll see."

Brid suddenly stopped talking and was staring over Caspar's head. The mysterious haunting song was growing louder. He thought he almost remembered the song. Surely, he had heard it before in his childhood dreams. Slowly he turned, aware of the intensity of concentration on Brid's face.

Before them stood a man, at least Caspar presumed he was a man. He was quite small, probably an inch shorter than himself, with bright blonde hair that looked almost golden in the shade of the leafy trees. He had enthralling features like those of an elf, though Caspar knew he could not possibly be one. Brid had assured him that elves were not listed in the *Book of Names* and so were purely mythical creatures. For want of a better word Caspar could only describe him as beautiful. His skin was a dark ivory and his eyes were a frightening, unworldly greenish yellow, almost glowing in the umbra of the trees. He had high cheekbones, widely set eyes and a small sharp nose. His legs were clad in emerald green hose and only a leather jerkin covered his naked torso. A gold-trimmed baldric, angled across his lithe body, supported a quiver of arrows and a horn hung from a red sash around his neck. He stood with legs astride, staring at them with the arrogant air of a grudging landlord eyeing his wayward peasants.

"So, we've found the little thieves at last," he declared in a firm but musical voice and stepped with slow deliberate strides towards them. Unhurried and decisive, it was the sort of approach Caspar might use on a frightened horse.

There was a quality about the man that the Torra Altan instantly understood to be magical; the voice, the movements were all so fluid. To his shame he realized he was afraid of this man. Fern was hiding behind Brid, trembling.

"A verderer," he murmured. "A singer of Rye Errish." He cowered behind Brid and squeaked at the being. "It was nothing to do with me. Nothing at all. It wasn't my idea."

The verderer, as the woodwose had called him, looked from Fern to Brid, half his mouth rising into a laugh, the other half remaining unmoved. Caspar couldn't begin to guess at his thoughts.

"You have the Pipe, my lady." He gave Brid a bow that conveyed not the slightest hint of deference. "You are very brave to offend the High Circle so."

"My hand was pressed," Brid replied by way of excuse. "I have no desire to offend, merely to return – to return the Pipe to you and for ourselves to return to—"

"Return, eh? So, you know where you are and what you are doing? You know more than most."

Brid tilted her head in a slight nod of acknowledgement. "I still need to return. There is work, much work that I have to do."

"I have heard that too often of late." The verderer seemed to be talking almost without thinking, his eyes strolling across Brid's body in pleasured absorption.

"And I would amend that!" Brid retorted stiffly, her voice rising.

Caspar felt his protective instincts aroused and he stood in front of Brid. "Leave her alone, whoever you are," he demanded, bristling.

Those greenish-yellow eyes fixed on his and he shuddered, recoiling from their strength. Quite unexpectedly the verderer stepped forward, raised his hand and slapped Caspar across the mouth.

The Baron's son was sent reeling to the ground, stunned by the impact of the blow. It was too powerful, much too powerful for just a slap. Caspar looked up at the man in amazement. "Who are you?"

"I am Talorcan, chief verderer. I have charge of all souls who pass through the forest," he said with a satisfied smirk. "And you, boy, are in my way."

Nobody, apart from Morrigwen of course, had called Caspar boy in several years. "You cannot speak to me like that." Caspar felt his emotions as pure intense energy, resentment welling uncontrollably up out of his heart. "I have powers," he boasted, thinking of Necrönd.

"Spar!" Brid snapped icily, her eyes widening, desperately warning him to hold his tongue.

"You can't tell me what to do, Brid. Not here, not anymore."

"Please." Brid's tone changed to one of cajolement. "Please, Spar, for me, be quiet and let me sort this out."

"Yes," Fern added from his position cowering behind the Maiden, "be quiet, Spar. Do as the lady says."

Talorcan gave both Fern and Caspar the same dismissive glance before confidently raising his hand out towards Brid. "The Pipe is mine. You had no right to take it. You must give it back."

Brid shook her head. "No, not yet," she said with quiet composure. "I suspect I may need it to bargain with. I shall give it back but not without first seeing the High Circle. I presume you can take me to them. We have to get back."

Talorcan laughed. "No human has to get back. The

songs of magic do not allow mortals to pass happily back and forth between worlds. Why should you have such a privilege?"

"We didn't mean to come here," Brid explained patiently. "It wasn't our fault and we have to get back – not for our sakes but for the sake of the greater good."

"Hmm." Talorcan sounded sceptical. "I saw it happen. You picked up the Pipe deliberately and if you hadn't the wolves would have got you. Isn't that true? So, by rights you should be here anyway. You cannot cheat death."

Caspar's blood ran cold at the thought. They should have been torn to pieces by wolves. He slowly drew his arms across his body and squeezed his forearms reassuringly to check he was still whole.

Brid looked down at her feet and then back up at Talorcan, evidently having difficulty meeting him in the eye. "I grant that might be true. But it was no meddling on my part that put such an artefact into my grasp. That I knew its worth was part of my training but I used no unnatural magic to draw the Pipe to me."

"No," Talorcan agreed. "No, but someone is doing that; there are chasms and maelstroms in the channels of magic. And now you appear. You are the first humans to break through like this in a very long time." His fingers moved towards his horn while his dark piercing eyes remained steadily pinned to Brid. A faint smile broke his lips before he said, "Forgive me young lady, but I must summon the Circle. Only they can deal with this matter."

He took a deep breath and blew long and hard on his horn. Caspar had expected a deep tuneful blast but instead the sound was like the buzzing and moaning wind rushing through the twists of a ravine. The noise grew until the wood was filled with the sound of wingbeats as the air was buffeted by some unseen force. Then all was silence, an unstill silence of anticipation as if the world had just paused for breath before a moment of great import. The quiet was broken by a haunting lament that echoed through the air and invaded Caspar's mind.

The air at the edge of the glade shimmered. Bursts of coloured light, like sunlight pouring through the spray from a great waterfall, flecked the atmosphere, casting microscopic and fragmented rainbows into the air.

"The ealdormen of the High Circle," Fern moaned pitifully. "They come to punish me."

Caspar pressed himself a little closer to Brid, feeling as small and ineffectual as Fern who quivered and twitched at the sight of the dancing lights twinkling at the edge of the glade. They were mesmerizing in their beauty, fascinating in their strangeness. Fairy lights, Caspar thought; surely that's what they were. The thought made him want to laugh as he pictured the tiny delicate creatures of childhood stories.

The air began to still and the lights gradually dimmed.

As the hazy dazzling effect of the disturbed air settled, he realized there were figures standing amidst the dazzle. None of them were minute. Thirteen men and women with burnished golden hair were singing, the sound beautiful and yet painfully disturbing. Their dress was bright and colourful: crimsons, violets, emeralds and saffron, all as resplendent as any forest flower. Each wore a sash marked with an emblem. Tree runes, Caspar thought in surprise. One central figure amongst the thirteen seemed to shine more brightly.

Though she was not the tallest she had the greatest presence. Dressed in a flowing gown of pure white, she had long golden hair that fell in waves to her waist, twists of silver thread laced through the tresses. She had a small, neat face with a pert nose and big almond-shaped eyes upturned at the outer corners. Caspar looked at the marks of her emblem. It was the tree rune for ash, or Nuin in the old tongue. He remembered his lessons in tree magic: Nuin unlocks the understanding of how all individual beings and deeds, however small, are linked to the greater design.

As she came closer Caspar was disturbed by her eyes. The pupils were elongated slits like a cat's and they were yellow, a fiery yellow that blazed with emotion. She was gliding towards them, the aura of lights dazzling about her person.

Talorcan dropped to one knee and reverently bowed his head. "My Lady Nuin."

Caspar felt Brid stiffen at the approach of the ealdorwoman. He couldn't take his eyes off the lady of Rye Errish. It wasn't because she was beautiful, which indeed she was, every inch of her radiant and shimmering with light, but because she appeared to be floating, gliding on thin air towards them.

Her twelve companions continued to sing. Caspar wanted to scream at them to stop. The noise filled his head, resonating back and forth, scrambling his mind. He couldn't think straight. The ealdorwoman in white stopped just a few paces from Brid, the shimmering aura around her dwindling as she gracefully floated to the ground. The naked pearl-white of her feet, just visible beneath her flowing gown, brushed the dark earth.

Caspar pinched himself. He knew his mouth was open as he stared in disbelief, but his will had left him and he couldn't force himself to close it.

In a demanding gesture, Nuin held out a long thin hand towards Brid. "Give me the Pipe of Abalone. You are a thief and will be punished."

Fern collapsed into a heap on the ground, gibbering incoherently. Nobody paid him the slightest heed though

Caspar wanted to reach out and grip the woodwose's hand, offering at least some comfort but he could not; he was too dazzled and overwhelmed by the ealdorwoman's eyes that lit up like a smouldering fire stirred by a blast of air.

"I cannot give you the Pipe," Brid replied softly. "I came upon it fairly. I came upon it in my world. I could have kept it there and you may never have retrieved it."

The lady seemed agitated and a faint buzzing hummed around her as the sparkling aura reappeared. She rose ever so slightly and hovered over Brid.

Caspar frowned. The ealdorwoman had wings, fine gossamer wings that moved so fast that he saw them only as broken light. Though she was only just a little smaller than Brid, she was like a fairy, after all.

"I am Nuin, the spirit of the ash. You risk your soul by meddling with me, frail creature."

Caspar couldn't believe that Nuin dared speak to Brid like that and nor would he let her. Nobody scoffed at Brid. He stepped forward to confront this creature but as he did so, Talorcan barred his way. The verderer thrust out his hand and with one finger prodded Caspar's chest. Fiery pain stabbed out of the finger and the youth sprang back in dismay.

"Don't fret," Brid said softly to him. "We have done nothing wrong; they cannot harm us."

"Done nothing wrong!" There was a chorus from the other twelve members of the High Circle as they hovered closer. Their singing ceased and Caspar felt the instant relief of the silence.

"Done nothing wrong?" they chorused. "You have cheated death."

"That's not fair," Caspar protested. "We did nothing but pick up a pipe."

"Fair?" A very dark-skinned ealdorman echoed grumpily. "Who said there was anything fair about death? You should have been eaten by the wolves. You were gaming with death the moment you entered the forest."

Caspar looked at his emblem. Straif, he thought gloomily, the spirit of the blackthorn tree.

Nuin spoke, "So many of you come begging to the High Circle with lame excuses. 'An accident, a mistake' I hear and I hear it too often. Your kind must learn to accept your fate. Only when death separates two souls unified in love will I contemplate any discussion about reuniting them in some way. But for you there is no excuse, no mitigating circumstance. Your choices are finite! You can move on through the cycle or you can remain here to be punished until you feel ready to do so." Her voice was terrible. Though the woman looked youthful, only a little older than Brid, she sounded ancient. Her voice didn't quaver or croak but it sounded as old as the wind, timeless, endless, sweeping through him like the murmuring breeze soughing through the leaves of a tree.

"You have no justice," Caspar blurted.

"Spar, keep quiet," Brid warned him without taking her eyes from Nuin. "These are things you cannot understand."

Caspar felt crushed and looked down at Fern. Perhaps to Brid he was no more important than this little woodwose here. How could Brid dismiss him like that when he loved her so. He was miserable in the knowledge that she did not return his love. He had been miserable for three years but had suppressed his burning passion for her and had turned his thwarted affections on May instead. Poor May. He had told her a thousand times that he loved her while all the while he dreamt of Brid.

"How dare you speak?" the ealdorwoman danced in

the air, her golden hair shimmering in the sparkling lights. "I am the spirit of the ash, that links all parts of the universe. Nobody defies me."

"I am Brid and One of the Three. How dare you speak to me in such a manner?" Brid, in her faded hunting leathers with her hair in a tussled braid, stood up to this terrible being with defiant confidence. Caspar's heart burst with love for her.

The other members of the Circle bristled at this remark and Talorcan shifted his weight on his feet. He looked uncomfortably at Nuin and then more slyly at Brid. A half-smile lifted his solemn features. He was evidently impressed by Brid's strength of character.

"I am above your laws," Nuin raged. "I hold the ultimate threat. I can keep you here for as long as my whim pleases, from now till the end of time."

"You cannot," Brid sounded indignant though there was a hint of trepidation in her voice. "I have your Pipe and I will send it back into the world if you threaten me."

"Threaten?" Nuin's voice was suddenly soothing and gentle. "I do not threaten." Her eyes fixed on the oak Pipe inlaid with mother-of-pearl that Brid was raising very slowly to her lips. "I have no need to threaten because you cannot possibly know the tune that would conjure such magic. It is easy enough to play the notes that will take mortals from your world to Rye Errish because that follows the natural flow of the cycle but it takes immortal power to work the magic against the grain of Nature. Nor is there any place in your world or mine from which I could not retrieve the Pipe of Abalone."

"Ah, but isn't there?" Brid said, her voice hushed and breathy, making Nuin strain forward to hear her. "There are things you don't know about me, Nuin. You may rule here in Rye Errish but you do not have ultimate powers in my world. I am One of the Three and the Trinity can reach into the natural magic of the Great Mother."

Talorcan's eyes flared as she spoke and he licked his dark lips sensuously.

"I am Nuin. I hold the keys that unlock the channels of magic and link the universe, and my power flows straight from Him." She looked heavenward to the great glowing orb of the sun whose energy was more brilliant in this world. The power of the sun radiating down on them seemed to intensify for a moment around Nuin as if emphasizing her words. "The Sun lends me His powers. He is first amongst Gods and I answer only to Him. I and the twelve others of the High Circle rule here in Rye Errish."

"There are dark places on the Earth," Brid murmured, "where His light doesn't reach and there are spells I can weave that will banish the Pipe to such places – places from where your slaves will be unable to retrieve it." Brid's eyes stabbed towards Talorcan.

"Slaves," he echoed, his voice laughing lightly, though his gleaming sun-shot eyes held Brid's stare without wavering. Though bright with energy there was a cold look of design in him that Caspar distrusted.

"Talorcan, be silent." Nuin flashed with anger and the very air around her seemed to sizzle. "I will discuss this matter no longer here in the woods. Bring the three creatures to the palace where I will decide what to do with them at my leisure. The Circle will sit in counsel."

The Lady Nuin in her silvery white dress stepped up into mid-air and spread her wings. Translucent webs like strands of glass, they clasped together on her back but when she unfurled them, they were like swans' wings, soft and feathery, though seen only as a slight distortion in the light. The twelve other members of the Circle spread their wings and followed. Talorcan, it was evident, didn't have wings. He was joined by a score of verderers, dressed much as he was though none quite caught the eye in the same way.

Caspar noted how Brid looked at the chief verderer for just a little longer than he would have expected. She caught Caspar's eye and flashed him a look full of indignation. "Have you suddenly become my conscience?" she demanded.

Caspar flushed. "You were staring at him," he accused.

"So were you," Brid retorted. "What of it?"

"Not in the same way. You're betrothed to Hal." Caspar felt his emotions leap across the restraining bounds of expediency. "You shouldn't look that way at any other man."

Brid laughed dismissively though there was a cold edge to her voice as she spoke. "He's not a man; he's a being of Rye Errish. He has no place on Earth and nor can he attain the bliss of Annwyn. I was merely thinking how very sad it must be to live forever outside the wheel of life."

"Do you mean they are immortal?" Caspar asked in disbelief.

"Of course. But to never be born and never to die, I can't think of anything worse." The anger was momentarily dispelled from her voice but then she turned on Caspar again. "And who are you to chastise me? You, who constantly covets your kinsman's betrothed."

Caspar looked away, mortified. Brid had never spoken of his infatuation for her before. They had been friends all these years, both pretending that the problem simply didn't exist but now she had finally voiced the painful truth. He didn't know how he could face her. This place was too painful; it exposed too many raw emotions.

Brid caught his expression. "You are meant to feel like this here in Rye Errish. It is a place of reckoning, a place of honesty where you can no longer hide from your feelings. Here one must face the truth of one's life in order to move on, cleansed and free to Annwyn."

"But I don't want to move on to Annwyn; I want to live. I want . . ." His voice trailed off.

The verderers armed with silver-pointed spears and short hunting bows closed ranks about them. They were so confident in their superiority that they didn't even bother to take Caspar's bow or knives from him.

Talorcan bowed in front of Brid. "We can inflict considerable pain: it will be far easier for you if you do as you are bidden and follow the High Circle."

Brid inclined her head gracefully in a gesture of acquiescence. "Lead on, Talorcan."

"Brid, don't," Fern begged. "Please use the Pipe and get us out of here before it's too late. They might never let us go. We could be here forever."

"I know, Fern," Brid replied gently. She stooped and whispered so the verderers couldn't hear, "But Nuin didn't guess one thing. I can neither send the Pipe to a place beyond her reach nor do I know the tune that will take us home from here. I only know how to wrap it with binding spells that will stop anyone from releasing its magic. We have no choice but to obey these people and wait until we can find some way out of our predicament."

Caspar wondered what forever really meant.

CHAPTER TEN

The little tawny wolfling was dead.

Pip looked at it sorrowfully, connecting the fate of the helpless wolflings with his own. The youth scraped out a shallow grave amongst the roots of the tree and slid the limp little body into the ground before smearing the earth back over it. He hadn't quite dug the grave deep enough and the tip of its brushy tail stuck out above the ground. Too exhausted to dig deeper, he swept some dry skeletal leaves over the top and edged away.

His neck was sore where the rough shackles chafed his flesh. He pressed at the skin with his fingertips; it felt damp and he looked at his hands. They were smeared with blood. He wiped his fingers on his breeches. I'll get blood poisoning, he thought in disgust, though he was not truly worried. He had survived the great siege after all; he could surely survive anything.

There was an odd sense of pride in living through such atrocities though it brought agonizing memories of his mother. He had told her that he would die defending her and yet in the end it was she that had died defending him. He had failed her. With his father already dead, it had fallen on him, as the only son, to protect his mother and he had failed. Though he had been only ten at the time he had been fully aware of his responsibilities. Now all he wanted was prove that he would never fail again.

He tried to wipe the thoughts from his head by scowling at the kobolds who had climbed into the lower branches of the tree for the night. One of them began flicking acorns at him, rotted split acorns from the previous autumn, and they fell with irritating regularity on his head. He would ignore it. Clenching his teeth, he refused to flinch. He would not give the devilish creature the satisfaction of showing he cared.

Trog was affectionately nuzzling the two remaining wolflings. They were curled up against his belly though he growled in warning if they went anywhere near his injured leg. Pip curled up round the back of the dog for warmth and threw his thick cloak over them all, wondering when the trappers would return.

"Oh Trog," he whispered, "when's Master Spar going to find us?" Surely, they would have been able to track him down, especially with all those kobold prints. Master Spar wouldn't leave him out here alone as a punishment for his ill-discipline, would he?

"Oh, Master Spar, forgive me," he said out loud. Trog whimpered at the sound of Spar's name and Pip patted him reassuringly. "He'll come, Trog. If not for me he'll come for you. Brid dotes on you and Master Spar would never allow the priestess to suffer."

He suddenly felt resentful towards the Baron's son, deciding that he must value Trog above himself. He then thought of how Master Spar was upsetting his sister. May was all he had in the world and though she had become irritatingly fussy towards him since their mother's death, she was still his sister and he didn't want to see her hurt. Pip sighed. She clearly wasn't Master Spar's first choice; everyone said so. But what could he do? The Baron's son could not have Brid because she was betrothed to Hal and as second best – clearly as second best – he chose

May. Of late May had not welcomed Master Spar's attentions but how could a peasant girl ever refuse a nobleman? The Baron's son placed May in an impossible position and the last thing Pip wanted was for May to enter a loveless marriage for his benefit and promotion.

He remembered how Master Spar had spent day upon day trying to teach his sister to ride but May still couldn't manage any horse fast enough to keep up with the hunt. Brid, however, could even ride Firecracker – on those rare occasions that Master Spar allowed it. If there was one thing that the Baron's son was more possessive of than the priestess, it was his horse. "Second fiddle not only to Brid but to a horse as well," Pip told the dog. "It's not right."

The dog grunted and Pip took that to be a sign of agreement. He was stiff, hungry and cold and he prayed that Master Spar would find him before the trappers got back.

He must have dozed for a while because he was stirred blurrily awake by the sound of whining. He pushed the cloak back off his head and shoulders and blinked at the two little wolflings nuzzled pathetically up against Trog. The dog licked them, making soft, purring sounds in his throat.

"Who'd have thought an old bruiser like you would be so soppy?" Pip said as he sat up, sadly wondering how long the cubs would last without more food. He was ravenous himself and at last stopped praying for Master Spar to hurry to his rescue but for the trappers to return with some food. He regretted it, however, when his prayers were shortly answered.

The kobolds were suddenly falling out of the trees and scuttling to take up their positions in an aggressive circle around him as if they had been there all night. Pip kicked dirt at them in disgust and rose stiffly to his feet, his joints aching and his skin raw from the shackles. He looked around to see what had alarmed them.

The two trappers came gliding through the mist, leading a string of ponies laden with a grisly cargo of wolves and traps. They were arguing and grumbling but fell abruptly silent as they saw Pip eyeing them in disgust. The horses were streaked in blood that had dripped from the wounds of the dead wolves slung across their backs.

The bearded Ceolothian threw the reins of the lead pony over a stump and slumped straight onto the dirt without bothering to tend to the animals. The Ovissian looked tired too. He gave his companion a disapproving but guarded glare, took in a deep resigned breath and began unloading his horses.

"Here, Ryder, we'll have to get this lot skinned before we go, else the flies and maggots will ruin the skins."

"I know," the Ceolothian grunted in irritation as he lay back against the stump, crossing his legs and shutting his eyes. He held an object in his hands, which he twiddled irritably. "A bloody rabbit's foot. What kind of payment is that? And now we've got to waste time with another rendezvous."

Pip looked at the object the Ceolothian flipped over in his hand and thought that stupid man didn't even know the difference between a rabbit and a hare.

"So, what do we do now?" the Ovissian asked.

"Make this new meeting where the two rivers join and hope they've got some decent payment and some news from the mountains. I'm not doing all this running around without payment and I don't want to make the meet at Flag Scarp without any news to pass on. After that we can go on into Ceolothia and sell the pelts," the squat grubby-looking foreigner said impatiently. "We've got to look after ourselves. You can make a start on the wolves while I rest. And get some breakfast going."

Pip was aware that, though the trapper appeared to be asleep, he was in fact watching him through slitted eyes. "You still playing nursemaid to those wolflings?" he scoffed. "Here, and where's the third?"

He was on his feet, angrily striding towards Pip who, despite himself, recoiled into a ball, fearing that the man would hit him. He forced himself to relax and stare the big gruff man in the face.

"It died in the night and little wonder," he said defiantly, nodding towards the leaf-covered grave. "It was too weak to feed properly. I gave the others what food I had and they'd be dead too if it wasn't for me."

The man stared at the mound. "That would have been worth two hundred ducats," he moaned and glared angrily at Pip. "You'd better keep feeding the other two." He smiled smugly at the boy. "Belbidians pretend to be so tough in these northern parts but they're as soft as bone marrow. Fingers, have you got those pheasants? This little sprat can do some work for us."

Pip found a brace of pheasants dumped in his lap. Well, if he were to get any breakfast, there was no point complaining and he set to work, stripping off the feathers. The two trappers, who had long since taken his precious bow and quiver, didn't trust him with a knife to draw the birds and Fingers finally decided that he would do this himself. After the pheasants were set over a fire, he turned his attention back to the ponies and their bloody cargo. Pip sat back gloomily against the tree and watched with detached horror at the messy way the man sawed and wrenched at the wolves as he struggled to skin them. He was more hampered by his mutilated hand than Pip had expected.

"There's only meant to be a hundred a year from the whole Barony," Pip complained, irrepressibly.

"Oh, aye? Well, these ain't nought to do with King Rewik," Ryder laughed. "A hundred a year. What good's that? It'll never clear the devils from Belbidia. No, this lot's going to the markets of Castabrice where the merchants – good fellows all – pay handsomely for the beasts. I get twelve guineas from the Baron of Torra Alta but fifty ducats in Ceolothia."

Fingers looked uncomfortably at the two wolflings kneading Trog's belly forlornly. "Disgusting little creatures. I still say we should kill them."

Ryder laughed. "Trouble with you, Fingers, is that you can't spot an opportunity. They'll be worth a fortune to us live. Put a bit of spice into the best line of fighting dog these would. Cross them with the right animal and he'll be right royal pleased with me. Them wolves and that fighting dog'll make a grand present for his personage. Buy me a lot of favour."

"Us," Fingers objected.

"Us then, but I don't see you contributing much beyond grumbles."

The pheasant was soon charred in places and partially cooked in others but it still tasted good. Pip ate his share hungrily while feeding scraps to Trog and chewing up mouthfuls for the pups. "Who'd have thought I'd become a kennel maid," he complained though he felt grieved when Ryder took the grey wolfling off him and dropped it back in the sack.

"Hey, you'll hurt him," he shouted.

Ryder's boot thumped into his thigh and he was pulled up by the chain around his neck, gasping and spluttering. He was somewhat appeased when the Ceolothian picked up the female cub. It bit him hard, drawing bright red blood from his thumb. Pip couldn't help smiling though he regretted it when the Ceolothian struck him hard across the mouth. Pip tasted blood.

The trappers bundled Trog onto one of the pack ponies along with over a dozen wolf pelts. Pip knew there were many trappers operating in the Chase and thought that soon there wouldn't be any wolves left. Not any Yellow Mountain wolves anyway, he corrected himself. Amongst all the skins he couldn't see a single hooded pelt.

"Where are we going?" he asked sulkily.

"Are you still talking, boy?" Fingers snarled. "Can't say I enjoy listening to you. Why don't you learn what's good for you and keep quiet?" The Ovissian suddenly looked away and glared at the kobolds. They were chattering nervously. "Ryder, there's some large animal out there," he warned in a low voice.

The Ceolothian shrugged dismissively. "Just a hog, I reckon. If it was a hooded wolf they'd be at the top of the trees, squealing, by now."

Pip heard a twig snap and relaxed. It wasn't wolves.

They moved off but the kobolds remained agitated, one or two running off into the shadows and scampering back, whispering in scratchy voices to each other.

"Remember what I said about Hobs Slack and what would happen if you don't behave and help me," Ryder threatened. He gave a shrill whistle, summoning his dogs to heel. The liver-coloured long-muzzled hounds panted and slobbered, crowding around his legs. A kobold yelled and pointed.

Pip raised his head and saw a shadow in the birch trees ahead. Ryder was immediately alert and snapped his fingers, shouting something in his own tongue. The dogs leapt forward, baying in pursuit. Quickly, they were out of sight. A hound shrieked, silencing the others for a moment, but then their baying returned and amidst their howls came the sound of a man running, branches snapping and the rustle of disturbed leaves. Ryder sprinted after his dogs.

Hurrying the horses, Fingers dragged Pip forward until they found one of Ryder's dogs lying dead on the ground, an arrow shaft sticking out through its chest. The point of the barb was just visible, poking up through the skin on the back of its neck where it had driven right through. Pip looked at the goose feathers of the quill. A Torra Altan arrow! His hopes leapt with delight. Master Spar had found him. But he could still hear running and the baying of dogs. He looked round expectantly. Was one of the party drawing Ryder and the dogs so that the rest could rescue him? Yes, that would be it. But where were they?

His blood ran cold as he heard snarls from the dogs and a man scream ahead. Ryder was still shouting in Ceolothian and Pip knew the rescue attempt had gone horribly wrong.

Fingers led the ponies on and Pip stumbled forward in sickened dismay. Brock was lying face down on the ground, breathing hard and moaning. Ryder rolled him over and kicked him in the ribs.

"That's for my dog. Get to your feet, man."

Brock used his elbows to push himself up, carefully guarding his right hand. Blood oozed out through the fingers of his good hand as he clutched the wound; his right hand had been horribly gashed. With his face twisted in pain, he stumbled forward as Ryder pushed him towards the horses. The dogs growled and snaked their necks down to snap at Brock's heels.

"Tie him up," Ryder ordered the kobolds who jostled and tripped over one another in their eagerness to lace a length of rope around Brock's struggling body. "Oh, get out of the way." The Ceolothian kicked at the thin, twig-like creatures. "Bloody incompetent varmints." He cinched the rope tight around Brock's wrists and the Torra Altan stifled a gasp and paled. Ryder dragged him forward to stand by Pip and the two looked helplessly into each other's eyes.

"Where are the others?" Pip asked in despair.

Brock didn't answer him and Pip realized with horror that Brock had come alone.

The harsh metal collar fashioned out of the jaws of a wolf trap snagged at the flesh around Pip's neck as he was jerked forward. Swearing loudly, he was forced to an unbalanced trot to keep up with the horses. Eventually the trappers stopped by a stream and Fingers undid Brock's ties and sloshed water over his hands. After slapping on some of the sulphurous witch-salve, he tied him up again. "Don't want it going bad on us otherwise you won't be able to walk and I don't want you burdening the horses," he grumbled.

Brock's colour slowly began to return though his face was still taut with pain. As they stumbled on through the Chase he turned to Pip. "Why did you have to be such a damn fool running off like that? Look at the mess you've caused."

"I didn't run off and I didn't ask you to rescue me and, anyway, where's Master Spar? At least he wouldn't have got himself caught. He's not a blundering old fool like you." He felt sorry for Brock but he didn't know how to say so. Torra Altans didn't like to admit to pain.

"Young lad like you, the Baron's too soft on you," Brock growled. "Impudent boy. If you had some decent respect for your elders we wouldn't be in this mess. You just marched off in a huff, didn't you?"

"I didn't march off. I found Trog's prints." Both of them looked at Trog who lay slumped next to the sack of wolflings that bumped against the flank of the skewbald pack pony in front of them.

"You should never have gone off alone."

"You seem to be alone," Pip reminded him.

"That's different. I didn't want Lady Brid searching the forest for you when it's thick with hooded wolves."

"So now she's searching it for Trog, me *and* you," Pip pointed out.

Brock muttered away to himself, "Youngsters. It's never been the same since the siege. No whippersnapper like you'd have dared speak to me like that in the old days."

The trappers were taking them further east into the depths of the Chase, away from even the most remote forest hamlets and Pip doubted there would be any foresters or even charcoal-burners so deep in the forest. Their only companions now were wolves and the occasional roe deer, barely discernible against the pale grey and brown of the winter forest. Gradually Pip became aware of the sound of a river ahead. He guessed it must be the Whitehart, which flowed down from the Jaws of the Wolf and eventually joined the Sylvanrush.

Ryder, too, must have heard the drone of running water because he changed course to join the river. The forest crowded thirstily down to the water in an impenetrable mass of tall trees, old brambles and winter dog roses. At first, they couldn't get to the river's edge because of the dense thicket of trees that lined the banks, but finally they found a track where cloven hooves had cut a path to the bank.

Gently shelving, grassy banks gracefully bowed down to the water's edge where smooth pebbles shifted restlessly in the flow, giving out a soft babbling chatter. On the far side, sipping silently at the clear water was a huge stag with a thick shaggy mane and impressive branchlike antlers. A very old stag, Pip thought, judging by the number of points. His coat was white, pure white. The boy gasped. He had lived long enough in the forest to know this was a very rare sighting. As a young child he had heard the woodcutters tell that the white hart was only to be seen once every hundred years. It heralded a time of great change. "Father Forest," he murmured. The kobolds fell silent.

"Wolf's teeth, look at that," Ryder breathed, his hand reaching for his bow. "The hide of a white stag! And those antlers!"

Pip stared at the man in horror. He couldn't kill the white stag, guardian of the forest. Never!

"No! No!" he yelled. "Get out of here! Run!" he shouted maniacally to startle the animal. The kobolds shrieked in dismay.

The beast's ears were pricked in an instant. He looked at them for one split second before fleeing. As his elegant hindlegs powered him through the water towards the cover of the trees, Ryder loosed his arrow. Just as the stag disappeared under the shade of an alder tree, it gave out a squeal and stumbled, and though the arrow had pierced the muscle just above its hock, the stag kept running.

Fingers struggled through the river, water gushing about his thighs, and on into the trees in pursuit.

"Damn!" Ryder looked at his bow as if it were its fault that he had missed and then he glowered at Pip. "Bloody meddling child." He yanked viciously at the boy's chain before Pip was ready for him. Sickening pain jarred his neck. Caught off balance, he stumbled to his knees. Ryder strode over and kicked him viciously in the stomach.

"Leave him be! He's just a lad," Brock shouted, shouldering into the Ceolothian only to be pulled up short by his rope.

Ryder bunched his fist and piled it into Brock's face. The old man coiled up, spluttering and spitting blood.

"Just a lad, eh? What makes you so high and moral, eh, lad? You so special that you don't want no supper today? That stag would have fed us well."

"I would die rather than eat the flesh of the sacred stag," Pip said quietly, stooping over Brock and trying to help him to his feet.

Ryder wrapped a length of chain around his hand and knocked him to the ground. Pip wasn't afraid of pain. He'd suffered a great many knocks and cuts during his childhood and even more of late, sparring with the other boys of the castle. Determined to prove himself, he had learnt to suppress pain because, if he felt no pain he could fight longer, harder and more determinedly. He wasn't daunted by a boot to the stomach.

He lifted his face from the earth and looked at the palms of his hands. They were speckled with blood where the gravel had bitten into his skin. Pip stared coldly at Ryder and then very slowly smiled. "If you've injured the white stag, your soul will pay for it."

The bearded Ceolothian trapper choked into laughter. "Ha! You think I'm afraid of your foolish earth magic. I worship the true God. His merciful, all-forgiving being will protect me from such primitive superstitions.'

Brock had staggered back to his feet by the time Fingers returned. Pip was heartily relieved as he read the expression on the trapper's sour face.

"He got away, vanished without trace." The Ovissian had cut his eye. He stooped and cupped his hand in the stream to bath the wound.

"What happened to your face?" Ryder asked without sympathy as he unhooked several canisters and leather bladders from the saddle and began to fill them from the stream. Pip stumbled to the edge of the waters and dipped his smarting hands into the fast-running river. It gushed straight from the bleak snowbound peaks and the freezing cold numbed the pain.

"Bloody holly bush whipped back at me," Ryder was muttering. "It just seemed to lash out."

Pip looked up, trying not to smile. The forest was alive like fire; it had a spirit of its own.

Ryder pressed a fast angry pace now, marching them northward along the banks of the Whitehart river, heading for the Sylvanrush. Dripping with a heavy sweat despite the cool of the wintry forest, Brock was labouring. Pip was worried for him and worried too that the ground was stone hard; they were leaving no tracks.

"At this rate Master Spar will never find us, however hard he looks," Pip fretted quietly to Brock. "If he hasn't found us after two days what are our chances?"

Brock didn't answer for some while and took in a deep breath almost of resignation as if he feared Pip were right. But then, after sucking at his lip, which was cut and clearly niggled him, he said, "We'll need to leave a trail, any mark or sign that shows we've passed this way."

He scuffed his heels in an attempt to mark the ground but it had little effect other than to make him trip. Pip followed the old man's lead and whenever Fingers took his wide-spaced eyes off him, he moved sideways to the limit of his chain and onto the softer earth and bracken at the edge of the trail. Finally, he managed to grab at a stone. He looked at it in satisfaction: a hard sharp-edged rock that fitted neatly into the palm of his hand.

Brock winked at him in approval.

The wolflings were beginning to whimper within their sack and Fingers snarled at them irritably.

"They need food," Pip spoke out. "They won't make much of a gift to your precious ringleader if you hand over a couple of corpses. And the dog too."

"Ringleader?" Fingers choked on the title and turned in amusement to his comrade. "Ringleader, Ryder! What do you think he'd say if he heard that, eh?"

Pip didn't know what to make of their amusement and turned back to worrying about the two cubs. He was relieved when Ryder ordered a halt and told him to feed the animals. He slipped his treasured rock into his pocket and hurried forward to take the sack of wolflings.

Brock sagged to the ground, wheezing, his rough breathing rasping in his throat. Pip was worried for him. It was too fast a pace for an old man and his swollen hand was obviously sapping his strength.

Brock caught the boy's concerned frown. Red in the face, he sniffed at him. "Don't you go round feeling sorry for me, Pip. I'll outlast you any day. You just worry about the trouble you've put Master Spar to – and that sweet girl."

Pip wondered what Brid would think to being called a sweet girl. Why was it, he thought, that old men like Brock would never accept their limitations and always puffed themselves up, trying to look after everyone long after they were capable. Brid wouldn't have been captured by these men, he thought. No, only he and the old man were stupid enough to let that happen.

Pip was given a loaf of stale bread and the remains of the pheasant. He chewed hard at the bread and, though ravenous himself, spat out the mashed-up food for the cubs. The grey male cub hissed and snarled though the little white she-cub came forward eagerly towards his hand. For the first time the little creature looked straight up into Pip's eyes and mewed. Pip tentatively stroked her head and smiled when she no longer recoiled from him.

"Poor little mites," Brock sighed.

Pip was so absorbed in feeding the little cubs that he nearly forgot Trog who was whining softly. Pip held out the last of the bread, which the dog gulped down in large dry chunks.

They were jerked to their feet and dragged on again by the horses. The sound of flowing water was swelling to a churning babble and Pip reckoned they must be nearing the point where the two rivers merged. Fingers seemed more alert and was looking round into the darker shadows between the trees to either side. Pip didn't miss the opportunity to swing to the edge of the track and mark any tree that came within reach, hoping beyond hope that somehow Master Spar would pick up his trail.

Surely, he would find them soon. But then he was pricked by self-doubt. How long would Master Spar search for him when he had been so rude and irresponsible? He would have to leave some mark that would catch Master Spar's eye and insure he followed the trail. Runes, he decided. He knew no spell-runes but he could form words with the characters.

He had to wait some while before he had an opportunity to carve his message but eventually, as Ryder deliberated on the way ahead, he found himself halted by an ash tree, its greenish-grey bark deeply fissured with age. As surreptitiously as he could, he slashed the bark with his stone.

"What are you doing that for?" Brock demanded. "You and your ideas won't get us anywhere."

"If you don't try something you'll never know if it'll work or not," Pip retorted.

"I've never tried walking on water but I'm not about to give it a go."

Pip merely narrowed his eyes, thinking the comment unworthy of a retort.

A little while later they reached the point where the Whitehart River flowed into the Sylvanrush. Ryder called a halt and they made camp. They sat there for two long hungry days, eating stale bread and scraps of pheasant, while the trappers became increasingly uneasy. As the afternoon of the second day wore on, Ryder jumped decisively to his feet and told his comrade to stay put while he took a look around. He then slipped away into the woods.

The fish-eyed Ovissian sat down at the edge of a clearing just within view of the sharp V formed by the two rivers. Pip wondered how they merged together without complaint, the two clean and separate lines of water blending so suddenly into one, like the hands of long-time lovers sliding naturally and easily together.

Ryder had been gone quite some while and Fingers was clearly agitated and impatient. He checked the packs over and looked thoughtfully at Pip's and Brock's bows strapped to the leading horses. Grunting decisively, he began untying Pip's ivory-inlaid bow and plucked a couple of arrows from the quiver.

"Bloody fine bow for a common lad," he muttered, still glancing anxiously into the shadows after Ryder. He growled at the kobolds and then twitched at the bowstring. "What's taking Ryder so long?" he angrily asked himself as he slumped back against the bole of a willow tree.

With Ryder gone, Pip decided his opportunity had come. He moved forward inch by inch to examine how his chain was secured to the pack pony. Fingers wasn't watching him. His pulse quickened as he took one careful step after the other, inching towards the pack pony. He was within one foot of the pony when the trapper nonchalantly tightened his grip on the bow and, holding it sideways so that the wood didn't touch the ground, aimed an arrow at Pip's belly. "Listen boy, you just take yourself back and sit down."

"I was only going to see to the wolflings," Pip said innocently.

Ryder nodded. "Yeah. Funny, that was just what I was thinking. Young lad like that wouldn't never dream of escaping. He's only worried about petting them bloody wolves, I tell myself. I was born with gold teeth, I guess too. Bloody Ryder, where's he got to? Him and his meets."

"What are you doing paired up with a Ceolothian anyway?" Brock asked. "Not a natural choice for a Belbidian."

The Ovissian looked away and kicked at a pinecone with his toe. "I'm doing this because I want to, old man, so don't you go thinking you can stir me up because you can't. These wolves killed my boy and I'm going to kill as many of them as I can before I die. Hundreds, thousands, I hope. I'm proud of what I do, old man. Proud of it, you hear."

Brock raised his eyebrows. "Yeah, maybe," he conceded, "though I'd lay odds that it weren't these type of wolves killed your lad."

"A wolf's a bloody wolf, ain't it?"

Brock shrugged. "That's like saying a man's a man and there's no difference between a Belbidian and Vaalakan."

"You're just trying to be smart. What's an old man, too old to be a real soldier, think he's doing trying to be smart? All you know is lapping up to your baron, I dare say. I've seen your livery, that little dragon broach you Torra Altans wear." The man was on his feet now, stooping impassioned over his captives. He flicked aside

Brock's cloak and snatched at the silver pin threaded into the man's collar and yanked it away, stamping it into the hard ground. "So proud of it, aren't you? Well, it's your bloody barony that's causing all these troubles. It's your paganism that's brought the Devil's work on us all. Anyone would think your baron was breeding the wolves the way they're pouring over the Yellow Mountains like some plague."

"That's not true." Pip's voice was rising with emotion. He yanked at his chains in frustration but could do no more than kick dirt at the trapper.

Fingers laughed at him and provocatively twanged Pip's bow. Thwarted, the boy sat back against a tree and stared moodily at the converging waters. "You can't trust a Ceolothian," he said as a last resort.

Fingers smiled. "I don't need to trust him now, do I? All I want is the wolves killed off and, if it so happens I can earn good money doing it, what do I care?"

The big Ovissian groaned, stood to his feet and went to inspect Trog. "His leg's doing well," he announced after a moment and cast a look of utter hatred at the wriggling sack of wolves. Disgustedly he unhooked the sack from the saddle and flung it at Pip. "Here, you do your nurse-maiding boy. If Ryder wants them alive, you'd better see to them. Money is money, even if it means the varmints live."

Pip fed them both and replaced the grey wolf in the sack though he continued to soothe the soft fur on the white wolfling's head. She was so pretty. Such lovely eyes, a deep mysterious green. They seemed to study him thoughtfully. He laughed at himself for such a fanciful idea. As he sat back, cradling the wolfling in the crook of his arm, she made a small purring sound and he felt himself relax and grow in confidence. Yes, he was hopeful;

Master Spar couldn't be that far behind them now. They had been moving slowly and had stopped regularly; they couldn't be hard to track.

Pip found his eyes closing. Sitting for so long was almost as tiring as stumbling after the ponies. With the she-cub nestled in his lap, he let his eyelids shut out the soft daylight and drifted off to the borders of slumber. He must have finally succumbed to full sleep because, all of a sudden, he knew he was dreaming. He was looking at a narrow arrowhead of land formed by the sharp fork of the two rivers where a ring of gnarled oaks stood waving their top branches in the breeze. Then, as with many dreams, strange things began appearing from nowhere. He thought for a moment that he could see a castle, not a blocky fortress like Torra Alta but a cluster of tall turreted towers with rounded walls. The stonework was a magical colour, glinting with pearl and silver and extraordinarily beautiful. But it was impossibly small, like a fairy castle. Everything, the outer walls, the moat, the drawbridge and keep, all were built in miniature and contained within the ring of oaks.

Then it was gone. Still the oaks looked wrong and it took Pip a moment to realize that was because they were in leaf. Oaks were always one of the last trees to clad themselves in the verdant cloak of spring. It was only mid Horning; how then could they be leafy? A strange dream, Pip told himself, trying to shake away his slumber. He found the dream disturbing and couldn't quite wake himself up.

As if from afar, the haunting sound of singing, beautiful but so sad, came drifting to his ears. It was such a lost, lonely sound, immeasurably beautiful and sweetly seductive.

"Ow!" Suddenly he was wide awake and clutching at

his finger. Beads of brilliant red sprang up on his flesh where the wolf cub had bitten him with her needle-sharp teeth. Pip grimaced, unable to speak as he sucked at his stinging finger.

He was still disturbed by the dream; it had seemed so real. He took a deep breath, trying to clear his head but found himself frowning. How strange, he thought as he stared at the bare branches of the ancient oaks by the rivers; he could smell bluebells.

His thoughts were immediately distracted by Fingers leaping to his feet at the sound of Ryder approaching.

"Well?" the Ovissian demanded but Pip couldn't hear all the reply as the two men muttered to themselves while glancing furtively at their captives. He only caught snatches of Ryder's angry words. "There's no one about for miles. We can't wait to make this meet with his minions. We'll have to go on to Flag Scarp."

CHAPTER ELEVEN

Caspar held Fern's hand. He wanted to hold Brid's but she was too distracted and aloof.

They were led eastwards, deeper into the heart of the forest. The sweet song of a blackbird followed their course and, beneath the soft shade of the trees, gorgeous fields of daffodils washed by seas of bluebells carpeted the forest floor for as far as the eye could see. Wild primroses and tulips burst in spangles of brilliant colour around the skirts of the beech and oak trees.

Curiously, Fern's hand was beginning to feel less coarse in his. The short black nails appeared softer and more human, though the skin was still covered in a fine pale mustard down. Fern, too, was looking at his hands and blinking his big doleful eyes. He tried to mention Sorrel's name but the words were lost in a choke of tears.

Caspar squeezed Fern's hand a little tighter.

Their escort marched effortlessly beside them, singing in counterpoint and descants, each with their own individual song, the combined effect powerful and enchanting. Though small in human terms, the verderers were all perfectly proportioned, young and healthy with well-formed muscles, and marched with an arrogant swagger. Hal would hate them, Caspar thought. Hal would hate their haughty conceit.

The little woodwose whimpered, "I'm afraid, Spar."

"You don't need to be." He tried to sound reassuring. "We're with Brid. She's the Maiden and will look after us, you'll see."

Fern snorted. "With deer, the stag has antlers because he is the one that defends the hinds. Is it different with humans?"

"No, it isn't. Of course it isn't different." Caspar blustered feeling the shame rising within him. Fern was looking at him quizzically and Caspar knew he was stumbling for a sensible answer. "No, it's just that Brid is different."

"She's angry with me," Fern said by way of reply and clung a little tighter to Caspar.

The sound of rushing waters filtered through the trees. It must be the Whitehart River, Caspar thought, or its equivalent here in the Otherworld. He frowned at the turbulent sound and then remembered that it was spring here and that the mountain snows must already be melting and swelling the streams that tumbled from the yellow crags to the Boarchase below.

Fern stiffened and sniffed the air, his nostrils twitching and his neck stretching up in alarm.

"What is it?" Caspar asked.

"Blood," Fern replied breathily. "I can smell blood." His eyes opened wide. "And him! I can smell him."

"Who?" Caspar asked, not truly understanding the little creature.

"The king."

"Fern, you're not making sense."

"The king of the forest." Fern was swinging round excitedly on the end of Caspar's arm as if he had forgotten the troop of verderers around them.

Alerted by Fern's excitable dance, the verderers began looking ahead towards the tumbling waters of the river. One of them pointed. For just a second Caspar saw it, a white flank and antlers. The animal was wading painfully downstream in the shallows of the Whitehart River, its body heaving with deep, laboured breaths as the ice-cold torrent washed around its legs. A scarlet sash of blood coloured one hindleg and its head hung low. The animal was in pain. Caspar blinked. Perhaps it was the reflection of the dazzling spring sunshine on the broken waters, casting light upwards on the cream beast that deceived his eyes because the stag seemed to shimmer and ripple just like the river. Caspar blinked again and the stag was gone.

Fern was speechless, tears welling up in his eyes. The verderers swept on but the woodwose dragged at Caspar's hand, wanting neither to let go nor to leave the vision of the stag behind. "He's hurt," he cried. "We must do something."

"There's nothing we can do." Brid who had been silent all this while turned to look back at them, her dark green eyes sparkling with tears. Her hands were trembling slightly though she still had perfect control of her expression and voice. "He's not in this world – we saw only his shadow – and I can't help him."

"Who is he?" Caspar asked.

"The one the kobolds begged help from. The old white hart, father of the forests." Anxiously she looked back over her shoulder. "He protects the woodlands."

The procession swung north to follow the fast-flowing waters that bubbled their way to join another river. The verderers' song became louder and more insistent. All had seen the stag and it was clear that it had disturbed them deeply.

The sight before him broke his thoughts and he gasped in astonishment. Where the two rivers met, a ring of magnificent oaks stood tall to over a hundred feet high, their spreading branches draped in the pale green of spring. But that was nothing. Set amidst the circle of trees was a castle, a miniature castle, looking as if it were made from icicles dusted with snow rather than any masonry material known to Caspar. The glittering fortress was a mass of clustered spires and towers, flamboyant flags fluttering from each pinnacle. The portcullis appeared to be made from solid gold, and the barbican above glistened with statues and minarets inlaid with mother-of-pearl. Though there was no curtain wall or heavy earthworks, the whole dazzling structure was surrounded by a moat.

As they approached, the glinting castle seemed to swell, growing up into a vast structure that soared up out of the valley, stretching for the heavens. The trees grew proportionately so that by the time they reached the oak circle, the base of each giant tree was over fifty feet wide.

The castle towered above them but, despite its size, Caspar thought it in some way feminine. Its intricate facades were decorated with delicate figurines and stonework flowers and birds. Twisting ornate spires elegantly spiralled to the sky. So unlike the blocky solidity of Torra Alta, the masonry here was almost fragile; light and airy in its aspirations.

Talorcan worked up and down the ranks of the singing verderers, organizing them into smart rows, their songs growing louder, until suddenly they formed one voice. Caspar found the singing maddening. It sapped his will and sucked him into a sense of subordination. He tried to stop his mind being drawn into the chanting, tried to retain his identity but knew it was slipping helplessly away. Fern stood, quietly submissive at his side.

Brid, he knew, was fighting it as she fought everything. He could feel the sparks of energy flicking out from her mind as she repelled the chanted magic, defiantly clinging to her own thoughts. She wrenched her eyes away from the castle and studied the forest floor as if trying to distract herself.

Talorcan appeared to be singing only for her, his voice subtly different to the chorus; compelling, wooing sweet, even. Caspar sensed the powerful desire in the verderer, desire focused on Brid, and yet he was powerless to do anything about it. Hatred boiled within him. How dare Talorcan look at Brid like that or use his cold, Otherworldly magic on her? He could see it, how she struggled against it, her head turned angrily away. But then, for a moment, she relaxed and looked towards the verderer, a sweet smile spreading across her lips.

"No, Brid no!" Caspar stepped beside her and grabbed at her hand, pulling her towards him.

Talorcan paced forward. Suddenly his song stopped and, brushing Caspar aside, clasped Brid's chin in his long, elegant fingers. "Not in ten thousand years have I seen a mortal as beautiful as you. You will love me," he declared as if he spoke a prophecy.

"She cannot." Caspar pulled Brid back.

The verderer laughed in amusement as if scoffing at Caspar's impotency. "And why not?"

"Because she loves . . ." Caspar stumbled for words, feeling Talorcan's blazing eyes slip into his soul, scorning the fragility of his mortal body. "Because I love her!" This place had something about it that forbade him to speak anything other than the honest truth in his heart. "I love her," he protested

"So, you love her," Talorcan shrugged, "but that doesn't make her yours. Many, many men must love one so fair as this creature but that means nothing. She is free to love me and she will; my magic is powerful."

Caspar possessively squeezed Brid's hand and she looked

at him almost helplessly – with affection and friendship yet, he knew, without love. Talorcan began the song again and Caspar felt Brid stiffen. Fiercely she turned her back on the verderer and stared into the forest. Her eyes blinked and focused for a moment on the nearest tree. A great ash tree, its graceful feathery leaves dancing in the soft spring breeze, casting moving shadows over the ground. She blinked.

Silently and without the expected clank and whirr from the winding mechanism, the drawbridge gently lowered to span the waters just where the two rivers slid unprotestingly into one. There was a trumpet blast from the far side of the river as the drawbridge eased down to rest on a plinth of stone set between two huge obelisks. The song changed and Caspar felt himself dragged forward again by the will of the musical voices. He strained against it, his head still twisting round, trying to focus on what had caught Brid's eye. Then he saw it, scratch marks on the smooth silvery green bark of an ash. Deep scour marks. The column of verderers then blocked his line of vision.

"Did you see it, Spar?" Brid demanded as they were swept forward.

"Runes," Caspar replied, trying to make sense of what he saw. "Do these people use spell-runes?" He'd only caught a glimpse of them. He closed his eyes, trying to recreate the image. "Tiw's rune," he began. "Tiw's then Rad's." Suddenly it came back to him. "Then Os's and finally Gifu's." He was trying to puzzle out what manner of spell that made, thinking through the significance of each character but could make neither head nor tail of it. ᛏ, Tiw, the rune of war; ᚱ, Rad, a journey; ᚩ, Os, governing wisdom; and ᚷ, Gifu, a gift. He put all four meanings together as Brid had taught him but could make no sense of it. He could only conclude that the spells here in Rye Errish were obviously wrought in a different way.

"You're looking too deeply." She released Caspar's hand and wiped her brow. She smiled deeply. "He's alive. In fact, they must both be alive."

Caspar looked at her blankly.

"It's not a runespell at all," she laughed.

"But they are runes?"

"Of course they're runes but not skilfully used. They are only being used as characters to spell out a name."

Brid didn't have to say more. "Trog," Caspar sighed. "And only Pip would write the word Trog. He must have found him. I hope Brock is with them." Caspar's delight suddenly fell from him. "But if they are here in Rye Errish, they must be dead."

Brid shook her head. "No, not at all. The runes are the writing of the Gods. They are not confined by normal laws but work through the channels of magic. If they exist in the real world they exist also here and . . ." Her words suddenly slowed as if struck by a thought.

"If they exist here, they also exist there?" Caspar finished for her.

She nodded. "Pip might be right here in the equivalent spot in the real world," she gasped. "Right this very moment sharing the same space. We might at least be able to tell him we're here." She sighed in despair. "But what good would that do? He can't do anything to help us."

There seemed no point in even trying but, as the procession narrowed to file across the bridge, Caspar found himself momentarily halted by one of the two huge stones and decided he must do something. He felt for the ring on his little finger. No one would notice. The inlaid metal, showing the design of the Dragon Standard of Torra Alta, would be hard enough to mark stone. Surreptitiously he dragged it across the surface, forming the simple runic characters that spelt out his name. It was no good writing anything else since Pip wouldn't be able to read a signature rune, so he had to write four characters and they were messily done. He didn't know what good they would do but he had to try something.

They crossed the bridge and passed under the portcullis into a small courtyard, with stables to one side and falconry mews to the other. The drawbridge eased closed behind them and Caspar watched the great oiled cogs of a wheel turning so smoothly; he wondered at the skill of such silent engineering. But his wonder turned sour at the sight of the trolls that the verderers used to drive the great wheel. The verderers' song also controlled them, Caspar realized, aware of how his own will was bowed into submission by the sound.

The castle smelt peculiarly of honey and everything sparkled in the brilliant sunlight as if covered in a film of water. A huge pair of doors embossed with a magnificent golden sunburst faced them across the courtyard. They swung silently outward as the procession approached and Talorcan led them forward into an airy green hall with high arched ceilings and stained-glass windows. Rainbows fell through the lights, dancing on the tiled floors, creating a moving mosaic of colours. The chorusing verderers fell silent though music still filled the air.

Birdsong, Caspar thought in surprise and followed Brid's gaze up towards the capital of a green marble pillar inlaid with spirals of silver. A golden cage swung from a hook and in it piped a song thrush, on the next pillar a sky lark and on the next a nightingale. Caspar slowly turned his head, staring giddily at the hall that in so many ways resembled the tall nave of a cathedral. The crown of each pillar split and branched into arches that fanned out to form a roof in cold parody of an avenue of trees. In each tree there was a caged bird, singing its own sad song.

"It's horrible," Brid whispered to him. "At first it looks so sparklingly clean and magically ornate." She waved her hands at the gold leafing that spiralled another pillar. The design was of a honeysuckle. "Green marble decorated with gold and silver, the craftsmanship is finer than anything I have ever seen, finer even than the work of the ancient smiths who fashioned my torc and amulet. But it's all so sterile, so dead."

They swept on through a hall thickly lined with tapestries, gold and silver plates, sashes and trophies, as well as row upon row of antlers and horns. Everything was beautiful but lifeless. He stopped in his thoughts. But that was how it should be since this was Rye Errish, the land of the dead.

The next hall they entered was similar only it was draped in scarlet sashes and ruby tapestries. Caspar could hear grunts, snuffles and the rattling of chains. Behind the pillars and hiding amidst the drapes were tufted-eared mountain lions chained by the neck. They looked old, tired and rather sad and Caspar found it hard to imagine them as the dangerous, wild beasts that stole ibex from the highest peaks in the Yellow Mountains.

Talorcan marched uncomfortably close to Brid. "They are so very beautiful. We like to keep beautiful things," he explained, keeping his eye intently on Brid. "My own collection is lacking just a little."

At last, they came to another closed door embossed with a central golden sunburst. One of Talorcan's men knocked with a staff and the doors swung outwards. Before them lay a circular room ringed by white marble arches with mirrors set in each arch. Silver leaf veined the pillars and creamy marble covered the floor. The mirrors, holding reflections within reflections, made Caspar feel giddy. In each mirror was an image of a single pillar. It was the reflection of a lone column, twelve foot high, set in the middle of the hall. Made of a pearly stone that Caspar could give no name to, it supported a vast circular plinth high above their heads.

"It's like a table for giants," Caspar mumbled to Brid.

She looked at him, her vivid green eyes flitting back and forth distractedly. "We must be very careful what we say. We don't want to be here forever."

Though her voice was firm and steady, just as it usually was, there was something about the look in Brid's eyes that troubled him; she wasn't quite in control of herself. Strong hands pulled him towards the edge of the hall, separating him from Brid. Talorcan grasped her wrist.

"Brid!" Caspar struggled to get to her but found himself pressed back by a chorus of voices, the will of Talorcan's men pinning him to the wall.

He was powerless to do anything but stand and watch the proceedings. Out from each of the mirrors stepped one of the thirteen ealdormen. The High Circle touched hands and approached the central plinth. A hum resonated through the chamber as they unfurled their wide-spreading translucent wings. Caspar was thrilled by the sight of them, his heart racing.

The High Circle took to the air, spiralling round the lone pillar and climbing upwards to hover around the slab of white stone. Their wings beat so fast that they were barely visible except for the shimmering air around them.

The verderers, in their green jackets and leather hunting breeches, stood patiently, listening with eager ears and submissive eyes while the Circle debated. They seemed to be in no hurry, arguing unconstructively amongst themselves in voices too low for the rest of the assembly to hear. As the minutes wore into hours, Caspar found himself feeling more and more drained, and his exhaustion was amplified by his frustration at being powerless against Talorcan. Even his patience towards Fern was fading as the little creature, again, tugged at his hand.

"Master Spar don't let them hurt me," the woodwose begged.

Caspar looked down at the little horned creature and blinked. The fine hair across his face had gone though he still had the look of a deer, with his short velvety horns, big round eyes, slender limbs and quick nervous movements.

"I have no power here to protect you," Caspar replied honestly. He, too, felt vulnerable but still considered himself responsible for this creature.

"I wished for this," Fern muttered at his hands, the fingernails still abnormally coarse and black. "But I feel so weak. Do all men feel so weak?"

"We are weak," Caspar told him.

"But, how can such a weak being control the rest of the animal kingdom?" Fern asked innocently. "It doesn't make sense to me."

"Nothing makes much sense anymore," Caspar agreed. He wasn't really listening. Since he could not understand much of the unending discussion of the Circle above their heads, he had been concentrating on Brid who stood at the far side of the chamber. She was surrounded by verderers and had defensively drawn her brown bearskin cloak tightly about her.

Although beautiful there was an earthiness about her that made Caspar smile. Yes, that was precisely what she was. She was a high priestess to the Mother Earth and she had that same strength and solidity. She was fresh like the forests, wild like the mountains, alive like the dancing streams, dangerous like waterfalls, comforting and homely like lush meadows; so many facets. Caspar sighed. She was lovely.

So much more lovely than the brilliant colourful radiance of the verderers' women who peeked through the open doors of the chamber, clearly forbidden to enter while the Circle was in session. From where he stood, Caspar could hear their magical voices and see them with their dresses of shimmering satin, their dazzling golden hair, perfect faces with smooth ivory complexions, and wide golden green eyes. Where Brid was earthy, they were ethereal, the stuff of sunbeams; sparkling but insubstantial creatures.

Caspar scowled. Talorcan was standing too close to Brid, whispering in her ear. There was no doubt that the male verderers, like the females within the castle, were beautiful to look at and he wondered how that affected Brid. He was distracted by a sudden outburst above their heads. The High Circle appeared to be arguing vehemently. Flashes of purple light burst between them as they angrily thrust short staves at each other and sparks flew off and sizzled and snapped in the air.

With a detached sense of unreality, Caspar found the spectacle almost amusing. He wondered how these creatures had ever managed to pass into folklore as tiny little things no bigger than butterflies with flimsy delicate wands. They were small, standing to only about his shoulder, but by no means unimaginably minute and their wands, far from being fine white rods of energy, looked like strong solid staves cut from the forest and were used with energetic aggression.

At last, the High Circle glided down from their elevated

position, and wordlessly swept out towards a further chamber. After a respectful moment Talorcan and his verderers followed and Caspar found himself compelled forward by the waves of energy that surrounded him as they struck up their song again. He tried to close his mind against their will and battled to find his self-control but it seemed shackled in the deepest dungeons of his mind. He felt impotent. It was only willpower, he told himself, nothing more, and yet he could not summon any and found himself moving submissively forward with the procession.

He felt invaded, possessed. Bitterly angry, he scowled across the hall at Talorcan. Brid was smiling at the verderer now as he serenaded her – with lies. He was cheating. Brid didn't love him but she was being forced by his song. This was violation.

The next chamber was smaller though the ceiling was even higher. Caspar blinked as they entered, dazzled by the light. Everything was golden, even the marble floor was inlaid with a vast golden sunburst which reflected the sunlight that fell through a circular opening high in the roof above. A crescent of thirteen carved wooden thrones dominated the chamber and the High Circle swept towards them. Behind the thrones was a small wooden door made of one vast board engraved with the spreading boughs of a tree. He felt instinctively drawn towards it and somehow knew that behind the door lay home.

There seemed to be some confusion as to which order the thirteen ealdormen should sit and there was a purple flash as two wands clashed. Caspar had originally assumed that Nuin would take precedence but it seemed that the thirteen members of the Circle all had equal status.

"It is mine!" a lady with white sweet-smelling blossoms

in her hair announced with conviction. Caspar looked at her emblem and recognized the tree rune Huathe, the spirit of the hawthorn.

"No mine," a grey skinned, bearded man objected. Phagos, the ancient tree of knowledge, Caspar thought. Unlike the others, he carried a book and not a wand. His beard was entangled with beech nuts.

While they squabbled, another member of the circle hurriedly sat down in the central throne. She was simply dressed in green and brown and seemed unable to sit still. She kept her wings outspread and every now and then hovered just a couple of inches off her chair. "I am Coll, and spokeswoman for this day," she announced blithely.

Hazel, Caspar thought, the tree of intuition. He smiled, thinking how Brid would be pleased with his knowledge of the different properties of the trees. He had learnt a lot since he first met her.

Now that Coll was seated, the rest of the Circle seemed content until the dark-skinned one with a staff spiked with treacherous thorns, waved it threateningly. Caspar didn't have to read the man's emblem to know this was Straif, the spirit of the blackthorn, the tree of ill-fates.

"It was truly Huathe's turn today. I remember because in the last counsel it was Nuin's and the time before that Tinne's . . ."

A solid-looking ealdorman, his head crowned by a circlet of acorns stood, frowned and, in a deep sensible voice, said, "Straif, it's decided. Now, stop causing trouble."

"But it is my turn," Huathe protested loudly, swinging her head around defiantly at the other members of the Circle and casting out petals from her tiara of white blossom.

"Does it matter? It doesn't matter so long as someone

sits in the chair and it might as well be Coll. She's very good at it. It can be your turn next," the most solid-looking member of the circle sensibly advised. Duir, the spirit of the oak, Caspar thought, looking at the acorn circlet and finding the ealdorman more likeable than most of the others. He felt reassured when he spoke.

"That might not be for another hundred years." Huathe seemed very upset. "We haven't had a dispute like this in centuries and why should it be Coll who takes the chair?"

"Why indeed?" Straif chipped in. The flashes of purple and yellow spat back and forth between their staves as they began to squabble again.

Caspar was aghast. They had seemed so regal, so perfectly in control and yet they were reduced to this squabbling, this childish bickering. He could do nothing but stand and wait and his legs began to ache with exhaustion. How long were they supposed to stand here?

Fern was dragging at his arm. Caspar looked at Brid. Why wasn't she doing something about this? Brid had so much will; surely, she could break through their spells and sort them out. He found he was forced to stare straight ahead and it was beginning to feel like he had been standing there weeks though the sun had swung round only a little and still poured in to light the golden sunburst on the marble floor.

If only Hal were here, he suddenly found himself thinking. Hal wouldn't tolerate any of this nonsense. A pricking of conscience at the back of his mind told him that if Hal wouldn't stand for it then nor should he. He screwed up his eyes tight, determined to wrench his body free from their grip. He struggled and twisted, coiling up his energies, preparing to burst free. He felt the blood vessels pound in his head as he struggled to snap the invisible bonds of will that constrained him. He felt them give, just flex minutely and with one last effort he fought to break loose.

All he managed was to raise his head and let out a low bestial moan. The Circle stared at him, a sudden look of surprise gaping on their faces. Coll stood up, shaking out the ruffles from her green and brown dress. "Since I am spokeswoman today," she announced smugly, producing a sour look from Huathe, "I shall speak to the prisoner. Have him released from his bonds."

The four verderers surrounding Caspar stood back and released their burning gaze from him. Caspar felt like a gasping fish released back into the water.

Coll glided forward and prodded him with her wand. "A little small, aren't you?" she asked. Caspar thought this rather ripe coming from an ealdorwoman. He stood a good head taller than the tallest of them. "What are you doing here?" she added without waiting for him to say anything. "You should not be here, not without passing through the cleansing of death where the soul is freed from the mind and so free to go on. No one cheats the pain of the separation. It is short but necessary. There must be pain to move on and you have tried to cheat it."

"I didn't try to do anything. I need to go home, that's all," Caspar protested.

Straif rapped his thorny staff on the marble floor. "You don't *need* anything. You are just a mortal, to be toyed with at the whim of the Gods."

Phagos tapped at the book in his hand, then thoughtfully combed a beech nut from his beard. "You belong to the cycle, the wheel of life, and it is forbidden to cheat its course. The law says you must be punished."

Duir interrupted, "I would hear what he has to say

first. He is interesting. Did he not just break free from the verderers' will, be it all but briefly?"

"They must be punished. The law is clear on this point," Phagos argued unemotionally.

"That matter is yet to be resolved," a sweet little voice interrupted. The air was filled with the tantalizing smell of honeysuckle as she spoke and Caspar knew this was Uilleand, the honeysuckle, tree of hidden secrets. "The law is not finite. We are here to resolve the unwritten truths in it."

"You always have to involve yourself, Uilleand, don't you?" Straif complained. "You cling to every little conversation and try and entangle yourself in it."

Uilleand's wand was supple and she used it more like a whip to flick purple flashes of dust into Straif's eyes, who recoiled sharply. "As I was saying before I was so rudely interrupted—"

"I am spokeswoman today. It's my turn." Coll hammered her rod into the ground. "You can only speak through me."

They are like children, Caspar despaired. They could bicker like this eternally. He could be stuck here forever and he thought with bitter frustration of his responsibilities at home, of Torra Alta, of Morrigwen growing old and the death of the sacred mother wolf. We'll never find the wolflings, he thought grievously, and Pip, Brock and Trog are missing. They had to get back.

"I'll never speak through you," Uilleand sulked. "I want to speak. Why shouldn't I? Who says we have to have a spokesman?"

"We always have a spokesman, otherwise we would all be talking at once," Duir said patiently.

"And nobody is listening to you, Uilleand," Straif added, rising from his throne. "Nobody's listened to you in ages. Now what we need is some order."

"And who says you're taking charge?" Huathe was on her feet, stamping up and down. "It was my turn."

"Just shut up! Shut up!" Brid suddenly shouted.

Caspar relaxed. At last, she had broken free! He hadn't believed that Brid could be bound so much tighter than he was by the will power of these creatures and at last she had spoken. The Circle fell silent and looked at her in amazement.

"You don't realize how important this all is," Brid told them quietly. "You have to let us get back. I am the Maiden." She said the words as if expecting them to have a sobering effect on the Circle but, clearly, they did not.

One of the male members of the Circle laughed, a sharp prickly laugh, his pointed fingers spiking aggressively towards Brid. Caspar looked at his emblem and recognized it as Tinne, the holly. "She makes demands on us. I say she must be taught a lesson so that when she speaks again she is more respectful."

"They all must be," several of the council agreed in unison.

"They must be punished until she gives us back Duir's Pipe," Phagos said, nodding his bearded head sagely.

"Never," Brid replied defiantly. "Never. I will destroy it first."

"You cannot do that," Straif hissed.

Brid smiled. "Oh, but I can. The Pipe might not be of earthly matter but it is not beyond the world of magic."

She held it up to the light and Caspar could see that she had engraved the wood with an inscription of runes. So that was what she had been doing, keeping quiet all this time. "These are the runes of concealment and undoing, wrought so that only runes known to me will release them. They will distort its song and you will be unable to play the Pipe. I will only release the runespell if you allow us back."

There was a silence from the Circle, a hot brooding silence like the stillness in the atmosphere before a storm.

"The dungeons!" Nuin, who had not spoken in a while stood up. "To the dungeons with them! Talorcan, see to it!"

"I beg you, reconsider." The chief verderer stepped respectfully but insistently forward. "Let me put them in my hunting tower first. From there they will be able to look out from the castle of Abalone on the beauty of the forest and despair that they will never be able to cross it and reach the bliss of Annwyn unless they return the Pipe and accept that their lives are over. They appear to have a strong tolerance to pain. A spell in my hunting tower might be more effective."

He turned and whispered softly to Brid. "And while you wait, I will be free to visit you. You will grow to look forward to my company."

CHAPTER TWELVE

The Ceolothian winter was particularly wet and gloomy that year. King Dagonet was even more gloomy at the prospect of his daughter's imminent departure.

"I cannot possibly have Cymbeline travelling so soon after the rains. The floods are worse than last year; crossing the plains will be impossible. We really should consider waiting." The king's words went largely unheeded since they were but the latest in a line of reasons he had provided to delay his daughter's departure.

He was at that moment overseeing the wagons that his men were preparing for Princess Cymbeline, her entourage of ladies-in-waiting and her vast dowry. Hal had been rendered almost speechless by the mountain of jewels that had been arriving daily from the sunburst ruby mines to the north. The Belbidian escort had rested three weeks while Princess Cymbeline's dowry was being prepared.

There were sixteen wagons in all. Some carried Ophidian gold, others Lonisian silks and Oriaxian painted pottery. Hal wondered how so delicate a cargo would survive the journey over the rough winter-ruined roads to the coast. The rest of the wagons were filled with necklaces and amulets crafted by Ceolothia's finest white-smiths and of course sunburst rubies, some still uncut in great irregular nuggets and some set in tiaras, chains, shields and swords. No wonder King Rewik had suddenly decided to marry, Hal decided.

King Dagonet and the Belbidian noblemen stood within a quadrangle of stables, watching the bustle of activity around them. The men were checking for the last time that the cargoes were evenly distributed over the base of the wagons; axles were being greased and harnesses rechecked. Hal looked at the six-wheeled wagons and up at the rolling grey clouds that muffled the sky. It promised more rain and he didn't think the wagons would travel well through the mud.

"It wouldn't do any harm to wait, sir," he addressed Prince Renaud. "We'll make better time when the roads are dry and we'll probably arrive no later in Narwhal Ria than if we left now."

"Perhaps, but if—"

"We could of course go north through the old forest and overland," Tupwell spoke out of turn, overriding Prince Renaud's words before he had time to finish. "Although the route through Vaalaka is longer, we would avoid the worst of the floods on the plains."

Prince Renaud continued listening to Tupwell and led him aside to discuss the matter with King Dagonet. Hal wondered how Tupwell knew so much about the northern route through the forest. He scuffed at the shining, rain-washed cobbles in annoyance, sending up a spray of water, before sauntering away from the noblemen in irritation. Prince Renaud never listened to anything he had to say, always preferring to look to Tupwell or Hardwin for advice. Not that Hardwin ever gave any advice; he was too eager to agree, which was even more irritating than Tupwell's presumptive suggestions.

"Why can't we just wait here like is sensible?" Ogden muttered, looking up at Hal from the underside of a wagon. His hands were smeared in grease and he had a black stripe across his cheek where he had inadvertently wiped his face. "Master Hal, can't you say something that'll get us out of this folly?"

Hal shook his head. "I've been trying for hours," he admitted, "but they seem set on finding a way and it probably would be drier in the forest. That spoke's rotten." He kicked at the nearest wheel. The wood gave out a dull thud rather than a crisp firm rap.

Ogden wriggled out to inspect the wheel. "Master Hal, I've been talking to the Ceolothian sergeant, Cai, and that forest Prince Tudwal's talking about, sir, is Trows Forest and within it is Hobs Slack. We don't want to be going there."

"Ceolothian superstition, Ogden. I'm sure Cai had a high old time filling your head with all that foolery."

"Oh, it ain't just stories, sir. It really is an old fairy wood. Strange things happen, Cai swore."

"Oh, come on, Ogden, you're not afraid of a few tiny fairies, are you? Little creatures that sit on toadstools?"

"I don't recollect nothing that says they're that small. It would be a lot wiser to bide our time and move on once the spring is blossoming, sir. These are big heavy wagons."

Hal chewed his lip thoughtfully. He saw no reason to avoid this wood but all the same he didn't see any harm in staying in Castabrice either – though Tupwell seemed utterly against it. The very fact that Tupwell wanted to go made Hal even keener to stay. He didn't like the man. Not one tiny little bit. He stuck his chin out and returned to the knot of noblemen, determined to say something that might sway them.

"I don't know, I'm not sure. Lord Hardwin?" Renaud was stammering indecisively.

"Believe us, sir," Tupwell interrupted, "we should head home. It's not wise to be abroad this long and your brother will be worried and may be needing you at home."

Ceowulf was frowning at the Ovissian nobleman and Hal caught the knight's sceptical look. Hal agreed it was highly unlikely that King Rewik would have any special need for his brother.

"I think we should stay," Ceowulf remarked. "We need only wait a couple of months till the rains cease."

"Well, it's not for you to say, is it?" Tupwell's voice rose to a shrill, cutting note. "I outrank you, remember. I am the *eldest* son of a Baron."

"You don't outrank the prince," Hal reminded him and turned to Renaud. "Sir, I concur with King Dagonet and Ceowulf; it would seem best if we stay. What are your orders?"

Renaud looked flummoxed. "I— well, let's see." He looked between Ceowulf's patient face, Hal's indignation and Tupwell's insistence.

"I am thinking of the wolves pouring southward through Belbidia. We are men of action and should not be away from Belbidia too long. King Rewik will have need of us," Tupwell pompously declared. "And I need to get home to ensure these wolves are exterminated." He flashed Hal an accusatory look.

"Yes, yes, I believe you are right. We should not shirk our duties, however pleasant it would be to remain here. We shall use the old trade route through the forest, as Tupwell suggests," Renaud confirmed.

As Tupwell orders, Hal thought bitterly to himself and not for the first time found his fingers wandering to the ornately carved hilt of his sword. Its skilfully crafted design of two warring dragons felt solidly comfortable in his grip.

Prince Tudwal swaggered in on the conversation. "If you are overly concerned by our wild country," he sneered with practised condescension, "then I shall ride with you for protection."

"Protection!" Hal sniffed in disgust.

Prince Tudwal smiled condescendingly and continued in the flat dull notes of his Ceolothian accent. "There is nothing to fear in Trows Forest. Though it's named for the trolls, the last of the beasts were hunted down many generations ago by my illustrious ancestors. So, you don't need to worry on that account – unless you're afraid of Hobs Slack." He laughed deeply. "Of course Belbidians are bound to be afraid of ghostly rumours."

"We are not afraid." Hal swallowed the rising indignation in his voice and fixed a courtly smile on his face. He was determined to deny Tudwal the satisfaction of rising to his bait. "It merely seems foolish to go north over hard terrain with a young princess and her ladies when we need only wait a little longer until the rains have passed and then travel by the larger roads to the sea."

"Princess Cymbeline is a Ceolothian. She is not so frail as your Belbidian ladies. She is not afraid of the old forest."

"Belbidian ladies are not frail," both Ceowulf and Hal rejoined in unison.

"No? Then it must be you who are afraid of the wood," Tudwal taunted with a satisfied laugh, flicking back his head to toss his straight blond fringe out of his eyes. Hal found the movement affected and irritating, especially since the man's lank fringe promptly flopped straight back down to dangle against his white eyelashes again.

"We will go north through the forests," Hal announced abruptly as if he were the one making the decisions. Remembering that he was not in charge, he turned back to Prince Renaud and said heavily, "I agree we should go via Trows Forest since Prince Tudwal has so graciously volunteered to *serve* as our guide."

"Protector." The younger Ceolothian prince sought for a more suitable role for himself. "I shall gladly *lead* your party through my kingdom."

"*My* kingdom," King Dagonet corrected. "Neither I nor your brother show any signs of terminal decay yet and while that is the case, Ceolothia is not yours. So, mind your tongue!"

Tudwal sucked in his lower lip and chewed on it broodingly.

"How does Tupwell know so much about this part of the world?" Ceowulf muttered to Hal as they finally strode to their quarters to pack their meagre belongings.

"I have cousins in Ceolothia." The Ovissian nobleman was unexpectedly behind them. He had a way of sneaking up on them and had evidently overheard their conversation. "I'm surprised, Hal, that you of all people wanted to stay so long. Won't your little priestess chastise you for so long an absence?" He snorted contemptuously and walked away, leaving Hal prickling with anger. His hand jerked to grip the hilt of his sword but a nagging feeling that these jibes were founded in truth stayed his hand. Shamed, he ground his teeth and vowed once more to prove Tupwell wrong.

Secret was eager for the exercise as they prepared to leave King Dagonet's court. Hal busied himself to take his mind off Tupwell though Princess Cymbeline did much to distract him. She was still dabbing at her eyes after her father's long farewell. At the very last moment he had pressed a full purse of gold into her hand and then, as if that hadn't been enough, tugged all his rings bar his signet ring from his fingers, working them over the fleshy knuckles with difficulty, to add them to his gifts.

"If you ever want for anything, just tell me. Promise you'll tell me," he begged as she finally rode away past the chained bear at the bejewelled golden gate. The beast snarled and jerked at its chain.

Tudwal, surrounded by half a dozen long-legged black hounds led the escort party. He was seated on a sweating charger, veins standing proudly out on its arching neck. With one brief wave of his hand, the prince commanded the party forward. His sister rode beside him with five of her ladies-in-waiting while seven others sheltered in the central wagons. A score of Tudwal's own men fell in alongside the Belbidian troops.

Rather than take the circuitous route through the city, he led them down a marble-lined slope that dipped underground into a broad tunnel lit every dozen paces by braziers on the pale walls. Hal's ears were ringing with the echo of rattling hooves on the smooth stones before they finally emerged into the grey Ceolothian daylight again. Ahead lay the vast marshy plain dotted with tree-covered knolls. The plain stretched to the hazy horizon where pale purple escarpments rose to meet the heavy rain clouds. As they headed north-west, Hal ignored the landscape and sought the princess instead.

Dressed in a verdant riding habit, she looked as lovely and as regal as she did in her formal gown. Rich green hemmed with silver, her skirt hugged her hips and waist in such a way that made Hal feel guilty about his thoughts. The hairs on the back of his neck prickled. He had the disconcerting sense that Brid was watching him.

He snorted at the thought. Brid might be truly enchanting – and of course he loved her – but he couldn't let himself be entirely governed by her. He thought of

Tupwell's scornful words that still stung in his ears. He stiffened and blocked out the thought by returning his mind to Princess Cymbeline. He couldn't help but admire how she sat elegantly on her side-saddle – and with seemingly no loss of control. She reached down her right arm to take a hooded blue merlin from one of the waiting falconers. Hal smiled. Now here was a capable woman who didn't ride in hunting leathers, which Brid professed was essential. However much he tried to overlook the matter, he still wished Brid would occasionally behave like a real Belbidian lady.

Tupwell cantered forward to ride ahead of the company while Tudwal kept alongside his sister, jealously guarding her and ensuring that no one else was able to engage her in conversation. Princess Cymbeline glanced in Hal's direction and he nodded back gallantly. He was sure she was blushing – just slightly.

Someone nudged his shoulder. Ceowulf leant forward and gave him one of those looks. Not quite disapproving – the knight wasn't apt to be openly disapproving – but more a look of warning.

"What do you want?" Hal demanded.

"Nothing," Ceowulf replied gently. "I just wondered if you knew what you were doing."

"I'm only looking. You've got to admit—"

"Tupwell was right," Ceowulf interrupted, a dry smile on his lips. "You've been away from home too long. Besides there's no such thing as only looking."

"There is! I've done nothing, said nothing."

"Mm." Ceowulf sounded entirely sceptical. "You can't look without thinking. And she knows you're thinking. She's a woman as well as a princess, Hal. Think how you offended the merchant's wife outside Farona. You can't go around offending princesses in the same way. Forgetting the problem of Brid for the moment, Princess Cymbeline is King Rewik's bride. You'd be putting your head in a noose."

"I was only looking," Hal insisted. "And who's to say I'll offend her? She might actually like me."

"Princess Cymbeline entertain favourable thoughts about you, a lesser noble with no lands and no wealth, when she has the King of Belbidia to look forward to? Don't be ridiculous."

"And why not?" Hal felt himself rising to the challenge, then added more light-heartedly, "Do I not cut a fine figure with my knightly paraphernalia and fine horse?" He raised his chin and grinned wickedly.

Ceowulf laughed.

"I'll lay a wager that I can get her to look on me with favour," Hal declared more earnestly. "I'll wager my horse. You know what a fine war-horse she is, well-schooled in close combat. I'll put up my horse!"

Ceowulf's laughter rolled out. "It's a good thing I know you're only joking."

Hal smiled congenially back but didn't contradict his friend. He couldn't have people laughing at him, not Tudwal, not Tupwell, not even Ceowulf. He would prove to all of them that he could win Princess Cymbeline's favour. She wore a silken yellow scarf embroidered with the Ceolothian bear and he vowed to himself that before the end of their journey to Farona he would win it as a token of her affection. The only real obstacle was getting the princess away from her ever attentive brother.

The whole idea caught Hal's imagination and he began to fantasize further. Princess Cymbeline was not yet claimed by King Rewik. Of her own will, she could refuse to marry him if, in the meantime, she made a better choice for herself. Think of the dowry! Ceolothia was a tremendously wealthy country. All those sunburst ruby mines! He would have lands, titles of his own. He would have power.

He found himself pouting. True, she was not so beautiful as Brid: a little plumper, her eyes lacked that striking vitality and her face was almost too perfect. She was like an ivory carving, whereas Brid's features were so alive with character and joy.

But people laughed at him because of Brid. He glowered at Tupwell's back. Marrying a priestess brought no titles, no land and no dowry. But if he married a princess like Cymbeline the dowry would be substantial – huge! Dagonet would do anything for his daughter's happiness, he was sure, and would, no doubt, bestow lands on them if she asked for it. Then he would have his position.

Why had he been so foolish as to propose to Brid? He had been too young and innocent, he told himself. Marrying her would only decrease his standing in the community. It would be bad enough now but when his brother eventually died and Spar became the Baron of Torra Alta . . . Imagine answering to Spar! Why hadn't he thought of it before? Cymbeline's dress alone must be worth a ransom.

His conscience pricked him and he scowled at Ceowulf, blaming the knight for his sour feelings. Then he laughed: he was being preposterous. It was no good dreaming about dowries and titles and inheriting a share of King Dagonet's wealth, though the thought of all those sunburst rubies made him tremble. No, it was useless thinking about that when Princess Cymbeline had not yet shown the least favour towards him. Still, she amused him. Brid would never have to know. It would be pleasing to see if he could win the princess even if it was just to prove to himself that he could.

Riding through the marshy plain that ran to the north-west of the capital, Hal respectfully eyed the treacherous bogs lurking in the reeds beside the path. The air smelt dank and stale and he decided they had made the wrong decision moving out of Dagonet's court so soon. Though the rain had briefly ceased, he thought the weather was far too grim for Cymbeline and her ladies-in-waiting. They were making slow progress, constantly having to wait while the men levered yet another wagon out of the mud. The princess, however, seemed quite unworried by the sharp breeze blowing down from the north and had tossed back the hood of her cloak so that the wind caught her silvery blonde hair. Hal felt himself shiver. She plucked the hood from her merlin and sent the small hawk screaming out into the air, circling away from them with easy beats of its curved wings.

Hal's thoughts were broken into by Lord Tupwell's voice. "A race. We should have a race."

"We should?" Ceowulf groaned under his breath to Hal. "Just look at the terrain. What on earth does he want to go rushing about for? The horses will have a hard enough time as it is in this mud."

"Is no one man enough to take up the challenge, eh?" The Ovissian nobleman aimed his goad at Hal, carefully removing his feathered cap from his head and stowing it in his breast pocket for safe keeping.

"Should we not wait for a more suitable place?" Ceowulf diplomatically suggested.

"Ha! Everyone knows that a mercenary is the biggest coward of all and now you are proving it," Tupwell taunted.

Hal was heated on his friend's behalf but Ceowulf smiled. "My dear man, I feel no need to prove myself to the likes of you."

"I'll take you up," Tudwal declared in his flat monotone

accent. "Myself and two of my men against you and two Belbidians. What do you say, Renaud?" he asked with familiarity. "Shall we see the cut of your princely steed?"

"Oh Mother," Hal grumbled at the whole preposterous idea.

"Don't you dare include yourself in this," Ceowulf warned. "Any man of action would know this was entirely inappropriate."

"I wouldn't dream of it," Hal tried to look indignant though he was not about to let on about the real reason he wouldn't race. He very much doubted that Secret would beat Tudwal's feisty horse and he'd rather leave the impression that he would have won if he had entered than prove to everyone that his liver chestnut mare, despite her flashy tack, superbly schooled head carriage and high-stepping action, was altogether slower than she looked.

Tupwell pointed. "See that knoll on the far side of the woods with that strange-looking rock on top? What do you say, gentlemen? That's about the right distance."

Everyone raised their heads and followed his pointing finger down into a dell where the road led through reeds, indicating sodden ground to either side, and into a wood. After that it emerged as a thin thread in the distance to rise towards a smooth hill crowned by a rock that nature had weathered to resemble an anvil.

It looked at least a league away but Tupwell, Renaud, and Hardwin – after much persuasion from the others – were lining up against Tudwal and two other Ceolothians, their horses already sweated up with anticipation.

"Wait one moment." Princess Cymbeline halted them and rode forward towards her brother. She unwound the yellow scarf from her neck and loyally offered her kinsmen the trophy. "You must win for the honour of Ceolothia," she told him with a lingering smile.

"Too far, it'll ruin the horses," Ceowulf murmured in despair. "The older I get the more thankful I am that I no longer feel the need to make an idiot of myself."

"Would you like to make odds on which one we'll have to pull out of a bog first?" Ogden asked. "We've got three of us betting on Lord Hardwin and six for Prince Renaud. Would you care to make a wager, sir?"

"I think that's entirely disrespectful," Hal laughed. "Shouldn't we be betting on who will win the race?"

"Foregone conclusion, sir. It'll be Prince Tudwal so we didn't think that would be so much fun."

Hal thought about it more seriously and frowned. He wondered why on earth Tupwell would have suggested the race when clearly Tudwal had a far superior animal. No one suggests a race if they don't think they can win, not a man of ambition at any rate.

He didn't have any time to ponder further as the six contestants spurted forward, sending sodden turves up into the air and splattering the horses behind. One of the ladies-in-waiting shrieked as her horse snorted and danced, kicking its heels out at the princess's dappled horse behind, before bolting off after the others. A Ceolothian guard spurred after the lady-in-waiting who was bouncing precariously, her arms flung round the horse's neck, but Hal's eyes weren't on her. He was concerned for Cymbeline. The bolting horse had kicked fiercely into her palfrey's chest, and the animal was now backing anxiously while the princess struggled to control it. Keeping her head, she managed just in time to loose the merlin into the air before her horse bolted after the others.

Hal battled to manoeuvre Secret alongside in an attempt to grab the reins but the princess's peppery animal was kicking out viciously as she plunged into a gallop. Far too fiery for a young woman to be riding, he thought to himself, glad of Secret's calm nature as he charged after her. Thankfully, the princess was keeping her head, though it was not what he had expected. Sitting back in the saddle and hauling on the reins, she was doing her best to control the bolting animal though it wasn't responding to her efforts.

Hal was grateful that at least he wasn't losing ground. He stood up in his stirrups and hunched over Secret's withers, urging her faster, sodden turves spraying up around them. He prayed Cymbeline's steed would slow as it swerved off the road and into the heavy black mud that sucked at its hooves.

After seeing where she had ridden into difficult terrain, Hal had the advantage now. He steered to the left to avoid the wetter areas, so gaining several lengths on her. The ground was beginning to rise and he hoped that, as they reached the wood, the going would be firmer and less treacherous. But he had forgotten about the dangers of the trees.

It hit him with a momentary flash of panic. "Turn!" he shouted. "Turn before the trees."

"I can't," she yelled back. The flapping merlin was swooping and darting to either side, adding to the horse's alarm.

Damn, Hal swore to himself, infuriated that Secret simply didn't have the turn of speed. He wasn't gaining fast enough. A horse bolting in open countryside was one thing but through closely packed trees was quite another. He yelled at her to throw herself to the ground but she clung on in fear and was no more than two paces ahead when she was swallowed by prickly branches. Dry twigs snapped underfoot and dangling boughs snagged at her clothing. Hal could see very little as he flinched and screwed up his eyes against the whiplash of younger shoots that flew back in his face. He needed to guide Secret but the trees were coming up too fast to think.

It would only take one low branch to wipe Cymbeline from her saddle or smash her skull. The consequences were dreadful. What would King Dagonet think if the Belbidian escort allowed his precious daughter to be so endangered? Such things could incite war. War between such two powerful nations was unthinkable. But if Dagonet's prized daughter was injured through Belbidian foolishness . . .

Brambles snarled around Secret's legs and she stumbled onto her knees but was quickly up again. Suddenly Hal was enveloped in a white veil that wrapped around his neck and covered Secret's face. The horse squealed in panic as he fought to rip away the garment that must have been wrenched from the princess's head.

A stifled scream stopped his heart for a beat. He hauled Secret to a slower but urgent trot as he dipped and dived between the branches of the hawthorns. Cymbeline lay face down in the leaf mould. Her horse had galloped on after scraping off its rider on the vicious branches of a blackthorn.

As he dismounted, he was relieved to hear her groan and see her tentatively move her head and stretch out her fingers. He rushed to her side, wishing he had at least a few words of her own tongue with which to comfort her. He flung himself down beside her, "My lady, are you hurt?" he gasped.

He wondered whether he should examine her in any way but decided it was best just to allow her a moment to catch her breath. He knew that if he were hurt himself the last thing he would want was to be hauled to his feet. She looked up at him and blinked, muttering uncertainly in her own tongue before finally stuttering into Belbidian.

"I couldn't hold her. I just couldn't do anything to stop her."

Hal offered his arm, relieved that, evidently, she had suffered no damage. "Can you get to your feet?"

She nodded but winced as he helped her up. Hal was beginning to enjoy a few moments alone with the princess. It was an ideal opportunity to gain her favour as her brave rescuer but presently the sounds of the Ceolothian troops hacking through the woods grew louder, and soon she was rapidly surrounded by fussing hands and worried faces and Hal found himself crowded out. He dusted himself down and retrieved Secret who was calmly chewing at some dead-nettles clustered beside a rotten tree stump.

"I'm going after her horse," Hal announced but no one seemed to be listening as they fussed over their princess.

At a sedate jog, he wound through the woods northwards away from the road, following the palfrey's tracks and half expecting to find the horse dead after running headlong into a tree. He slowed when he reached a small clearing in the leafless trees; the dappled palfrey was grazing at the far edge of it.

As he crossed the glade, a thin cry high in the air made him raise his head to see Cymbeline's blue merlin hovering above the trees further ahead. He was distracted by the bird's flight, as it swooped and plunged into the thick of the wood, and, as a result, he came up on Cymbeline's horse much too quickly. It flicked up its head and smartly trotted away from him.

Hal cursed himself and followed more cautiously into the thickening wood. He heard noises ahead like the sound of flapping wings and Hal was suddenly worried for Cymbeline's merlin. Forgetting the horse for the moment, he wound his way forward until he came across a small though unnatural clearing. A ring of hazel trees, entangled with clambering honeysuckle, marked its perimeter. The merlin swung from a rope, flapping its wings intermittently as it pecked at something large dangling from the rope. The bird's flapping made it difficult to see exactly what it was. He hurried forward and shooed away the merlin with great wafts of his arms.

It was a wolf's skull. The rope was looped through the animal's empty eye sockets. Hal instantly thought how Brid wouldn't have liked to see the head hanging there like that of a criminal to be picked at by carrion, so he took his knife and cut it down.

It was freshly killed, the flesh scraped away with a knife though bits of dried browned meat still clung around the jaw. He frowned at it, wondering at its significance. At first, he thought it must be there as a part of some pagan worship though he found that unlikely here in Ceolothia. He looked around him for any other oddities and his gaze fell on some deep tan-coloured toadstools bubbling up around the roots of an ivy-strangled tree. Almost camouflaged amongst the fungus was a scrunched-up ball of torn parchment. He dismounted and made towards it. The screwed up parchment was smeared with blood as if it had been pulled from the inside of the wolf's skull. Filled with curiosity, Hal stooped for it and unravelled the tatters. He tried to piece them together.

Fragments of the parchment carried words written in Belbidian, which he found strange here in the depths of Ceolothia though not entirely improbable. Belbidian was always used when any two nationalities of the Caballan Sea wished to communicate. Even when Hal had finally laid all the pieces out and pressed them flat, the writing was barely legible for smears of mud and missing sections.

He could discern several single words but on their own they meant nothing. He rearranged the sections and found that as he pieced the upper part of one and the lower part of another together, the words *Princess and her 16* were suddenly discernible. He instantly thought of the sixteen treasure-laden wagons and his heartbeat quickened as he studied the rest of the smeared pieces more diligently. Eventually he identified a few words though none appeared to mean anything significant except for the word *Trows*, which he thought must refer to Trows Forest where they were headed and more ominously *waylay*.

His mind raced. Examining the torn-up message, he wondered at it, almost with disbelief. Had he really uncovered a plot to kidnap the princess and her dowry? The parchment looked like it had been hastily pulled from the wolf's head, scrunched up and hidden. He wondered if he had disturbed the conspirator in the process of retrieving or writing the message. He must inform Prince Renaud and Prince Tudwal at once.

He turned and, as he did, glimpsed by chance a second scrap of parchment poking up through the crisp leaves at the edge of the clearing. He snatched it up avidly. Judging by the smooth edges of the paper this was the bottom section and it was very much less creased and smeared as if the man who had screwed up the other sections had inadvertently dropped this part before scrunching up the rest to destroy the evidence. Hal turned it the right way up, his lips suddenly dry with anticipation.

She must not enter Belbidia.

Hal was disappointed; he was hoping to find a signature but there was none.

But what did it mean? Who would write such a secret

letter? He strode towards his horse, eager to warn the others but stopped in his tracks as he realized the significance of that last line.

He looked about him for any sign of someone about to collect the message but there was none. He stuffed it into his pocket, collected Secret and then stalked Cymbeline's animal who was now calm enough to catch easily. He mounted quickly and rode out into the open to rejoin the escort party. They were making their way towards the knoll where Prince Tudwal and Prince Renaud were still small figures in the distance. Red faced and flustered, Hardwin joined the wagons at the same time as Hal.

"My horse shied and I got caught up in the wood. I took a fall," Hardwin was explaining in obvious embarrassment but no one apart from Hal was listening to him. Everyone else was worrying over Princess Cymbeline as she insisted on remounting her wayward palfrey. When it was clear by all the commotion around the princess that something untoward had happened, the two princes thundered back towards them. Prince Tudwal's horse barged its way through the entourage and the Ceolothian went almost white as he saw his sister's soiled dress and tousled hair. "Cymbeline, you've been hurt!"

"It's nothing. My horse bolted and I fell off," she said sharply, brushing out her skirts. She was clearly annoyed that she had shown herself lacking in horsemanship.

Hal disguised his grin, thinking that Brid would have been furious too, though he had to admit that Brid would probably have been able to halt the horse. But on the other hand, it was very appealing in Cymbeline that she wasn't quite so accomplished. It gave him the opportunity to shine as her protector. Cymbeline had needed him whereas Brid would not have done.

He found himself smiling at her, the thought warming within him and she caught his eye. A slow uncertain but intrigued smile widened across her face. With her head slightly on one side, she gave him a long look and then with a girlish grin turned quickly away and kicked into a fast canter, scattering her entourage into disarray. They scrambled after her.

Hal found himself staring into Tudwal's slitted eyes as the squarely built prince pushed himself in front of him, blocking his path. "Keep away from her," he snarled with typical Ceolothian ferocity. "I don't want her talking to pagans."

Hal shrugged away Tudwal's affront. He quite enjoyed upsetting Tudwal and was too busy thinking about the man's beautiful sister to take offence. It would be a dreadful shame if the girl were to marry Rewik. Such life, such spirit would be wasted.

"You're glowering," Ceowulf spoke beside him and Hal jumped.

"I am?"

"Dark thoughts, Hal?" Ceowulf asked though it was not entirely a question. "Has the princess done something to displease you?"

"She's too good to marry an old vulture like Rewik." Hal firmly clenched his lips shut as though dismissing the conversation but a broad grin soon broke out on his young face. The princess had at that moment turned to smile at him from beneath her ruby-studied tiara.

Ceowulf studied his face and raised a knowing eyebrow. Hal knew that look and scowled, waiting for the big solid Caldean to lecture him but Ceowulf kept silent, which was all the more infuriating. Still, he needed to talk to Ceowulf alone. He signalled with his eyes that they should meet at the rear of the column and twiddled Secret's mane whilst pulling her to a slower pace, waiting for the rest of the escort to overtake them.

The flat boggy landscape was beginning to fold into low hills and in the distance sharp escarpments broke the skyline. Prince Tudwal loudly ordered several of his men to out-riding positions to ensure there were no lurking dangers as they moved into rockier terrain. "Too many places for bandits to hide around here. The sight of sixteen wagons is bound to attract trouble," he explained.

Prince Renaud hurriedly followed suit. "Sergeant Otho," he ordered, looking directly at Ogden. The sergeant looked blankly back for a moment and then smartly saluted.

"Sir?"

"A scouting party. Organize a few men and see there's no one sinister about. Sixteen wagons are bound to attract trouble," he repeated Tudwal's words as if they were his own.

Hal caught Ogden's eye and threw his own heavenward as the two princes hurried forward to head the column. "So, no one won their bets, did they?" he remarked affably. He didn't really care who had won the race but he liked to take what opportunity he could to talk to the men. It was something that he had learnt from his brother to always keep an open discourse with the troops. It made them trust him and boosted general morale. Besides he enjoyed it.

"Oh, but they did, sir. I guess everyone else was too busy with Princess Cymbeline to notice. I lost my bet; we had to pull Lord Tupwell from the bog."

Hal hadn't noticed and he stood in his stirrups to catch sight of Tupwell ingratiating himself with Prince Tudwal. Somehow the Ovissian nobleman had already changed into a fresh doublet and hose and, infuriatingly, he still had his peacock feather.

Hal grinned, leaving Ogden to his duties, and waited for Ceowulf to join him at the rear of the column. When his friend was alongside, he looked all around and then told him of his find in the woods.

"Can I see it?" Ceowulf asked when Hal was done.

Hal patted his breast pocket where the parchment was hidden. "Shh!" he warned him to keep his voice down. "All that's legible is a section about waylaying Princess Cymbeline and her dowry and then the very last bit that warns she must not reach Belbidia."

For a brief moment Ceowulf's eyebrows looked like they would disappear into his hairline but he quickly composed himself. "We must inform . . . But, no, we can't, can we?"

Hal smiled at Ceowulf's quick thought. "No, we can't. At first, I thought we must tell both princes but then I thought about the last bit. Why would anyone be determined to stop Princess Cymbeline reaching Belbidia? The answer can only be that they wish to prevent the marriage to King Rewik and the only person who would want that is Renaud. The letter was written in Belbidian too. We can't say anything in case it's his message."

"And nor can we warn Tudwal." Ceowulf sucked in a deep breath and rubbed at the back of his neck. "He might assume that all we Belbidians are part of this conspiracy."

"Beyond that it could mean war. What do you think King Dagonet will do if he hears of a Belbidian conspiracy against his precious daughter?"

Ceowulf nodded. "Men have gone to war for far less. We must keep this to ourselves. All we can do is ensure that nothing untoward happens to Cymbeline."

"And keep a wary eye out on Prince Renaud and whoever else might be in his league," Hal added.

Ceowulf was studying the column of men ahead. "Hmm,

yes, like Tupwell and Hardwin. After all, Tupwell suggested the race. We said it was a daft thing to do. But what if he wanted the race as a distraction?"

Hal thought for a moment about what Ceowulf was saying. The race couldn't have diverted attention away from Prince Renaud because Prince Tudwal had been alongside him all the while but not so Hardwin or Tupwell. Both had been mysteriously delayed.

Ceowulf suddenly laughed. "But Hal, it's all ridiculous. Renaud couldn't contrive anything like that."

"Why not?" Hal asked, thinking that he already knew Ceowulf's answer.

"He's just too stupid."

"Yes, but he's the only one with a motive. The prospect of losing his chance of the Belbidian throne might have sharpened his mind."

Ceowulf nodded. "You're right, he has a great deal to gain, but Hardwin is no conniver. Now Tupwell maybe. Renaud might have offered him lands, money . . .'

"Tupwell has enough already: the entire barony of Ovissia. What man would want more?" Hal asked.

"You're only saying that because you don't have a barony. Now Ogden," Ceowulf raised his voice as Hardwin slowed to within earshot, "for instance, who, no doubt, doesn't even own the cottage he lives in, would think that you must be entirely content just by being a nobleman. Whereas you think owning a barony would bring utter satisfaction. Yet if you did—"

"I know," Hal interrupted. "Most of us always want to be just one rung higher than we are. It's the nature of man to be discontent." He thought it was a pompous thing to say but he couldn't think of anything else and didn't want Hardwin to suspect that they had been discussing anything of importance.

"Except of course for the few that have nothing," Ceowulf philosophized.

"That doesn't make sense." Hardwin joined their conversation

"Haven't you ever noticed how sometimes the woodsfolk and the commoners who have so little seem to be the most content of all?" Ceowulf asked.

Hal thought about it and was reminded of May's sweet nature. He then remembered how she had shunned Caspar so coldly when she had finally grown old enough to realize that Caspar's affections might not be entirely focused on her. Still, none of that mattered right now. He gave a sidelong glance at Hardwin and then forward at Prince Renaud's back. The question now was what to do.

"Sir, my Lord Hal!" Ogden was rushing to his side. "Sir, there might be trouble to the north." The man was blowing hard and his horse sweating. He had been acting as a scout on their right flank.

Hal turned seriously towards the man. "Tell me."

Ogden nodded north towards the rising line of an escarpment. "You can't see it now but you will on the next rise. There's vultures circling and ravens gathered in the trees. Too many of them just for an ordinary kill – if I'm any judge of such things."

CHAPTER THIRTEEN

Brid sat alone at the far side of the cold, airy tower room. Caspar had tried talking to her but she wasn't prepared to listen. He was close to despair.

At first, he had been dazzled by the view that overlooked the river. The glinting waters coiled through the lime-green beeches, dark evergreens and rustling poplars, like a cast off sash. Countless paths crossed and recrossed the forest around it in a dense network of irregular lines. He could see animals flitting amongst the trees and what looked like small herds and troops of humans moving sedately along the paths. He didn't know what to make of them.

Distracted by hunger, he turned to look back at the inside of the tower room and wondered how long they would be kept here without food. They were in the very top turret room, a circular chamber that spanned the width of the tower. On the way up they had passed several closed doors and Talorcan had made a point of stopping at one of them, opening the door wide enough for them to glimpse inside. It was richly furnished with tapestries on the walls and cushions on the floor and seeped a heady smell of wine. Fruits were laid out on a low table alongside a couch where a naked girl lay sobbing quietly into her hands. Sitting forlornly at her side were two other women wrapped in soft silks. All three were beautiful though contrasting in looks; one black-haired and pale skinned, the second blonde with bronzed skin and the third was tall and statuesque with ebony skin and deep brown eyes. And Brid, fair with her coppery brown hair, would complete the collection, Caspar thought in disgust. Brid looked into the room with slitted eyes and Talorcan studied her reaction.

"They are pitifully sad, I know, but I cannot be happy without their beauty," he admitted to Brid. "But I would set them free, all of them, for you. You hold the key to their freedom and happiness. As soon as you give yourself to me, I will allow them to move onto the bliss beyond the forest where they yearn to go." Talorcan began his song again, wooing Brid.

The girl's sobbing was pathetic and Brid looked white with the strain of witnessing her suffering. "It's not my fault. You cannot lay their suffering at my door," she began, sounding confused.

Talorcan sang ever more sweetly, a self-satisfied smile faintly lifting his lips as he ushered them up to the top room. "Think about it, my sweet. Listen to them crying and remember that it is you alone who holds the key to their freedom," he told Brid before he locked them in.

Caspar was now slumped against the wall and stared at his boots, examining the scuff marks in great detail to distract his mind. How long had they been here? Days, weeks? He wasn't sure. He found himself grinding his teeth. Hal often ground his teeth and it had always infuriated him so he bit at his tongue instead. The constant crying cut through to his soul and he could see how it played on Brid as she kept herself quietly to herself at the far end of the room. She plucked at her plait in agitation.

Caspar was losing his restraint. Why couldn't Brid see

that Talorcan was trying to trick her? He relented momentarily, knowing that he wasn't being fair. He had felt the strength of the verderer's song when it was turned on him and yet he expected Brid to defy it. Still, he couldn't help thinking that Brid wasn't trying hard enough. He couldn't help himself. He was angry.

Now that he finally recognized the emotion, it sprouted out from his soul like a canker to consume his entire body. He was angry with Brid. Until now he had always thought her perfect but here she was, wallowing in self-pity. She should be putting her mind to getting them out of here, to using the Pipe; but she wasn't. She was just toying with it distractedly. He was no longer studying his boot but glowering at the Maiden.

"You've got us into this, Brid, so now get us out," he snapped, no longer even noticing Fern who wept wild sobs in the centre of the room and looked in despair at his lengthening fingers.

"How dare you speak to me like that?" Brid was clearly every bit as angry as he was and Caspar was taken aback, suddenly aware that he was afraid – afraid of losing her friendship and afraid of her scorn. As an all-knowing high priestess, full of wisdom and understanding, she always seemed so strong, so much above him. He had worshipped her since they had first met but now, for the very first time, he had seen her as fallible.

"And how dare you blame me for this?" Brid continued to rage hotly.

"I'm not blaming you. I just think you should be getting us out of here rather than mooning over Talorcan," he replied bluntly, knowing instantly, as her green eyes flashed, that he had hit the mark.

She stood up dismissively and looked out between the bars of the narrow window slit. "I don't care one jot about

Talorcan." She sniffed in a way that made it quite clear she did.

"What about Hal?" Caspar asked coldly, rising to his feet.

"What about him?" Brid's face was red with anger. With clenched fists, she stalked towards him like a threatening lioness. "Are you trying to tell me what I should think and feel?"

"Yes!"

"How dare you? Hal isn't even in this world. We're in the Otherworld. It's like being dead, don't you see? Would you expect me to love Hal through my next life and my life beyond?"

Caspar didn't know. He didn't feel particularly dead. He felt just as alive as ever if not more so – and barely in control of his emotions.

"How can you love Talorcan? How dare you succumb to his song! It's nothing but fairy magic. How could you love him when I'm here!" There! He had said it, said what he had wanted to say for years. Finally, he admitted to himself that he loved her beyond all else. And May? What of May? Brid was all that mattered. He didn't care about anyone, only his wounded heart. He felt ashamed, bitter and misused all at once.

"You?" Brid was contemptuous. "You!"

Fern was on his feet, butting his head between them. "What's the matter with you? I don't understand. Just stop it. Why are you fighting? You were friends before."

Brid looked down her nose at the little woodwose and for a moment Caspar thought she would shout at the poor confused creature but then the corners of her mouth crinkled and her face melted into an expression of sympathy and remorse. She knelt down by the small horned woodwose, hugging him close. "I'm sorry," she murmured. "I don't know what's happened to me. I've been trying to keep calm but my emotions keep sweeping through me like a storm." She looked at Caspar. "Forgive me."

Caspar didn't want to forgive her. He was too incensed and hurt.

Fern stared at him. "What's happened to you? Why are you so angry?"

Caspar knew why he was angry. It was because he loved Brid and she didn't love him.

Suddenly the studded oak door swung open and Talorcan, shining and brilliant, stood in the doorway laughing. "You are in the land of the spirit now and can no longer hide from your emotions. For you, this is the place of reckoning." He laughed at their suffering. "It always amuses me to observe human souls as they pass through Rye Errish. I know of your world, of how men strive for control of themselves, each in their own small way contriving to create order within their short lives. Then when they arrive here, they simper and weep, wallowing in their repressed hurts against one another. Such unknowing, self-deceived creatures!"

"I still don't understand," Fern said honestly.

Brid gripped Fern's hand, giving him support and sympathy. "No, of course you don't understand," she told him gently though her eyes still reached out towards Talorcan. "But you will learn that human beings are perverse, complicated creatures, simmering with conflicting emotions. We are often dishonest with ourselves as well as others to achieve our goals or avoid conflict."

"You are?" Fern sounded incredulous. "But why?"

Brid shrugged. "Because life would be too painful otherwise. Like it is now." She stared deeply into Talorcan's eyes. His lips opened and he breathed out his song. Like a sunburst piercing brooding thunderheads, the beautiful, mysterious notes promised joy and freedom from woes and responsibilities. Caspar looked imploringly at Brid's dragon-green eyes and was appalled to see them tainted by the golden reflection of Talorcan's eyes. Trembling, Brid held the verderer's stare for a long moment before she managed to wrench her mind away.

Talorcan clenched his jaw. "You will be mine, lady. You are too beautiful for the sullied Earth. This is where you belong." He marched forward and kissed her zealously on the lips before turning smartly and leaving the room. Brid spat and rubbed at her lips in disgust though she was still trembling and her eyes had followed Talorcan and remained long on the door that closed behind him.

Caspar turned on his heel in disgust and went over to the window to look out at the view. The forest stretched out for miles; everything, for as far as the eye could see, was lush green. Caspar felt terribly lonely. Here in the Otherworld Hal didn't exist; his mother and father didn't exist; maybe even Torra Alta didn't exist. He wanted desperately to go home. He would do almost anything to get back to the real world. He belonged to the Earth and he missed it more than he missed anything. Talorcan had been right. He felt utter despair as he looked out over the never-ending forest.

He turned furiously on Brid. "We've got to get home. Why can't you get us out of here?"

She slumped to the floor and hugged Fern even tighter. "We can't get home," she admitted softy. "I don't know how to get home. I can't play the Pipe and . . ."

"And you don't want to go home," Caspar accused.

"Of course I want to get home!" She held out her hand to Caspar in a truce of friendship. "We have to get home and not just for the sake of the Trinity but simply for our souls. But we'll be here forever unless we can persuade the Circle to let us return." Brid stood up decisively, marched towards the oak doors and began hammering on them. "I demand to see the High Circle. They must listen to me." She hammered for several minutes without getting a response and finally kicked the door in frustration.

Just like Hal, Caspar thought, finding the comparison quite amusing. He had never seen Brid in that light before. She was normally so calm and self-possessed but here her emotions were cut bare to the bone, pure and unclouded. Underneath it all she was just like Hal, quick to lose her temper.

He found himself laughing and Brid glowered at him. "What's funny?"

"I was just thinking how Hal is always being reprimanded for having no restraint but how he would cope better than all of us here because he wouldn't be any different."

Brid laughed too. "But that's what I like about Hal. He's so honest. He doesn't put up an act."

"Hal! You're talking about the man who put three curb chains on Secret just to make her look vicious and unpredictable when she's the best trained war-horse I've ever seen."

"You're not meant to know that," Brid chuckled. "After all he's never let you ride her."

"I know," Caspar laughed, having no idea why it was all so funny. "But it's so obvious that she doesn't need them – despite the fact he's trained her to bite and kick on demand. But that's the point; she bites at his request, not out of viciousness."

"But that's what I mean about Hal. He knows why he's doing those daft things. He doesn't pretend to himself. He knows exactly what he's feeling whereas the rest of us try and kid ourselves it's for some higher motive. It makes him difficult because he's blunt and doesn't understand the meaning of compromise but when he says he loves you, you know he means it."

"And I don't?"

"No, and you don't," she retorted.

Caspar frowned. "But I do love you, Brid." He blushed crimson as the words gushed unbidden from his mouth.

"Oh, I know that – in your own way," she replied lightly as if he had done no more than compliment her dress. "I mean you've been telling May all these years that you love her and never truly meant it." She continued her hammering at the locked door.

Caspar was consumed by guilt. It was true. Fleeing from himself, he tried to hide in a bluster of activity and leapt to his feet to hammer on the door alongside Brid. They had to get home, back to where he could at least pretend that he no longer loved her. It was all becoming too painful.

"Let us out. We must see the High Circle. You must give us an audience. Help us to return or the Trinity will be lost," Brid shouted.

There was no reply that day nor the next. During the long tedious days Caspar found it impossible not to argue with Brid about even the smallest issues. He felt too raw and too wounded to be pleasant. During the cold, comfortless nights he sat on the far side of the chamber from her, listening to the bestial shrieks and sudden howls that erupted from far off in the forest. His blood ran cold and his nightmares were filled with images of half-formed creatures bursting open the shell of Necrönd to crawl out into the pit. In the dank dungeons they grew unnaturally fast, filling the chambers and crushing him to the walls, before rampaging through Torra Alta, gouging and tearing at the people with voracious hatred.

Caspar was sure they had been forgotten and left to rot. They had been given no food and he was ravenous with hunger. When he felt he had little strength left to fight off the maddening panic that gnawed at the roots of his mind, the door finally swung open. Talorcan stood in the doorway, a green sweeping robe cloaking his leathers and golden jacket. He strode arrogantly forward, singing a song that was more lovely than the sound of fresh running water. It was wild and free and offered the promise of eternal happiness. Caspar could feel all those things and could see the effect it had on Brid. She was biting her trembling lower lip in her struggle to restrain her warring emotions.

"You're cheating her," Caspar roared.

Talorcan laughed. "Cheating a mortal?"

"She doesn't love you. You mustn't use magic on her."

"Love is magic."

Caspar knew he was being goaded. Talorcan was smiling, smugly aware of their helplessness. The auburn-haired youth could feel the blood pumping inside his head. He would kill this creature! But some tiny voice in the back of his mind squealed at him to resist and summon his self-control. If he lost his self-restraint, he would be no more than an animal. He took steady deep breaths, struggling with his anger but when Talorcan reached out a hand for Brid, he could not contain himself. He flew at the verderer only to find himself repelled by the sudden notes of Talorcan's song that flung him back against the wall.

"You have no power against me here, mortal." Talorcan stood over him, his bright yellow eyes scorching into Caspar's. "We are the source of all magic; we know all the words of the song. Whereas you are no more important than an insect here in Rye Errish."

"You have to let us go home," Caspar stuttered irrepressibly, his mind shaking from the intensity of the magic.

"You have cheated the divine laws. Those who belong to the Earth must pass through Rye Errish and then on to Annwyn from whence they are reborn into the endless cycle. You have cheated that cycle. We immortals that live here in Rye Errish, we are creatures of the sun and we are not tied to the cycles of time. We stand in judgement over you."

"How can such soulless, pitiless creatures stand judgement over us?" Caspar forced the words through his lips. "You must let us go home."

Talorcan shrugged. "You will remain here and that is an end to it! When you walk through the forest you will have time to come to terms with your past life."

"I don't want to be a man," Fern suddenly sobbed. "I need to go home. Who will look after Sorrel if I don't?"

"The forest will look after her," Talorcan said patiently.

"You know that means death. My fawn must live," Fern wailed helplessly. Caspar felt intense sympathy for the poor creature and his own face was wet and sticky with tears as he took Fern's hand. Apart from the velvety horns, the creature now looked mostly human although he still had black cloven hooves for feet and his skin was still the sandy colour of a forest deer and his movements were too quick. He swung his head from side to side with nervous jerks and his eyes were wide and startled. "I have to go home," he said softly, looking up into Caspar's eyes. "I have to."

Caspar nodded and stared towards Brid. "So do I." This was purgatory.

Brid had not spoken in a long while. She was staring at Talorcan, her eyes glazed, caught up in the magic of his song. The verderer smiled at her in satisfaction and she took a few tottering steps closer to him as he reached out for her.

Caspar grabbed at her sleeve. "Brid, you don't love him. Don't you see that it's just a spell? It's not real."

She wasn't listening. Her eyes were melting into Talorcan's as his song soared into intense notes of passion.

"Come, Brid, lady of the Great Mother, come live with me in the paradise of Rye Errish and taste the bliss of timeless happiness. Come live with me forever. Forever!" Talorcan breathed, his words like smooth honey enveloping her in a warm stickiness from which she was powerless to escape. Just as his song had the force to hurl Caspar across the room, so did it have the power to compel Brid towards him. "Together we can do much good. You have great power in your own world. Join them with mine and we can set worlds to rights. Together we can heal and prevent all suffering."

"Resist him, Brid," Caspar begged, instinctively aware that there was no truth in the verderer's words. "The world needs you, Brid. Resist him or the Trinity will fail."

Brid looked at him helplessly and then back towards Talorcan with longing in her eyes. "Forever," she murmured, as if pondering the idea. "Thwarted by King Rewik and the other nobles of the New Faith, even with Keridwen and Morrigwen, I had little enough power to help put the world back to rights. But with you . . ."

"Brid, we must get back." Caspar found his voice rising in fear. Brid's eyes were changing, losing the natural green of the earth as they caught the brilliance of the sun reflected in the eyes of the verderer. "What of Keridwen and Morrigwen? What will they do without you?"

She turned back to him. "Yes," she said slowly as if fighting an inner conflict. "Yes, we must get back. I have Duir's Pipe." Her voice was faltering and uncertain.

Talorcan held out his hand again. "Yes, and you will give it to me."

Brid looked at him uncertainly. "No, I— Not yet."

Caspar was holding his breath, wondering how he could reach Brid, the real Brid that he knew. Here in this forsaken land, she was almost a stranger to him and he felt lost without her. His thoughts were interrupted by a noise from the stairwell. Talorcan stiffened and withdrew abruptly from Brid, a flash of guilt tightening his features.

Cloaked in pale green, Uilleand, the most lissom and sweet smelling of the High Circle glided into the room accompanied by Duir, in contrast the most sturdily built figure of the thirteen. Caspar found the stout ealdorman strangely reassuring and Brid whispered in his ear, "Duir and Uilleand; oak and honeysuckle."

Caspar didn't need her to tell him; he already knew but her tutorial manner was at least familiar and so reassuring.

"My Lady Uilleand. My Lord Duir." Talorcan bowed.

"Chief Verderer." Duir looked at him solemnly, his deep voice rumbling in the confines of the room. He vaguely reminded Caspar of his father. "What are you doing here? You have more pressing tasks. We agreed they were to be left alone to contemplate their fate." He smiled gently at Caspar, Brid and Fern. "Come, tell me, have you been comfortable?"

"No," Caspar replied succinctly.

While Duir looked saddened at this response, Uilleand nodded sympathetically. "Well then, we shall make you comfortable – since your stay here is likely to be a long one," she added ominously, in her sweet silky voice. "You must be starving; come, join us for the feast. You will find it pleasant. Verderer, see that these creatures are brought to the feast."

Creatures! Caspar thought. Are we know more than animals to them?

The two members of the High Circle glided towards

the door but then Duir turned unexpectedly. "I will have my Pipe."

Talorcan, who had been standing stiffly to attention, relaxed the moment the door was closed. "Huh! They always think they know best. The feast indeed! All prisoners should be left entirely to me." He glowered at the closed door.

Caspar fixed him accusingly. "You want the Pipe for yourself and are using Brid to get it."

Talorcan laughed. "I don't care about the Pipe. The Pipe is nothing, its powers limited. I want her!" He pointed at Brid. "And if she has the Pipe, she may yet escape me." He smiled and said ominously as he left, "She is very beautiful and I won't let her leave. Ever!"

Later, a troop of Talorcan's verderers escorted them to a great hall. Vast beams arched over their heads and elaborate candelabras swung on gold chains from heavy crossbeams. There were candles everywhere, their flickering light bringing tapestries to life so that the animals stitched from scarlet and emerald, copper and bronze threads seemed to run within the forest scenes around them. The middle of the hall was dominated by a vast table of polished elm. Around it innumerable carved chairs, studded with silver, seated a host of laughing verderers and their women in brilliant array, all feasting on exotic fare. The High Circle looked down at them from a raised table at the far end of the hall.

The diners were served by other dazzlingly beautiful people of their own kind but as Caspar came closer, he noted amongst them one or two brown- or black-haired men with plain, unremarkable eyes. They looked pained and weary, their skin pocked with sores and cuts that wept as they stumbled around the table. Men! Mortals like himself, used as slaves, he thought with revulsion – and fear.

Despite his anger towards these people of the Otherworld, Caspar found his mouth watering. Roast duck, jugged hare, saddles of venison, honeyed hams, marchpane and fruitcakes, suet puddings, fine breads, sparkling wines, creamy thick ciders – and apple cake. Caspar adored apple cake. He looked at the festivities before him; the beautiful ladies, dressed in the glorious natural colours of bluebell, daffodil, field pansies and bryony, dancing and singing. They floated to and fro from the kitchens, carrying silver dishes of desserts and puddings, and pewter platters of savouries. Caspar's eyes lingered on the salmons dressed in pastry crusts and the tartlets and flans. Cook would have been amazed to see all this, the young nobleman thought ravenously. He was starving.

Fern shrieked in horror as a plate of venison, in fact a roasted saddle, the juicy meat glistening on the ribcage, was carried past his nose. "How could they?" he screamed hysterically. Brid clutched at his hand and put a protective arm around his shoulder.

"Come, you three will sit at the high table with the ealders," Nuin pleasantly invited them. "I'll see we have no venison." She stroked a ring of plain, long-shafted keys that she held in her hand while eyeing the Pipe clutched determinedly by Brid. Caspar was reminded that the ash tree bore seed pods resembling keys.

One of the High Circle took Caspar's hand and whispered in his ear, "Come and sit by me." She was slender and her eyes were exquisitely sorrowful. Caspar glanced at the sash across her shoulder. She was Saille, the spirit of the willow. "Come, tell me why you think you should go home when, by rights, you should be here. You cheated death at the jaws of the wolf. Tell me what is so important that we should break the rules for you."

"Because if Brid doesn't get home and find her successor,

the Trinity is lost and the people will forget the worship of the Great Mother and they will destroy Her."

"So, you do not ask for yourself? In fact, you give me no reason that you should go back at all. It is only the lady who needs to return," Saille surmised.

Caspar hadn't thought of that and he felt tears welling up inside as he grieved for his lost life. "It is true. I can give you no reason why I should go back," he said honestly. "But Brid must."

Saille nodded her head thoughtfully. "You are in pain, child. Drink of the sweet drink, eat of the sweet food and you will forget the pain. It is always hard for humans when they arrive here. They spend so much of their lives hiding from the truth of their wants and desires so that, when they pass on, the unbridled passions bite deep into their souls. It hurts me to see it."

"Where are they?" Caspar asked. "Where are all the people? I can see only ealdormen and verderers and only a handful of men serving."

"Apart from the ones that are below the castle of Abalone, the rest are in the forest of course. Everyone must go to the forest. Some take a long time on their journey and others hurry to move on. All must pass through the dangers of the forest before they reach Annwyn."

"What about the ones below?"

Saille nodded sadly. "They are the ones that seek to cheat death. They remain here beneath the castle until the Circle decides what is to be done with them or they are finally persuaded to move on of their own accord."

"And how long does that take?" Caspar queried.

"Persuasion is quicker. The verderers are very good at it. And it's difficult for all of us in the High Circle to agree. Even if most of us do, Straif never agrees. I lose track of the time. It's hard to tell here exactly how many years . . ."

"Years!"

"Oh yes, years. Tens, hundreds maybe."

Caspar was near despair.

"You see," Saille continued, "what we offer them is perfectly reasonable. All we want is for them to move on to the next part of the cycle, where they will find perfect bliss and forget all before being reborn, but some won't accept it. They would rather suffer miserably in the hope of returning to their loved ones – or their enemies. I don't understand it myself but I can't bear their pain. I think they should go back but Phagos and Nuin never agree with me. Now eat; eat the food and drink the wines and ciders. You will find them all more wonderful than anything you have ever tasted."

Caspar was eager to accept but was silenced by someone treading on his toe. He was about to exclaim in protest when he realized it wasn't a radiant-eyed, golden-haired being of Rye Errish but a man, though he was strangely dressed.

He stared hard at Caspar as if willing him strength. "Don't y' eat the food. Don't y' touch the apple wine."

"Don't be silly; you'll feel better." Saille used a motherly tone.

"Don't touch it. Y'll never get home if y' touch it," the man warned.

"Verderers!" Saille shouted. "Verderers, take this creature away! Take him away!" Her voice was like the soughing wind rising in tempest and several of Talorcan's men were soon at her side, marshalling around the poor man. He was dressed in old fashioned cotte and hose and could have stepped out of any period of the last seven hundred years. His accent, though, was familiar to Caspar: Torra

Altan but with a lilting breathiness to it like Brid's but more so. "Don't be touching the vittles, sir," the man shouted over his shoulder as he was dragged away. Brid had a piece of apple in her hand but froze just before it touched her lips. She was seated next to the prickly, stern-looking member of the High Circle. Tinne looked furiously at her. "Eat it, girl, eat it!"

Brid stood up. "No! I will not." She held the pearly Pipe in her hand, ready to put it to her lips by way of threat. "And if you won't listen to us, I will send your Pipe into oblivion, where you can never find it. I am One of the Three and I have the power to do that," she menaced.

Caspar prayed they wouldn't call her bluff but at the same time smiled. At last! This was more like his Brid. But then Talorcan was not in the room to confuse her.

"You've tried to trick us," Caspar said more loudly than he had intended, "with enchanted food." He flung the platter in front of him across the table, spilling wine and milk everywhere. "We didn't mean to be here at all. You promised us a fair trial."

He was disgusted. There was no order, no sense to this place. Nobody seemed to care. He should be dead, but he didn't feel dead. He had so much to live for. It was all so important and these immortals were playing with him, just fooling with his life as if he were no more than the fluffed seeds of a dandelion clock being blown apart by their careless breath. It was a horrible world and Caspar wanted to go home. He felt cheated of his life. "If we give you Diur's Pipe, will you let us go home?" he demanded.

"Why of course not, dear," Saille said smoothly, looking at him as if he were quite absurd. "Just calm down and taste the apple wine. I know you will like it. All the pain will go." She held out a gleaming goblet to him and, with no thought for his safety, Caspar hurled his fist at it and sent the metal cup clattering to the ground.

"Verderers!" Straif shrieked. "Have this creature restrained. Saille, what do you think you are doing? You always cause trouble with your over-sympathetic ways. You should know by now that it's no good feeling sorry for people like this. They are thieves of time, outlaws. And we are here to see that they obey the law. The divine law must be enforced; they shall all be punished."

"Not without trial," Duir said solemnly. "They must all undergo a trial."

All thirteen of the High Circle fell into arguing amongst themselves though Straif was still yelling for the verderers. "Have this slave taken away with the other one," he demanded.

"You've no feelings," Saille rebuked him. "You didn't give him enough chance. It's you that causes trouble."

Caspar found himself being dragged after the man in the cotte and hose. Without bothering to use the magic of their tongues, the green jacketed verderers roughly manhandled them to a spiralling stairwell that led down into the dark. Talorcan, holding a firebrand in his hand, did nothing to repress the pleasure on his face. "It is well that you will be out of the way. It will be easier for me to speak to the fair lady who so despises you."

"Brid has never despised me," Caspar vehemently shrieked back as he was forced to descend the stairs.

After a while he thought he heard the sounds of running water but soon realized he was wrong. It was the wails and sighs of men and women weeping in utter despair, unable to forget, unable to hide from their own emotions. He shuddered. This was the underworld of the afterlife; hell itself.

The steps ended in a long, dark corridor hewn out of

the rock. They were marched along it, passing many grilles set low down in the wall, from which emitted the groans and screams of trapped souls. The man who had been at the feast seemed to have difficulty walking and stumbled regularly, clawing at the walls for support. He was breathless by the time they finally halted. Talorcan produced a bunch of keys and unlocked a grille, no more than two foot high by two foot across, and shoved the man down and through it. He then raised his voice and compelled Caspar onwards along the dark tunnel.

CHAPTER FOURTEEN

Foreboding filled every fibre of Caspar's body. Beneath his feet the stone was hot and the air smelt of burnt fat. Choking as acrid fumes caught the back of his throat, he could see little for the fug of smoke and steam belching from pits and furnaces. Sweat drenched his back and dripped from his forehead.

A shriek of agony cut through the groans. The hairs on the back of the youth's neck bristled. It was a scream of horrible pain. Caspar fought to stop himself quaking. From the sound of tortured screams and roaring flames, he knew what lay ahead.

The sweltering interior of the domed dungeon was illuminated by a vast firepit, the flames licking at the feet of men hung from chains about their wrists. One was spitted through the gut and was being slowly twisted over a leaping tongue of fire. His fleshed sizzled.

Jerking his head away in revulsion, he found himself looking directly into a prisoner's eyes. The man's body was stretched taught, his ankles lashed to a post and his arms stretched away from him to a winch. Caspar had never seen one but he knew what it was. The rack. The man's face twisted with agony as he was dragged by his dislocated arms then swung up into iron hand cuffs and hauled by a series of pulleys onto the bar above the firepit. Caspar knew what that smell was now. It was the charred smell of burning flesh. The black greasy slime that coated the floors and walls was melted human fat.

Bile spumed into his throat but he bit back his revulsion and braced himself against the sight, substituting his shock with anger. He swung his clenched fist at Talorcan's beautiful face. The chief verderer caught the blow with the lightest touch of his open palm and laughed at the youth's weakness.

"You will never hurt me, frail mortal. But you will come to know and respect my power, and the suffering I can inflict. I shall show the fair maiden your pain. She will know that only she can stop it by giving herself to me. It is cruel, I know," he said lightly, "but necessary to break her spirit."

As Talorcan swept away, two verderers grabbed Caspar's arms and dragged him, yelling and struggling, towards a leg-shaped iron brace. He jerked his body away from the device. It had clamps that would grip his shins and spikes that were designed to be screwed down to split the bone. A verderer grabbed a clump of his hair and forced him to look up. Through the smoke he saw a viewing gallery cut into the side of the cavern high above his head. Behind its wooden railing, Talorcan was gripping Brid's hand. She stood emotionless, unable to do anything but watch as the chief verderer's song embraced her.

Their eyes met and Caspar's heart sank. In that instant he saw the inevitable. Brid's shield of defiance against Talorcan would break to save him pain, and then the enchanting song would enter her soul. She would be lost forever. To save Brid, he must not scream. He struggled to close his mouth on his yelling, shaking with the effort, but as they stripped away his boots and the brace was clamped down over his naked leg his control snapped. Iron straps clamped his other leg at knee and ankle.

His scream went on as they turned the screws though he fought to find his self-control. He was losing himself to fear. The screws tightened. His body from the hip down was a fire of agony but he knew he must endure the pain. The perfect white ridge of his curve-stressed shinbone was clearly defined through the horribly tight skin of his lower leg. The sight focused his pain. He tried to pull away from it and clawed at the verderers around him but it had no effect. He squirmed and wrenched, arching his back, but he could not distance himself from the pain of the brace. He bucked and strained and hit out wildly.

Just before he knew the bone would shatter, they reversed the screws and released his leg from the brace He gaped at them breathlessly like a landed fish.

"More!" Talorcan's terrible voice swelled out from above.

Caspar froze. The sharp-pointed screws wound down towards his flesh. His skin puckered and whitened under the pressure. His body went rigid as he anticipated the pain.

"No, no!" Brid yelled. "Don't! Don't do it to him."

Caspar gritted his teeth and looked up at her, willing her not to give in, not to give up her soul on his behalf. He needed strength and didn't know where he would find it. He was afraid, horribly afraid. He could see the vein-raising fear and pain on the other tortured men around him. He had to close himself against the pain.

As they wound the screws down on his shin another set of blunt off-set screws pressed from the other side, slowly pushing the centre of his shinbone out to the side. It would break his leg. The pressure was slow to build up and he saw the bone curve before the more acute pain of the sharpened screws pierced the skin. He yelled and flung his body rigid, fighting against the agony. He had to fight and could never beg for mercy. If he begged for mercy Talorcan would not give it unless Brid yielded her will to him.

He screwed his eyes up tight, biting at his lip. His lower leg was curved now to a splintering bow. His control snapped. He screamed and writhed, his mind a red wash of pain.

Far off he heard Brid's entreating cries.

Suddenly the pressure was released. The impenetrable golden eyes of the verderers stared unemotionally at Caspar's agonized face. "It hurts. We promise you it will hurt more. Give in. Ask for mercy. It's for your own good. You must move on through the cycle."

Caspar breathed in gasps. A human voice, gruff and rumbling in comparison to the musical tones of the verderers, called out, "Don't listen to them. It's lies, all lies." The man looked too exhausted to struggle as he was dragged towards the flames. His feet already claws of bone where the skin had been scorched away, rasped over the stone floor.

Caspar clenched his teeth and shrieked as the verderers closed the screws again. Jolts of pain shot up through his leg. Rather than writhe and wrench as he had done before, he pulled his body taught and glared fixedly at his leg. Focusing his will, he began to shout, "Torra Alta! Torra Alta!" the battle cry of his forefathers. He was a noble Belbidian, more he was heir to Torra Alta itself and he would not shame the proud blood of heroes that ran in his veins. "Torra Alta!" he shouted over and over, rage not fear filling his voice and lending him power.

Blood gushed over his shin, hiding the bow in his leg. He fought from his mind the image of the bone snapping, as he knew it would. He filled his mind instead with the thought of all the hundreds of souls that had nobly given their lives for the great castle in the Vaalakan war. "Torra

Alta!" he shouted in their name, fighting to retreat to the steel chamber of his inner mind that could not feel pain. He looked up at Brid and screamed the words. "Torra Alta!" It was all he could do to show her that he had the strength to bear this.

The pain receded, distanced from his mind, as he glared at the limb, telling himself that it was outside of him, not his essential self at all.

But Brid never saw his expression of defiant courage. A verderer was already leading her away while Talorcan smiled down with satisfaction. He signalled to the torturers below and they reversed the screws on Caspar's leg.

They pulled his leg clear of the brace, and hauled him upright, blood puddling around their feet. Caspar threw back his head and yelled again in violent defiance, "Torra Alta!" his voice filling the chamber.

From somewhere at the far end of the cavernous room came an echoing cry steeped in loathing.

Through the smoke and writhing mass of tortured souls, Caspar saw the man who had returned his yell. A metal brace circled his head, obscuring his face and, as Caspar watched, the verderers brought down a hinged metal plate attached to the circlet and thrust it into the man's mouth. Two screws gouged into the prisoner's tightly closed eyes. The scream that shrieked from his gagged throat, filled Caspar with dread. Talorcan's blazing gaze swooped down from the gallery above to fix for a long moment on the man as Caspar was dragged out of the fearful hell chamber and back into the cell-lined corridor.

One of the low grilles in the wall grated across the stone as it was drawn aside and Caspar found himself looking into the eyes of the man who had warned him not to touch any food. Still clutching his bow that the verderers had never bothered to take from him, the youth was shoved forwards and kicked through the opening. His legs screamed with pain as he dragged them across the dry floor into a circular cell. A shaft of ghostly sunlight lit the centre of the cramped space and the merest breath of air wafted reluctantly down. The grille slammed shut behind him and Caspar was left with his pain and the man in the cotte and hose.

The man looked from his leg to his face, acknowledging his pain with no more than a nod. Caspar was relieved when he didn't mention it. Somehow the terror of the torture chambers was less real if it remained unspoken and this man seemed to understand that.

"Y' didn't eat it, did y'?" he asked almost roughly.

"Eat what?" Caspar gasped for breath and slumped onto the beaten earth that formed the floor of the cell.

"The food at the feast."

The youth didn't reply for some while as he heaved himself up against the wall, trying to ease his pain and struggling to gather his strength. He wanted to cry. Finally, after wrapping his bleeding leg in a strip torn off his shirt, he risked looking into the man's face. It was an open honest face. He was fair skinned with straight thick hair the colour of dried cloves. His hazel brown eyes were typically Belbidian but they seemed saddened and weary as if from carrying a great burden.

"No." Caspar's voice trembled slightly. "No, I didn't eat the food."

"Good."

"Why, was it poisoned?" The thought of food took his mind from the sickening throb of his leg and he was reminded of the gnawing ache of his hunger. "I've got to eat soon or I'll die with hunger."

The man smiled. "Y' can't die here. We're dead already. At first the hunger is terrible but y' grow no weaker from it."

He was about to ask more when the grille was pulled aside and Saille's sympathetic face peeked through the opening. Her golden eyes looked at him sorrowfully and she held out her hand to offer Caspar a coiled strip of pale bark. "I'm sorry," she said simply before withdrawing.

"Eat it," the man advised. "'Twill heal any wound inflicted here in Rye Errish save the wound of y'r death. Eat it. There ain't no danger. The rest of the ealdormen only allow Saille to give it us so that the verderers can inflict new pain."

Caspar recognized it at once as the pain-relieving willow bark but was surprised at how much more potent it was here in the Otherworld. Shortly, his leg no longer troubled him. Gingerly, he pushed himself to his feet, hunching his shoulders in the cramped hollow of the cell, and was surprised to find he could put weight on both his legs. Tormented by his worry for Brid, he impatiently circled the room, stooping to the grille on each circuit to grip the bars with his fists. Other than the weak light from the shaft overhead and the glow of flickering torchlight falling in patterned squares through the grille, it was dark. He was beginning to feel claustrophobic.

"Sit y' down, sir," the man begged after a while. "There's nought to settle on but the hard floor but y' might as well sit and try and calm y'rself."

"How can I calm myself? I have to find Brid and get her home. How can you be so complacent?"

"Sit down, sir. Y'll be here a long time so y' may as well. And stop shouting. It does nought but hurt my ears. Y'll get control of y'r emotions again, one day at any rate, but y' may as well be sat down."

"No! I will not sit. How can you just sit there?" Caspar snapped.

"Because I've been sitting here, on and off, for the better part of four hundred years by my reckoning."

Caspar froze and stared hard at the man. He looked no more than forty. His hands were rough and the fingers of his right hand callused in the way of all archers. "Don't be ridiculous," he snarled.

The man shrugged as if not caring whether the youth believed him or not, which Caspar found infuriating. He continued to march up and down at a most agitated pace and stamped in front of the other prisoner but without arousing any further reaction. Finally, Caspar sat down and twitched at his sleeve. The man was studying him curiously.

"Well?" Caspar demanded. "Are you going to explain all this madness?"

The man raised the corner of his mouth in a sad half smile. "Y'll go mad here if y' don't calm yourself. What's it y' don't understand?"

Caspar shrugged. He didn't want to mention the chamber full of roasting flesh and tortured men. He couldn't trust himself to speak of it in case his lips trembled or his voice cracked.

The man studied him and then began to talk in a comfortable and slow manner as if giving Caspar a chance to gather his self-control. "They do this to make y' give up on y'r life. This Otherworld is the place where souls confront their lives, a place of cleansing before they move on. It's like saying farewell to y'r entire life before y' move to the next one but sometimes people like myself – or evidently y'rself – won't let go. Then the verderers use force to make us relinquish our self-will so as we'll move on into the forest. Of course, some of us are more stalwart than others."

"But I can't move on! I have to get back," Caspar sighed.

"Aye, and so do I," the man replied solemnly. "But I haven't yet figured on a way. Though I will."

"What's your name?" Caspar asked.

"What's a name matter here?" the man retorted. "How can a lost soul have a name?"

"Well, what shall I call you then?" The Baron's son was feeling agitated. This conversation was getting nowhere.

"Abelard, bowman to Baron Pellidore of Torra Alta." He saluted Caspar. "And by the insignia on y'r tunic y're of that noble lineage. I saw the mark of the dragon when I first spied y' in the great hall and that was why I bid y' not to eat."

"Pellinore!" Caspar was staggered. "He was the baron who built the outer ramparts and the north tower."

"Yeah, that's right. We were just building the new tower when it happened." Abelard had a faint smile growing on his face. "They completed it then, did they?"

"Oh yes," Caspar assured him.

"And we did win the war? I have heard from others that we did but it makes me feel good to hear it again."

"Which war?" the youth asked.

Abelard frowned. "The one with them treacherous Ceolothians."

Caspar laughed. "Yes, of course we did. We've been allies for centuries."

Abelard spat. "Never trust a Ceolothian, sir – whatever treaty they've signed. But tell me how I address y', sir?"

"My name is Caspar. I'm the only son of Baron Branwolf, Lord of Torra Alta." He nodded in greeting to the man and held out his hand.

"Lord Caspar," the archer saluted.

Caspar frowned and proffered his hand again. "Please, Master Spar, if you will. Most everyone calls me that. Or just Spar, seeing I'm master of nothing here," he added with a humbling sense of realism.

Abelard gripped his hand. "Well, what Baron Pellinore would've thought if he knew his successors were so familiar, I don't know," he said with humour. "So, Spar, what brings y' here?" he asked, seemingly comfortable with the friendly form of address.

"We were attacked by wolves and Brid found a pipe."

"A pipe?"

"Yes, a pipe. The High Circle was very upset about it," Caspar explained.

Abelard stared at him, sudden comprehension and excitement freezing his features. "The Pipe of Abalone? Lord Duir's Pipe?"

Caspar nodded. "And what brings you here?"

Abelard sighed and swallowed hard as if choking back tears. "The Ceolothians had made several attacks on the castle and Lord Pellinore decided to make a sortie into the canyon, to take the action to them as it were, and drive them back. We could see they were digging earthworks just out of range and we were fearful of them tunnelling forward to undermine the castle."

Caspar listened intently. He had read about the episode in the Barony's history many times but to hear the account from an eye witness . . .

Abelard continued, "The young Prince Galland had come to see action under Baron Pellinore, seeking to learn how to be a leader and such like. Lord Pellinore instructed me, as a trusted bowman, to keep a special eye out for the young heir. I was honoured of course . . ."

Suddenly it dawned on Caspar and he looked at this simple man in a new light. Abelard! He mulled the name over in his mind. Abelard the archer, it couldn't be!

The ancient Torra Altan continued, "I were right by Prince Galland but the Ceolothians were dug in much closer to the Tor than we realized and I didn't know it had happened until I saw the arrow stuck in my chest. I were right before Lord Pellinore as it happen, though I didn't realize that were the way of it until I thought back on it later. 'Twere even a moment before the blood started to ooze out and I felt the pain. I couldn't breathe. I knew then my lung were pierced and I were drowning in my own blood. Still clutching my bow, I fell from my horse."

There were tears in Abelard's eyes and he paused a moment to draw breath. Caspar watched him peel back his coat to expose a pustular, festering wound, its edges blackened where the skin had necrotized. "The verderers say they can heal it and take away my pain but if I let them mend the wound of my death, I would be accepting my death and forgo my right to return. The verderers can mend any wound." He sighed regretfully.

"I know," Caspar muttered, looking at his leg.

"Prince Galland were only a lad, a young lad and he didn't deserve to die that young. I saw the Ceolothian take aim. I could have shot him. It was an easy shot and I struggled to pull back the string but I just couldn't do it. I was weakening too fast. The prince died and happen I followed him a few minutes later. There were no other casualties. The last I saw of earth was Lord Pellinore as he cut into the Ceolothian force. If only I'd had the strength, I could have saved Prince Galland."

"But I still don't understand. Did Prince Galland mean so much to you that you would endure four hundred years of torture for him?"

"Not the prince himself, no," the ancient Torra Altan admitted. "But the old king had no other direct heirs. It meant the throne would pass to his cousin."

"Sorstan," Caspar concluded running through Belbidia's history in his head.

"Yes, and if I'd done my job Prince Galland would have succeeded."

Caspar frowned, wondering why this was so important but then realized. Of course, Sorstan was from Ophidia. Sorstan's mother had married an Ophidian and he had been brought up in that country, which had long since turned away from the Great Mother to the one true God from the south. It was Sorstan that first introduced the New Faith to the noblemen of Belbidia. "The root of the decline of the Old Faith," Caspar said heavily.

Abelard sat with his back to the cold beaten-earth walls and looked glumly at his hands. "And y' see it were my fault. I was there to look after him." He sat forward. "All my fault. I need to go back and put it to rights. I have been to the High Circle seven times now and each time they've ruled against me. They say there are only two reasons to go back."

"There are?"

"True love is the first," Abelard told him. "The love that be above death, the love that melds souls so that even in death they cannot be parted. For them the bliss of Annwyn is unattainable unless they pass on together. Unfortunately," he said more dryly, "the second reason Phagos describes as 'a just cause' and they find that too difficult to agree on. At my last hearing the Circle decreed that there were no special reason for me to return, but how can I face the Great Mother when it's my lack of action, my failings that be the cause of the decline of the faith? How can I face Her? I cannot go on."

"So you didn't cheat death?" Caspar asked suddenly shuddering. He was talking to a man that had truly died, and of a horrible wound. He had died slowly, drowning in his own blood as it filled up his lungs. He must have fought death until the very last second and even now he was fighting it after passing on to Rye Errish. But Abelard seemed very much alive to him.

"No, I didn't cheat death but when I arrived here, I would not stay in the forest to be guided by the verderers along one of the many paths to Annwyn. Instead, I escaped and braved the woods to get back to the castle. I begged to be given audience and here I've been ever since. I cannot go on because I ain't reconciled with my death. They've offered me food so that I might forget and tried coercion to make me go on of my own free will but I cannot. I must go back. And when I saw y'r insignia, sir, I felt it my duty to warn you. So . . ." Abelard opened his hands in a simple gesture that indicated he had bared his soul. "Here I am. Y' know all of me. Tell me of y'rself. Why must y' go back?"

"Because I came with another – One of the Three, Brid the Maiden. And if she dies now, we will not find her successor. The Crone's health is failing fast and the faith is held together by trembling threads after a decade of persecution. If we lose the Trinity now the world is ruined."

Abelard looked at him speechlessly for a long hard minute, his mouth gaping and his hands dropping weakly to his sides. Then a fire seemed to light up behind his eyes and his whole body stiffened with energy. "Now I know why I am still here! The Great Mother has Her design in all things. I cannot return to put things right in my own time but I'm here to help now at a time of greater need. We must get her home. Y' say y' have the Pipe of Abalone?"

"Brid does, but she doesn't know how to use it."

"It's not how you use it, it's where you use it."

"But she played it to get us here," Caspar objected.

Abelard waved his argument aside. "She didn't. The Pipe was merely returning home to Abalone, to Duir's ring of oaks, of its own accord, and it simply brought you with it. To direct its power is too difficult for us mortals, however learned, unless we reach a gateway between the dimensions. There are points in the universe where the divide between the two worlds is no more than a thin veil. It's like if y' want to go from one room to another it's easier to go through the door than to pass through the walls. The Pipe is a key to open the door."

"How do you know such things?"

"I've been here four hundred years. Nigh on six lifetimes. Happen a man can learn a lot in that time. I've shared this here cell with a great many souls, learned and otherwise, even a shamaness who knew more than any of them. But the man that was already here when I arrived was an old Druid. He said there was only three artefacts that had the power to enable souls to pass between Rye Errish and our world: Duir's Pipe, Nuin's Keys and the Druid's Egg, Necrönd. Lord Duir controls the Pipe, allowing the verderers to move between the worlds. The High Circle need no such instrument of power since they are the only beings able to cross the divide at will. Nuin's Keys unlock the door in the throne-room. It leads back to the world of the living and many are instinctively drawn to it. And Necrönd belongs to the world of man and is in his precarious guardianship."

Caspar shuddered at the mention of Necrönd.

"We have to get the Pipe. It's our only hope of getting the Maiden out of here," Abelard continued. There was a sudden glow to the man's face as if at last the cloud of utter despair had left him. "If I can do this and see her safely restored, I won't no longer need to go back."

A cold finger of truth crept into the youth's heart as he realized that he didn't have to go back either. It was Brid that mattered. He, like Abelard, was already dead.

CHAPTER FIFTEEN

Hal galloped to the middle of the column, pulling up alongside the two princes to point out the circle of vultures hanging ominously in the sky to the north-west.

"It's a little of the road but still too close for comfort. Renaud, what say you? Shall we give our horses a chance to stretch their legs? We ought to investigate this matter in case there's something that poses a threat to the princess."

Prince Renaud looked at him askance and then hastily turned to Hal and Ceowulf. "You will accompany me and Prince Tudwal while we investigate this matter. Lord Tupwell," he called forward to the Ovissian, "I'm leaving you in charge with Lord Hardwin." He never dropped their titles, which Hal found irritatingly formal.

The Torra Altan's eyebrows rose at this arrangement. The more he thought about it the less he liked it. Any number of roving robbers could be lurking in the woods that dotted the landscape to either side. Escorting the princes meant leaving the princess and her dowry extremely vulnerable. Of the six knights, only Tudwal, Ceowulf and himself carried swords, lances, spare javelins, battle-axes and throwing knives; Tudwal even carried a mace. The three of them were almost a private army in their own right while the rest of the escort party was armed only with short swords and pikes.

Was Prince Renaud distancing himself from the wagons so that, if a crime were committed, no one could point the finger of blame at him? Hal wondered what part the other Belbidians might play and surreptitiously eyed Tupwell who was busily strutting up and down, pompously displaying his authority. Hardwin rode at the head of the column, still fussing over his torn silken hose. Hal remembered how it was Hardwin who had been so long in the woods during the race and reminded himself that it was often the quiet ones you needed to be wary of.

"I don't think this is a good idea," he muttered to Ceowulf. "It leaves Princess Cymbeline too vulnerable."

"I think you're being over cautious," Ceowulf said reasonably. "We're leaving forty men behind and Cai and the Ceolothian troops are well-trained. King Dagonet likes to keep his men well prepared."

Despite Ceowulf's reassurances, Hal was still disturbed by the arrangement. He might be outranked by all but Hardwin but he wasn't going to keep quiet. "Sir, this is preposterous, leaving only Hardwin and Tupwell to guard the princess!"

Ceowulf groaned, "Well done, Hal. Ever the diplomat."

Renaud looked thunderously at Hal. "The decision is mine! My brother will hear of your insolence on our return."

Hal knew that he, also, had much to tell King Rewik and so was not in the least intimidated. "By taking both Ceowulf and myself with you to investigate what may well be nothing, you leave too few knights to protect the ladies. Or is that what you want?" he accused; his voice tightening to a viperous hiss as he held Renaud's gaze.

Renaud stiffened in surprise, almost shock. He blinked nervously. "What are you talking about? Are you calling me a coward? Do you think I'm afraid to stay and protect the ladies without you?"

This was not quite the reaction that Hal had anticipated. But then Renaud was clearly far cleverer than he had credited, even hoodwinking his brother into allowing him to escort his bride. He was about to publicly accuse Renaud of complicity until he caught Tudwal's wide-eyed stare. No, he would not shame the name of Belbidia by accusing his prince in front of the Ceolothian. It would dishonour himself and his country.

"No, sir, never." Hal quickly altered his tone.

Prince Renaud looked utterly relieved. "Good, good I'm glad to hear it."

Hal continued, "I would never accuse a Belbidian of cowardice. Any one Belbidian is as brave as ten Ceolothians. It was proved in the Ceolothian wars four hundred years ago."

He had expected Prince Tudwal to hotly uphold Ceolothia's honour but the man's attention was fixed on the black cloud of ravens hovering above the escarpment to the north-west, and was clearly eager for action rather than squabbling over politics.

Tudwal waved his hand irritably. "When you Belbidians have stopped bickering, I wish to proceed. Of course, I can go alone; I need no escort. I am a Ceolothian prince and fifty bandits would be no match for me." It was a large boast though not necessarily a false one. Hal had seen this man in the tournament ring and he was both determined and skilful with every one of his deadly weapons.

Prince Renaud smacked his lips together in indignation, opening his mouth as if to speak but then turned his horse and headed for the escarpment.

"What are they trying to prove?" Ogden muttered as Tudwal spurred his horse after the Belbidian prince.

Hal did not want to be left behind by either of the

princes but neither could he leave without first ensuring the princess's safety. "Stay close to the wagon," he ordered Ogden and then lowered his voice. "No matter what Hardwin or Tupwell order, make certain you are not diverted away." He gave both nobles a hard stare before setting off after Ceowulf and the two princes.

Tudwal and his black dogs had long since overtaken Prince Renaud, the blocky quarters of his war-horse powering him up the rise towards the gathering of mocking ravens and beneath the circle of vultures high in the sky. Wary of danger, Ceowulf was making a more cautious approach, standing high in the saddle and casting his gaze to either side. As Hal caught up with him, the seasoned knight advised, "No need to sweat the horses up and blunder in like fools."

Hal nodded in agreement as they broke over the bare rise to join the two princes. Together they looked down as the ground fell sharply away from their feet. Though the climb to the ridge had been steep and the horses were blowing heavily, it was nothing like so sheer as the drop to the river below them. What they had presumed was a flat-topped escarpment was actually a narrow spine of rock, whittled and thinned by Ceolothia's winds and rains, the sides so steep that little more than Ceolothian bog myrtle and moss clung to its slippery rocks moistened by the spray from the river. Tudwal's steaming charger climbed the air, snorting and plunging despite the prince's efforts to steady it.

Prince Renaud looked anxiously at the two Belbidian knights. "What kept you so long? We need to keep together. You have your sword ready, Lord Hal?"

Perhaps he really is afraid, Hal thought but reminded himself not to be duped by the prince's ability to act.

Tudwal disappeared over the crest. They could barely

hear anything above the caw of the birds that dipped and swooped in and out of the gorge. Hal followed Ceowulf's experienced example and paused on the crest of the ridge, allowing himself the opportunity to survey the scene. The gorge was steep, cut by a fast-flowing river thick with silt. He had never seen such a big river. It writhed like a caged animal in the tight confines of the sheer-sided valley. On the opposite side of the gorge, several black-mouthed caves holed the sheer rockface some dozen feet above the water.

Below him on this side of the gorge an overhang of rock jutted out over the water. The twisted carcasses of three Ceolothian black bears were slumped on the ledge of rock that moved with flickering shadows where the vast carrion birds passed before the sun. He couldn't tell whether caves also undermined their side of the valley because of the steepness of the ground.

Instinctively he knew something was wrong. Both he and Ceowulf paused in their tracks.

"What are you waiting for?" Renaud demanded. "We can't let Tudwal think we're cowards."

"Indeed not, sir," Ceowulf shouted above the roar of the river and the cackle of birds. "But we don't want him to think we're fools either." He looked upwards at the circling birds that dived and mocked at the carcasses without ever once landing. "Tudwal hasn't stopped to think what's keeping the birds at bay."

Renaud looked up in sudden alarm and for the first time Hal thought the man couldn't be pretending; he looked genuinely afraid. But a Belbidian afraid! The idea was preposterous.

Ceowulf nudged his black charger forward, an old stoical stallion, long used to campaigns. Hal admired the animal as, with great trust, it obeyed Ceowulf and began the descent. He knew Ceowulf didn't like heights but the knight had visited Torra Alta enough of late to be accustomed to such sudden drops. He sat well back in the saddle, easing his weight off the horse's forehand and allowing the stallion plenty of rein to pick its own way down. He looked round at Hal and gave him a self-effacing grin. "I never told you. I thought it was too early to say yet but Cybillia's pregnant. And here I am sliding down scree towards dangers unknown!"

Hal shouted his congratulations but Ceowulf had already turned to concentrate on the descent. Allowing a safe distance between them, Hal followed on. The going was steep and Secret grunted with the effort, but Hal had every confidence that she would cope and relaxed into the saddle; she was a Torra Altan mountain horse after all. He turned around once to see Prince Renaud still hesitating on the brink, his face ash white as his mount shied away from the drop. Hal wasn't surprised. He had seen many brave men pale at the precipitous drop from the top of Torra Alta.

"Prince Tudwal, be careful!" Ceowulf shouted but even his deep voice was drowned out by the roar of the river.

The Ceolothian prince had reached the platform of rock and had already dismounted. His steaming horse stamped and snorted at the end of its reins. He made towards one of the great carcasses and prodded it with the tip of his outstretched sword. From above the prince appeared almost as square as his horse. Not a tall man like Ceowulf but he had a deep barrel chest and legs as solid as tree-trunks. There was no denying his strength – nor his bravery. He hadn't flinched at the drop from the ridge and approached the bears without hesitation. He briefly frowned up at the vultures and ravens above before prodding each bear in turn.

Hal could see that the Ceolothian's instincts troubled

him. Why did the ravens shy away from the bloodied flesh that oozed from the bears' gaping wounds? Hal knew the only explanation but evidently it had not yet occurred to the Ceolothian.

He could smell the bodies from here; the sickening thick smell of blood and the pungent aroma of a full gut torn from the belly. Whatever had killed the bears was still lurking close by.

Hal's first thoughts were of trolls. Only a troll or, more likely, several trolls, would be capable of tackling three fully grown bears. That or wyvern . . . ? Ceowulf was sniffing the air and raised his light lance from its slot in the saddle and shouldered it in readiness, while shouting a warning to Tudwal.

Again, Hal glanced up behind him, wary of attack from above but also curious as to Prince Renaud's movements. The tall lean Belbidian, however, was still dithering on the brink of the gorge, turning his horse back and forth along the skyline as if hunting for an easier descent. Hal brushed away all thought of the prince, returning to the more immediate unseen threat, knowing that danger lay in an unfocused mind.

But it was so difficult to centre his thoughts with all the noise. The mocking call of the ravens filled his brain, hassling his mind and scattering his concentration. He fixed his eyes on the broken bodies of the bears, their contorted carcasses lying as if only recently discarded by some giant hand. He squared his shoulders at the thought of wyvern. Perhaps this would be his chance to kill one. He picked his way carefully down to the rocky ledge and noted that there were indeed caves on this side as well, just a little way to his left above the dead bears.

"What took you so long?" Tudwal demanded angrily as the Belbidians approached.

"There has to be some predator here," Ceowulf yelled above the clamour of the torrent.

"I'm not afraid of bears," Tudwal sneered. "Where do you think my saddlecloth came from? I'd killed bigger than these before I could count."

Hal didn't doubt it. Tudwal was brave to the point of being stupid.

"It might not be bear." Ceowulf looked towards the black gaping mouths of the caves in the side of the gorge above their heads.

"I know these animals; they were probably killed by other bears quarrelling over the fish in the river," Tudwal told him casually.

Ceowulf dismounted to examine the carcasses, prodding them with his boot that came away with a thick sticky coating of blood. "Not been dead long; they're just beginning to stiffen. But I think you may be right; they certainly weren't killed by wyvern. They wrench their prey limb from limb." His nostrils twitched. "There's a strange smell but it's not pungent enough for wyvern."

Hal, too, could smell it, an unpleasant stale aroma.

"Wyvern!" Tudwal snorted in laughter. "Never yet met a man who's even seen one. All fairy tales. But then you Belbidians like your fairy tales, don't you?"

Ceowulf didn't rise to the taunt but nodded calmly towards the nearest cave. A streak of blood smeared the rocks at its mouth. "Whatever it is, it's in there!"

"Pagans! So melodramatic," the Ceolothian prince sneered and began to climb towards the cave.

"He's a fool," Ceowulf said as they scrambled up over the blood-smeared rocks after the prince. Hal wiped his hands on his thighs and drew his sword. The sun caught the magnificent blade, highlighting one of the blood-red runes that decorated the fuller. Greedily, he drank in the feeling of invincibility with which it imbued him. The Belbidians stood shoulder to shoulder as they stared into the black of the cave.

"There's nothing here," Tudwal announced, looking back scornfully at the sight of Hal's raised sword. "What are you so afraid of? I guarantee there's nothing here at all." He marched deeper into the blackness.

Hal was inclined to think him right as he peered into the dark of the cave. Its muffled interior smelt mustily of bear but it appeared entirely empty. Only there had to be something here. His skin prickled as he waited for his eyes to adjust to the gloom.

"We'd better be getting back," Tudwal snorted.

Hal stared in horror as a dark shape swallowed the prince's outline. He tightened his grip on his sword. "What in the blessed name . . . ?"

The air rang with the clash of metal as Tudwal's steel breastplate crashed into the cave wall. Rolling over, he sprung to his feet, his sword tip up and ready for action. He was well-trained, practised in the jousting arena and his mind was quickly focused but he still stumbled back as the cave was filled with a bellowing roar.

It was not the thunderous roar of a dragon, booming like a distant storm, but more the bellow of an enraged bull mixed with the snarl of a tiger. But Hal could see no sign of the hulking creature. It had vanished like a shadow on a bright crisp night when a cloud slips across the face of the moon. He blinked and took a step forward. Whatever it was must have retreated, menaced by the threat of their armed presence. Despite the screaming birds crying out in frustration for the moist fresh meat below, his confidence swelled. The great runesword would protect him, whatever it was. He took another step towards Tudwal and offered his hand to help him up.

"Don't move, either of you," Ceowulf hissed.

"It's gone back into the cave," Hal dismissed his warning. "The best thing we can do is get out of here and back to the princess. Bears are never friendly but it's not really a matter for us to deal with at the moment."

"It wasn't a bear."

Ceowulf's voice impressed him with its icy calmness. Slowly he inched the tip of the great blade up before him.

It came at them again, fast and furiously, bellowing in enraged anger. It swiped at Tudwal and lashed sideways at Ceowulf but kept warily away from the reach of Hal's sword. The three men retreated step by step, cautiously keeping behind the runesword. It was too dark to see, which unnerved Hal far more than the deathly smell permeating the caves and the echoing howls of rage, and he had no idea what might, at any moment, stab out of the blackness. Still dazed after being flung against the cave wall, Tudwal stumbled. Ceowulf gripped his arm.

"Don't break your concentration," the big Caldean warned Hal.

"I can't see a damn thing!" Hal complained as he strained his eyes to pierce the gloom. But he knew it was there.

They reached the mouth of the cave and stepped back into the grey Ceolothian daylight. Hal knew instantly what he saw though he had large satisfaction in hearing the great Prince Tudwal suppress a yell of terror as they beheld the apparition. Hal had seen the like before and was better able to steel his nerves against the sight. It was a bear, standing to at least ten foot as it swayed towards them, but it wasn't whole. A feathered outline as if made of cobwebs glinting with early morning dew, the light glancing off the insubstantial surfaces, emerged before them. The huge ghostly bear staggered forward on its hindlegs, its coat of thick shaggy hair trembling in the translucent image.

Its roar, however, was not that of a phantom and Hal roared back to bolster his courage. The bear halted for a moment and then, with a clumsy swinging stride, swayed forward into the full sunlight, the rays piercing its body. Its forepaws lashed out and Hal heard a rattle of chains. He couldn't quite make it out. Then he saw it, a length of chain dangling from a studded iron collar about the beast's neck. The end of the chain trawled on the cave floor. Hal dragged his gaze upwards towards the dark face and leapt back as the definition hardened into more solid form. Two heads snarled at him from above the shoulders of the huge black body.

One head was the natural head of a bear, the mouth wide open as it bellowed its hoarse roar, large teeth gnashing viciously. The other head was smaller and twisted, the eyes offset and unfocused. Though it, too, roared and gnashed, its teeth were crooked and loose. The skull was concave as if it had been beaten with a club. Claw marks around the neck showed where the animal had tried to tear away the mutilated head. That at least accounted for the stench.

"A beast of Necrönd! This is Spar's doing!" Ceowulf exclaimed. "What in the name of the Mother has he done?"

Though the knight's words might have seemed inexplicable, Hal understood them. The only way such a monster, a ghostly two-headed bear could appear, was through the necromantic power of Necrönd. And only Caspar had access to it. Clearly the youth had persisted in ignoring the priestesses' warnings to leave the Druid's Egg alone. Hal resolved to strangle his nephew when he got home.

He brandished his sword as the beast made a sudden

half charge. It retreated, snarling. Hal refocused his mind. Clearly this bear had died at the hands of man. Nothing else could have wielded a club to crush its head like that and Hal read the hatred in its eyes as it beheld them.

"Great Mother, let me send this creature back to the depths of the Otherworld," he prayed, preparing to strike with the runesword, but the Ceolothian prince was suddenly in his way, thrusting boldly forward.

"Out of my way!" he demanded angrily and flung his javelin at the bear. It swept clean through the beast and clattered uselessly against the rocks at the back of the cave.

"Get back!" Hal shouted. "Tudwal, get out of the way!"

"I'm a Ceolothian. We're not afraid of bears – however many heads they've got."

Tudwal was evidently determined to show his prowess and pressed forward, chanting the Ceolothian battle cry. Rather than rushing forward in attack, his ugly dogs snivelled behind his legs. For a brief second Hal thought of Trog. He wasn't as found of the animal as Brid was but he knew Trog would have launched himself at the bear without hesitation. For all his faults the dog was fearless. These mongrels lacked the spine of the Ophidian snake-catcher.

Tudwal was shouting in Ceolothian, evidently ordering the dogs to draw the bear's attention so that he could make his attack, but the dogs remained cowered.

"Stand aside! You'll just get yourself hurt," Hal bellowed as Tudwal slashed with huge strokes at the beast, the black metal of his sword almost invisible in the semi-darkness.

"I'm not standing aside for a Belbidian. Weak, lily-livered race. Your prince is probably still cowering at the top of the slope. And I'm not standing aside for you, the lesser son of a lesser baron."

"Ceowulf, get him out of my way," Hal cried in desperation. "Do something before this fool sends us all to the afterlife before time."

Ceowulf tried to come up on the Ceolothian from behind but couldn't get near him for the long thrashing strokes of Tudwal's sword as it swung in great arcs about him. The prince yelled and lashed forward again, his sword sweeping clean through the apparition. But this time the two-headed bear lashed back, the membranous outline of its claw swiping across Tudwal's chest. Though the shape was barely real, the cut was vicious enough. Claws screeched across the smooth steel of Tudwal's breastplate and raked into his neck, ploughing up a single furrow in the soft flesh. The force lifted him from his feet and hurled to the ground, his hand springing to his torn throat as he rolled over. Ceowulf wrapped his arms around the prince's legs and struggled to drag him clear.

Hal strode forward alone, the stench of the bear's breath thick in his face. "Great Mother," he prayed, "send this creature back to the world where it belongs." The bear's crushed head, with its concave skull and squashed eyes, was alert, the rotted eyes swivelling towards him. He stifled the moan that pushed at the back of his tightly clenched teeth.

He had to get close enough to strike yet there seemed no sensible way of doing so. He closed his eyes, for a blind second summoning his courage and letting the strength of the Great Mother well up from the solid rock at his feet to infuse his body. He rushed the beast like an enraged child, the words of Torra Alta's battle song howling from his mouth.

He thrust and stabbed without risking a backstroke with his blade for fear of allowing the bear time to make a strike with those vast curving claws. He aimed high for the neck where the hide was thinnest. He heard the screaming chime as his blade struck the iron collar and swept straight through it. Though the beast was no more than a shimmering outline in the darkness, his muscles jarred as if he had hit the bole of an oak. A spurt of blood burst onto his face, momentarily blinding him. He flinched away but the sword had found its mark, severing the vital artery that fed the two brains.

The animal staggered, stumbled and was gone. Other than the pool of blood seeping into the cracks in the cave floor and merging into further dark pools, there was nothing left except the broken collar. It rolled and rattled on the stone before eventually coming to rest. Though Tudwal still clutched at his neck he was recovered enough to take in the scene. All three of them gaped at the iron ring and the length of chain, though all were too exhausted and dumbstruck to do or say anything for a full minute.

Hal wiped the blood from his face. He was eventually aware of a difference in the noise from outside the cave: the caw of the ravens had changed. He looked out to where they squabbled and fought on the ground for strips of intestine dragged from the dead bears.

Tudwal looked stupidly at his blood-covered hand. "I don't understand," he muttered at the Torra Altans. His show of bravado and anger had evaporated.

"It wasn't of this world," Hal tried to explain, "but a beast banished to the Otherworld. Somehow it has returned." He didn't add that the only way such a beast could appear was through the power of Necrönd and that his nephew had been the only person to wield its power in aeons.

"You're talking like a madman." Tudwal spat in disgust.

"Well, you saw it for yourself," Ceowulf defended his countryman. "The bear was an apparition, a shadow. It wasn't wholly formed."

"Bah! Creatures from the Otherworld! You're not expecting me to believe your pagan fairy tales?" Tudwal sounded disgusted.

Hal had some sympathy for the man. He had himself once believed only in the one God of the New Faith and a single life that led to heaven – or hell. All the same it was folly to deny evidence beheld with your own eyes.

"You saw it," he said as Tudwal brushed away his offered hand and pushed himself to his feet.

"Yeah, some kind of devil. And I've heard about the devil wolves that are swarming out of Torra Alta. It seems that wherever you go, you pagans bring with you the creatures of the Dark Lord."

Hal didn't know what to say. He had to admit there was much truth in the Ceolothian's words.

Tudwal dabbed at his neck with his hand and looked disgustedly at the blood. He bound the wound with his kerchief but refused to let either Hal or Ceowulf look at it. He sat down again, breathing hard and shouted at his dogs who were sniffing and whining around the dark stain of the bears' blood.

Ceowulf disappeared into the back of the cave but came out mumbling to himself and then stooped to pick up the strange metal of the bear's collar. He looked at the design and frowned. "Never seen the like. Must be Ceolothian though," he said, "judging by the scrollwork. It looks like the same patterns that decorate Castabrice's city gates."

Tudwal didn't bother to look at it. "No doubt. We have many bears for entertainment. Such a beast with two heads would have been worth a fortune. My father paid a substantial price for the huge beast at his palace, but one with two heads . . ."

Ceowulf raised his eyebrows in distaste but kept his

thoughts to himself. "It's ancient though. No smith in the last thousand years would use iron rather than steel to shackle a bear."

"It was coming home," Hal said in sudden realization. "It must have been captured as a cub and taken to the cities for the man's amusement, where perhaps it ran amuck and so was killed with a club. One of its heads had definitely been clubbed. Then when it was somehow recalled to this world it must have made its way home to the place of its birth. Yes," he decided with conviction. "It returned to this cave only to find it taken over by a new family of bears. He was merely protecting his home."

Tudwal finally got to his feet once more and stamped towards the dead bears. In a mad rush of anger, he took a swipe at the scavenging vultures with his sword and they scattered into the air. He looked at the mess of dead bears on the rock, already heaving with flies, and took one of his throwing axes from his saddle. With vicious strikes, he hacked off their claws. Hal wondered at this act but then realized that the prince wanted the claws as trophies. His dogs looked on and slobbered avariciously.

"We'd best get back to the wagons," Tudwal said when he had finally finished his task. He pressed at the wound on his neck as they began the steep climb.

Prince Renaud was peering anxiously over the edge for them but, the moment Hal caught his eye, Renaud tilted his nose into the air and looked away. Hal wondered what excuse the man would give for failing to follow them down the steep slope. He expected some laughable excuse; that he had spotted a different danger and gone to investigate alone or that his horse was lame, but Hal was taken aback by the prince's apology.

"I'm sorry, I just couldn't face the slope," he said sincerely as the three sweating horses heaved themselves and their riders to the top of the climb. "Prince Tudwal, you've hurt you neck. Are you hale?" he asked with concern.

Tudwal disgustedly muttered about ghosts and a mutant bear. Prince Renaud looked at him in disbelief.

Tudwal growled in his throat. "I'll not talk of it. We should get straight back to the princess."

The two princes cantered briskly southwards to rejoin the slow-moving wagons but Ceowulf held back and Hal realized that he wanted to tell him something.

"If there was one bear there might be more," he warned. "We need to be vigilant."

"It's Caspar's fault, isn't it?" Hal said almost apologetically, feeling ashamed for his nephew.

Ceowulf gazed anxiously westward across the rough-hewn hills to the thick dark mass of the forest in the far distance. "Perhaps. But would either of us have resisted the lure of its power any better?"

CHAPTER SIXTEEN

Only a beggarly circle of light, diffuse and stuffed with slowly falling dust, penetrated the deep shaft to the dungeon of lost souls; but it was enough. Caspar had seen their doomed faces. Through the narrow grille came the soft sounds of their hopeless misery, their groans, their sighs, the sonorous knock of their lonely movements. He saw they knew no escape from the dungeons of Abalone.

He crawled to the back of the cell and slumped his head into his hands, unable to judge time as it slipped through his fingers. He sat there for what may have been hours or even days until the actions of the ancient archer roused him from the darkest depths of gloom.

Abelard was rattling the iron grid that spanned the low opening to their cramped cell. Caspar grimaced at the purple wounds encircling the man's wrists and ankles. The skin was raised and knotted with swollen cysts that seeped a foul-smelling liquid.

The old archer caught his eye and self-consciously rubbed at his wrists.

"They caught me trying to escape once and clamped me in irons for longer than I care to remember. Not even Saille's bark could fully heal me. That Talorcan took pains to beat me too. It's his job, y' see. He has to make sure the souls go through the forest and he was herding us across when I escaped back to the castle, thinking I'd find me a way to slip through Nuin's door but all I did was get me back to Talorcan's torture chambers. He's in charge of too much, if y' asks me."

"He's done something to Brid," Caspar said coldly as he stared through the bars at the pool of light mottling the beaten earth floor. He was impossibly hungry. He wasn't sure how many days he had been down there, listening to the screams and demented moans of the other prisoners. He was no thinner, in fact his body had changed in no way, even the graze he had suffered running from the wolves still seeped blood, yet his hunger was worsening by the moment.

Abelard told him that they were often forced to serve at the high feasts in order to intensify the awareness of their hunger. Caspar could see it was the one thing they all found so hard to bear: the hunger and the thirst. He dreamt of it at night and images of bread and cheese and cool running water constantly played at the back of his mind, making all other thought confused and fuzzy.

"What do y' mean, he's done something to the Maiden?" Abelard demanded after a long pause. "And stop looking through the bars. Listening to the anger of souls who can't accept their death and move on will only drive y' mad."

Caspar dragged himself back into the cramped confines of the cell, its walls rubbed smooth by the years of hunched backs rubbing against it. Huddling his knees, he had to crane his neck to one side to keep his head from pressing against the bell-shaped curve of the earthen roof. He would go mad. He wondered how Abelard had remained sane all this time, especially with the persistent, repetitive beat and moans from the neighbouring cell. All the time they had been there, the inmate had kept up the same series of three notes over and over again.

"'Twere the song he sang as he died. A great composer, a great bard," Abelard explained. "'Twere to be his masterpiece but he died afore it were finished. His king were to pay a thousand gold crowns for it, a wedding gift for his bride. The bard looked all his life to find the world's most beautiful tune then died before it were finished."

Caspar remarked that it didn't sound the least bit beautiful now.

"Of course, it ain't beautiful, Spar." Abelard laughed but not unkindly. "Would the face of the most beautiful maiden on earth be fair if it were cut from her body?"

Caspar thought that the sound of those endlessly repeated notes more maddening than his hunger.

"Focus," Abelard told him. "Y' must focus else they'll take y'r soul. If y' succumb to the madness of self-pity that chief verderer will have y' as his slave. Talorcan has scores of slaves, broken to his will and he loves the power. Y' can see it in his burning eyes, the way he thirsts for it. And happen the Maiden would bring him greater power still if he had her in his grip." Abelard ran his tongue over his dry cracked lips.

"Brid," Caspar murmured in despair. The knowledge of his helplessness swelled like a tumour within his brain. He was powerless to save her from Talorcan's slavery.

Abelard shrugged. "No one knows much about the ways of the verderers or the ealdormen of the High Circle. No one has been here long enough to know." He laughed sardonically. "Immortality. There are many as pray for it but they know nothing of what they seek. I long to join with the Great Mother, to return to her womb and the bliss of forgetfulness but I cannot, not without righting the wrongs that I have caused. Now gird yourself and focus, Spar. Y' must focus. Concentrate on one thing at a time otherwise the madness of forever will overcome y'."

He sighed, drew in a deep fortifying breath and stared levelly at the youth. "Tell me about Brid and Talorcan."

Caspar tried to concentrate. He hadn't seen Brid in days – or was it weeks? In a confused fashion, he slowly recounted his tale, eventually explaining that Fern was still with her. He didn't know what the little horned woodwose could do to help but Fern was all Brid had now. Poor Fern, Caspar thought, staring hard at the cell wall and again finding his mind wandering because of the maddening effect of the bard's monotonous singing.

"Tell me more about Brid." Abelard gently placed his hand on Caspar's shoulders and drew him round to face him.

"I love her," Caspar said simply. "I love her and she's going to marry my kinsman. These past years I'd persuaded myself that I love another but now, here, I can no longer lie to myself."

Abelard took Caspar's hand and patted it. "The truth of y'r life is so very often painful to bear. I know; I've spent hundreds of years trying to come to terms with it, but in the end, I've had to accept life's failings. Life cannot be perfect and y' cannot blame y'rself for such complications."

"But I told May that I love her and now I discover that I don't: I love Brid. I always have and I always will."

"Does she love y' back?" Abelard asked seriously.

Caspar dropped his head into his hands. "No. She might love me as a brother or a friend but never in that way."

"Then y' mustn't torture y'r conscience over it. Unrequited love is a painful love, which in some ways intensifies the passion, but it ain't true love."

"How do you know?" Caspar demanded angrily. "And how can you judge my love?"

Abelard shrugged. He had nothing to lose and spoke

honestly with considered thought. "Happen I've seen many souls pass through and only those with true love ever return. Nuin lets them back through her door so as they don't face the commoners nor the terrors of the forest. The High Circle knows they have true love as their soul ain't able to survive the journey to Annwyn without its other half. Their souls are joined and cannot be parted by death. With unrequited love there is no joining of souls."

"But I do love her," Caspar protested.

"Of course, y' love her," Abelard said gently and uncritically. "She is the Maiden. She is life and nature to you. Of course, y' love her, but y'r souls ain't joined."

"But if I love her, how then can I love May?" Caspar continued.

Abelard frowned thoughtfully. "There are many types of love. Until love is requited, it can't grow and y' could as well call it infatuation. It ain't the same thing as true love. But more importantly, does she love y'r uncle, this young man Hal y' told me of?"

"Why is that important?" Caspar demanded, resentful that his own feelings had been so lightly dismissed.

"Happen it might protect her from Talorcan."

"I don't see." Caspar looked at him intently. For the first time he was able to fully concentrate on their problem and forget his hunger and the maddening noise of their neighbours.

"If she falls in love with Talorcan she'll give him what he wants," Abelard warned.

"What can Talorcan want from Brid?" Caspar asked innocently.

"She has Lord Duir's Pipe. Who knows what manner of mischief Talorcan will undertake with it? Already he gathers those of ill content. Listen to the horrors here in this foul stench of a dungeon. Listen to it. When he finally breaks their will, he does not send all on through the forest but keeps some, mainly those with black hearts, for his own ends." He looked up at Caspar. "I must help the Maiden return to the land of the living to prevent the collapse of the Trinity. Happen all these hundreds of years as the High Circle was right not to send me back since I find that it's now as I am needed." He smiled weakly at the thought of it as if suddenly accepting the suffering he had endured. "But they'll argue for eternity whether it's right to send Brid back or no."

"We will have to escape and—" Caspar began but Abelard laughed before he had finished what he was saying.

"Escape! And to where?! Into the forest? The forest is dangerous. The beasts, the commoners . . . And then there's Talorcan with the hunt to chase us down. If the hunt catches us, we'll lose our souls and never be reborn. We'll be like the poor souls that linger near the gateways where the veil between the worlds is thin, ever hungry to return, trapped in this world of Rye Errish yet able to glimpse the world of the living. Y' don't want that. To be for all time a shadow!"

"How can the forest be dangerous? Surely that's where all souls must eventually go in order to reach the bliss of Annwyn. I thought the journey through the forest was to help us come to terms with our lives so that we pass on cleansed into the next."

"There are things in the forest that no soul would wish to meet. That's why we need the verderers. They guide souls through the forest and protect them from the wild beings lurking in the shadows of the woods – and the commoners. We cannot make it without the protection of the verderers."

"Could we not pretend to go willingly and later escape?"

Abelard smiled. "Clever lad!" His face then dropped. "But what of Brid? She would need to know of our plan and would she agree? What if she won't leave Talorcan?"

Caspar could see this wasn't going to be easy. They sat there for a very long time, mulling the problem through, though it was hard to concentrate for his agonizing hunger.

"Abelard?" he eventually asked.

"Hmm?"

"How do we get a meeting with the High Circle?" The light falling through the shaft was beginning to fade and he could hear the sounds of merrymaking seeping down from above.

"That's easy," Abelard said as if the solution were obvious. "They always fall for it. Beg for mercy. Say as y're ready to move on if only y' can talk to the High Circle. They always allow it though y' always come straight back again when y' start and argue y'r case with them. They take y' straight to the hell chambers but at least y' get out of here awhiles," he said with a laugh. He looked at the youth as if enlightened. "And we must do that. We must beg for the Maiden to be allowed to return. Happen they might accept a bargain. Perhaps if we say as we'll go on willingly, they'll let her return. We could try."

"We have to try," Caspar said urgently. He would never see Torra Alta, nor his mother and father, nor even Hal again. He crawled towards the grille and rattled the bars. "Verderer," he cried into the gloom. The cells echoed with his cries.

"Verderer! Verderer!" came back the crazed mocking yells from those who had lost their minds in the dank dark solitude. Caspar clapped his hands to his ears, trying to blot out the noise. How many souls were down here in these endless dungeons he didn't care to imagine.

"If we could get Brid through the forest to a gateway, she might be able to use the Pipe to return us to the world," Abelard said thoughtfully. "But if we can persuade the High Circle to send her back through Nuin's door, it'd be better. The forest is dangerous."

The verderers came eventually and ushered them out of their cell, taking them deeper into the dungeons rather than back up the long dark corridor that led to the stairs beneath the refectory hall.

"Try not to look into the cells," Abelard warned him breathlessly. The twisted misalignment of his knees meant he hobbled awkwardly and had difficulty keeping up with the smooth easy strides of the verderers.

But Caspar couldn't help looking. Most stared vacantly, but some screamed at them as they passed and one woman, who chewed at the grille of her door, salivating and growling like a caged bear, her teeth virtually worn away, spat at them viciously. Another knelt on the earthen floor of his cell and beat his head against the imprisoning bars, a trickle of blood winding down his face.

Abelard stiffened as the air around them began to warm and Caspar knew they were nearing the hellish torture chamber. The ancient archer rubbed his chin and smiled encouragingly. "They take us through here to weaken our resolve but we are men of Torra Alta," he said proudly.

"Backbones of steel," Caspar assured him, feeling his insides liquefy at the sound of the haunting cries of anguish.

"It helps if y' avoid looking into their faces," Abelard advised. "It'll do y'r soul no good to see their distress and it could take many lifetimes to forget, if y' ever do." Protectively, he took a step closer to the youth though Caspar could not help looking at the writhing bodies that dripped fat from their blackened skin into the spitting flames. A man, waiting for his turn on the rack, met Caspar's gaze.

"He has no fear nor pity in his eyes," Caspar pointed out.

"I know. Most of those here wish to return for an evil cause. Consumed by revenge, hatred or jealousy, they're obsessed by some evil in their past life; their only thought is to return to that wickedness. Until their souls are cleansed, they cannot pass on. These are hard men who have endured endless years of torture. They're toughened by their hatred. Remember their hatred was so vivid that they carried it with them even across the barrier of death."

Despite his stiff bearing, Abelard shuddered as he hobbled past the ankle stocks on the wall. Three men hung crookedly upside down. The stocks were so angled as to hold their shins parallel to the floor so that the weight of their bodies hung from their bent knees, causing them to slowly dislocate as they weakened. Caspar knew now why Abelard had such difficulty walking. Unable to endure the thought, he turned away and his gaze fell on the man in the head brace.

He stiffened; Talorcan was standing right next to the man, watching almost with admiration at the way he silently endured the pain of the screws embedded deep into his eyes. Closer to the man now, Caspar could see his face and hands sprouted dark grey hairs, and his jaw protruded. He had the look of a wolf and Caspar decided that he was metamorphosing like Fern.

The wolf-like man jerked upright and, despite the spikes gouging his eyes, seemed to stare straight back at Caspar. Suddenly he was free from the grasp of his torturers. A throttled scream of hatred escaped from his gagged mouth and his arms flayed wildly with his chains as he lunged at Caspar.

Taken off-guard, Caspar could do no more than duck

beneath the assault as the man's hands raked and yanked at his head, ripping out a clump of his auburn hair by the roots. Three verderers hastily pinned the eyeless man down, while Talorcan looked at him thoughtfully.

"Are y' all right, Spar?" Abelard asked anxiously.

Caspar couldn't respond. Blinking rapidly, he tried to steady himself. As he had been attacked by the frenzied wolf-like man, the image of Necrönd had sprung into his mind. He couldn't explain it.

Abelard gripped his hand fiercely. "Keep y'r mind on y'r purpose. We have to help Brid."

"Yes, Brid," he murmured, turning to see Talorcan nodding in wonder at the way the eyeless man had broken his bonds.

"So much hatred!" Abelard repeated, as they were ushered towards the far end of the chamber where a hole in the wall led to a stairwell.

Caspar couldn't shake off the notion that the man had tried to devour his soul. Aware of a prickling in his scalp, he rubbed at his head, drawing comfort from Abelard as they climbed the seemingly endless winding stairs. At first the steps were cut from the earth, but after a while they were lined with old, rotted timbers, then well-worn stone and finally, as they reached the lower levels of the palace, the pearly marble of Abalone.

Caspar looked back and saw how his feet left dirty footprints on the immaculate surface and somehow felt ashamed. At last, they climbed to the levels of the palace that housed the dazzlingly white stately chambers. Tall marble pillars were gilded with golden threads mimicking vines clambering up graceful tree-trunks. Colourful caged birds sang sorrowfully from the capitals. Caspar looked round at Abelard. "They must be singing of their longing for the bliss of Annwyn?"

Abelard nodded.

"Everyone calls it the bliss of Annwyn," Caspar said quietly as they marched through hall after hall, their footsteps echoing on the cold hard stone. Small elf-like faces peeked out from behind half-closed doors as they passed and, soon, they were being followed by verderers' children who laughed at them and danced alongside gleefully as if they were part of some jesters' act. "But how do they know that it's bliss?"

Abelard frowned. "I asked that same question to a shamaness once, a very ancient woman. She said we don't need proof of the bliss of Annwyn. If you search inwardly you know in your heart that the bliss is there and that, one day, we'll all be joined with the Great Mother. It ain't something you know but something you feel."

When at last they reached the judgement chamber it was empty. The vast, ornately carved wooden thrones were set in a circle in the middle of the hall and looked almost lonely. Brilliant sunshine flooded down from the opening in the vaulted ceiling, giving life to the burnished gold that plated the door mantles, pillar capitals and the thirteen thrones. A sudden blasted fanfare made him jump as the thirteen members of the Circle swept in. followed by a host of verderers who lined the perimeter of the hall. All began to sing, their voices compelling Caspar and Abelard to stand motionless before the thrones.

"Don't resist the song," Abelard told him. "It's possible but saps y'r strength and distracts y'r concentration."

They were bidden forward by Nuin, spirit of the ash. Her soft feathery hair danced about her shoulders and a circle of keys jangled at her neck. She possessively covered the keys with her hand as she caught Caspar eyeing them.

"My lords, ladies," Abelard acknowledged in his thick

Torra Altan accent. "We are here to beg not for our lives but for the life of another."

"Another!" A flurry of excitement ran through the Circle and their fluorescent wings unfurled and buzzed in a soft hum at their backs.

"Whose life do you beg for?" Duir demanded, toying with his tufty whiskers, a ready though dispassionate smile spreading across his broad features.

Abelard watched the ealdorman's changing expression and when he spoke again his voice was soft but insistent. "For Brid, for Brid the Maiden. She must go back to prevent the chain of the Trinity being broken. At the time when she slipped across the divide, she sought the infant that would in time replace her. The Crone is nigh on her time to pass on and, with only one of the three high priestesses left, the faith'll be lost," Abelard explained without fluster.

"She cheated death and we cannot allow her under any circumstances to go back," Straif burst out, thumping his thorny stave on the smooth floor. "Never!"

"We will hear more," Duir interceded. "For this affects us all. She holds the Pipe of Abalone and Talorcan keeps her captive with his song."

"Unwise, unwise," Phagos muttered, fingering his book. "Most unwise. Talorcan has too much power. Is she not already his thrall?"

Duir sighed. "Few mortals can resist the love of a verderer. We of Rye Errish are all marvellously beautiful to them."

"We beg for her life," Abelard interrupted and as one the Circle turned towards him. "If the Maiden dies other faiths, unsympathetic to the Mother Earth, will fill the vacuum and disturb the balance of the world. We gladly offer ourselves for her."

"You cannot offer your souls in exchange for hers because you have already passed over and your souls are under our jurisdiction. You can make no bargains," Phagos informed them knowledgeably.

"But she must go back," Abelard insisted.

Phagos tutted and the sound of his displeasure rumbled around the hall. "There is no must. The only cause that the law is clear about is when two souls are joined in love. Does she have such love, for only then can we grant her return?"

"Most clearly not, since she has fallen under my spell," Talorcan interrupted as he strode into the hall without offering an excuse for his tardiness. Brid followed him, with Fern beside her, the little woodwose clutching and patting her hand.

"Brid!" Caspar cried but she showed no sign of hearing him.

Gone were her plain, stained and worn hunting leathers and, in their stead, she wore a shimmering white satin dress covered in sparkling rubies and a fine pearl-edged veil. She was as beautiful as a rose veiled in dew-dropped gossamer. But it was an alien beauty, so very unlike Brid, who normally shunned such frivolous adornments, her usual decorations being only the torc and circlets of her office, which she still bore.

In one hand she clutched the Pipe of Abalone that she had engraved with binding runes. As she was led triumphantly into the circle, she stumbled as if near blind and clutched fearfully to Fern for support. Talorcan swept the veil off her face and smiled proudly at the Circle. "She is my bride and is to stay here with me in Rye Errish."

Caspar's hopes plummeted into the cold depths of despair. "But, Brid—" he muttered in feeble protest.

Duir was on his feet in outrage. "No! These humans

are creatures of the Great Mother, not the stuff of the sun and stars like ourselves. You cannot deny her the bliss of Annwyn."

"She loves me," Talorcan stated clearly with a wide sweep of his arm to illustrate the extent of the emotion.

"You mean, she has fallen under the spell of your song," Nuin corrected.

Caspar's mouth gaped. Brid looked wan. She seemed faint with weakness as if she struggled with a losing battle and her once brilliantly dazzling green eyes had lost much of their depth of colour and were now tinged with yellow. A faint far-away smile spread across her features.

"See!" Talorcan declared. "I offer her eternal life here as a creature of the sun and her heart is accepting."

"Brid!" Caspar cried helplessly. Though she was standing quite close to him she seemed impossibly remote. "Brid, please, Brid, come back to us. I love you, Brid. I love you."

For the first time she looked up at him, her eyes welling with tears. It was as if she were drowning and no longer had the strength to save herself. Feebly she raised an imploring hand towards him but she collapsed and Talorcan caught her in his arms, her depleted body motionless as he began his song, the sound sweet like honeyed wine. Though she wept and clenched her fists, her lips smiled in surrender. Fern reached up and grabbed her arm, shaking it violently though he could not draw her attention.

Talorcan swirled Brid up into his embrace, her body as lifeless as a puppet in his arms. "I have promised that I will teach her to play the Pipe," he declared. "Think, Brid, what good we can do. Together we can set the world to rights." He licked his lips as if tasting the heady drug of power.

"No." Saille moved gently towards Brid. "Do not listen

to him. Do not play the Pipe for him. He is a verderer, not one of the Circle and his motives are not governed by justice."

"What justice is there when you do nothing but deliberate? There is no virtue in your indolence," Talorcan stormed.

"How dare you address the High Circle in such a manner?" Tinne leapt to his feet, thrusting forward a long arm and lancing a spiky finger at the verderer.

Talorcan smiled confidently and held his ground. "Because now I have control of the Pipe. She will unbind it only for me and then your purpose as the High Circle will be done. I alone shall hold judgement over all that pass through the forest. My people suffer every day, trying to protect the souls as they make the long journey. I will end their hardship. I will rule instead of you squabbling fools. Thirteen is too many. One is enough."

"Careful, Talorcan, she does not yet play the Pipe for you," Nuin warned. "And I still hold the keys."

"Things change. I will shortly hold a second power," Talorcan announced.

Straif laughed. "There is only one other power and you cannot reach that. It has always lived in the world of mortals."

Talorcan raised a half smile and nodded knowingly. "Indeed. But as I said things are about to change. Soon you will all revere me. You are not fit to rule. You have spent too long in the castle and have forgotten what it is like in the forest. My rule will ensure that the right creatures cross into Annwyn and the rest shall remain here or make the final journey to the sun."

Caspar's heart pounded in his throat and he felt sick. Abelard had spoken of three powers. Two of them he could see; the Pipe of Abalone and the Keys of Nuin. The third, Abelard had said, was Necrönd.

Talorcan, as if unconcerned by the displeasure he had generated within the throne-room, turned and placed a tender kiss on Brid's forehead before beginning his hauntingly magical song again. Caspar saw her strength fading. She fought to turn her head away and Talorcan laughed. "Resist me and it will only hurt more." He scooped up her hand, which was still holding the Pipe, and kissed it. "You will sit in judgement beside me and put all wrongs to right. You will be able to prevent such suffering. Remember how you felt thwarted and powerless in your last life? All those powerful noblemen, preventing you from achieving your aim of restoring the balance? Here things will be different. We shall stop the confusion caused by these fools." Tenderly he placed her on her feet beside Fern and with one last look at her beautiful face swept towards the huge double doors. "Verderers, we will leave these fools to their bickering. It is time we swept the forest and gathered the newly arrived souls."

Caspar knew it was lies, knew that Talorcan was deliberately offering the one thing that Brid was too ready to accept; the chance to ease suffering. She blinked at the chief verderer's retreating back and smiled faintly. Her eyes softly glowed.

As the great doors to the judgement chamber slammed shut, Tinne shouted, that he must be punished. The rest of the circle buzzed with agitation, arguing animatedly while Straif muttered that he knew all along that something like this would happen.

Phagos stood tall, coughed and waited patiently for silence. "We cannot punish him. Talorcan is already too strong and his verderers would support him."

Again, there was a great deal of muttering amongst the ealdormen before they were silenced by Nuin. "Then we must bargain with the girl and allow her to go back. We cannot risk Talorcan getting control of Duir's Pipe. She promised she would return us the Pipe if we sent her back."

"The law does not allow us to send mortals back simply to achieve our own aims," Phagos told her, plucking a beech nut from his beard, dropping it to the floor and crunching it underfoot. "We who uphold the law cannot be above it."

"I wish you wouldn't do that," Tinne hissed angrily.

There was silence for a moment and then Straif finally sighed and stood, though more calmly than usual. "We have no choice. She must carve her own fate and make the journey through the forest. All we can do is release her and see if she can reach a gateway on her own."

"She will never escape the commoners, not without the protection of the verderers," Duir worried.

"And Talorcan will raise the hunt to bring her back again," Nuin pointed out.

Straif nodded at Abelard, Caspar and Fern. "She has friends. We can set them loose to protect her. They may make it. Talorcan might not raise the hunt till they are deep in the forest. He'll be some time gathering fresh souls and he's been preoccupied with the dungeons of late."

Nuin swept back her feathery hair and thoughtfully fingered her Keys. "For once, Straif, I will not argue with you. We will set them free and pray they outrun the hunt." She swept elegantly forward towards them. "You must try to understand, fair mortal, this is the best we can do. We cannot use our powers to send you back but we can allow you to use your own wits. If you manage to reach a gateway and have the skill to play the Pipe so that you return to the world of the living, will you then return Duir his Pipe?"

Brid nodded weakly and Caspar's heart leapt with joy as he saw that she was not fully succumbed to Talorcan. He had feared that she would refuse to leave the verderer.

Uilleand coiled her hands through her tumbling hair and looked deep into Brid's eyes and nodded in satisfaction. "She hides no secrets. She will return the Pipe as she says."

Nuin looked relieved. "I can offer little guidance other than warn you not to go south to the nearest gateway. Talorcan will expect that. Head north-west. It is a harder route and trod only by those that need a long journey to come to terms with their last lives but it may give you more time to get ahead of Talorcan."

CHAPTER SEVENTEEN

Pip was giving up hope. For several days he had been sustained by a discovery of runes, but they had neither heard nor seen anything since and his spirits were sorely depleted.

Just after fording the confluence of rivers where the Whitehart and the Sylvanrush met, he had been about to scratch tell-tale marks into the side of a prominent upright stone, when he had seen four distinct runes already scratched into it.

The runes formed the name Spar. He and Brock were immediately sure that Master Spar and Brid had finally tracked them down and were merely waiting for the right opportunity to rescue them. But that had been days ago. He wasn't even sure how many now as they stumbled across the iron-hard ground of southern Vaalaka.

Trog now limped alongside, his head craned round in the direction of home and though he wasn't tethered as they were, he showed no inclination to desert them. Pip was annoyed. He had told Trog a hundred times to go home but each time the terrier had looked hurt and turned his head away. "You wouldn't disobey Brid," he said angrily.

The dog pricked up his ears at the sound of the Maiden's name, stopped and looked expectantly around before sullenly trooping off after Pip and Brock. Pip had begun to resent that Trog remained unbound while he and Brock still suffered the dragging weight of the heavy chains around their necks.

At first the boy had thought that Trog remained out of loyalty to him and Brock but had changed his mind when, every time they stopped, the terrier rushed to nuzzle up against the sack of wolflings. The two trappers had originally used a length of rope to leash the dog but, since he had gnawed through it three times and still showed no inclination to run away, they no longer bothered.

"Go home! Just go home and get help. Go home to Brid," he ordered insistently as they trudged across the broken stony ground. The dog craned his head south-west towards Torra Alta and whimpered before limping on, keeping his nose tilted towards the squirming sack that thumped against the flank of the skewbald pack pony in front.

"I don't know why you keep grizzling on at the dog, lad. It's yourself you should be cross with. It's you that's got us in this situation," Brock reminded him. The old man looked weary and was lagging on the end of his chain and, though Pip had much sympathy for him, he resented his censorship.

"I didn't ask you to try and rescue me," he mumbled sourly. "I'm not taking responsibility for you."

Brock didn't bother to turn his head as he muttered in reply, "When you get older, you'll realize that you and me are both Torra Altans so that makes us responsible for each other."

"I'm my own man."

"You're just a whippersnapper, a whippersnapper with a lot to learn. No man's their own master and, besides that, you've got a great many years to go till you're even a man."

"None of this is my fault!" Pip protested. "I was trying to find Trog. If it's anyone's fault it's his. And he's a wretched disobedient animal because he won't go home!"

Pip relented momentarily as he looked at the dog's swollen leg. Trog was a stoical animal, bred to kill the dangerous vipers that plagued the seas and sandy beaches of Ophidia, and he was fearless of pain. The trappers had seen his qualities instantly. Such a terrier, fiercely compact with crushing jaws and an undaunted spirit, made for a perfect fighting dog but Pip knew it was not really in the dog's nature. He wondered what type of man these trappers worked for, a man that would want a fighting dog. Baron Branwolf dealt harshly with such practices if he discovered them, so much so that man sometimes joked that he treated his dogs, horses and hawks better than his men though Pip knew that wasn't true. He admired the Baron. He was a fine leader just like his young half-brother.

Pip did not, however, hold the same opinion of Master Spar. He liked the Baron's son but he couldn't respect him in the same way; he was too soft with the men and too uncertain of his commands. If Branwolf or Hal had been leading the party he would never have gone off on his own so this whole situation was really Master Spar's fault. And where was Master Spar now? A baron's son should be able to overcome two degraded trappers.

He slowed to draw breath as the ground steepened. Vaalaka was a godforsaken world, he thought. They had long since left the woods behind and now travelled east across the high plateau, dipping in and out of the dry river beds that, come late spring, would roar with the sound of rushing meltwater from the northern ice-caps.

For now, the lifeless ground was frozen solid, the horses' bruised hooves leaving no tracks as they clanged and clattered on the barren earth.

Ryder and Fingers had argued long about whether to follow the main trade route on their return to Ceolothia or keep to the wilderness. Unsurprisingly, Ryder had won. Clearly, he was wary of meeting other travellers as he led them across country where the going was hard.

Pip yelped involuntarily as the brutal chain around his neck snagged tight. He had unwittingly ground to a halt to take his bearings and the skewbald pony ahead had trudged on regardless, taking up the slack in the chain. His jarred neck was sore and made him feel sick. He could think of little else beyond his own misery as they began a slow climb through a wide shallow valley.

"Not so brave as you like to make out, eh?" Fingers sneered at his captives. "And did I hear a little squeak from the brave Torra Altan warrior? Ain't you going to tell us your name yet, Squeak? Or are you too frightened to talk?"

"Leave the lad alone," Brock snarled. He straightened up stiffly and closed protectively alongside the boy.

Despite his pride, Pip was grateful. Still, it vexed him that the two trappers were more wary of the old man than they were of him and he resented Brock for believing he was there to look after him – though, as yet, the old man had achieved nothing except getting himself captured.

Brock continued to grumble at the trappers, "Are you so wretched you can only slink through the dark, picking on dumb animals and a helpless kid?"

Helpless kid! Pip ground his teeth, a habit he had picked up from Master Hal, and peered venomously at Brock in cold silence, before sourly eyeing his precious bow that swung from Fingers' saddle pack.

"The little Torra Altan warrior can't even speak for himself now," Ryder taunted. "So, wolf-lovers, what do we call you, Grumble and Squeak?"

"Don't say anything," Pip hissed at Brock. He had vowed to ignore the men and he most certainly wasn't going to tell them his name, particularly not now since they had called him Squeak. The humiliation of combining Pip with Squeak would be just too much to bear. Guiltily, he found himself cursing his dead mother for giving him such a silly name. Why couldn't he have been called something noble like Ceowulf? Even something plain and solid like Dunstan would have done but Pip . . . How could he become captain of the Baron's garrison with a name like Pip? Captain Pip! It sounded ridiculous.

The Captain of Torra Alta's guard had held his position for many years and Pip had vowed that, when the tall gaunt soldier finally stood down, he would fill his shoes. Pip smiled, suddenly thinking that the Captain was never addressed as anything other than Captain and he wondered whether he too suffered the disgrace of an ignoble name.

By late afternoon they had crossed the windswept plateau and now stumbled down to a stony valley where only spiny gorse and the occasional stunted rowan struggled to survive on the barren surface. The escarpments to either side had sharp jagged crests but they flared downwards in a gentle slope that must once have been tall and steep before the aeons had weathered them, leaving only the spine standing where the flesh had flaked away and sloughed down the sides in broken flakes of black-grey rock to clog the valley floor.

Pip was exhausted though he desperately tried not to show it. He might be young but he was a Torra Altan and any Torra Altan was tougher than a sheep-minding

Ovissian or a foreigner. Copying Brock, he gritted his teeth and kept his eyes down on the broken ground. To his relief, the horses were setting a slower pace, puffing and grunting with the effort of their loads.

Ryder, the short square Ceolothian trapper, his beard entangled with burrs, impatiently cast back towards the dark red glow of the sun that was sleepily heading for its bed on the western horizon behind them. He grumbled and shouted at his comrade, "Get those animals at the rear moving. We need to get over the next pass and into the valley below Flag Scarp before sundown."

Pip winced as the fish-eyed Ovissian whipped and sliced into the flanks of the trailing ponies. "This time we'd better get paid more than a rabbit's paw for all these messages," Fingers complained sourly. "Your schemes do us no good. We should concentrate on selling pelts."

Ryder snarled at him irritably. "It don't pay enough. Not compared to what he gives us."

The troop of kobolds continually trudged in single file after them, always keeping a wary distance from Trog whose self-control was clearly tested by these squeaking creatures. The dog chomped and snapped at them whenever they came close but otherwise his attention was rarely torn away from the wolf cubs. The kobolds were apprehensively studying the two trappers. Pip had noticed that since they had seen the white stag in the Boarchase they had become less co-operative.

"Evil little creatures," Fingers said distastefully, squinting back at them with his wide-spaced eyes and making them titter anxiously.

Ryder grinned slyly. "They'll do as they're told. There's been little rain in Hobs Slack this year and it'll take to flame as well as an oil-soaked rag."

There was a shriek of dismay from the kobolds. Ryder

smirked at them, clearly relishing his power. Surrounded by his snarling dogs, he paced ahead, leaving Fingers to whip on the rear ponies. Their coats were heavy with sweat-encrusted grime from the wind-torn plateau.

Brock looked at him in disgust as he and Pip were dragged behind the last pony. Great wealds swelled across its patterned flank. "What's a Belbidian doing in this evil trade? Have you no self-respect?"

The Ovissian snatched up the rope that tethered Brock's hands and yanked it taut on his maimed wrist. Pip winced on Brock's behalf but the old Torra Altan drew in a sharp breath and let it slowly out. "What are you doing pairing up with a Ceolothian and his foul schemes? There must be easier ways of making a living, even the sunburst ruby mines in northern Ceolothia must be easier than this." Brock cited the infamous pits.

"I used to be a shepherd, like I said, but now I'm a trapper of wolves. It's as pure and simple as that," the fish-eyed Ovissian told him rigorously. "Selling the skins to the Ceolothians is the only way to get a good living at it since Baron Branwolf won't let us kill enough of the vile beasts. Besides it's the moral right I'm upholding here. Belbidia needs to be cleansed of every last wolf. I'm just doing Baron Branwolf's job for him."

Brock visibly restrained himself with a deep breath. "You ain't trappers by trade, neither of you. I've seen your friend fumbling around, trying to skin the wolves and he's no expert."

Fingers looked indignant and inadvertently blurted, "Well, he's better than me."

"Maybe," Pip smartly agreed, "but you've just said yourself that you're a shepherd not a trapper. He's not been trapping wolves all his life otherwise he'd be quicker with his knife. I've seen foresters skin deer in a tenth of the time."

Brock looked at the Ovissian in disgust. "How could you team up with a Ceolothian against your own countrymen . . ."

"Bah! Countrymen! Nobody believes Torra Alta's part of Belbidia anymore. Not for much longer, any road. King Rewik's been weak on you but the other barons will eventually persuade him that something has to be done. Everyone knows that Torra Alta won't last much longer."

Pip scowled and looked back at the darkening ground as they were dragged onwards. They reached the pass just before sunset. Catching the glow of the fading sun, the treeless landscape behind them was a warm golden sea flecked by the dark lines of loose stones that cast out long black fingers of shadow towards them. The valley ahead of them dropped away into a dark world. Pip thought he saw trees in the gloom but it was just too dark to tell for certain. Foreboding dimmed his spirits as they passed from the warmth of one valley into the darkness of the next. The kobolds, however, seemed a little more cheerful, one or two skipping ahead, pointing excitedly ahead into the dark.

"Ceolothia at last!" Ryder exclaimed, lashing out with his whip to catch one of the kobolds across the back of the neck. It squealed and the others postured round, their tangle of arms and legs like a thatch of hawthorn waving in a strong gale. "Just don't forget about Hobs Slack," the man threatened. "I've got friends there and one word, just one word . . ." He looked from the kobolds to the darkening landscape. "We'll stop here," he ordered.

Pip was so tired that he slumped down on a rock and could do no more than watch as his captors prepared themselves for the night. The fire was welcome though it plunged the rest of the world around into a thicker blackness. Ryder rationed out salted venison and smoked boar, giving Trog a very large portion. He slapped the dog and petted him in a clumsy attempt to win the animal's favour.

"I thought you wanted him sharp and vicious for fighting?" Fingers complained.

The man smirked. "Oh, he'll fight all right; it's bred into him. No, I want him fit and healthy and amenable enough to be handled. He's got to look like he can father healthy pups and he'll be worth more to us like that. He's a dog of war if ever I saw one. The way he's so loyally kept by this boy's side and the way he'll keep walking on that leg as though it don't pain him though clearly it must, he's a wardog and, like I said, he'll win me a lot of favour with his personage."

Pip set about the task of feeding the wolflings. It amused Fingers that his captive would work so willingly. Though Pip had no particular liking for wolves, he couldn't bear to think of these poor creatures starving alone and motherless. He knew what it was like to lose a mother and just as Baron Branwolf had looked after him, he would look after them.

"We could set the creature's free so these men can make no money out of them," Brock hissed at him.

"They'd starve," Pip protested. "Besides Brid was looking for a wolfling. She wouldn't want them to suffer."

"But they ain't the right wolflings, are they? She said plainly that we'd know them when we saw them. There ain't nothing to set either of them apart from any other Yellow Mountain wolf."

Pip shrugged. "But they trust me; I can't let them down," he said lamely, clutching the cubs possessively towards him. He was responsible for them and he swore silently that he wouldn't fail them like he'd failed his mother.

Pip concentrated on feeding the two wolflings. It was slow work chewing the meat up fine enough for them to swallow but the boy persevered though he became increasingly irritated by Trog's constant licking of them.

"You're like an over fussy bitch," he told the terrier as he spat out his last mouthful of meat to give to the cubs, reasoning that they needed it more than he did. He then concentrated on the dry crust of bread, which was all he had kept for himself.

"You shouldn't waste all your food on them, lad," Brock grumbled. "Leave them be otherwise I'll have to give half my food to you."

"I don't want your food," Pip retorted. "You worry about yourself. It's my food. I know there's nothing special about these wolflings but they've done no wrong." He couldn't explain that he saw his own life mirrored in theirs since he and his sister had been left similarly orphaned.

Brock shook his head. "That ain't no way to speak to your elder and better."

Pip made a face. "We'll see who's better. I'm going to be captain of the guard one day." The boy couldn't understand why Brock was laughing.

"You? The trouble with you lad is you don't know the place you were born to. No amount of learning's going to change who you are."

Pip grunted in irritation and curled up under his bearskin. The wind had risen and the night was cold so he was more than usually grateful, not only for his cloak and Brock's back against his, but also for Trog's company. The dog was warm and curled up close, his snuffles drowning out some of the irritating snores from the trappers, who relied on the kobold to keep watch during the hours of darkness. It was almost an unnecessary task since the Torra Altans had no means of escape and it would clearly be suicide to try to cross back through the Dragon Scorch of Vaalaka alone without provisions.

Though he was tired, Pip found it difficult to sleep. He wanted to know whom Ryder planned to meet here beneath the head of the pass. He looked up at the black outline of a twisted rowan tree bent over by the prevailing wind at the head of the valley. Standing out alone like a flag, it formed a distinctive silhouette against the moonlit sky, a clear landmark for many miles around, and had evidently given the pass its name.

Pip pulled the cloak up around his neck and watched the stars brighten in the midnight sky. Sleepily, he fell to wondering what his sister was doing and if she was worried for him, and whether the Baron had sent out a search party. He decided resentfully that Master Spar had abandoned his search for them. Though he was tired, he had no problem staying awake because of the thoughts churning in his mind and for the grey wolf cub that kept nibbling at his hand. Aware that the kobolds were also keeping a lookout, he kept his eyes on the ridge. Finally, the half-sized creatures began chattering. Ryder stirred from beneath his hunched mound of wolf skins and kicked his companion.

"They're here," he growled then nodded up towards the ridge. A lone horseman was silhouetted against the western sky.

Pip wondered whether it was just the illusion of looking up at the man from so low that made him seem so unusually thin and tall. His tallness was emphasized by the mean stature of his horse. He was shortly joined by another horseman, his outline less distinctive. Together they broke over the ridge and plunged into darkness, descending to halt twenty yards from the fire. Ryder walked out to greet them. Blinded by the firelight, Pip could see little but the dark shapes of scrub but he could hear the heavy breathing of the horses and snatches of conversation from the men's lowered voices. He nudged at Brock to wake him.

With the wind gusting, the Torra Altans had difficulty overhearing the secret moot.

"They're arguing about payment," Brock muttered.

"I know," Pip hissed. "Keep quite so we can hear."

The wind gusted in a different direction for a moment, blowing away the sound of the voices and the Torra Altans strained to hear anything at all until the night breeze swung round again from the east. One voice was Belbidian but not rustic: it had clear clipped tones like those of the Baron and his family, quite distinct from the regional accents of the common folk. What on earth would a noble Belbidian be doing creeping around here in the dark, conversing with a Ceolothian? It couldn't just be about wolf pelts.

"I'll be glad to tell my brother that you've kept the men driving them south. There's not enough food for them in the Yellow Mountains, not for that many . . . they'll keep on into Ovissia . . . and hooded wolves won't just kill sheep. They'll take the odd man . . . then we will have our excuse . . . They must be brought into submission . . ."

Pip frowned. Torra Alta, surely, they were talking about Torra Alta. He jumped as the wind brought the sound of the conspirators' voices to his ears again.

"Now, what news of the other matter?" the crisp tones of the Belbidian nobleman continued. The wind blew away the low, muttered reply but Pip caught the sharper words of the nobleman again. "Good, you will be well rewarded. The prince will see to that."

The prince, Pip thought, his heart beating hard. Was this some plot devised by King Rewik's brother against Torra Alta? Everyone knew he was ambitious; Hal had told him so many times, but a traitor? Pip puzzled over what he had heard and wondered what to make of it.

CHAPTER EIGHTEEN

The castle of pearly spires grew smaller with every step that Caspar forced Brid to take.

"Talorcan," she whispered and stared accusingly at Caspar. "Let me go. I have to be with him." She dragged against his arm, straining backwards, her gaze frantically clinging to the view of Abalone.

"He's poisoned your mind with his song," Caspar tried to explain. "It's all deceits."

"He promised me eternal life," Brid said. "And the power to restore the balance of nature in our world."

"All lies, Brid," Abelard said gently. "Such power is only for the Gods."

Her yellowed eyes brimmed with tears of confusion. Frantically, she scrabbled at Caspar's arm, clawing with her fingers until beaded lines of blood sprang up on his forearm. He ignored the pain and his distress at her behaviour. All that mattered was getting her through the forest.

"Come on, hurry! We won't make it if you don't hurry." Fern stood on a log fifty yards ahead and was jumping up and down with impatience. "Hurry up!"

Brid sighed. "I need the music, his sweet voice . . ."

"Please, Brid, think of home and what we have to achieve. Morrigwen is dying and the chain of the Trinity will be broken, if we don't get you home," Caspar reasoned.

"Talorcan promised he would put all that to rights for me. With the Pipe we can do anything. He promised!" Brid insisted.

"With great respect, my lady," Abelard said kindly, "Talorcan is not renowned for keeping his promises. He seeks to have power above that of the ealdormen and though the Circle may have its drawbacks such power in the hands of a single verderer—"

"But he wouldn't be alone; I would be there to guide him," Brid objected.

"My lady, I've been here long enough to know that the verderers do not hold their women in very high regard. He merely seeks to use your runecraft – after all you have bound the Pipe with runes."

"You are a liar. You only want to use me to get yourself back across the divide," Brid cried acidly.

This was not the woman Caspar knew and loved so dearly. How could he counter Talorcan's song when all her wants and desires were fulfilled by the verderer's conjuring?

"Brid, you must fight off this cloud. You are not yourself. Remember how you fought the magic before you surrendered to save me from torture. You must fight it again." He wanted to sit down and weep. Brid had always been so utterly resolute in her purpose and he didn't know how to cope with her like this.

"Please, please," Fern cried, running back to tug at Brid's arm. The little creature was distraught. "I have to get back to look after my fawn. I have to, don't you see? Sorrel will be savaged by the wolves. I have to get back. Brid, you are my only hope."

The Maiden's shoulders drooped and she tottered forward as the woodwose tugged her on. "Yes," she said uncertainly. "I must help your fawn but if you could just wait until I have some power in this land, I could send you back without facing the hunt. Talorcan will help me."

Fern started at the mention of the hunt and stretched his neck up, nervously twitching his nostrils.

"My lady, he won't never give y' power," Abelard said heavily.

Fern's body shook as he began to weep uncontrollably. "I must get back. Please help me get back. I must!" he shouted, his uncomplicated mind fixed only on his one purpose.

"The magic works well on Brid," Abelard sighed, turning to Caspar. "Now if she were a simple creature, like Fern there, the tune would drift in and out of her head. Animals, I've learnt, have a great strength in the simplicity of their nature. It makes them so very incorruptible as their needs and wants are pure and straightforward. But a human now . . . Ah, we seek so many things and there's always a promise that'll buy our souls."

"But not Brid's." Caspar refused to believe it.

"Probably most particularly Brid's. As a high priestess she's so many cares, so many things to look after, so many others to care for; yet she's just a girl, just a young girl and her soul must cry out for its own needs. There's no person that ever lived entirely for others. She didn't after all choose her office. Some part of her must resent such heavy responsibilities, must cry out for the childhood lost and yearn to be just herself. She believes him y' see because some small part of her needs to believe him."

Abelard and Caspar each took one of Brid's arms to drag her forward but her determination increased her strength and, though small, she was strong. Caspar was afraid of hurting her. If only Hal were here, he thought. His mind was full to bursting with the complexities of their situation. But to wish for Hal was to wish Hal dead. How could he think such a thing? He wracked his mind, thinking how he could reach Brid beneath the dark clouds of Talorcan's spell.

"Think what will happen if Morrigwen passes on to join us here in Rye Errish before a new Maiden is found," Caspar shouted at Brid as she kicked and struggled.

"Morrigwen," she said the name slowly as if trying to remember. "It's hard," she choked. "Everything from before seems lost in mist. A turbulent haze. Morrigwen . . ."

"Morrigwen will be very angry," Caspar said slowly.

Brid bit at her tongue and seemed to think about it. "Morrigwen . . ." Her eyes narrowed as if she were trying to pierce the grey gloom of her mind.

"She's losing the memory of her life," Abelard sighed. "I've seen it happen before. The verderer's song is so very powerful. Think of it compelling y' to stand or move or jump at their will. It's a simple thing for him to slip into Brid's mind and give her hope of things she wants and needs."

Brid was quiet between them.

"For a plain simple archer, you have many a wise word," Caspar said softly.

Abelard rubbed his free hand across his face and looked sidelong at Caspar. "Spar, you make the mistake of thinking a man is a plain simple anything. Never judge a man by his profession: judge the man by the man, for very few are what they first appear to be. The goatherd may yet be a prince in disguise, learning the ways of his people; and the prince may yet be a pirate seeking to conquer new lands; and an archer is never only an archer. He may be a father, a husband, a friend or a foe and he mightn't have led the narrow life that those who ain't archers might think. Don't judge a man till y've tried to draw his bow."

Caspar humbly muttered his apologies and laughed at himself. So often he had thought people fools for judging him only as a baron's son, thinking him sheltered from life, spoilt and arrogant, without first hearing him speak. Just because a man had property and subjects didn't mean that he felt important. In fact, Caspar had always felt rather unimportant, having always compared himself to Hal who always seemed so very much more capable than himself. Hal would have been able to make Brid forget Talorcan and see the trickery in the false promises. Caspar wondered if Brid would be able to remember Hal any more clearly than she could remember Morrigwen.

"Don't you want to get home to Hal?" he asked, looking straight into Brid's sun-bright eyes. They were frightening, alienating, and he could not hold their gaze. He could not see into them. The glow made them impenetrable and they seemed to stab out towards him.

"Hal . . ." Brid muttered. "Was he . . . ? No, I don't remember."

"She's lost to the song," Abelard sighed.

Caspar tried to pick her up but she was struggling too much for him. Abelard was a much bigger man and, though hobbling painfully because of his crooked knees, he was able to throw Brid's slight weight over his shoulder. Caspar wished he could bear some of the archer's pain.

Avoiding the paths for fear of the verderers, they struggled through the forest, moving too slowly for Fern, who ran circles around them, continually bounding ahead though he never strayed more than four score paces in any one direction before scurrying impatiently back. He was like a sheep dog, Caspar thought, as the little woodwose rounded behind them for the umpteenth time.

Fern's inability to contain his impatience only made his own frustration worse. "You should go on alone,"

Caspar snapped at him, sorely aware that they had precious little time left before Talorcan would raise the hunt.

"He can't go on ahead," Abelard said patiently. "He's never lived as a man and knows only the ways of the herd. A deer abandons the herd at his peril. He'll not go far from us."

Brid was wriggling and kicking, and Abelard stumbled.

"Here, let me," Caspar offered.

Together they carried Brid whilst tripping on bramble briars that crawled through the grass in their springtime efforts to conquer the forest undergrowth. After what seemed to have been no more than half an hour, Caspar was utterly exhausted and shamefully aware that the ancient hobbling archer was bearing most of the burden.

"It'll not take them long to search all the paths leading to the nearest gateway from Abalone. Happen their horses are swift and we'll not have much of a head start. And they know the forest. We'll not make it," Abelard sighed. "Please, my lady, I entreat y', please, y' must help us."

She shook her head and inhaled deeply. "No, I cannot help; it isn't right. We should have been eaten by the wolves. One cannot cheat death any more than call back an arrow after it is loosed."

Fern took her hand and began to shake it. "Please hurry. Brid, please! They will eat my fawn. You must help me. You must."

The yellow in Brid's eyes dimmed.

"The wolves will tear her limb from limb. Sorrel's not fast enough to outrun them. Please, please, help me. I need you to get to the gateway. Take us there. Take us there and play the music."

Brid suddenly ceased to struggle and was glaring at Caspar and Abelard. "Let go of me, you blundering fools," she cried irritably. "I must help this poor creature. Don't you realize that we must get him across the forest before the hunt catches him?"

Her voice was so compelling that they immediately released her. Hitching up her silken skirts, she ran after the woodwose, her dress snagging and tearing in the hawthorns and briars that choked the forest. She irritably drew to a halt and ripped the glistening material off just below the knee so she could run more freely.

Fern leapt with great bounds over the criss-cross of fallen trees and undergrowth that littered their way and it was not long before Abelard began to lag behind. Caspar berated himself for allowing the archer to carry Brid for so long. Abelard stumbled awkwardly on his tortured legs and grasped at Caspar for support. The arrow wound in his chest had opened up and his breath came in rasping bursts.

The blast of a horn wailed out across the forest, its tone distorting and swelling as it swept over them. Fern's neck stretched up several inches and his large eyes blackened. The song of the forest was abruptly stilled by the terrible sound.

"Go on without me," Abelard cried as a second blast trembled the air. "The hunt is on."

"They will go south first," Caspar said, boldly daring to hope he was right and slowing to grab Abelard's arm as he stumbled. "What will happen if they catch us?"

"They'll take our souls," he panted, "so we can never return to our past life nor move on to the bliss of Annwyn. Then we'll populate the forest like the other creatures out there."

"And they live here forever?"

"Unless they're caught by the commoners, of course."

"What do the commoners do with them?" Caspar asked breathlessly.

"They are scavengers and they eat them and then that's it," he said simply between gasped breaths.

"What do you mean that's it?" Caspar asked, slowing further to help Abelard. Brid was now running ahead with Fern.

"Once y' die here, y' no longer exist. There is nothing left of y'," the archer said enigmatically. He was lagging, unable to maintain even Caspar's careful pace and finally stopped and clutched at his ruined knees. "And nor do they return to the glorious burning light of the sun like the verderers do. They simply cease to be. That's what the verderers are here for; to stop souls being poached by the commoners."

Caspar was struck by the horror of it and pulled at Abelard's arm to speed him through the forest.

Abelard's face contorted with pain. "I can't make it; y' must go on without me. Y' must get the Maiden to the gateway."

"But we will need your help to do that. You know the forest and the ways of the Otherworld," Caspar said sensibly though his mind was tossed by other fears. What if he were caught by the hunt? What would happen to Torra Alta? What would happen to Belbidia, to all the people he knew and loved and to the delicate balance of Nature if the Trinity were broken? The New Faith would rise again and the rape of nature would be complete; the forests felled, the fields over-farmed – and all this just when they had started to get some sense of order back into their zealously over-productive lives. Brid had to get home. And so must they all lest they became nothing but dust blowing in the unquiet winds of Rye Errish.

The sound of running disrupted his thoughts. Hooves, he thought, running fast like a horse only lighter. Perhaps a deer, he wasn't sure. To his left a dappled white flank flashed between the trees and then suddenly it was ahead, joining other creatures, all running faster than anything he had ever seen. The galloping herd wheeled through the thick undergrowth, leaping in and out of the bracken, towards a glade where they halted and dropped their heads to graze as one animal. Caspar let go of Abelard's arm and ran on breathlessly until he was at the edge of the clearing. The dappled white animals were everywhere, grazing contentedly in the spring sunlight.

The horn sounded again and Caspar clenched his fists. The beautiful creatures let the noise pass unheeded. They appeared to be the only creatures in Rye Errish that were untroubled by the invasive call of the hunting horn drifting across the rolling forest. Fern stopped momentarily in his tracks to watch the grazing herd. For a moment Caspar thought they were white ponies but, as they raised their heads above the level of the long grass, he saw he was wrong.

Abelard smiled wistfully. "So, it's true. I'd heard of them but never seen them before."

"I've seen unicorns before," Caspar said, "but big lean strong ones with the bodies of powerfully fast horses. These are small and cheeky like goats."

"The shamaness told me they were the souls of the stillborn and newly born infants," Abelard explained. "They are considered blessed by commoner and verderer alike; neither party hunts them. They pass their lives here in the Otherworld as carefree unicorns dancing through the forest until it is their time to move on to the bliss of Annwyn. For them there is no pain of reckoning that the rest of us must go through."

"Come on, come on!" Fern cried from the far side of the glade and set off at an exhausting pace through the dappled shade beneath the lime-green leaves of the beeches. Very soon even Brid began to tire.

"We can't keep up," Caspar gasped as Fern circled back to them. The cry of the hunting horn seemed to be more distant and he was beginning to relax a little, allowing himself to believe that the High Circle had been right about Talorcan's initial movements.

He was just about to congratulate Abelard on his expertise as their guide when the earth disappeared from beneath his feet and he found himself tumbling down a steep bank.

"A river!" Brid gasped with delight. "It's like the Sylvanrush!"

Caspar sat up and watched her, drawing hope from the sight of Brid's awakening awareness as she waded eagerly into the sparklingly clear shallows. Fern was running around in excited circles while Abelard glowered at him in irritation and even Brid waved at the woodwose to keep still. Her movements became more insistent and she covered her lips with one forefinger, warning them to keep quiet. Caspar inched forward, curious to know what she had seen.

A magnificent stag stood not fifty paces from where they were, the shaft of an arrow jutting from its hock and its ribcage heaving with laboured breaths. Its head sagged low, the twelve points of its huge antlers brushing the water and he could only guess that it was the same one they had seen before entering the castle of Abalone. Evidently, it had kept to the line of the rivers.

"He's hurt," Brid cried in dismay and waded out towards the great stag.

"Be careful, my lady," Abelard warned but she paid no heed and, instead, held out her hand to the wounded animal. He snickered, his breath casting ripples in the shallow water.

The forest dimmed as a cloud wiped across the face of the sun and the stag vanished in the umbra. Points of white flickered and sparkled in the space he had occupied. Caspar started, but Brid waited, unfazed, until the shading cloud had passed and the stronger light filtered down through the trees once more. The creamy white stag was visible again but only partially. Below the water that gushed around its hocks and knees, only the silvery outline of his hooves was visible.

"He ain't fully here in the Otherworld yet. He's dying but he's not yet dead. The verderers'll come for him presently," Abelard warned. "We must hurry."

Brid still held her hand out towards the stag's muzzle. "He's hurt," she said softly. "I cannot leave him. Here, old friend, stand." She put her hand to her breast and drew out her herb scrip from beneath her silk dress. She fumbled through its contents and produced a small spray of sorrel, offering it to the stag as a token of friendship. He raised his muzzle and blew at her hand. Brid sighed in satisfaction and slowly reached forward to touch his neck. He quivered and twitched but remained standing, his eyes full of fear.

"I can help you," she soothed in the most lulling of voices, slowly inching around to his quarters.

Too weak to run, the stag slumped to his knees and, with a sigh, fell on his side. He craned his head weakly round towards her as, careless of the water swirling around her thighs, she knelt beside him.

"The arrow's pierced right through the leg and the wound's infected," she muttered to herself as she examined the swollen flesh of his hock. Acting quickly, she reached for her sacramental sickle on its chain about her neck and cut through the wood of the arrow to remove the barb.

"I'm sorry, this will hurt," she warned as she moved to put one hand on the stag's leg and the other on the arrow shaft. Caspar instantly realized she would need help and hurried around the back of the animal to grasp its antlers. He carefully averted his head to protect his face lest the creature suddenly swung at him. Breathing in the stench from its injured hock, he knew the wound must be infected.

Brid looked up at Caspar and he nodded back, indicating that he was ready. With one quick movement and a grunt of effort she yanked the arrow shaft back through the wound. A spurt of black blood jetted from the hole. The stag kicked its leg out stiff and struggled to rise but Caspar forced his weight down on its head, pinning it to the ground.

"Well done, Spar," Brid grunted gratefully as she pressed one hand to the wound and deftly fingered through her herb scrip with the other. Caspar's heart leapt with joy; she spoke as if she knew him. "Hyssop, loosestrife and ribbed melilot," she muttered, twisting sprays of herbs in her hands to extract the juice and mixing them with mud from the riverbank to pack the wound. "Well, it may help." She sighed with partial satisfaction and moved slowly round to soothe the stag's muzzle before cupping her hands into the river and dribbling water into the creature's mouth. "He's been too weak to drink. Water is the best curative of all, and especially with some of Morrigwen's finest bloodwort." She crushed it in her hands and, opening the stag's mouth, eased it under his long, rough tongue.

She mentioned Morrigwen! Caspar raised his eyes in hope towards her but kept his grip tightly on the stag's antlers, fearing that he might lose an eye on one of the great points if the beast suddenly swung its head. After a moment or two the stag pushed his nose towards the river and Caspar released his grip, flinging himself backwards and clear of the vast span of antlers. The stag lay still for a while but then, grunting, heaved himself up and stumbled deeper into the river. He nuzzled the water and then drank deeply. Blood ran freely from the wound in his leg and Caspar hoped that it would wash out the poison.

"Will he live?" Fern asked anxiously.

"The wound is deeply infected and it will take a while for him to fight off the poison but his chances are better now," Brid told him calmly as they moved downstream and out of sight of the beast where she began washing the blood from her hands. She rinsed them in the river before scooping up a mouthful of the cool water. She sipped some and then watched in delight as it trickled from her fingers. "It tastes just the same." She looked at her hand and then the silver torc twisted around her upper arm. Runes engraved on the torc told of her office as the Maiden and One of the Three. She blinked slowly and turned round to look at Caspar with horror. "Spar, forgive me, please forgive me." Hurriedly she felt for the Pipe of Abalone that she had tied to her waist and gripped it determinedly. Her eyes were again a deep forest green.

"It must've been the stag," Abelard pondered. "She touched him while part of him was still in the living world. It must've awoken her mind to the memory of her life."

"He stole my mind!" Brid whitened with the horrified thought of what might have been. "He promised me freedom to do so much good. He was so proud and handsome and there was such joy in his song. Oh Spar, will you ever forgive me for my weakness?"

Brid didn't wait for his absolution and Caspar suspected that it wasn't *his* forgiveness that she sought. She looked quickly at Abelard and Fern and then at the river. "Even if they've gone south, they will catch our scent soon. We must not follow the river; it's too obvious."

"We should head for home," Caspar sighed, looking longingly south-east towards where Torra Alta should be.

Abelard shook his head. "There's no castle there, just the great Tor – and dragons. It's many leagues that we must travel and a direct course will be best, I'm sure."

"We'll never stay ahead of the hunt for that long," Caspar said pessimistically.

Brid took his hands in hers and looked him straight in the eye. "We have to make it, Spar. There are no ifs nor buts; we just have to. Too many people, too many souls depend on us. We cannot let the Old Faith die."

Caspar's spirits soared. The priestess's courage fortified all of them and gave Abelard new strength as they jogged on, brushing through the leafy trees until Abelard sprawled to the ground, his feet entangled in creeping brambles. Caspar gripped his shoulder and hauled him back up to his feet. The three Torra Altans struggled on after the tireless Fern who, despite his greater speed, still berated the frailties of his new form.

"To think I've held humans in awe the whole length of my life and it turns out they'd not be able to keep pace with a new-born fawn."

"I wish you'd stop twitching your nose like that," Caspar complained. "It makes me want to sneeze."

Fern looked him straight in the eye and twitched his nose even faster, a look of complete incomprehension writ large on his long face.

"By the time he reaches the gateway I should think he'll be a regular man – if any man can be called such. Come, we must hurry," Abelard urged. "It's a long way to the gateway."

"How do you know so much of the forest?" Brid asked.

"As I told Spar, I made the journey before. It were in my head that I could pass on to Annwyn to be reborn to a new life where I thought I could take up my cause and do all I could to fight for the Great Mother. I prayed I would retain the memory of my purpose and I even scribed it into my arm, hoping the marks would be there in my next life. Look."

He rolled back his sleeve and, there, etched into his flesh, were the words *Protect the Trinity* written in plain Belbidian.

"It wouldn't have worked," Brid told him flatly. "Only runes will pass through the dimensions. They are the writing of the Gods and only they are unbounded by physical laws."

"Well, it made no odds. I couldn't pass on to Annwyn but for a moment I saw it; the land of paradise," he said with wonder, "but I couldn't step across the great divide because my soul weren't willing to give up on my last life and the Great Mother wouldn't accept me."

"What did it look like?" Brid gasped, transfixed by the thought.

"It's hard to say. Shrouded, like, in a soft swirling mist, the land of the forest seemed to blend into a lake. I couldn't make out a definite shoreline, nor could I honestly say that I saw anything special; it were just like the thought of going home, of returning to y'r mother when y're a child. I could almost smell the freshly baked bread and the wood smoke; could almost hear her voice, soft and sweet. I was tired and frightened and alone and it were as if my mother were just across the divide with arms wide, waiting to embrace me. I wanted so much to go home but still I couldn't leave behind my last life and, though I watched others blend into the mist, She wouldn't accept me till I was truly willing. The mist thickened around me, becoming like treacly mud and I couldn't move forward and had to return. The verderers marched me back and they were none too pleased about it."

"We will make it back," Brid told them decisively. "We have to."

They had left the clear fast flowing waters of the river far behind when they first heard the sound of fast-moving beasts. They pressed themselves into the cover of a holly bush as the ground shook beneath their feet shortly before a herd of boar, several score strong, charged through the undergrowth. The noise passed and Caspar heard the deeper grunts and ponderous movements of a larger animal. He wondered what it was and looked to Abelard for an explanation. The archer was biting his lip anxiously but raised a bright smile when he caught his eye.

"There's no need to worry the Maiden," he whispered to the youth as they hurried on. "It's just a beast of the forest."

Caspar nodded in agreement. The last thing they wanted was to distress Brid unnecessarily. "Is all Rye Errish under forest?" he asked, longing for the sight of open mountains and broad skies.

"All Rye Errish is forest but not all the forest is wood," Abelard said.

Caspar frowned at him. "That doesn't make sense."

"Oh, come on, come on. It's obvious, isn't it?" Fern whimpered, running round to butt Caspar in the small of the back.

"What do you mean, it's obvious?"

"Forest is all land governed by forest law. All creatures know that. Anywhere under the jurisdiction of the verderers is forest, be it heath, marsh or woodland, though it's true that the vast majority is woodland."

"Yes, of course, like the Boarchase," Abelard added,

frowning at Caspar as if bewildered that he didn't understand.

"There are no special laws governing the Chase," Caspar said.

"Ah well, in my day the Chase were kept solely for the use of the Baron. Commoners were banned from touching any of the game. That's why it were called Boarchase Forest and not Boarchase Wood."

"I thought a forest was just a bigger type of wood," Caspar panted.

"No, not at all and in my day the forest laws were very harsh. Any man felling a deer would have his hand cut off so as he could never draw a bow again. And if a man living in the forest owned a dog, he had to have the toes of its hind feet cut off so that it couldn't outrun the deer."

"That's terrible," Caspar exclaimed.

"Doesn't seem so terrible to me," Fern retorted. "All hounds could rot in the dungeons of Abalone for all I care."

"You are heartless," Brid scolded him.

The little woodwose tilted up his head in disgust. "None of you understand the fear of the hounds."

"It's not their fault. Besides it's natural for a dog to hunt. He's a carnivore," Caspar breathlessly argued with the little woodwose. He had no idea that deer were so argumentative.

"I don't see how any creature thinks he has the right to eat another," Fern muttered. "No right at all. I mean, all we want to do is just eat the grass and the tops off a few fresh saplings. Must say I'm very partial to the odd fresh beech or hazel shoot."

"Well, just think what the fresh shoots think about you," Abelard pointed out. "It's no good you going on about dogs when you do the same thing to the saplings."

"That's not the same thing and you know it." Fern looked hurt. "And can't you hurry up? I suppose you eat deer too."

"We all eat deer," Brid told the woodwose gently. "And so will you one day. If we get back to the real world, you'll be a man and a man must live."

"Well, I won't eat deer. I won't eat the flesh of any animal."

"That's all very well in the lowlands where there's plenty of grain and fruits and cheeses but in the high mountains, it's different and you'll have to eat meat," Brid quietly explained.

"Well, I shall eat dog then."

Abelard looked horrified. "You can't eat dog!"

"Why not? What's the difference? Are you telling me that humans hold deer so low that they will eat them and not their wretched dogs?"

"It's not as simple as that, Fern. It's just that man makes friends with his dogs and you really can't eat your friend now, can you?" Brid pointed out gently.

"That creature's really getting on my nerves," Abelard complained as mile after exhausting mile the little woodwose muttered on and on about the treacherous morals of humans.

"It's confusing for him," Brid defended Fern. "He comes from a completely different way of thinking and now he has to see through human eyes. It can't be easy."

"You know, in life there's always one man in every crowd who seems somehow lost and never quite gets things right. You know, always misunderstands the joke or is always waiting for everyone in the wrong place, that kind of thing," Caspar said. "Do you think they are people that have been animals in their past lives and haven't fully made the adjustment to being human?"

"I hadn't thought of it before," Brid said between breaths as they pushed their way through a particularly thick tangle of brambles. "Yes, I guess that's very probable."

"What's a little creature like Fern think he wants to be a man for?" the ancient Torra Altan complained. "He was surely happy being a deer."

"He wanted to kill the wolves," Caspar explained.

"That was before I realized that man was such a hopeless creature," the little horned woodwose muttered bitterly, not even slightly out of breath.

"You're saying that now," Brid argued, "but that's before you've come to learn what qualities you'll have as a man. It's not till you are reborn that you can learn the skills of being human. Haven't you wondered why some babies cry so much? The process of learning to be human is a very painful one."

Fern looked at them all disdainfully before leaping on ahead.

"Quiet!" Caspar warned. He felt the blood drain from his flesh and his knees go weak.

"What is it?" Brid hissed.

Caspar pointed to the deep shade beneath a tree where Fern had suddenly halted. His neck was stretched up in alarm.

CHAPTER NINETEEN

Tudwal examined his collection of claws that he had strung across the front of his saddle. Blood stained the saddlecloth as it dripped from the trophies. Hal was disgusted with him for desecrating the bodies of the three bears and listened sceptically to the prince's claims for their medicinal properties. Hal prided himself on not being sentimental. He was raised in a frontier garrison where, to survive men had to be tough, but it had turned his stomach to see the relish in the Ceolothian's face as he hacked off the bears' claws.

He was relieved to see the train of wagons just ahead so that he could forget the incident but was troubled at the sight of Lord Tupwell thundering towards them. The Ovissian panted his greetings to Prince Renaud but was evidently more eager to talk to the Ceolothian prince.

"Sir," he saluted smartly. "There's some trouble."

"Princess Cymbeline?" Prince Tudwal was instantly alert.

Tupwell shook his head. "She's fine but one of the scouts found strange footprints." He turned to Prince Renaud. "The Belbidian sergeant has been most unhelpful on the matter. He refused to leave the wagons to examine the prints even when I ordered him to do so. I wish to see him most severely reprimanded."

Hal smiled, glad that Ogden had taken him seriously about not abandoning the princess.

Tudwal seemed remarkably calm. "We'll take a look."

"You've had no trouble yourself then, sir," Tupwell asked, ignoring Hal and Ceowulf.

"Trouble? No, of course not." The Ceolothian prince stroked the bears' claws. "No, no trouble at all."

Hal growled in his throat as they rode on towards the long lumbering trail of wagons ploughing through the muddy ground. The teams of horses struggled under the effort.

"You should use Jotunn oxen," Ceowulf remarked. "My father-in-law would be happy to trade, I'm sure."

Tudwal looked unimpressed. "A royal wagon shouldn't be drawn by anything but horses."

"Well, they're hardly being drawn now," Renaud remarked rather sharply as if, somehow, to regain some face after his display of cowardice above the steep slope.

The women seemed startled and even Princess Cymbeline was quieter than usual when she emerged from the central wagon at the sound of her brother's voice. She spoke to him in Ceolothian; some words of concern for his safety, Hal guessed. His command of the language was getting better but it was still not good. She seemed deeply troubled by Tudwal's wound and, when she reached up to move aside the kerchief he had tied about his neck, he caught her hand and squeezed it reassuringly. She fixed on his eyes and smiled but then, as if suddenly aware of the Belbidians around her, stiffened her expression and broke into formal Belbidian.

"My brother, thank goodness you've returned."

"What has happened in my absence?" the prince asked, searching his sister's eyes.

Hal had forgotten just how beautiful Cymbeline was. She stared at Tudwal for a long moment and, while Hal waited for the princess to explain what troubled her, he became briefly absorbed in studying her grace and charm.

She had not one hair out of place and, even in the wan Ceolothian sunlight, it glistened like polished silver. It was twisted into a fine rope and held in place by a spiral of gold thread. Soft ringlets, painstakingly teased into place by her ladies-in-waiting, he presumed, feathered her brow. She had naturally straight hair like her brother, but he liked the ringlets, however many hours it took to create them.

"One of the soldiers found some strange footprints," she informed them. "Hardwin and Tupwell hadn't seen the like before so everyone began to worry, of course; but I think it's nothing untoward."

Tudwal rode off with Cai to examine the find while the wagons rolled laboriously westward, groaning under the weight of the jewel-laden dowry. Cymbeline's gaze followed him for a moment before she continued, "Noblemen, like Tupwell and Hardwin, from the soft plains of Belbidia can hardly be expected to distinguish the print of a hog from a stag." She looked sideways at Hal. "Unlike your fine self, of course."

Her gaze lingered. He liked to think she was admiring his manly figure, array of impressive weapons and the fine carved horn strung from a silver chain round his neck. Made from the long horns of a Jotunn ox, the horn, when well used, gave out a particularly powerful note. Self-consciously, he touched the hilt of his sword.

The princess looked disappointed with her brother, however, when he shortly returned. His pale eyebrows rose meaningfully as if to tell her to keep away from Hal. "Ceowulf, Hal, come with me," he ordered imperiously. "It's possible you may have better training in—" he started to admit though clamped his mouth shut on his words. "Follow me!"

Hal didn't like being ordered about so abruptly but he was pleased that his opinion was not only sought but needed. It must have galled Tudwal to ask for his help and he enjoyed the prince's discomfort. He wasn't so pleased, however, when he saw the tracks.

Tudwal slid from his horse and pointed to the deep marks in the moist ground. They peered at the plain crescent imprint where even the sculpting in the central, under part of the hoof had left an impression in the soft ground. It was clearly an unshod horse and, Hal judged by the open shape of the crescent, that it was probably a hind hoof. Ceowulf nodded in agreement.

"That's what I thought," Tudwal agreed. "Nothing strange in itself until you see this."

The next print along showed the same horse's hoofprint but with it the unmistakable clawed print of a large predator, four times the size of a wolf's. It was neat and round, unlike the long print of a bear, though it was almost as big.

"That's a very large cat," Hal said without hesitation. "Very, very large; bigger than the mountain cats around Torra Alta. More the size of a lion. And that's odd—" he stopped, the words dying on his lips.

"The men were concerned because of the sheer size but clearly it's odder than that," Tudwal agreed, his tone reasonable for once.

Hal slid from Secret's back to study the spoors more closely. "The horse is unshod so probably a wild horse." He looked up at Tudwal who nodded in agreement before continuing. "A large cat stalking a horse? It would seem logical."

"Only you can see here how the horse's print is overlying the cat's." Tudwal pointed to another mark further along. "We do have a large number of wild horses so I thought the same as you but what wild horse stalks a cat? And a very big cat at that."

Hal felt the hairs on the back of his neck prickle. He stood alongside the print and let his weight fall naturally onto his foot and then stood back to examine the marks. He had sunk a good two inches into the mud, yet this great cat had left only a slight indention.

"It's a recent spoor of course," Ceowulf added as if reading Hal's thoughts. "The ground's too wet and the rain's too persistent for any track to last long. But the print seems too shallow. An animal that size should sink deeper into this mud. It's like it has no substance."

"Just like the two-headed bear," Tudwal added. "All very unnatural. On no account are you to tell the others. I won't have the ladies alarmed."

They all agreed this was sensible. For the first time Hal decided that, despite Tudwal's overbearing arrogance and inbred conviction that as a Ceolothian he was naturally superior, he did at least possess common sense.

"I'll tell the men to look out for a big lion of sorts," the prince said. "You two, have a further look around and report back to me if you find anything else. Is that clear?" He looked steadily at Hal to impress his authority further before spurring back to the wagons.

As ordered, they tracked the shallow prints while their own horses left a ploughed trail in the mud. In rising puzzlement and apprehension, they followed the trail as it swept parallel to the course of the wagons.

"You know, Ceowulf, it's very curious," Hal began uncertainly for once. "I don't understand it; we've only found prints from the hind hooves of a horse and the fore paws of a cat. Look at this claw mark here. We've never once found one with the elongated heel mark of a rear paw, but only the neat round prints of the front."

"So, what you're saying is that not only do we have a large cat being followed by a horse but the cat seems to be walking on its front legs and the horse on its rear," Ceowulf hypothesized with a laugh at the ridiculous notion.

"Brid would know what a half cat and half horse is called," Hal said bluntly.

"A lequus," Ceowulf told him, all trace of humour gone. "We had better get back to the column."

Renaud snapped his fingers at them as they approached. "Well, my lords? What did you find?"

Hal saw no point in shouting about mystical beasts: the prince would never believe him. "A large cat, maybe a lion or a tiger, something like that," he said matter-of-factly.

The prince nodded and cast to left and right. "A word with you a moment, Hal." He coughed as they drew aside from the column. "I wasn't afraid of the bears, you know. And I'm sorry I wasn't there to help you. I saw the bears from the top of the cliff and heard your shouts but I just couldn't face that slope."

Hal forced a smile onto his face. "I've seen a great many men of undoubted bravery who have balked at the climb to Torra Alta and more that's driven wagons up but can't bring themselves to drive them down again."

"Well, I apologize. I'm not a man for pretence. I failed you and I'm sorry. When we return to Belbidia I will redress the situation by paying a visit to Torra Alta and accustoming myself to its heights."

"You should have got off the horse, sir," Hal advised him in retrospect. "On horseback you're another five foot off the ground and that can make all the difference."

"The world just seemed to fall away."

Hal couldn't help but be warmed by Renaud's candid honesty. Perhaps, like Prince Tudwal, he wasn't so bad after all. He checked his thoughts, reminding himself that Renaud had already proved himself to be more cunning than he had first believed. This show of openness might just be a ploy to distract him.

He fell in behind the rest of the noblemen, who listened

to Prince Tudwal explaining that their road was the main trading route into Vaalaka. Hal idly wondered how anyone could describe this river of mud as a road.

Princess Cymbeline had retired to the wagons. She was weary from riding after her horse had struggled and slipped through the mud for so long and Hal was disappointed because it gave him no opportunity to talk to her. If only he could engage her in conversation, he was confident that he could win her scarf. Tudwal had returned it after the race and Hal had not forgotten his promise to himself. He was fully aware that he had the dark features that women so often found irresistible and he had never yet failed to win the affection of a lady if he so wished.

He raised his head and looked at the dark expanse of rising ground before them. Trows Forest spilt like a flood over the undulating terrain. The road, as Tudwal insisted on calling this sodden line churned by wheels and mule trains, headed straight for the trees. Hal thought again of the bear in the cave and the strange tracks they had seen and decided that the last place he would choose to be was in the confines of a forest where oncoming danger would be difficult to spot.

"Wouldn't it be better if we steered left and dipped to the south of the forest?" he suggested.

Ceowulf nodded at this but Tudwal laughed. "Afraid of the woods, eh, Belbidian? What was the point of King Rewik sending a *Belbidian* escort? We are going through the forest whether you like it or not. The terrain to the south is far too difficult for wagons."

Finding that there was nothing more he could say, Hal growled in his throat.

Tudwal glowered angrily. "You don't believe me. Ask any of my men. South of here the valleys run north to south; we would be working against the grain of the land, up one slope and down the other. This route at least sticks to the plains and valley bottoms."

Hal nodded, conceding the point.

Tudwal beamed in triumph. "Thought you might know more about my lands than I did, eh?" He sniggered and Hal thought how well Tudwal would look with Secret's teeth marks across his rump and returned the smile.

"When do we stop?" Hardwin asked expectantly. He sat crookedly on his saddle, evidently sparing his sores.

"Wudskert, just before the forest. We'll pick up supplies and get a good night's sleep under a real roof. It'll be many days before we reach the village at Tallacs and it'll be another two weeks or more before we reach Gortbarrow, which is the last hamlet before Hobs Slack, the uninhabited heart of the forest. The ladies will welcome a proper rest," Tudwal explained.

After a comfortable night's sleep on real beds for once, they left Wudskert behind and entered the gloom of the forest. At first Hal found the woods irksome but when the road began to climb through the trees and the wagons rolled a little more easily on better drained soil, he began to feel less apprehensive. At least the forest protected them from the raw wind and drenching rain.

After many slow days trudging alongside the wagon and uncomfortable nights sleeping rough, they at last saw the braziers at Tallacs' gate shining dimly through the drizzle of the early evening gloom. Hal moistened his lips in anticipation of a good meal. The village prefect had ridden out to greet them and escorted them to the inn. Hal led Secret towards the stables. He twitched at her bit and she obediently flung out her heels. One of the Ceolothians' horses skittered away, hooves striking sparks on the cobbled yard.

"Sorry! She's a dangerous beast," he apologized loudly, enjoying the awed looks from the grooms as they stood aside to let him lead the "dangerous" animal to her stall. "Good girl." He patted her affectionately and fetched in his pocket for a slice of apple that she politely took from his palm with her velveteen lips. There was a grunt from the next stall and Hal winced as two grooms were flattened to the boarding by Tudwal's stallion. He was all the more grateful for Secret's nature and Brid's skilful training of the horse.

He wondered briefly how she fared without him in Torra Alta and whether she was missing him. He liked to think she was but he wasn't sure. She had been preoccupied of late, worrying over Morrigwen's health, and it had made him feel so unneeded at times.

The inn was typically Ceolothian and exactly what Hal had come to expect. It was dark inside and most of the travellers had gathered to the far end where charcoal fires glowed in open stoves and meat sizzled on grills. Ceolothians liked meat. It didn't matter from what animal as long as it came in large slabs scorched and charred over the flames. Their heavy bread was salty rather than yeasty and, though Hal knew little about it, he suspected it was soda bread. He liked it, just as he liked meat, but he was becoming heartily bored by the lack of variety.

The walls of the tavern were made of dry stone and were hung with all manner of hunting trophies, from bear to goats' heads and even a stuffed stoat in its winter coat of ermine. The windows were small and already shuttered up against the night with thick wooden battens. The ceiling was low and both Prince Renaud and Ceowulf had to stoop beneath thick beams.

The innkeeper clapped his hands and ordered the space around two long tables to be cleared. The tables were already set. A Ceolothian soldier had ridden ahead several days before to warn him of their imminent arrival and had only just rejoined them. Hal could tell, by the shining faces and fresh white smocks of the serving women, that they had all taken extra care to present themselves.

He placed himself with his back to the fire, basking in the glorious warmth that eased his aching limbs. He hoped that the firelight at his back would throw him into sinister silhouette; he liked to make himself appear mysterious. The other nobles, with the exception of Ceowulf, headed for the chamber at the rear of the inn, calling for fresh clothes and hot water as they went. Hal didn't see the point. He would be just as wet and dirty tomorrow. He would dry out quickly enough by the fire and he was too hungry to wait. Tudwal's dogs slunk towards the fire but cringed and retreated, snarling, when he bent to stroke them.

"Spineless creatures," he rebuked them. "And I bet you've got fleas."

At least Trog never had fleas. Brid always saw to that with unctions of lavender and cypress oil. The terrier spent so much time curled up on her bed that she never failed to ensure that the fleas were kept at bay. Humph! That was another thing about Brid. She even put Trog's feelings before his at times. He knew how obstinate the dog was and wondered how he'd ever get Trog away from Brid's bed. He wondered whether Cymbeline had such a dog. He hoped not.

Hal perused the patrons of the tavern. Apart from the serving women, every one of them was male, mostly with shaggy beards and ingrained dirt in their hard-working hands. Traders, he guessed, judging by the number of mules he had heard braying and coughing in the stables; but not all of them. Three wore shabby, stained clothes made from bear and wolf skins, roughly stitched into hard-wearing jackets. They had quick eyes, and still bodies and he knew them at once for hunters. There was an air of steady patience and commitment in their movements. They shared a table with a finely dressed gentleman, wearing padded leathers and a tailored cloak clasped by an expensive broach.

Tudwal joined him at the table as he was still studying the gentlemen and their bearded guides. "There's good sport to be had in the mountains south of Trows Forest. The guides take them into the rougher country for the goats."

"Goats!" Hal echoed in surprise. What sport was there in hunting goats?

Tudwal read his contemptuous expression aright. "You Belbidians have no notion of real game. The Ceolothian goat that roams these territories is huge. Bigger than a stag." He nodded at a head hanging on the wall. Its face was the size of a pony's and it had huge curling horns like a giant ram's.

"That's a goat?" Hal exclaimed, genuinely impressed.

Princess Cymbeline gracefully descended the stairs and sat next to her brother and opposite Hal. The Torra Altan's attention was immediately caught by her sparkling earrings, the huge sunburst rubies glinting in the firelight. Tudwal sat back while Hal began to fidget, wondering where Prince Renaud had got to. But he quickly forgot Renaud as he put his mind to graciously filling Cymbeline's cup with the sweet mixture of milk laced with treacly Ceolothian mead that was provided for the ladies. Hal thought the concoction sounded quite revolting but Cymbeline liked it and it brought colour to her cheeks.

Her earrings fascinated him. He could not stop himself from thinking that they would buy a full bard of armour for his horse at the least. It would be gratifying to ride into Farona like one of those proud knights of old, marks of combat on his horse's fine armour bearing testament to the slaying of a dragon or wyvern.

He had asked Branwolf for enough money to commission a smith to make him a steel bard for Secret but his brother had only lectured him about the cost of rebuilding the castle.

Even *one* of those earrings would be enough, Hal decided.

Close shaven and freshly scrubbed, Prince Renaud, shadowed by Hardwin, finally joined the supper party. As he crossed the room, the Belbidian prince took great pains to avoid brushing against any of the bearded huntsmen, and then he had the innkeeper swab down the table in front of him before he would sit.

"Disease," he explained. "You can never be too sure."

Hardwin visibly brightened at the prospect of food and grinned congenially at Hal but the Torra Altan found it hard to return the smile since he suspected the man of duplicity. Hardwin lowered his gaze at this rebuff and, with a ruddy face, tried to strike up a conversation with Princess Cymbeline.

"You will like Farona, Madam. All the ladies at court will be so anxious to meet you. And there is so much for a fine lady to see: the rose gardens, the tapestries, the pageants. And we have jesters, tumblers and mime artists. The plays are delightful. So much art, such gaiety."

Funny, Hal thought. He found Farona rather dull compared to the wild expanse of the mountains where the air made him tingle with vitality.

Tudwal looked bored with their conversation. He turned to idly study the richly dressed man of the hunting party. The man looked up and caught his eye, his mouth dropping open a full inch. Hurriedly, he stood to offer a bow. "Your royal highnesses," he stammered. "Forgive me, I didn't recognize you."

Tudwal waved the apology aside. "Has your hunting been good?"

"We have fared well and plan an early start in the morning. With the weather being so bad in the high country, we thought to take to the shelter of the wood."

"Mm, a wise plan. Nice-looking dogs." He nodded at the man's clay-red hounds, who much to their master's embarrassment growled at the prince. Tudwal merely smiled in appreciation and struck up an involved conversation about hunting and hounds.

Hal was disappointed when the evening drew to an early close without any remarkable incident. He had hoped that either Prince Renaud or his shadow, Hardwin, might inadvertently say something incriminating. Feeling less than content, he took himself off to the back chamber that he was to share with Ceowulf, Tupwell and Hardwin. The bedclothes were damp and smelt musty. Shivering, he fell asleep and dreamt of horses, armour and sunburst rubies.

The sheets still felt just as damp when he woke the next day. He crawled from his bed and the prospect of another cold drizzly day did nothing to encourage his spirits. The Ceolothians, he noted, were anxious about the journey ahead, and there was much checking and rechecking of harnesses and weapons. Even Tudwal showed signs of concern, his pale blue eyes roving over his men as he gave orders for them to move forward. Hal had not expected anxiety from the prince who usually made such a point of displaying his Ceolothian bravery.

Prince Renaud and Hardwin stayed close to the ladies, which conveniently placed them safely in the centre of the escort party. "Must see that they are well protected through the forest," Renaud said loudly.

The woods immediately around Tallacs mainly consisted of giant oaks but these quickly gave way to the commoner tall, red-barked pines, whose tightly cramped branches broke the wind and sheltered them from the Ceolothian drizzle. But it was dark beneath their evergreen shade and the men automatically closed around the rumbling wagons that disturbed the lull of the woods. Hal halted for a moment to listen to the sounds from the woods. A blackbird rustled in the undergrowth, foraging for food and somewhere in the distance the unmistakable hammer of a woodpecker drummed out across the still of the woodlands and a chattering squirrel with red tufted ears was busily gathering pine kernels. The air smelt sweet with resin and one of the soldiers started to cough and sneeze.

Hal found the trees oppressive. They gave excellent cover for predators and he continually worried about the strange footprints that Ceowulf had credited to an unnatural lequus. As they crested a rise where the trees were thinner, he looked distrustfully at the dark swath that blanketed the land below, hiding its secrets behind the thick layers of vegetation. The great wagons rumbled happily on through the half-light and, as the day wore on, he gradually forgot his concerns.

They ground their way deeper into the forest, the pines giving way to oaks, ancient trees with twisted boughs and folded bark. He surprised himself by remembering that the oak was the tree of strength and protection as well as the doorway to the mysterious. She had also pointed out how most front doors were made from oak because it gave protection to those within. He must have been paying more attention to Brid's words than he thought.

For much of the journey Hardwin, Tupwell and Renaud

had kept themselves to themselves and so it came as a surprise when Hal found Tupwell, not only beside him, but moodily complaining about Prince Renaud. The Ovissian tugged at one of his sticking-out ears and snorted in disgust. "Mmm! Look at him hiding by the wagons. He just gives himself an excuse to get surrounded by armed troops. How can he call himself a prince?"

For a moment Hal thought to tell him of Renaud's fear on the steep slope above the dead bears but he held his tongue. Firstly, he didn't like Tupwell – the man gave him a bad taste in the mouth – and secondly, it would shame the noble name of Belbidia to dwell on the incident. He was surprised, though, that Tupwell had spoken out against Prince Renaud; they had been so close of late.

Hal's thoughts were curtailed by a sudden stiffening in the Ovissian's bearing. "I can smell wolves," Tupwell warned.

Hal drew a deep breath. He could smell leaf mould and sap but nothing else. He laughed derogatorily. "Your imagination's getting the better of you, dear friend. Wolves wouldn't go near so many men and you've a keener sense of smell than I have if you can smell wolves more than ten paces away." Hal had absolutely no doubt that this over-dressed man with his peacock feather still flouncing brightly in his cap wouldn't possibly know what a wolf smelt like.

Tupwell filled his lungs, his eyes wide with indignation. He looked as if he were about to burst forth in outrage, but he pursed his lips and held back his indignation.

Someone else was quarrelling ahead.

Hal could hear Cymbeline's high voice at counterpoint to Prince Tudwal's groans but he couldn't catch the gist of it because they were shouting in Ceolothian.

"She should stay in the wagon as he says," Tupwell

voiced his thoughts and so enlightened Hal to the nature of the royal quarrel.

His lips rose in a faint smile as he realized that the silver-blonde princess was getting the better of her brother. He thanked his stars that he didn't have a sister. Brid was hard enough to cope with, and sisters clearly didn't know their place either. He couldn't prevent a smirk lifting one side of his face as he watched the belligerent Prince Tudwal being put down by a woman.

The Ceolothian prince stormed ahead and Cymbeline turned her horse toward the rear of the column. The men politely drew aside to give her room and Hal seized his opportunity to speak with her alone, his thoughts already focusing on winning that scarf as a token of her favour. He had no intention of failing. It was a point of honour, he told himself.

He slowed Secret until he was several lengths behind the rear guard and met Cymbeline's flushed face with his most charming smile. Her reaction showed that she wanted to be alone but, brashly, he ignored her unspoken words and positioned Secret firmly in the centre of the road, now deeply rutted by the passage of the wagons.

"Fair Princess Cymbeline, your presence is like a rainbow gladdening a rain-lashed sky." He was pleased with the simile though it was hardly spontaneous. In the days before Brid, he had used it on numerous occasions and had found it most effective. The words were not his own; he had discovered them by chance in a thick leather-bound book full of exquisite illustrations and painted letters while searching for pictures of armour.

Cymbeline scowled but as Hal's smile grew wider, she finally succumbed to his charm and laughed. Hal was pleased. It was the first time he had the opportunity to speak with Cymbeline for some time and her laughter promised much. Tudwal's vigilant and disapproving presence had been a problem, but clearly, this once, she had grown tired of his brotherly protection.

"You have been hiding away in that wagon far too long. Such beauty should not be caged." Hal searched further for something winning to say and decided that, since her quarrel was with Tudwal, he could not go far wrong by taking her side even if he didn't know what the argument was about. "Your brother doesn't understand you."

"He always thinks he knows best. But I can't sit in the wagon all day," she complained ardently before falling silent for a moment, searching beyond the line of wagons to where her brother, a fine figure of a man Hal had to admit, was shouting harshly at a section of the column. A cloud of birds burst into the air in startled dismay as he vented his anger. Cymbeline looked equally angry but as she turned back to Hal her countenance melted into sudden sweetness "What's he like?" she asked abruptly.

"Your brother?" he asked quizzically.

She laughed. "No, no. King Rewik."

"Not good enough for you." Hal was direct. He found that most girls were flattered by such unrestrained forwardness. It was all a matter of lavish attention followed by indifference to make them all the more hungry for his adulation. Too much of one or the other estranged them but he felt he had perfected the balance, besides Cymbeline was easy prey. With such a doting father, no doubt, she had been sheltered from suitors and knew little of the wiles of men. He had started with open and unrestrained admiration and he could see it was beginning to work. She was blushing.

Hal grinned to himself, thinking how men complained about the wiles of women. He was only doing his bit to redress the balance a little.

But what was he thinking about? What would Brid think? A pang of guilt surfaced from his subconscious but it was only fleeting; he was having too much fun. King Dagonet's daughter was too big a challenge, too big a conquest to be passed by. She had already nibbled at his bait and he wasn't going to let her go now.

She laughed at his flattery. "King Rewik of Belbidia is every bit a perfect match for a princess of Ceolothia," she corrected him.

"But you can't marry him just because he's a king. There is more to life than that."

"For you maybe but not for me. I have duties and responsibilities," she said heavily, narrowing her eyes and glowering through long deerlike lashes at Tudwal, whose gruff barracking of the men filtered back along the line of wagons. But when her brother stood up in his stirrups and stretched his neck up to look for her, she hastily turned away and drew closer to Hal. Again, that quick smile sweetened her face.

"We all have our duties," Hal said grandly though his thoughts were interrupted by an image of Brid. The distraction annoyed him and he felt angry with his betrothed. He was too young to be tied to just one person. Far, far too young to make such a choice. Why should Brid control his life and stop him from having any fun? Brid was too serious. She had higher concerns and was so, well . . . superior. If it had been Brid's horse that had bolted, she would have pulled the animal up. Brid never needed rescuing. She never needed his help. Did she really need him at all?

Whereas Cymbeline . . . Well now, she most certainly needed him; she needed to be rescued from that vulture Rewik. She would wither away, stuffed up in his dull palace. Cymbeline was vulnerable without him . . . helpless. The thought was so alluring. Chivalrously coming to her aid, he could be her saviour, her gallant knight; it was all that he had ever wanted. Again, his eyes focused on the priceless sunburst rubies as they sparkled in a rare shaft of Ceolothian sunlight that lanced through the trees. He pointed out the ray of light as it fell like a blessing on the drab earth, turning all about it to the vivid colours of life.

"You are just such a sunburst, brilliant and golden, brightness and beauty. You are like the first daffodil to break through the dun of the winter forest." He was very satisfied with his analogy. It dimly occurred to him that that was how Brid touched upon the world, but he decided it would not be the most seductive thing to say to the princess.

Her gaze lingered on his lips, eyes and raven hair and she smiled in undoubted pleasure, he was sure. "My lord, you should not be saying such things to me," she scolded though her eyes begged him to continue.

He laughed, knowing that if he went too far, he would sound like an obsequious page. "It would make a rainbow no more beautiful if I polished it with praise but I will say no more unless you have something to say to me." He threw the challenge back at her.

"I am a princess and betrothed to a king!" she rebuked him haughtily but her regal composure crumbled into girlish giggles. "Is he really so terribly old?"

"King Rewik? Oh yes, terribly. At least a hundred and five," Hal joked.

"He isn't, is he?!" The princess looked shocked until she realized he was teasing her.

These Ceolothians were so literal, Hal thought. "No, but he might as well be," he continued. "He's a wrinkly old terrapin and I doubt that he would let his bride ride out with her merlin. That's not the sort of thing ladies do in Belbidia."

"I shall set the fashion," she replied loftily though doubt clouded her pale face. She stroked her merlin which was perched on the ornate carving of the pommel that reared up on the front of her saddle. The bird stood on one leg and twisted its head round to scratch the back of its neck. "Anyway, why can't a lady hunt? My merlin is very much a lady's hawk."

Hal considered her in her very fine clothes, practical and yet intensely feminine with veils and silks and shimmering threads interwoven in the glorious green velvet. For a moment he thought how wonderful Brid would look in such a dress; the green would catch the colour of her eyes. But Brid would have scorned such a riding-habit. The trouble with Brid was that she always wanted to go to the wildest of places where no lady should ever be.

Hal was annoyed. Every time he gazed at Cymbeline some thought of Brid would slip into his mind to spoil his pleasure. Toying with his reins, he reconsidered the situation. He couldn't truly love Brid if he could think about Cymbeline in this way, could he? Surely, he shouldn't even notice another female. And what would he gain if he married a priestess? She was highly revered but had no lands and no power amongst the aristocracy of the country, only amongst the people. Marry the princess of Ceolothia, now that was quite a different matter. He dismissed the problem of how Dagonet would respond to him eloping with his most prized possession by deciding that fathers were easily won round by their daughters. If he made Princess Cymbeline happy then no doubt King Dagonet would approve, in time. And he could make her happy, he was certain of that.

She turned to look deep into his eyes and smiled so beautifully. "I'm glad you stayed behind," she said coyly.

"So am I," he agreed but his guilt deepened. Angrily he decided that if he were betrothed to Cymbeline and not Brid he wouldn't need to keep looking elsewhere because the princess would fulfil all his needs. Life was too sharp, too painful with Brid; she knew too much, knew him too well. Brid didn't see his glossy hair and handsome face, his fine figure or his accomplished mannerisms. She saw through him and it made him feel inadequate. Cymbeline would let him be the man he wanted to be, the man he would have been if he had been born the older rather than the younger son of a baron.

Hal continued to chat intermittently to Cymbeline but was careful not to be too attentive, instead encouraging her to speak about her blue merlin, something that the princess clearly enjoyed. After some while he noted a subtle change in her behaviour. She ceased to search ahead for the figure of her brother and relaxed alongside the Torra Altan. Hal was pleased. Given just a little more time she would truly be interested in him; he was quite confident on the matter. There wasn't a maiden yet that he hadn't failed to win though he had to admit he was a little out of practice.

The pleasure of the day was ruined, however, when Tupwell slowed to join them at the rear of the column. He gave Cymbeline a respectful nod of the head and fell in alongside without a word. Hal glowered at him, willing him to leave but the Ovissian seemed impervious to his hints. Hal was relieved when Ceowulf also joined them. The Caldean knight looked troubled but said nothing.

Tupwell was sniffing the air. "I can definitely smell wolves," he repeated his earlier assertion.

Hal was about to put the Ovissian down by telling him it was only his cowardly imagination when he too scented a distinct odour. But it wasn't wolf. It was stale and musty. Hal couldn't place it.

Ceowulf looked troubled and checked his weapons. "My lady, I think we should escort you nearer the centre of the escort."

"I'm fine here," she objected but the knight shook his head.

"No, my lady. I'm sure it's fine if you stay on your horse but for the moment you must ride at the centre of the column. You are too vulnerable here at the rear."

She quietly acquiesced, mainly, Hal suspected, because she had had enough of Tupwell's brooding company. "You'll ride with me, Lord Hal?" she asked and he grinned back at her in satisfaction.

"I'll follow you," he bowed gallantly. He wanted a word with Ceowulf first before continuing his pursuit of the princess.

As Cymbeline rode forward, Hal opened his mouth to speak to his friend but quickly clamped it shut. Ceowulf was frowning reprovingly.

"I feel obliged to warn you that there is little wisdom—"

"That smell!" Hal cut his friend short, determined to be spared any lecture about his conduct. "Tupwell keeps talking about wolves but it's not, is it?"

Ceowulf continued to frown while he shook his head. "I thought perhaps it was just a stagnant mire upwind of us but it's been too persistent. If it were, we should have passed it by long since."

"Wyvern?" Hal suggested.

Ceowulf shook his head. "No, not wyvern and not wolves; just death, the smell of death."

CHAPTER TWENTY

"We're being stalked," Abelard whispered, nodding towards Fern whose nose twitched and his body trembled with anticipation. "Look at him. He doesn't know it but his old instincts are still warning him of a predator. He's all a-tremble."

"It's the hunt!" Caspar spoke with alarm.

Abelard shook his head. "No, we would have heard their horns."

Fern relaxed as if the fearful presence had passed and they all hurried on, though the hairs on the back of Caspar's neck still prickled. They forced their way deeper into the forest until it was too dark to see. Exhausted, they retreated to a hollow but could only sleep fitfully for the moans and groans wailing through the trees, and the occasional cackle and caw of beasts that Caspar could give no name to. Far away a rumbling roar like rolling thunder boomed out over the forest and for a long, intense, breathless minute all other noises were quelled. A dragon, Caspar thought fearfully. The other sounds of large creatures trampling through the woods gradually returned, emitting the occasional startled shriek or low predatory growls.

After a few hours of uncomfortable rest, they forced themselves to struggle on before it was even light. The branches of the trees were thickly interwoven, heavy with leaf, drooping low to the ground and they were continually stooping beneath them and becoming entangled in thorns or brambles. By the time the sun was high, Brid's cheeks were covered in deep scratches and she was irritated by the ooze of blood that could not be stemmed.

"There won't be much of us left by the time we get through," Abelard observed, stumbling on exhausted legs.

"We must stop for a rest," Caspar panted.

"No, we must keep going," Brid objected.

He shook his head. "We can't think straight for the exhaustion, Brid. We must stop. Look at you. We need to give ourselves time to think otherwise we'll end up going round in circles."

Brid anxiously looked up at the fragmented bites of blue sky visible through the green canopy. She nodded. "You're right. We've already turned too far north. No wonder we're exhausted. We must have been climbing for hours up to what would be the Vaalakan plateau if we were at home but it's all so different here. I'm disorientated." She sat down heavily and rubbed at her thighs. All but Fern sat down beside her.

Abelard looked to the little woodwose, who twitched anxiously, and then at Caspar's bow strapped to his back. "It might be four hundred year since I've drawn a bow but they say y' never forget."

Caspar didn't know. He couldn't remember a day in his life when he hadn't, at some time, practised the skill.

"Do y' carry a spare bowstring, Spar?" the ancient archer asked the youth.

"Of course. Several."

"Good. At least the Torra Altan standards ain't slipped over the years," Abelard joked though Caspar couldn't imagine where he had delved for his humour. His own had long since departed. "Well, if y' have a knife too, I'll cut me a piece of yew. It might not be perfect but it'll be better than nought."

Brid quickly set about fashioning a quiver from the remains of her veil and Caspar divided his arrows. After some while Abelard reached a level of dissatisfaction with his strip of wood that he could not improve upon. "Well, it'll have to do but it certainly ain't a Torra Altan war bow. Bit small too but it had to fit your string, Spar." He rolled his shoulder, loosening the joint. Bracing the bottom section of the wood against his foot, he bent the bow sufficiently to loop the string into place. Thoughtfully, he plucked at it once or twice before reaching for an arrow and nocking it to the string. He took careful aim at a warty growth on the bole of a stunted chestnut not thirty paces away. It was a close target and a large one though he only managed to graze the outside of the knot. He shrugged regretfully. "I thought it'd do better than that."

Fern looked appalled by the bows. He looked down at his small body and straight spindly legs in disgust. "It's cheating."

Brid laughed lightly at him.

"It is," he objected. "Man is just a weak creature but he uses bits of wood and string to become a killer."

"Y' still think like a deer," Abelard grumbled. "Like a stupid deer. Y're so small-minded. Man has a brain. It's his biggest weapon though evidently y'rs ain't grown yet."

The little woodwose halted abruptly, his nostrils flaring.

Abelard nudged Caspar's arm and pointed at the little woodwose. "It's following us again, Spar."

"What is it?" Brid asked Fern.

He shook his head. "It feels like wolves," he muttered in horror. "It's flanking us like wolves would but it doesn't smell like them and there's only one, I think, one or maybe two."

"Why didn't you say earlier?" Caspar asked.

Fern frowned at him. "Didn't you know?" he asked incredulously. "You must have known!"

The four of them instinctively drew closer.

"Look; there's a track up to the right, the other side of that hawthorn," Brid murmured. "The light's brighter that way. Hurry! We should have a clearer view and more room to protect ourselves."

It was hard work breaking through the thatch of flowering hawthorn. Caspar looked at the white blossom and for the first time thought of its namesake, May. He suddenly wished for her comfort and longed to look into those soft hazel eyes and stroke her chestnut curls. It would be safe wherever May was. Here he might have Brid but the world was too wild and savage around him.

A twig snapped somewhere to their right and they all froze before hurrying on towards the path. Just as a beaten track came into sight ahead, Caspar heard a deep-throated growl from the undergrowth behind them. He shoved Brid forward and, bow in hand, swung round to defend her.

It was like staring into the face of his own death. He faced a wolf, a hooded wolf. Sunlight shimmered in the rich gloss of its ebony coat. He saw the teeth dripping with blood and a slobbering tongue. Icicles of saliva hung like extra teeth from the corners of its mouth and the deep red slice of its panting tongue dangled to the side. The tongue stiffened and quivered as the beast growled. He still couldn't see its eyes as it stalked forward out of the gloom towards him.

"Run, Spar, run," Abelard hissed at him but Caspar was rooted to the spot.

This, surely, was the same beast that should have killed him in the Boarchase. He needed Necrönd. Why had he been such a fool as to leave it in Torra Alta?

"Spar!" Abelard shouted, snatching him backwards by his shoulder. "Get to the path and stay with the others: they need you."

Caspar heard the man's words as if they were part of a dream. He couldn't take his eyes off the wolf. He expected to see the great creature's eyes glowing red in the dark but he could not pierce the gloom. A shadow enveloped the wolf and it sucked his gaze into the blackness. The shadow might have been created by the trees only Caspar somehow knew it wasn't. His head tingled where the hairs had been ripped out by the tortured man in Abalone's dungeons.

With his instincts to react too entangled in fear, Caspar couldn't move. He stared helplessly as the wolf ran forward out of the darkness, a flailing snarling mass of claw and tooth, its serrated black lips peeled back from the deep jaw line.

The thrum of a bowstring sounded behind him. Once, twice the great wolf shrieked but it blundered on despite the arrows buried in its chest and flank. Caspar was knocked flat by the weight of the wolf as it tore into his chest. He was aware of the blood moments before the sound of his own scream cut through to his conscious mind. He felt faint and giddy and terribly cold. Trees swirled about him. He knew he was losing blood fast and was vaguely aware of the distorted cries of dismay from his companions. Brid's face came close to his while Abelard dragged the great weight of the writhing wolf from his body as it suffered the same agony as himself, the agony of near death.

"Spar, Spar can you hear me?" Brid begged.

He saw her dimly, the blurred edges of his vision clouded with red. He moved his hand and for a second gripped hers before his strength failed him. To die here meant to die forever, to become nothing. He could not die; life meant too much to him.

He could hear singing, not sweet and light as he had expected on his departure from life, but a dirge of compelling sadness like a chant from a priory. There was no melody to the song. "Brid, please, please don't leave me," he tried to say but found his mouth would barely work.

"I'm here, Spar." She was kneeling beside him, pressing her face close to his. "Dear friend, I am here by your side. I won't leave you."

"I can hear the song of my death," Caspar croaked. "And it's sad. It should have been happy, it should have been triumphant, rejoicing in a worthwhile life. But I get no more than I deserve and it is sad."

"Spar, that's real singing. We can all hear it."

"But I hurt and feel so terribly cold."

"I know," she said with sympathy and understanding. "I know and I can bear none of the pain for you, but it's real singing, Spar. Believe me."

"Not the hunt," he choked urgently.

"No." She sounded distant and uncertain. He could hear the sound of hurrying feet retreating through the undergrowth, the noise trembling through the cold damp ground that pressed against his body. "No, Abelard says it's verderers guiding a group of souls through the forest. The path we've found is one of their ways . . ." Her voice trailed off and she pressed Caspar's hand. "Abelard has gone to look, so keep quiet."

The sound of singing grew louder and more insistent. Caspar found he could hardly catch his breath. His lungs were filling and he was certain he was drowning in his own blood. Brid tightened her grip on his hand, clinging to him for fear of losing him forever.

"Brid, I love you," he murmured in farewell.

She stroked his cheek, the deep green of her eyes reaching down into his soul. "I love you too," she replied, cradling his head in her lap.

In that instant he knew that it was not true love because she had to reach out for his soul and was not already a part of it. Caspar could feel the tears drip from her cheeks onto his face and trickle to mingle with the blood on his lips. He could barely breathe for the shooting pain that stabbed deep into his chest. His senses slowed and he ceased to struggle. Over the years, little by little, the carrion of Rye Errish would pick him clean and the worms and fly larvae would be left to ingest the very last of his being. Then his soul would be gone and with it the pain.

He could no longer feel Brid's hand and he closed his eyes. Too weak to move, he felt horribly cold. He tried to concentrate on Brid's voice and though he no longer had the strength to speak, he could still hear her and willed her to keep talking so that he didn't feel alone. He would be alone forever soon, denied the bliss of Annwyn, denied the right to become one with the Mother.

Brid didn't leave him. She seemed to understand and pulled him tight towards her bosom, rocking him back and forth like a baby in her arms, all the while murmuring prayers to the Mother. But none of it could take away his pain.

"I won't leave you, Spar," she repeated.

Caspar could hear other voices now and Brid was no longer whispering in his ear but had raised her voice to talk to Abelard. "You must summon them. We need the verderers and their healing powers, even if it means joining the party of souls that they are driving through the forest."

"What if they alert the hunt?" Abelard objected.

"It is either that or abandoning Spar. They may not

know of the hunt. You said they're moving slowly so they must have left Abalone long before us. You've been part of a column before; you know what to expect. You said yourself that the verderers can heal all suffering inflicted here."

"Hide the Pipe, my lady. And see y'r face is content and peaceful. I don't want to be with the column but it seems we've no choice."

Caspar could feel himself being hauled by his arms through the undergrowth. He knew they were risking their chances of crossing to the gateway for him but at that moment he could think of little beyond his pain. If the verderers could stop the pain . . .

He was aware of little else until he blinked his eyes open and looked into the bright sunlight reflected in the yellow glow of a verderer's eyes.

Abelard spoke out, "We are poor souls lost in our way through the forest. We need guidance across y'r lands to the life beyond and the Great Mother."

A cool long-fingered hand stroked Caspar's brow and a sweet melody, which he imagined was like the song that bluebells and daffodils might sing if only they could, filled his ears. A scroll of bark was pressed under his tongue. Minutes later the pain was gone as completely as if it had been no more than dirt that could be washed away with water. Though the youth was still carrying the savage tear wounds where the wolf had sunk its jaws into his chest and shredded his skin, he could feel his strength returning. He felt feather light.

"Join the column," the verderer ordered without emotion.

Caspar found himself on his feet, walking beside Brid. Her gaze clung to him as if she feared he might fall if she looked away. They trudged along in the centre of a large group of souls more than four score in number. Many of the faces were empty of expression; some looked ahead hopefully and a few looked behind as if wondering how those in the real world still fared; but all, judging by their step, were accepting of their deaths. Mostly they were human but there were some, like Fern, who were making the transition from beast to man. One poor soul periodically dropped onto all fours, tossing his head and throwing out his heels like a horse. The sight was quite preposterous.

Caspar decided that if he'd been born a horse, he wouldn't want to become a human being. Life as a man was just too complicated. Agitated and skipping ahead, Fern weaved in and out of the other souls. Many ignored him but some were irritated by his behaviour as he butted into them before rushing back to his three companions.

"We shouldn't have done this," the woodwose told Abelard. "Everything is lost now. Everything!"

"Just be quiet, little man, and think for a minute."

"No," Fern insisted on chattering on. "Look, they've guards flanking the entire column and they have silver arrows to fell us if we try to escape."

"Listen," Brid told him gently. "For the moment, this is our best chance. It'll take us right to the gateway and we'll be well protected from the creatures in the forest. Moreover, the hunt won't think to look for us here."

"Yes, but we're all going to Annwyn. The column is going to Annwyn and I have to get back, you hear me!"

"Listen, Fern, we understand," Abelard muttered with lessening patience. "But they'll take us to a gateway and Brid has the Pipe. We're best off in the column."

"I don't believe you. We should go on alone."

"No, Fern. This is best," Brid said smoothly and authoritatively.

The little woodwose looked up at her and twitched his nose appreciatively. He appeared to have a great deal more faith in Brid's word than Abelard's. He fell in alongside her, throwing in a few extra skips and jumps as he went, while casting irritated glances towards the ancient archer. Abelard looked more out of place than any other soul in the column. His clothes reminded Caspar of the glorious gilt illustrations in an ancient book of fairy tales that he had loved as a small child.

His mind was still reeling from the shock of being attacked by the wolf and it took him many miles of slow walking before he began to come to terms with what had happened. For the time being at any rate, they were safe. Like Fern though, he was now beginning to worry about joining the column. What if the verderers realized that they were not intending to pass on to Annwyn? Would they take them back to Abalone and the dungeons or turn them over to the hunt?

The elfin-like verderers marched alongside with a sprightly step, their unremitting song controlling the movement of the column. There was something about the set of their faces that warned Caspar of how they itched to use their beautiful gold and silver bows. Their bodies taut and alert, they were ready for the moment any soul might attempt to break away into the woods.

"What good will it do them if they try to escape?" Brid asked.

"Those as are unreconciled with death might, like Fern, seek a way to return. Mostly they head back to Abalone, hopeful that they can persuade Nuin to unlock the door at the centre of the castle for them."

Caspar tried not to look down at his chest. Though there was no pain, the grievous wound smelt and looked quite horrendous. His hand subconsciously rubbed at his scalp where the few hairs had been plucked out. The spot irritated him.

The sudden thunder of fast-moving beasts and the sound of snorting and grunting filled his head. The verderers hurriedly drove the column to the side of the path. Cattle! Each beast was similar to the next and he realized that they must all be part of one herd and, no doubt, had been slaughtered all at the same time.

Brid looked at him, her eyes widening fearfully. Caspar knew they had simultaneously reached the same conclusion that here in Rye Errish it was possible to meet any animal that they themselves might have killed or eaten in the world of the living.

"You know what's strange?" Brid said, keeping her voice low for fear of drawing attention.

"No, what?"

"They've been used by man, herded and controlled all their lives and then killed by man and yet they've still chosen to come back as they were to suffer the same fate again."

"The pastures are sweet and the life easy," Abelard ventured when Caspar could give no sensible reason for their behaviour. "All creatures have to die and a quick and sudden death is all that most would ask for. Why not choose to go back to graze the green fields again?"

Caspar thought about it and almost found the idea appealing but Fern was horrified. "I can wander the forests at will and never once be controlled by man."

"Well, you give up your freedom by becoming a man," Caspar told him. "We men are all beholden to someone."

"Surely as the heir to Torra Alta y' have freedom, Spar," Abelard pointed out. "Y're not a tied man and can do as y' please."

"Just as my people are tied to me so am I to them. I

can do as I please so long as it is for the good of the people."

Abelard tilted his head to one side, conceding the point but then added, "But it's y'r choice to serve them. I'm sure as there's noblemen who choose to do as they please regardless of their people."

Caspar considered that there probably were. "But are they ever free from their consciences?" he asked feeling that he proved his point.

"Men like that don't have consciences." Brid destroyed his argument. "Men like Rewik see themselves as great responsible leaders but do they know what their people need? Often the burden they feel is little more than the weight of their egos and their thirst for power." Suddenly she nudged Caspar's arm. "Don't look but there's a man behind watching us too intently."

Caspar nodded, trying to look surreptitiously over his shoulder.

"Stop it," she said. "Try and look contented and at peace."

"I can't. I'm not."

"Well, try a bit harder," Brid told him, lowering her head and relaxing her stride so that she looked more at ease with the general pace.

Caspar tried to follow suit but still found his eyes wandering over his fellow travellers. He felt uncomfortable. Someone was watching him and the compulsion to turn and look was building to unbearable levels. Caspar coughed to try and clear his emotions and felt his freckled skin begin to flush a deep crimson. He finally succumbed to his curiosity and, despite Brid's insistent hissing at him, cast a look over his shoulder.

At first, he noted only a verderer vaguely looking in his direction, his mouth working over the words of the song. For a moment Caspar feared the wolf-like man in the iron head brace from the dungeons was a part of the column but the thought was washed from his mind by the rolling tones of an old and familiar voice at his shoulder.

"Blessed Mother, not Master Spar."

CHAPTER TWENTY-ONE

Princess Cymbeline stuck her nose in the air and spoke a few hushed but acid words to her brother, in Ceolothian. Hal didn't catch them but presumed, by the way Prince Tudwal flicked back his blunt fringe from his eyes and glowered darkly, that they were not to his liking. Hauling on his reins, the prince dragged his horse round by the bit and spurred the heavy brute forward to head the column. Hal was glad. With Tudwal out of the way, he could once more enjoy the princess's company.

The days were long as the wagons crept along the narrow road through Ceolothia's seemingly boundless forest and he came to treasure her company. Cymbeline had sought his companionship more and more of late and he relished any opportunity to be alone with her. He was even more pleased by her attentions because it clearly infuriated Tudwal. Someone needed to put Prince Tudwal in his place and Hal admired Cymbeline's ability to do so. Sisters, it seemed always held great power over their brothers. Certainly, Ceowulf's wife, Cybillia, ordered all her brothers about, even the eldest who was to inherit the wealthy Barony of Jotunn.

Several days had now gone by without any hint of that disconcerting stale odour, which Tupwell had first noticed, nor the strange tracks and Hal had almost put all thought of them to the back of his mind. He was enjoying the ride, especially with Cymbeline by his side, until Prince Renaud joined their company. His smile fell flat and he began studying his surroundings, hoping that if he provided no amusing conversation that the prince would move on and seek out Hardwin or Tupwell.

Naked winter oaks, their gnarled bark and twisted limbs coiling upwards to the sky, were now interspersed with smooth-barked beeches. The months of Horning and Lenting were past and, with the coming of Ostara, spring was just beginning to peek through. Unlike the oaks, which were always the last into leaf, the beech trees were covered in tight sticky buds some of which had burst out to give a feathering of pale green leaves. Hal noted how no fresh shoots grew below shoulder height and deduced that the forest deer had neatly pruned off all the lower branches. A movement to his left caught his eye. Though he heard no more than the softest rustle, an entire herd of deer, over a score strong, galloped through the deep pile of crisp leaves fallen in the previous autumn. There was nothing untoward in the herd's behaviour but Hal was already on edge, still anxious because of the unfamiliar footprints they had seen in Ceolothia's soft mud.

Princess Cymbeline exclaimed with delight at the sight of the deer. Her amazed expression told Hal that she had rarely seen one before. Though much of Ceolothia was under large tracts of forest, the capital was surrounded by open plains where deer were scarce.

She tilted forward in her saddle. "Can't we follow them?"

"It wouldn't be safe to leave the escort, your highness," Renaud told her.

She looked disappointed. "But they're so enchanting. They move so quickly and yet so silently as if they had wings. I would like some deer. I shall have a garden full of deer."

Hal was about to tell her that if she did there wouldn't be much of a garden left but held his tongue.

"If we found a fawn, I could take it with me as a pet," Cymbeline continued. "You'll catch one for me, won't you, Hal?"

The Torra Altan found the idea quite absurd but he merely bowed. "Whatever your heart desires. I am ever your servant."

He spent the rest of the day trying to look as if he were scanning the surrounding forest for a mother hind with a small fawn whilst hoping that he wouldn't see one. Brid's voice, like a conscience, whispered in his ear that to even contemplate stealing a fawn would be wrong. Hunting for food was one thing but to kill a hind so that the princess could keep a little fawn tied up in her garden was quite another. He was thankful that the opportunity never arose, though, for appearance's sake, he continued to stoop forward onto Secret's shoulder so that he could see beneath the level of the fresh beech leaves.

As he rode, the perspective from which he viewed the trees was constantly changing so that those in the distance appeared to cross behind those in the foreground, and it was very distracting on the eyes so that when he first saw the beasts, he thought he was mistaken until he got a further sighting. To Hal there was no mistaking them; as large as an ox with tusks, hog-bare skin and a roach back. Though the animal's skin was black rather than grey, it was very similar to the Vaalakan trolls he had previously encountered.

"Troll!" he shouted to alert the troops. "Ceowulf, troll to our right."

The troops closed ranks and drew swords. "Stand close to the wagons," Hal ordered. "If it's a male troll he'll go straight for the women."

There were squeals of fright from the central wagon.

Tudwal, however, laughed. "Trolls, Belbidian? You're a fool. I told you there are none left. No doubt it's just a bear. Relax, men. Let's keep these wagons rolling."

But Hal was certain he was right and kept himself firmly positioned beside Cymbeline.

"Trolls!" Tudwal again snorted scornfully. "Fool, Belbidian, it was no doubt just the trunk of a tree distorted by shadows. You're all nerves."

Hal knew what he had seen and so felt no inclination to defend himself. Time would prove him right. Trolls were innately aggressive creatures and once they had identified a quarry they would soon attack. Tudwal whistled up his dogs and took the head of the column but not without first throwing a sneer at Hal and a long, hard resentful look at his sister. Hal briefly wondered how Cymbeline had so offended her brother but merely smiled confidently back and put his mind to preparing himself.

He called Ogden to his side and told him to pass the word to the Belbidian troops to keep close around the women and on no account to break ranks or pursue the trolls. He nodded at Ceowulf, gesturing that he was certain of his sighting. The big Caldean nodded back and turned his great black destrier so that he was pacing steadily on the right of the central wagon. Hal took the left side and placed Cymbeline between him and the wagon.

"Do you really think there are trolls?" she asked with innocent excitement. "My brother is rarely mistaken."

"There are trolls," he affirmed. "And whatever happens, keep close by the wagons. Trolls look clumsy but they'll outrun a horse without the slightest problem so do as I ask at all costs."

They paced on in taut silence for nearly half an hour and, despite his own convictions, Hal was beginning to feel slightly foolish.

"I did say Tudwal was always right." Cymbeline smiled teasingly. "Besides Trows Forest was cleared of the beasts long ago."

Hal nodded back with an uncertain smile. He had been certain it was a troll and just because it hadn't attacked yet didn't make him wrong. Still, he was beginning to feel as if he had been somewhat melodramatic until he noted that they were leaving behind the beech forests and entering closer mixed woods, dense with intertwined hawthorn, red birch and buckthorn. He was instantly alert. Trolls were intelligent animals and may well have raced ahead to find a more suitable place from which to launch an ambush.

He carefully checked his weapons, freed his horn from his clothing so that he could quickly raise it to his lips and lifted a light lance from its carrying pouch on his saddle.

A movement in the birches to his left caught his eye. He hefted the light lance and adjusted his grip. The stout saplings rippled like corn disturbed by a running dog and without hesitation he raised his horn to his lips and blasted out one single note. Reflexively, he hurled his lance as the short snout of a troll broke out of the thicket. Its skin was redder in colour than the troll he had spied earlier and Hal knew at once there was more than one beast and feared that the line of wagons would be attacked simultaneously along its length.

His lance shattered the bared teeth of the troll and stuck into the cartilage at the back of its throat. The noise, as it bowled over and twisted through the undergrowth, was drowned out by Cymbeline's screams.

Hal wished he had just a few Torra Alta archers to bring the trolls down at a distance but he didn't and it was pointless to dwell on such matters. It was focus that mattered. Riding bodily before the princess, he drew his sword and braced himself for the impact of attack.

"Keep a firm grip on your horse," he shouted with booming authority. For a moment he took in the yells from the men, grisly snarls and gnashing growls from the attacking trolls and the panicked shrieks from the women. Then his focus narrowed. Before him, a short-legged troll with a jowly mouth and protruding upturned tusks was working through the undergrowth towards him.

Using his legs to guide his horse, Hal wheeled Secret to face the beast so that she could absorb the shock of the troll's thundering weight into her hindquarters. With his sword in his right hand, he balanced in his stirrups to make a clean strike at the troll's throat. His mind was so focused that he even saw how its left tusk was splintered and cracked. Secret jittered beneath him and he tightened his gauntleted hand around the hilt of his sword.

He held contact with the troll's eyes as it burst towards him in sudden attack, its claws drumming on the soft ground. He thrust the sword up above his head and spurred Secret forward to meet it. The troll had aimed for Secret's head but the horse's sudden movements upset the beast's approach and it lunged directly onto the runesword. Hal grunted as the great weight of the beast shuddered through his braced arm, slamming him against the high cantle that reared up at the back of his saddle. Secret dipped under the shock as the sword twisted in the troll's neck, the creature's scream spraying out in a blood-red sheet that splattered over Hal's arms and face.

Once the beast was felled, he gave it no more thought and looked for the next. None came straight for him and he had time to glance quickly around. Tudwal, a whirl of flashing metal, axe in one hand mace in the other, was hacking his way through three trolls in his efforts to reach his sister's side. "Cymbeline!" he yelled in panic.

Fearful for her brother's safety, the princess craned upwards, scanning the mêlée for him. But Prince Tudwal was a solid man with a vicious panoply of weapons and took on the trolls with gusto. Ceowulf was spurring his horse to Cai's aid, his lance tilted to spear the tough hide of a roached back as the beast latched, like a lion, to the quarters of the sergeant's horse. The troll fell away and Ceowulf turned to face another attack.

Hal blotted from his mind the screams as men were dragged from their horses, their chests raked with lashing troll claws. The Vaalakan trolls' usual method of killing a man was to rip open his jugular with a sideways swipe of the claw and these Ceolothian beasts were no different.

The man to Hal's immediate right was in trouble. His horse was down and, as he rolled to the ground, the troll flicked him over and drew back a curving claw to strike again. Hal burst forward, swinging his sword about his head. It planed through the air, cleaving through the troll's claw and on to split its skull.

Hal caught the soldier's look of relief as he rolled gratefully upright and reached for his sword. In that instance Hal knew he had distanced himself from the princess's side but, as he turned Secret to barge through the tussling men, a cry from the other side of the column slowed his pace. His loyalties were torn. It was his duty to protect the princess, but the cry came from Ceowulf, his friend, and, in the midst of battle, his decision was made: he could not forsake him.

Two trolls attacked the knight. Hal switched the grip on his sword so that he could use his right hand to snatch up a throwing knife. He hurled it too quickly and it cartwheeled uselessly over a troll's head and into the thicket. He cursed. Knives were a treacherous weapon if handled clumsily and he could as easily have harmed his own men as kill a troll. He snatched up a second. This time he paused to take better aim and fixed his eye on the head of the troll lolloping away from him towards Ceowulf's rear. The animal jerked as the blade skimmed through its shoulder and embedded in the flesh of its cheek. It wasn't enough to kill the beast but it gave Ceowulf a moment's grace to concentrate on the other troll. It reared up before him, exposing its breast as it lashed at his destrier's head. With one lunge the knight powered his lance deep into its ribcage.

Hal trusted Ceowulf to cope with the remaining beast and turned to look for Cymbeline. The distraction, however brief, had lost him valuable seconds. The central wagon was exposed and there was a dreadful squeal from a horse as a troll charged the side of the wagon with all the force of a ten-man siege ram. Its great tusked head hammered into the wooden boards, the force bursting the spokes from the rim of a wheel on the opposite side. The troll's coarse legs powered on, tilting the wagon onto the ruined axle stub. The wagon swayed and, in a sudden rush, toppled over, dragging the team of squealing horses with it. A thrashing maelstrom of hooves scattered the men close by. Four trolls burst from the cover of the wood and charged straight for the wagon.

"The women! Look to the women!" Hal shouted as two of Cymbeline's ladies-in-waiting were dragged out by their feet, clawing frantically at the ground.

Cymbeline's horse was bucking and kicking in panic and Hal's only thought was to protect her. The other men would have to save her ladies-in-waiting. If she were thrown or the horse bolted, as he knew it was apt to do, all would be lost.

Secret's solid flank pressed up against her palfrey. He

didn't bother to grab Cymbeline's reins but gripped her about the waist as her horse plunged and bucked. She was heavier than Brid and it was awkward for him to hold her but she kept her head. As her palfrey ran from under her, she bravely scrambled for a hold on Hal's saddle.

Two trolls lurched forward but turned away at the sight of Hal's sword before him. A few more screams, some animal, some human, pierced the forest and then came sudden silence. The trolls were gone. All seemed to hold their breath as they waited for the next attack. When none came the air was soon thick with panting and excited shouts.

Ceowulf dismounted with a heavy thud and pulled his sword from a troll. Though dead, its claw still gripped fast to the leg of one of Cymbeline's ladies-in-waiting. She lay still, Hal hoped only in a swoon. The other one was on her feet supported by Ogden who looked down proudly at the hacked body of the troll at his feet. Black wells of blood oozed thickly from deep wounds that had split open its chest and abdomen. Flies buzzed and mobbed the wounds and clumped thickly around the eyes and tail.

The air was crammed with noise; shrieks from the horses, groans from wounded men and sobs from the women. Ceowulf was cutting the squealing horses free from the stricken wagon, while Tudwal, white faced with anxiety, came thundering from the fore of the column, searching for his sister. He saw her loose horse and his deep voice became a thin wail of dismay as he called her name. His cry was quickly swallowed, however, as she shouted to him from the back of Hal's horse.

The prince slumped into his saddle with relief at the sight of her face. There was a brief flash of gratitude in his eyes when he met Hal's gaze but it quickly soured and he glowered at him for a long cool moment before manoeuvring his horse through the debris towards them.

"Sister, let me help you to your horse. You are unhurt I trust?" he asked, grasping her hand.

Cymbeline snatched it away. "No thanks to you." She gripped Hal's waist tighter for a moment before allowing her brother's strong arms to lift her down so that she could remount her own horse.

She flashed Hal a gracious smile. "My gratitude is all for you, noble knight of Belbidia."

He bowed back, basking in the adulation. "Your servant, my princess."

He knew now was the moment to leave her as there were men to attend to, a column to reorganize, wounded to succour and dead to be buried. He turned to leave, acutely aware of her gaze following him.

Three men were dead and two badly wounded. The latter were placed in a wagon where they could be tended. The post-battle euphoria was over and a heavy silence hung over the men as they grieved their losses. Hal dismounted and worked his way through them, praising and cajoling and giving them simple but worthwhile tasks that would keep them busy.

They nodded respectfully back at him and Ogden risked a smile. "It's good of you, Master Hal. The men appreciate it."

He looked towards both princes huddled together with Tupwell and Hardwin. Prince Renaud was shaking and still held his bloodied sword before him. It seemed he had managed to stab it into a troll. Hal was faintly surprised. None of them had paid the least attention to the men. Since Ceowulf, who had cut the traces of the stricken horses, was still struggling with the practicalities of righting the wagon and fixing the wheel, he and Hal were the only noblemen amongst them to give the troops encouragement.

After the burials, Hal advised they should move on as quickly as possible. Activity was the best thing for morale and, though it evidently galled him that he should be seen to follow Hal's suggestions, Prince Tudwal reluctantly conceded.

The light was already fading and they needed to get to the next staging post at the small forest hamlet of Gortbarrow before it was fully dark. Hal took up his place by the central wagon and Cymbeline greeted him with an eager though exhausted smile. She looked pale. He expected her to say something about how awful she felt that men had died to protect her. He expected it because he knew that was what Brid would have said but the princess was a princess, accustomed to bodyguards, and Brid wasn't. Cymbeline had evidently thought little of it. After all, what was the point of an escort if they were not prepared to fight for her?

"Thank you, Lord Hal," she said graciously, unwrapping the scarf from her hair. "You were right; there were trolls. We owe our lives to you." She moved her horse forward so that she could wrap her scarf round Hal's neck. "Thank you, my knight. You saved my life." She leant closer and her lips brushed against his cheek.

A whoop of triumph rose in Hal's throat but he managed to choke it back. He had won her scarf! As she turned away his eyes lingered on her back and he stroked the soft scarf against his lips, inhaling the sweet smell of her body that lingered on the material. A broad smile of satisfaction spread across his dark features; he had proved himself. Someday, someone would write an epic ballad of how he had so heroically saved the Princess Cymbeline from the lustful beasts of Trows Forest and won her.

It was late that night when they eventually reached the tavern in the remote woodland hamlet of Gortbarrow. It was little more than a ramshackle ivy-covered log cabin but it would serve their needs, Hal thought. Inside it was devoid of customers: a messenger had ridden on ahead to warn them of the approach of the royal party and clearly the landlord had turned out his less illustrious patrons. Hal was just wondering where all the other travellers would sleep that night when Prince Tudwal launched into an emotional diatribe on the subject of trolls.

"Repeated hunting parties rid the forest of trolls many years ago. There have been no sightings for years and now, suddenly, there's an entire tribe of them boldly harrying the road."

"Like the wolves in Belbidia," Tupwell sympathized. "Lately they are simply pouring south from Torra Alta." He flashed Hal a meaningful look.

"Pagans!" Tudwal spat onto the tavern floor. "All the doing of pagans."

Hal jerked upwards from his seat, rage pulsing through every inch of his body, but he caught Ceowulf's troubled glance and slowly lowered himself down, thinking it expedient to remain tacit. He thought of the unnatural footprints and the ghostly bear and worried that the wolves might be conjured from the same necromancy. It wasn't until much later, however, after they had retired to bed, that he had a chance to speak with Ceowulf about the matter.

"Hooded wolves and trolls; more of the dark creatures of the earth," Ceowulf said in deep concern. "We'll be seeing goblins next."

"It's Spar, isn't it?" Hal felt sick deep within his stomach. "I knew all along he wasn't strong enough. The power of Necrönd has got the better of him and he's allowing all the creatures to return from the Otherworld."

"It looks like it," Ceowulf sadly agreed.

"I knew it," Hal repeated, feeling both angry with Caspar and ashamed for him.

He slept badly that night, his dreams troubled by trolls and wolves tearing at his legs though, thankfully, the dream finally gave way to Princess Cymbeline melting into his arms and pressing great nuggets of sunburst rubies into his hands. Then, with Secret's polished bard glittering with encrusted jewels, he was riding furiously up the Tor of Torra Alta to show off his new suit of armour to Caspar. But Caspar wasn't there. He could only hear Brid weeping forlornly. He couldn't find her at first and, in panic, ran wildly through the castle, crying her name. He found her at last, lost, alone and terribly frightened, curled up in a dark oubliette at the very depths of Torra Alta's stale-smelling dungeons; but he couldn't pull her out. The leaden weight of his new armour clanking and crashing against the sides of the dungeon wall prevented him from moving freely. He panicked and began wrenching at her arms and the sound of clanking grew louder until suddenly he was awake. Ceowulf was rising from his bed, stamping his feet to get warm, and outside the yard was alive with the general hubbub of morning activity.

The dream had unsettled him and Hal was eager to get moving, though Cymbeline's warm smile of greeting cheered his spirits considerably as the noble folk convened in the tavern for breakfast. After a brief breakfast, where he had little opportunity to talk to the princess, he was again impatient to be moving though Prince Tudwal showed no signs of hurrying. Hal gave Secret a brisk grooming to vent his frustration as he waited.

It was only when they were at last heading east on the road again that he noted an uneasiness in the men. He had expected them to be dour and sombre after their losses but they seemed unsettled and anxious, many snatching at their reins and sitting stiffly in their saddles.

After some hours, the birch trees gave way to majestic

oaks with more space around the trees. The taller trees gave way to coppiced oaks, with vast trunks and clumps of thin short branches, sticky buds just forming on the tips of the bare branches. The oak wood was so old that Hal fancifully felt they were travelling back in time. They passed a charcoal-burner's where round structures of piled wood and turf looked like a miniature village but after that they saw no further evidence of human habitation. The woods became silent except for the rustle of leaves and the swish of horses' hooves brushing through the crisp golden carpet of fallen leaves.

Only then did Hal sense the enormity of the Ceolothian forests. They had been travelling through it for weeks and now, suddenly, he had the horrible realization that if he left the road he could become forever lost.

The Ceolothian soldiers were muttering amongst themselves and he wished his command of the language were better. He nudged Secret further ahead of the wagons to ride alongside Ogden.

The man nodded politely at him. "Morning, sir."

Hal grunted and tilted his head towards the Ceolothian troops. "They seem unsettled. Have they said anything to you?"

"All too much," Ogden replied, widening his eyes expressively. "Cai and the other Ceolothians have been saying how they don't care for Hobs Slack, sir. Isn't that right, Cai?" he called over to the Ceolothian sergeant. The man nodded sternly while Ogden continued, "They're as superstitious as any soldiers I've met. They say the wood's elf-shot, a fairy wood. Myself, I'm glad to be out of the worst of the rain but this way does run us perilously close by Hobs Slack. Cai was all for suggesting a southern route to Prince Tudwal just now but in the end, he didn't dare mention it. The Prince is not an easy man to approach."

"But there isn't a southern route," Hal objected. "It would mean travelling across the valleys and we'd be forever crossing streams and broaching ridges. We've got sixteen heavy wagons."

Cai nodded at a narrow-shouldered youth who rode five men in front of him. "See that lad there. He was telling me earlier that he used to live in the hills south of Trows Forest before his overlord sent him to work for the king. Anyway, he says the first few hills are difficult but beyond them there's a road you could drive three teams abreast."

Hal looked at him sceptically. If that were true Tudwal surely would have opted for that route. It wasn't until much later in the day, when the column slowed to take on water from a stream, that he had an opportunity to ask the Ceolothian prince about his choice of route.

Tudwal flicked his hand at his floppy fringe in that irritating way and looked down disinterestedly at his horse's withers as the charger chomped at its bit and snorted. "You were foolish to discuss this with the men and you're a bigger fool than I thought to heed what they say! We never go that way. It's an old route. By all accounts the road is sound but there are no way-stations, barely a village where we might gain shelter or supplies and it's a well-known area for bandits. They use the deep waters of the River Nar to gain access to the interior. Not safe or suitable for the princess at all. Does that satisfy you?"

Hal could feel his anger burning up his neck but managed to merely nod at this explanation. He would gain nothing by disputing the facts with Tudwal in his own country and he prided himself that the days when his temper ruled his actions were gone. He quietly congratulated himself on his self-restraint and considered Tudwal's words. It was, of course, most conceivable that the prince had a fuller understanding of the routes of his country than the young soldier.

Later on, however, Hal considered that Tudwal had been somewhat awry in his judgement, whatever the demerits of the more southerly route, when they were faced with a swollen river.

"Skins Gutter," one of the Ceolothians muttered at the dark waters rushing past. The river was brimming to its banks, fat bulging waters thick with pine-needles and twigs that formed a blanketing skin over the surface. A low wooden bridge supported by rickety posts spanned the river, water splashing up to the underbelly of the structure and lapping at the planking. Debris caught on the posts partially dammed the flow and the water level upstream was building rapidly. The bridge timbers creaked and looked rotten.

Tudwal's face fell.

"I knew we should have waited in Castabrice," Renaud muttered.

"We'll just have to head upriver until we find somewhere to ford it," Tudwal said, his face unsmiling, discouraging anyone from accusing him of making a misjudgement with his choice of route. "These bridges are supposed to be repaired each spring. Someone will pay for this."

The Ceolothian soldiers muttered and flashed each other anxious glances. Ogden drew level. "They say heading north with the wagons will be difficult."

Fortunately, this part of the forest harboured a great many hogs and deer that kept the undergrowth to a minimum, allowing the wagons to wind their way laboriously between the widely spaced trees, wheels crunching over twigs and beech nuts as they went. Tupwell made a big show of defending the rear of the column while Tudwal took the lead. Prince Renaud, who had looked anxious all day, kept close by the central wagons. Hal only hoped that they wouldn't be forced too far out of their way and that another bridge would shortly be forthcoming because he was certain there wouldn't be a suitable fording point. Not for miles. The spating river of Skins Gutter was black with mud torn from its banks

He was broodingly thinking that it would be ages before he received his next hot meal when Secret, who was usually so calm and sensible, skittered unexpectedly as the breeze stirred the leaves.

"Steady girl," he soothed. "What's getting to you?" Hal glanced towards Ceowulf who also looked concerned and was soothing the sleek coat of his horse.

"Whoa there, it's nothing but the breeze," the Caldean muttered, urging his destrier closer to Hal. "Keep an eye out for the ladies," he warned. "The horses won't be uneasy for nothing."

They moved on for several minutes without anything disturbing the peace until one of Tudwal's dogs, which had been trotting right at the fore of the column, stopped and stiffened. The hackles rose along its spine and its tail bushed out as thick as a winter fox's. Snarling and grizzling unhappily, he was staring fixedly at nothing more than a tree. Another dog, tail between its legs, took shelter under Tudwal's horse. Hal noticed uneasily that the birds had stopped singing.

Tudwal raised his whip in threat and the dogs moved on. "Ceowulf's keen to sell me some oxen but what I really need is a decent hunting dog," he growled and cracked his whip at the nearest dog.

The Belbidian soldier directly in front of the princess suddenly halted and reached for his sword. The movement was so abrupt that Cymbeline was unable to react in time and her horse thumped into the halted animal.

"What are you doing?" she shouted at him.

The man looked deathly white. He stared fixedly to his right. Trembling, he raised his free arm and pointed into the forest. Hal could make out nothing other than the warty bole of an ancient oak, its roots split with age.

"Steady there now. There's nothing to be seen," he said, firmly pulling at the man's reins so that the princess could continue unhindered. She smiled her thanks, her head coyly tilted to one side as she blinked her darkened eyelashes at him. Hal was acutely aware of the scent of her silk scarf around his neck and held her gaze for a long moment before turning back to the soldier. "What's the matter?" he asked the stammering soldier.

"I saw a man."

"A forester, a charcoal-burner perhaps?" Hal said calmly. Although he was angry with the soldier for his loss of control, he knew it would only make matters worse if he rebuked him.

"No, sir, it weren't. He was bleeding from his eye and clutching at his shoulder. Dressed in a chain-mail shirt, he was."

Hal patted him encouragingly on the back. "I think yesterday's attack has shaken all of us a little," he suggested.

He was concerned, however, at the growing unease amongst his own countrymen. Many were beginning to fidget and start. Several exclaimed in sudden alarm and pointed at things he couldn't see. The others, who like himself saw nothing untoward, were becoming alarmed by the fears of their comrades. Worse though were the horses that snatched at their bits and began to squeal in horror, eyes rolling. Hal feared that at any moment there would be panic.

"The wheel's jammed," one of the waggoners in the middle of the train cried as his big six-wheeler failed to negotiate the narrow riverside track and stuck between two tall oaks.

"Leave it!" a younger soldier cried, near hysterics. "We can't stop here; they're closing on us."

"Stand in line," Tudwal ordered. "Back those horses so we can free this wheel." He then began to snap and growl in Ceolothian.

One of the younger men began to cry and thrash out hysterically with his arms. "Get away! Get away! Leave me be!"

Hal saw the apparition at last. Not ten paces away stood the wispy image of a young girl, the solid trunk of the tree behind her still visible through her hazy body. She was clothed in sacking cloth, her pale blonde hair hanging raggedly around her shoulders. Her bare feet bled where the brackens and thorns of the undergrowth had torn her skin. She was weeping hysterically and reaching out her hands imploringly to the nearest Ceolothian soldier. The man's horse reared as she snatched at its bridle.

"Get a grip man," Prince Renaud shouted angrily. "I'll have you thrashed if you don't get your horse under control."

His words were barely audible for a scream of alarm to their rear. One of the Belbidian troops had his sword held high and was thrashing at thin air. Hal heard the assailant before he saw it. Out of nowhere came a scream of attack, the battle cry of Ceolothia that he had heard before from Tudwal's lips, and every man in the column recognized it. Ceolothian swords were drawn instantly. For Hal it was as if the fetch had stepped out from one of the ancient tapestries that had dressed the walls of Torra Alta in his youth. Before him stood a Ceolothian foot-soldier distinctively dressed in antiquated style. On his head he wore a steel cap with protruding nose guard and over his tunic he wore a simple studded leather gambeson reinforced with metal plates across his breast. A motif of a bear was stitched at his shoulder and he brandished a short sword for close fighting.

"Belbidian murderers!" the fetch accused, launching his attack at a Belbidian soldier, whose horse reared up as the apparition's sword thrashed towards its throat. The blade made no impact but passed clean through the animal's neck. The horse panicked, rearing up onto its hindlegs until it toppled over backwards, crushing its rider. The men scattered and the air was thick with startled cries from the women.

"Get in control! Stand in line!" Prince Tudwal and Tupwell were both shouting, while Prince Renaud and Hardwin looked as frightened as any of the women.

Ceowulf's voice boomed out in deep confident tones, above all others, "They can't hurt you, men. They can't touch you."

Hal disagreed. The fear was enough to harm them. The horses were near uncontrollable and, as more of the men drew swords to thrash at spectres clawing out of the gloom of the forest, matters could only get worse. He knew it was no good telling the men that they were safe. They were too frightened; they needed positive commands, a positive lead; they needed to actively fight their fear. He drew his sword and stood up in his stirrups.

"To me, men! To me! Stand firm by the women. Draw swords and close ranks!"

CHAPTER TWENTY-TWO

"No, for the pity of it, not Master Spar! I saved you, lad. Oh, mercy on my soul, I died happy thinking you safe. I thought the old witch was protecting you but now I find you marching through this land towards the after-life."

Caspar could feel the tears pricking at his eyes. Of all the men lost in the Vaalakan war, Catrik was the one he missed most. He flung himself into the old wellmaster's arms and hugged him tight.

"There, lad, there," Catrik muttered, sniffing intermittently. "I died happy, thinking you safe but now . . . Whatever happened?" There was deep sorrow in the man's voice. Gently, he held Caspar at arms' length to look at him. "What manner of beast did this?!" he exclaimed, studying the youth's wounds.

"An ancient wolf, here in the forest."

"Shh!" Brid sidled alongside. "We're attracting attention."

Catrik looked steadily at Caspar's companions, noting each one as he was briefly introduced. "So, you left Hal behind," the old man commented wryly. Brid blanched and clutched at her chest, muttering a few words of prayer and Caspar knew they were for his uncle's protection.

"Well, I'd never thought I'd live to see the day when you, Master Spar, would be separated from Hal," Catrik began. Then his eyebrows nudged up and he nodded his head as if conceding a point. "But there again I didn't live to see the day, did I?"

"No, you didn't. But it's more complex than that: we're not, or at least we shouldn't be, dead," Brid interrupted.

"Ah, but I fear you are mistaken there, miss. Let me explain," Catrik said congenially. "There's rules, you see. Did the verderers not explain when you arrived? There's no going back. This place is like a river; it only flows one way and you can't swim against the current. It's too strong and if you do, in a manner of speaking, you'll drown."

"We got here by accident," Brid tried to clarify things.

"Ah, but didn't we all. Well, mostly all," Catrik philosophized. "There's a few here looking mighty miserable what's got themselves here deliberately and a few that's old to look at but walk along like they're in their prime again. Now me, I was contented enough, feeling I'd had a good innings and done me a good job of serving the Baron and I'd died happy knowing the lad here was safe; but he ain't. Did he get you in the end?" Catrik asked abruptly but didn't wait for the answer. "You know, after all the years I'd trusted Father Gwion and listened to him saying how he cared for you and all, and then down the well we go and he triggers the explosion to bring the rocks down on you. I thought you dead but the Baron told me not. I remember clear as day how he came to my sick-bed to say that I was the only one injured in the blast and that you lived. But I never recovered enough strength to warn of Father Gwion's treachery. So, he got you in the end. The shame of it. How now can I be reconciled with my life when I have failed my liege-lord?"

Abelard looked at Catrik as if he had found a fellow soul and nodded in approval.

"You didn't fail," Caspar tried to reassure him. "I wasn't hurt in the blast and Gwion fell to his death from a cliff in Camaalia." Somehow, he didn't wish to add that he had caused his uncle's death. It seemed unwise to mention such things here in the Otherworld.

"I didn't know there were any cliffs in Camaalia." Catrik frowned. He seemed unable to take in the whole story and focused merely on the simplest of facts.

"Well, of course there are," Caspar started to explain but Brid caught his hand.

"Let me. You're only complicating matters." She started from the beginning and explained how they happened to be in the forest and inadvertently slipped through to the Otherworld because of Fern, who had stolen the Pipe of Abalone. "You see, we shouldn't be here at all and we really do have to get back and, on top of all that, the hunt is after us," Brid concluded.

Catrik grunted in understanding. "But what of him?" He nodded at the archer. "You've mentioned nothing of your last companion."

"Abelard, friend," the man replied for himself. "Bowman to the Baron, first rank."

Catrik warmly offered his hand and smiled. "Wellmaster to the Baron and his loyal subject to the end. Baron Branwolf that is."

"Baron Pellinore," Abelard returned the introduction.

"You've taken a while to follow the forest trail but, no doubt, you've reason enough. Well, I'm privileged to meet such a hero: you took an arrow and saved your baron's life," Catrik told him with an admiring smile.

Abelard stared. "How did y' know?"

"It's written in the chronicles. They spoke well of you." Caspar laughed.

Abelard looked at him suspiciously as if fearful of being mocked.

"It is," Caspar insisted. "And there's a ballad too. The ballad of Abelard the archer."

"There's a ballad about me!" Abelard exclaimed.

Caspar took in a breath and sung in a hushed but melodious voice:

Prince Galland, young and innocent, heir to all Belbidia,
Rode with Baron Pellinore on that sad and bloody morn.
Brunghar and Beotoric, Atterton and Halgard
Rode fast at their heels to meet the Ceolothian storm.

But first, Abelard the archer, bowman to the Baron
Torra Alta's finest, charged forth from the Tor.
Fearless of the enemy and proud before his baron,
He was first into battle afore the dogs of war.

Abelard the archer, bowman to the Baron,
Braver than the dragons that once ruled this land,
Though Pellinore's saviour and Torra Alta's hero
Could not save their aethling, the noble Prince Galland.

But Abelard, brave Abelard, took the deadly arrow
That was meant for Baron Pellinore
Sing Abelard! Sing Abelard!
May his name live evermore!

"Stop! I can't take no more," the man cried in extreme embarrassment. "It ain't deserved. I failed. The prince died and I knew his cousin would inherit. I was meant to protect Prince Galland; I failed; I brought about the downfall of the Old Faith."

Catrik bowed his head towards the man. "Well, I for one am proud to meet you, Master Bowman. Ah! But they must have been fine men in those days. The young nowadays—"

"Have no respect?" Caspar anticipated the old wellmaster's inevitable remark.

Catrik nodded in satisfaction.

Abelard laughed. "I thought the same in my day too."

Brid waved at them to be quiet. "You're drawing attention to us."

Caspar looked over his right shoulder and decided that Brid was overreacting. The nearest verderer was not looking at them in particular but letting his eyes drift over the entire column. Other souls also talked as they marched though he had to admit the majority looked wistfully ahead, already at peace with themselves and their past lives, the cryptic question of the purpose of their last life already answered.

"You're looking the wrong way." Brid indicated to her left and forward with the neatest flick of her eyes.

"He's not looking at us though, Brid," the youth objected.

"No, but he's been glaring at Fern and he'll soon connect him with us."

Caspar didn't need to ask more. Fern looked more uncomfortable even than the horselike man. The other souls moved relentlessly forward while Fern weaved from one side of the column to the next, butting elbows to force his way through to peer back down the length of the column, his eyes forever watchful.

Brid slipped away from Caspar's side to impress some sense of propriety on the little creature. The woodwose still looked anxious though happier as he clutched Brid's hand and she gently slowed his pace until they were back alongside the other Torra Altans.

Abelard muttered in his throat, "Stupid creature. What did y' think y' were doing?"

"We have to escape," Fern piped. "Look at their bows!"

"You've got to learn to be more discreet," Brid told the little horned woodwose.

"Can't y' see, Fern, how y're making it worse?" Abelard growled. "Or are y're just too stupid?"

"You just doesn't care!" Fern wailed back at him. "You don't realize how important it is. It's not your fawn back there being torn apart by wolves."

"Oh, shut up," Abelard snarled. "What's one fawn compared to the fate of—"

"It's my child! Don't you understand, she depends on me? She needs me and I've got to get back to help her." Fern stamped his cloven hooves and wrung his hands in distress.

Brid soothed his anxious hands. "We will get back, Fern, we will."

Abelard growled, sniffed and looked sternly ahead.

Brid patted the woodwose's shoulder. "Fern, you can't explain it to people who have never had children."

"How do y' know I ain't had childer?" Abelard asked accusingly.

Brid laughed. "It's obvious. You wouldn't have ridden so boldly out at the fore, trying to protect your baron and prince. The need to look after your own children would have held you back."

Catrik looked impressed with Brid's deductions. "Now here's a lass too young to know the emotions that come with bearing young ones but still she knows."

"It's only a matter of watching how others behave," she said dismissively. "When you don't have children, the world is yours but once you have them, your children are the world. And it's right too because they are the future."

As they marched on through the dark forest, Caspar found his hopes rising. They hadn't heard the sound of the hunting horn in what felt like weeks and he hoped they would soon be nearing the gateway. The foliage was still that of spring but the ground here was wet and the bracken alongside the track had given way to reeds and bog myrtle with exquisite starry white flowers. Over several days, they had gradually dropped from the high ground towards the marshes where the flat sheets of mist lazed on the waterfowl beds. A lapwing weaved and dodged over its nest, piping out its distress cry and Caspar feared for its chicks, thinking there must be a stoat or a grass-snake amongst the reeds. Immediately ahead lay heath, a russet blanket of heathers and ferns with tall gorse in the jubilant yellow flush of spring.

It was beginning to rain. Caspar had assumed wrongly that it never rained in Rye Errish but now he watched as a dreary drizzle washed away the colours from the gently undulating landscape until they were no more than shadow and pale mist, the dark line of each ridge just visible between the milky-grey hollows. Though the land-scape was no longer wooded this was, as Abelard reminded them, still forest because it was under forest law.

"Are the birds here part of the cycle of life?" Caspar asked, trying to keep his mind from their problems.

"I wouldn't think so," Brid said thoughtfully. "Morrigwen believed that the creatures of the Otherworld are born and die just the once. They never die of old age only of violent or brutal deaths and then return to the burning energy of the great sun god. There the heat burns the soul away until nothing is left. They are unlike the creatures of our world who return to the Mother to be regenerated in her love and given substance by Her own solidity."

"The landscape looks just like Ceolothia, doesn't it?" Caspar asked.

"This is Ceolothia!" an archly dismissive voice sneered from behind them. The voice belonged to a woman dressed in a purple satin gown that spread wide over a hooped skirt with a fringe of bows arranged in a scalloped pattern about the hem. The bodice was low cut and the shelf of her vast bosom rolled and rippled as she puffed along in slippers that were built up with wooden soles to give her height.

"It's raining, isn't it? It's quite obvious to everyone that we're in Ceolothia. Or are you an uneducated yeoman?"

"What if I am?" Caspar replied, seeing no reason why he should give this woman the truth.

He studied the ruddy complexion of the middle-aged woman. Though she had a handsome face and probably once had a handsome figure, she had gone too much to fat. But it was not the healthy fatness of an enjoyed life of good food balanced by hard work or the necessity to keep out the cold; it was the puffy fatness of indolence. He saw no reason to say that he was a high ranking Belbidian noble.

"I thought as much. Ignorant riff-raff. I hate this place and I hate walking. I have nothing to eat and I don't know where all my servants have gone. You, boy, will be my servant," she announced. "And girl," she looked at Brid, "you will be my serving-woman. I am rich and will pay you well."

"Gladly! I would be honoured to serve so fine a lady." Brid thickened her normally mellow mountain accent and bobbed a clumsy but deferential curtsy. "But, Ma'am, with what will you pay me?" she asked sweetly.

"My husband sees to all that." She waved a bloodied hand dismissively. "Now when we stop next you must see to my hair."

Brid laughed and the woman looked shocked.

"I must settle with your husband first," Brid insisted.

"He's not here," the woman said archly. "I'll have none of your nonsense. Is my word not good enough? Do you know who I am?"

"Why no, ma'am, we're common folk us. We have no brush with gentlefolk," Caspar burred and Brid winced at his terrible rendition of a yeoman's accent.

"I see." She drew herself up a little taller and thrust

out her bosom an extra two inches. "I am the wife of the richest man in Nattarda, excepting Baron Wiglaf himself. My husband is the greatest cheese merchant in all the countries of the Caballan Sea."

"He is?" Brid said with the required awe.

"The big cheese," Caspar interrupted, unable to contain his giggles any longer. He had caught Brid's eye, which was twinkling with delight at their sport.

Catrik tutted at them. "Master Spar, pray it is unfair to mock. She doesn't realize yet."

A small mousy looking girl pushed forward. "She's a good woman really." "She doesn't mean no harm by her ways. She's had little love in her life, only gifts from her husband, and she used to weep something awful at night."

"I've dismissed you, girl, and I will not have you talking to my new staff in such a way. It's one of my rules. I just won't have it."

"She doesn't realize yet what's happened. She doesn't know we're dead yet. The shock was too much."

"What happened?" Caspar asked in his usual clipped accent that clearly distinguished him from the common folk.

"We were ambushed on the road for her money. They demanded her jewels and the silly creature decided to stand up to them. They even cut the wedding ring from her hand because she refused to give it them. Brave as an ox she was and twice as stupid."

"I will have my husband see that you are punished for your insolence, girl."

"She shouldn't be in this column at all. She should be on one of the longer journeys and when she realizes what's happened, I fear she won't be able to cross into Annwyn," the girl fretted.

Caspar was surprised that the poor serving girl had any pity for this harridan.

"Madam, your husband cannot punish me," she tried to explain again. "He's not here."

"What do you mean, he's not here? I know he's not here but he will return home soon and then he will come to find me. He would never leave me. I mean more to him than anything else in the world. He gives me jewels; emeralds and diamonds."

"Her father is very influential. He owns a great many trading ships and gives favourable rates for the export of her husband's cheeses," the serving girl explained. "The merchant couldn't risk his disfavour and so he endlessly bought her presents. But he never loved her."

"How sad," Brid murmured. "How sad to go through life with all that money and no love."

There was a look of fear building in the woman's eyes. "No one has ever dared speak to me like this before. I am a merchant's wife. I am rich and powerful and I will not walk any further. Someone will carry me."

Caspar looked at her. "I am the first son of Baron Branwolf of Torra Alta yet I wouldn't speak to my dog the way you speak to your servants."

"Well then, no doubt your men have no respect for you," the woman sniffed, her eyes widening in mortification as if she realized she had made a fool of herself. "You have to let your servants know who's in charge otherwise you'll get no work out of them. I pay them good money and I expect value. But you, boy, are lying to me," she said with renewed confidence. "Clearly you are no nobleman otherwise you would know such things and wouldn't fraternize with the riff-raff. Now, girl," she turned to Brid, "you must find my rings. I've put them down somewhere but I can't remember where."

"They were stolen from you." All Brid's mockery was suddenly gone from her voice. This woman might be objectionable to her servants but she was confused. "And you cannot have them now because you are dead and have passed on into the Otherworld. You can have no servants here and no money. You must come to terms with that. You have passed on to the Otherworld and you cannot take status, wealth or property across the divide."

The woman sniffed in disgust. "Liar," she sneered and drew away, shuffling and muttering, a look of rising distress growing on her face. Occasionally she looked round at the souls about her and particularly at her serving girl who had a deep wound across her face and an arm that hung at a horrible angle. She then stared at her hand where her ring finger had been sliced off. "Men!" she eventually whimpered. "Three masked men with swords and a crossbow. I remember. They attacked us. We should be dead."

"We are dead," her serving girl told her patiently. There was a look of contentment on the girl's face as she stared past her mistress towards the warm glow of the eastern horizon that increased in brightness daily. Caspar felt sure it must be the glow of love emanating from the Great Mother that projected towards Her children as they struggled home.

"I'm dead!" the woman shrieked. She tore at her clothing, threw back her head and howled. "I'm dead! My money, all my money, I need my money!"

"The bliss of the afterlife is worth a million jewels," the serving girl told her.

"Don't you dare speak to me like that. What is this column doing? We are walking away from life. My money. If I don't have money, I won't have servants. I can't die without my money. I must go back for it."

"You can't bring it with you," Brid tried to explain.

"But there is no happiness without money. There is nothing without money."

The verderers closed their formation around the travellers as they entered a series of water meadows that lay between heath and the mists of the marshes. Some had their bows pointing at the column but most looked outwards to where shaggy cattle and dun donkeys nuzzled at the rough grass amongst the thistles. Short-legged coarse-maned ponies ambled in single file in search of fresher pasture.

Abelard nudged Caspar's arm and pointed beyond the ponies. "That's them, Spar. That's the commoners."

Caspar saw them now. Two tall but thin men with flat faces and stooped shoulders, looked covetously towards the column. Their arms and legs appeared too long for their spare bodies. One had a short bow, another a knife. They tramped a parallel route to the column of souls and Caspar was uncomfortably aware of their hungry scrutiny.

"They're starving," Brid murmured.

Fern had already drawn close alongside Brid, instinctively aware of the danger. The verderers herded the souls into tight order as they crossed the open heath. All eyes were warily turned on the hunched commoners and their dogs that lopped awkwardly at their masters' heels.

"See there, Spar, like I said. By forest law any commoner as keeps a dog must've part of the animal's back paw cut away," Abelard explained in a hushed whisper as he caught the youth's expression, "so as it's harder for them to bring down—" he faltered for a moment, "the game, should I say."

"You mean us," Brid said flatly.

Abelard nodded while Catrik straightened up and pushed back his old shoulders. He stood protectively in front of Caspar and Brid. Caspar was about to object but thought better of it. Catrik needed to feel that he was protecting him so he swallowed his pride and let the old man bristle. Fern nervously gripped Brid's hand.

"Dogs! Dogs!" he yelped. "Why are we standing here? Danger! Danger! Danger!" He leapt high into the air with increasing insistence as he piped his warning.

Brid caught his arm. "Sometimes it's more provocative to run."

"We must run!"

"You're a man now, and it's not always our way to run."

"Run!" Fern insisted as if he had lost any other form of speech.

Abelard threw his eyes up in annoyance. "He's the kind of fool that gets everyone shot in a campaign; the man that looses his arrows when we've been told to wait to the last minute." He looked at Fern with scorn. "No substance and no nerve."

"Hush!" Brid scolded the archer. "It's his way. We don't know what it's like to be a creature one minute and a man the next. The transition must be painful."

Caspar thought on this and decided he couldn't have been a man in his last life either. No, people like Hal and his father had been men, secure and comfortable, and at ease with the ambitions of men. Pip too, he thought. No, he was certain he hadn't always been a man. Just as Firecracker was frustrated with being a horse, Caspar felt overwhelmed with his responsibilities as a man.

"No nerve," Abelard muttered on to himself. "He'll draw the commoners to us."

Caspar could smell the sweat of fear and anticipation from the commoners as they prowled alongside.

The verderers were singing loudly to produce powerful notes that bolstered the spirit and closely mustered the column, which at least calmed Fern a little.

"Right flank!" a verderer warned as a lolloping hound drew so near that they could see its ribs rippling beneath its mangy coat. The dog snarled at them, hunger driving back his fear of the verderers' bows that followed the dog's movements until it finally retreated. Caspar's breathing grew steadier as he realized that, while they had the verderers' protection, they were indeed safe in forest. So long as they kept to this neat orderly column, the commoners wouldn't attack.

He reached for Brid's hand and squeezed it, offering a thousand words of friendship, love and protection in that one pulse of his muscles. She returned it more lightly as if acknowledging his sentiments, accepting them, but not quite reciprocating them. They marched on with stiff anxious strides, sweat dampening their backs as they trudged through the mud. The dark swath of woodland was a welcoming sight ahead.

"The commoners won't risk the woodlands," Abelard told them. "The woodland creatures are too dangerous for them. We'll be safe there."

"Nearly there," Catrik said positively, trying to bolster their spirits. "I can feel it in my bones." He looked round protectively at Brid and Caspar.

"We'll need a plan," the youth told Brid. "You won't be able to play the Pipe with all these souls around. They must pass on to Annwyn. We cannot bring them home."

He never heard Brid's answer for the sudden howl that screeched from the merchant's wife. "I'm not leaving without my money! I can't leave without my money! Take me back! Someone take me back! I've enough money, gold, diamonds, rubies to satisfy all of you if you'll take me back. I can't leave my money," she screamed helplessly, her mutilated hand dragging through her hair in her anguish. "I want my money!"

The rest of the column drew away from her as if fearing to be contaminated by her sudden desire to cling to life. A small wan-looking girl, wearing a simple white frock and little wooden clogs, looked at the merchant's wife in horror. Her terrified voice cut through the lady's screams. "I want my mother!"

Caspar's heart was bleeding for her. The tail of the column was beginning to scatter and he looked around in dismay, knowing that he must do something to prevent the ensuing chaos. He stood there gaping, waiting to take charge and muttering, "We must keep together."

The verderers' song focused on the merchant's wife, trying to compel her into obedience though there seemed little of her conscious personality left to subdue. She howled maniacally and Caspar feared she wouldn't even hear the song. His own mind was filled with the panicked screams of the little girl.

"Ma," she howled. "Ma! I'm lost. You've left me. Ma!"

Her last cry of anguish was smothered in Brid's bosom as she swept the child off her feet and hugged her close. "She hasn't left you. She loves you," Brid tried to console the child.

The girl was weeping forlornly, dragging at her hair with one hand and clutching at Brid with the other. Too late, Caspar realized he was caught up in the tragedy of one soul while disaster threatened the rest. The men, women and children had scattered. Distracted from the commoners by the screams of the merchant's wife, the verderers had neglected the others, and now the wild men of the heath were amongst them. With a sudden rush they split the group from the column. Their rangy dogs dashed in, jaws snapping left and right. Souls scattered in panicked frenzy away from the column, the dogs biting at their heels. The man that was still half horse was brought down before the verderers could take proper aim with their arrows.

Caspar's heart sank as he saw more and more of the

emaciated giants surge out from behind the leggy gorse to attack the column. The verderers fired their silver arrows but, with the column divided and panicked souls scattered about the heath, they were unable to protect them all. Caspar uncertainly reached for his bow.

Abelard looked to him for command. "Sir?" he asked stiffly, dropping the familiar form of address. He stood smartly to attention, awaiting orders.

Caspar remained motionless, deciding what to do. What would his father do, what would Hal do? "To me! To me!" he yelled. "Close up. Hold tight in a circle."

Many of the souls mustered to his determined cry though the merchant's wife broke away in a frenzy of flailing arms and wild shrieks.

"No, come back, come back," Caspar yelled.

But it was too late. The verderers were concentrated on the larger body of the column, which was now some distance ahead. A young commoner whistled up his three dogs and, clutching his knife point-down, gave chase. A dog ran her close, its muzzle snuffling the ground. It snatched at her ankle and she fell heavily. The other two dogs were quickly on her, worrying her fat body and tearing at her arms and face. The screams wailed on until the commoner fell on her with his knife and cut her throat. As she squirmed and struggled, he slit her down the belly and gutted her as swiftly as a huntsman would gralloch a stag. One of the dogs tore off an arm and rushed triumphantly away into the gorse, holding it high like a trophy. A trail of dogs followed.

"To me!" Caspar yelled. "Stand close."

"A circle!" Brid cried. "Form a circle." The simple faces of the accepting souls heard her words as commands. As they gathered around her, she flashed a smile of comradeship at Caspar.

"Abelard, take one side," he ordered. "I'll take the other. Catrik, here's my knife."

"I have one," the old wellmaster said, fumbling at his belt.

"And I," another soul cried out.

The three men and the youth stood protectively around their isolated party. There were no verderers left to guard them; all the yellow-eyed archers of Rye Errish were preoccupied, desperately trying to defend the larger section of the column. Ahead, the air thrummed with their silver arrows that became beautiful streaks of white gold flashing across the dove grey of the misty landscape.

Rapidly retreating from the arrows, a band of commoners spied the splinter group. Caspar felt his pulse quicken and swallowed hard, trying to master his fear. He took careful aim but held off, hoping that the emaciated commoner would retreat from his threat. He had too few arrows to waste.

The commoner's gaunt face wrinkled into a hungry sneer as he looked into Caspar's eyes. He swallowed, promising himself that he would not die here, not forever, in a place where his death would pass unnoticed.

The commoner grinned, revealing jagged teeth and a pointed tongue as four of his fellows joined his advance. One had only stumps where his hands should have been, no doubt as a result of punishment for stealing game. They rushed him and Caspar loosed his arrow, nocked another to his string and fired again. One of the commoners, with huge bony hands, grappled with an old man. Once he had his victim on his knees, the commoner tore at his scalp with his teeth. Catrik pushed forward and, with two hands on his knife, bore the blade down on the exposed ridge of spine protruding at the back of the commoner's neck.

There was no fountain of blood nor did a glistening

pulse of tendons and veins burst through the skin. Instead, the commoner crumpled like the dry empty skin of a snake.

The sight did not deter the other commoners who stood amidst his dusty remains, hacking in all directions with their rusted knives. Caspar could barely think for the screams and fired at anything, commoner or dog, within range, concentrating only on keeping himself between the commoners and Brid. She was all that mattered. She must not die, not here, not now. She had to make it back.

One soul broke away from their party but, unlike the others before him, it was more in savage attack than fearful panic. He lowered his head and ran at them like a raging bull. He was a broad solid man and piled into a commoner's stomach, rolling him over and flattening him to the ground. For a moment the souls cheered, rejoicing in the individual's bravery but then the dogs set about him. He lashed out at them and lowered his head, threatening with horns that had long since shrivelled away.

Despite Caspar's best efforts to drive them off with the last of his arrows, it took them only seconds to tear the man apart. The youth shot one dog through the eye and another ran off with an arrow deep in its shoulder. Behind him he could hear the persistent twang and whistle as Abelard loosed arrow after arrow at the circling commoners. Far off, through the mist, they could see the verderers and the main body of the column entering the safety of the woods. The verderers' song, devised to drive back the commoners, drifted to Caspar on the breeze but was too distant and undirected to have any effect on the wild men of the heath. The last of his arrows spent, he drew his knife and waited for them to attack.

The damp misty air held the stench of blood on the commoners' breath and he could hear the gurgling of saliva and the gnashing of hungry jaws as the dogs fought over scraps torn off the still kicking remains of one poor soul.

They rushed him. The first dog punched into his stomach and he was sent flying back into the souls behind. Another tore at his throat. Catrik sprang forward and hacked at the hounds with his knife to drive them off. Caspar found himself on his knees, trying to struggle up. Both Abelard and Catrik stood before him now, both men of Torra Alta determined to protect him.

Caspar could not let his men stand between him and oblivion at the risk of their own souls. He tried to crawl forward but his strength was leaving him. Three commoners rushed forward together and he thought they had all seen their last when the air was filled by the miasma of enchanting voices. The commoners retreated, their gaunt figures melting back into the mist and gorse. Caspar lay helpless in the dirt, no longer having the strength to stand.

Verderers pursued the commoners into the mist only for two commoners to attack the section from the opposite quarter. All around, men and women were fleeing in panic. Soon only the knot of Torra Altans remained.

Catrik stood over Caspar's body. "I'll get you home, lad, don't fear."

The commoners seemed heartened by the sudden panic in their prey and circled through the gorse ready to attack again. Lying on the sodden comfortless ground, Caspar saw a dark figure. He was unlike the commoners, moving like a shadow through the mist. Hooded wolves snaked around him.

Great Mother, protect Brid, he prayed silently.

From the shelter of the woods the other verderers, who had remained to protect the major part of the column, raised their song, summoning the splinter group forward.

Caspar could not move. Though his mind was willing,

his body was broken and his limbs would not respond. He could hear the verderers' song compelling them forward but he didn't even have enough strength to drag himself to his knees. The column was moving on without him. He lay helpless in the mud, awaiting his grisly end. Only the Torra Altans remained, their loyalty still stronger than the song of the distant verderers.

"You must go. Brid has to get to the gateway. Abelard, take her," Caspar ordered. "Protect Brid. You must see her through to the gateway. Go!"

Caspar could see so little but he felt the ground tremble with the thud of retreating feet. He knew he would be left alone to the dogs.

A big hand grabbed his collar. "Move, lad. You ain't finished yet. I've seen you born and watched you grow. Torra Alta needs you. I swore an oath to your father that I would protect you with my life and that I will do."

"Catrik, no," Caspar whispered. "Your life but not your soul. Go on with the rest and meet the bliss of the Great Mother."

"My place is by your side, Master Spar. You're still just a lad and, whatever you say, I ain't about to leave you."

CHAPTER TWENTY-THREE

Pip fretted with the iron band that chafed his neck. He was concerned for Brock who looked sickly green, his face dripping with cold sweat. The old man stumbled onto one knee, and he stooped to help him up.

"What do they want with us?" Brock grumbled as he prodded gently at his festering hand. Despite Ryder's potion, the edges of the peeling scabs still oozed a thick green pus.

Pip couldn't answer. He had no breath left for speech as he stumbled on behind the skewbald pack pony. Flag Scarp was now far behind them and they trudged through the dappled shade of birch woods, which marked the western border of the great Trows Forest of Ceolothia. The air became heavy with resin as the birch woods eventually thinned, and they slid into the gloom beneath an evergreen canopy of pine, working their way laboriously along little-used and overgrown tracks.

Pip was overawed by the immensity of the forest; days passed into weeks without any break in the monotony of the trees. The kobolds seemed glad of the trees, stroking and patting one or two of the older specimens as they passed but always keeping themselves as far away from Ryder and his ill-natured dogs as possible. After a few weeks in the subdued lull of the forest, Pip was beginning to feel some empathy for them as he noticed how they too stabbed reproachful looks at the blonde-haired Ceolothian. The boy was thinking how he could use the kobolds to his advantage when they rounded a bend and the overpowering hush of the still forest was broken by the rush of a fast-flowing water.

Through the trees they presently saw the rolling, earth-brown surface of a swollen river. Fingers was frowning. "Skins Gutter wasn't this big the last time we were here. The damn thing's in spate. We'll never ford it."

"The spring rains," Ryder said distractedly. "They happen every year. We'll head upriver, which is best anyhow 'cos it keeps us out of the heart of Hobs Slack. There's more than one bridge that way and the first ain't far." They trudged upstream.

Bridge wasn't quite the word Pip would have used for the irregular planking and posts that joined the large flat-topped boulders spaced at random intervals in the torrent. Skins Gutter, though much smaller than the Silversalmon, was brimming its banks and sucked and stormed around the giant stones. Surprisingly, the kobolds were undaunted at the sight and skittered across to the other side without the least hesitation.

Ryder unknotted the ropes that tied the prisoners to the skewbald pack pony and waved his skinning knife in their faces. "Don't even think of making a run for it," he growled.

Brock simply sank in exhaustion to the ground and slumped his head forward onto his knees, though Pip did wonder if this was the moment to jump the trapper. He bit his lip hard; without Brock's help it would be impossible and the old man didn't look like he could take another pace let alone run. Still, he was free from the pack pony for the first time in several long miserable weeks.

Ryder continued to stand guard over them while the fish-eyed Ovissian gingerly led three pack ponies across the planking. The rear animal sniffed at the wooden boards suspiciously but tottered forward, encouraged by a thwack from Ryder's oft-used whip. Pip was then ordered to lead the skewbald pony that carried the sack of wolves.

"You won't be taking no risks with that pack there, I know, Squeak. But just remember any trouble from you and your old friend here gets another beating."

Pip flashed him a look of utter contempt and took a firm grip of the pony's head collar as he stepped onto the wobbly bridge. The river gushed beneath them, black and angry. The skewbald pony stumbled forward on its cracked hooves and was soon trembling above the first of the supporting boulders. Pip drew a deep breath, steadying himself. The dark waters divided around the rock, carrying brush and pinecones that had fallen into the flood. They were swimming past at a horrible rate and the rolling surface spoke of strong undercurrents.

"Get on with it, Squeak, or are you afraid?" Ryder shouted from the bank, dragging Brock to his feet and pushing him forwards. "You next, old fool." He cut the man's hands free and gave him a pack pony to lead.

Fingers was already on the other side and had Pip's bow levelled at the boy. "No tricks," he warned, quashing Pip's rising hopes of escape.

"I'm a Torra Altan. I am never afraid," Pip shouted back at him. He tugged at the pony's head collar but faltered in his tracks at the sight of a large black creature running through the forest towards Fingers's back. For a moment he thought it was a small bear.

The black shape ducked around Fingers and headed for the planking bridge, rushing towards him. It wasn't a bear but a cloaked man, running hard – running at him.

Pip squared his shoulders, lowered his stance and prepared himself for the impact – only it never came. He blinked. His heart and his breathing stopped for just a moment and it was as if a cold blade had passed straight through him. He was imagining things; the man had run straight through him. Pip spun on his heels but was too late. The skewbald pony, bearing the sack of two wolflings, reared up and twisted sideways where there was no room to turn on the slippery planks.

Pip held tight to its head collar as its hindlegs slid from the bridge, its front hooves scrabbling for grip. He wouldn't let go. The wolves, his little wolves! He dug in his heels and clenched his teeth in his effort but could do nothing as the pony began dragging him with it towards the racing current. "Help me, Brock! Help!" he yelled at the old Torra Altan who was already on the bridge.

But Brock didn't lunge for the pony's head collar but instead grabbed his wrists, weakening his grip. "Let go, Pip, or you'll be lost. Let go."

Pip struggled to resist the man's heavy hands but he wasn't strong enough. The pack pony was on its belly, its haunches submerged in the raging waters and then it was gone, plunging and spinning round and around in the eddying current, and thrashing to hold its head above water for a foothold. The packs on its back bobbed up and down on the dark surface.

"My wolves!" Pip cried. He had cared for them through the long, lonely weeks and they depended on him: he couldn't let them drown. "No!" he shouted at the roiling water. "No!"

But it was Trog who forced him to action. The dog took a standing leap, diving in after the horse and landing in a spectacular belly-flop. The terrier was spun round and all but disappeared beneath the brown surface in a mad mimicry of the pony's dance before his frantic forelegs won the struggle to keep his head above water. He was making for the pony, his head held high, and strained forward to reach the sacking, which was kept above the water by the rolls of skins beneath. It dragged out behind, a bladder of air bobbing in the current.

Pip took one look at the dog and wrenched himself free of Brock's grasp. He couldn't lose Brid's dog as well as the wolflings – not Trog, the baron's favourite dog. He'd set out to save the animal. What could he tell Master Spar if he failed?

Trog was gaining on the pony, his mouth wide like a crocodile's, snapping at the sack. The cloth was becoming waterlogged and was gradually sinking. With one sideways sweep of his jaws, he raked through the sacking.

Pip caught his breath at the sight of a white whirl of fur. The little female wolfling was out of the sack and spinning free in the water, her instincts not yet formed enough to make her struggle. She was revolving round in the black waters, her long legs splayed out wide. Trog plunged for her and the last Pip saw as they were swept around the curve of the river was the terrier gripping the wolf in his jaws as he was tossed in the swelled waters. Trapped inside the sacking, the grey wolf never appeared.

Pip braced himself to dive into the river but Fingers caught the back of his belt and spun him round. With his mutilated hand he thwacked him hard across the mouth.

"You vermin. You scum. You thought to escape by pushing the pony into the river. Get back to the other side. I'll have those pelts and if I don't, I'll sell your skin instead." Fingers shook the boy by his shoulders until his jaw rattled.

"I didn't push him," Pip protested wildly.

"I suppose the wind swept him off the rock."

"I didn't push him," the boy repeated more feebly. "Why would I push him? He had the wolflings with him."

His mouth began to bleed as Fingers hit him again. Pip shoved back. "I didn't push him! You must have seen the man."

"What man?" Fingers jerked him back across the bridge and dragged him along the bank, searching for where the skewbald pony might wash up. Pip didn't understand. How could Fingers not have seen the man?

"There was nothing there." Brock was panting beside him as they ran back to the flooded ford where they had first joined the river. "What's got into you?"

Pip felt deeply confused. Why would a man deliberately push a pony into the river and how had the others not seen him? He must surely have imagined it. Had his brain been softened by spending too much time talking to the dog and the wolves?

"There!" Ryder was pointing downstream to the inside curve of the river where the flow was less ferocious over the shallows. The pony was lying on its side, its head swinging limply to the rhythm of the current. "The animal's bloody dead. And all those skins ruined. Bloody ruined."

Pip wrenched himself free from Fingers's grasp as the man momentarily softened his grip at the sight of the pony. He splashed into the shallows to reach the packs and urgently worked the sack open. He pulled out a little curled-up ball of matted fur. "Drowned!"

Ryder picked the boy up by his collar and shook him. "You've ruined the skins and drowned the cub. You'll pay for this."

He plunged Pip's head into the water and held him

under. Pip fought and kicked, terrified at how quickly his strength left him. The black water boiled with white bubbles that poured from his mouth. His arms flailed limply in the river around him as the Ceolothian whipped him back and forth under the water, shaking him like a terrier would a rat. Breath rasped through his throat as Ryder hauled him above the surface.

"No," Fingers shouted. He dwarfed the Ceolothian several inches and hauled him away from the river's edge. "He might be a Torra Altan, and I thought I'd feel different about that, but he's still a fellow countryman of mine and you'll not kill a Belbidian while I stand by. He might be unnaturally caring for wolves but you'll not kill him."

Pip was thinking that if he'd lost Trog, life wasn't worth living anyway. How would he ever prove his worth to Master Spar if he failed now? While the two trappers glared at each other, Pip, now slippery from the river, wriggled free and ran as fast as he could along the bank. "Trog!" he yelled.

If he could only rescue Trog, Master Spar would forgive him and Brid would be forever grateful. The Baron too! He'd be a hero.

"Go on then, get the bloody dog," Ryder screamed after him. Trees and dense bushes lined the banks; Pip found it impossible to run as the undergrowth thickened. He knew the only way to catch Trog was to swim after him.

He jumped down the bank, which was steep at this point, and gasped as he slithered feet first into deep water. It was cold, not as cold as the mountain streams of Torra Alta but still it knocked the breath from him. He strained his neck back to keep his head above water as he pushed away from the bank only to find himself quickly entangled in weeds and mats of twigs that were being swept along by the river. It was hopeless to resist the current so all he could do was flay his arms and try and keep his head above water as he was rushed around the bend of the river.

He gasped for air just before the Skins Gutter rolled him under and ground him against hard rocks on the riverbed. He kicked out against the bottom and struggled up for air just as the rapids sped him forward into calmer waters. Trog was only yards away, nearing the next curve in the river where a fallen beech stretched into the water, calming the flow.

The dog still had something white in his mouth but, with the spray and his own splashing, Pip found it difficult to see. He was not a strong swimmer; he had never had the need and he cursed this failing, knowing that Master Hal, or even Master Spar, would have reached Trog by now.

He had thought when he had first come to the castle that the two noble youths were sheltered from the physical harshness of life, always having others to do things for them but he had soon learnt he was wrong. They always did what they could for themselves and were experienced in many fields and Pip had soon discovered that it was his own skills that were limited to the woods and a woodcutter's life. He had set his heart on expanding his talents but had not vaguely considered improving his swimming.

Trog had disappeared. One second his bulbous white head had craned up above the waters and the next he was gone. A whirl of current showed where he had been dragged under.

Pip dropped his head into the water and hauled himself arm over arm through the river like he had seen Master Hal do at last midsummer's festival. The Baron's brother had challenged all the men to a race across a wide bend in the Silversalmon and back. Hal of course had won, as he invariably did when the contest was at his suggestion. Pip struggled with the technique but for all his efforts he was hardly moving and his lungs burnt with the exertion. Spluttering out water, he splashed towards the point where Trog had disappeared. Twenty paces downstream, a flash of white spat out of the water and, for a second, Pip caught a glimpse of the dog beating the water with his stocky legs. Trog's head was clear of the river for one precious gulp of air and his mouth was empty. The wolfling was gone. Pip redoubled his efforts only to see Trog plunge headfirst back into the waters.

The dog reappeared three times more, each time a little further down river and Pip was losing hope of catching him. It was hard to see anything in the spuming waters and it was getting harder now as the river swept beneath a dense canopy of pine trees whose tall trunks and evergreen branches clamped out the sky.

A log buffeted him from behind. He tried to scramble for it to help keep him afloat but it was slippery and spun away each time he nearly had it. A branch hit him in the back and another caught against his cheek; he was beginning to tire rapidly. For a frantic moment, trailing weed wrapped around his legs but he kicked himself free before it pulled him under. Across the swirling waters, Pip saw the dog thrashing the surface again where the river was calmer in the lee of the bend.

He had to rescue the dog; his whole future in the castle depended on it. He kicked frantically but was spun round by a raft of debris and branches. One branch knocked him under but, when he broke back up, he was at last level with the dog.

Trog surfaced just for a moment before disappearing again, though he wasn't pulled down but clearly had dived deliberately back into the murky depths. Pip couldn't believe it; Trog must be going after the white wolfling. It didn't seem possible. The boy had already given up hope that the white cub could still be alive. He gasped for air and dived after Trog. Completely unaccustomed to swimming under water, it took him a moment to realize that he would have to open his eyes to see what he was doing.

He caught a ghostly glimpse of the dog's murky shape coiling beneath him as they were all swept down river together. Trog was wrenching his head back and forth, worrying at something that Pip could not clearly make out in the blackness. Too quickly, he ran out of air and kicked to the surface. Whether the wolf cub was alive or not, it was clear that Trog would not give up until the body was retrieved.

Pip plunged back into the blackness, his eyes stinging as he blinked and searched through the swirling gloom, the roar of the river muffled and deep as he kicked down into the churning current. His cheeks still puffed with air, he got a hand to the dog and pulled.

Then he saw it; a flash of silver tail and fins, the flank of a great fish as it spun in the water. And a face! Without thought he recoiled in horror and fought for the surface, all notion of saving the dog or the wolfling swept from his mind.

Something caught his ankle. He instinctively knew that it could be nothing but a hand; nothing else could have that all-embracing grasp. It was pulling him down.

Bubbles streamed from his mouth as he clawed for the surface but he couldn't get free. He daren't look down. He couldn't look back into that face, a thin face with a sharp nose but no eyes; the face of a man. The sight of the dark pits of its empty eye-sockets sucked all reason from his mind. Never had he seen such evil, each black pit a hole into the emptiness of death.

His lungs screamed for air. He kicked at the hand but when it still held fast, he doubled up and clawed at it with his nails, forced to look again at the monster. It was like a great six-foot pike with vast down-turned whiskers and a hooked jaw but emerging from its chest were a human nose, mouth and empty eye sockets. Arms jutted from its flanks just behind the gills. One hand throttled the wolfling's neck, the other gripped his ankle.

The water churned around him as Trog dived again, his great curving fangs embedding in the pike's head. The vast fish thrashed its tail back and forth, flinging them to the surface just long enough for Pip to gasp in air. They were snatched down into the water again, rolling over amidst a froth of fur and foaming water. Just when he thought his lungs would burst, he was in the air again, gasping for breath and catching a glimpse of the tall dark pine trees and Brock struggling to break free of the trappers to help him.

"Brock," he tried to yell but only gulped in water. He spat and gasped, gulping in air before being dragged back down into the murk.

Trog was still battling frantically and he thought he saw the wolf cub struggle but it was impossible to be certain in the churning waters.

Pip never thought he would drown. He was still too horrified by the face embedded in the underbelly of the fish to think of anything else other than the abyss of black in the non-existent eye sockets. The creature's arms were sucking back into the belly of the fish and he was terrified that he, too, would be sucked in through the flesh of the pike to the creature within. A swirl of red clouded his vision. He didn't know if it was his blood, Trog's or the pike's only that he was being dragged along the gravel.

Pip was weakening. He had gasped in as much water as air and he had little strength left to fight his way free but the grasp around his ankle was gradually weakening too. The great fish rolled over, crushing him into the gravel but then suddenly he was free and he found himself crawling towards the bank. Trog had the fish's whiskered head in his mouth and was beating it back and forth, his curving jaws sinking deeper and deeper into the bone. Pip might have known that Trog would never lose a fight.

The dog seemed to finally realize he was on dry land and that the pike was dead. He dropped it and his eyes flitted across the surface of the water. He whimpered pitifully before plunging back into the river.

Pip lay gasping on the bank, staring at the pike. It was just a pike; the hands and the diabolical face were gone. It was just a plain old pike. He blinked at it for several moments before he recovered his senses and remembered Trog. The dog was in the fast flow of the river again, being churned like a mouse in a butter barrel. Ahead of Trog was a speak of white. Though exhausted, Pip waded back into the current.

Too weak to swim, he let the force of the current tow him down river, spinning him against the outside bends beneath over hanging banks. Here the water sped with force before grating him over the shallows. The woods around were dark, thick dense conifers that prevented the sun from filtering through. Pip stretched his neck up, gulping in air and spray. Shadows, silvery forms, slid between the trees. His blood turned cold. Miserable creatures stared at him from the bank, their tortured faces harbouring cruel hard emotions. They were mostly humans though a few dogs, a bear and several mountain cats slunk through the undergrowth, the snivelling creatures snarling and growling at each other.

Pip wondered at first if it weren't the cold and exhaustion that was causing him to see the apparitions. A man waded out and reached for his hand but he slithered straight through its touch. He felt no more than a shiver of cold. He must be half drowned, he told himself reasonably but then remembered where they were. Ryder had said they would make their way north to avoid the heart of Hobs Slack; Skins Gutter had swept him a good distance south.

"Here, give me your hand," a hollow voice echoed through his head as a thin ranger strode into the water. "Let me help you."

Pip stretched up his hand but the man's fingers passed straight through him and the ranger's desperate cry was steeped with wretchedness. "I couldn't save him. I couldn't save my boy."

Pip tugged his mind away from the horror of the ghosts around him.

"Pip, come over. Swim to me." He recognized the voice with relief. It was Brock who must have broken free from the trappers. He was running towards him along the far side of the river.

The boy looked at this hope but turned away. Brock might have given up on the dog, but he wasn't going to. With renewed efforts, he flung his arms out in a brave attempt to swim with force. Again, he found that cart-wheeling his arms created more splashing than speed and he was soon choking and spluttering out grimy water and river weed.

Trog struggled towards the bank where a spit of gravel reached out like a friendly arm, soothing the waters and stilling the flow. He scrabbled up onto dry land, a white raglike body sagging from his jaws. He shook himself like only a dog can, spraying out a halo of water, the limp wolfling being spun and whisked in the process.

"No," Pip began to yell, "no don't, Trog." He was worried for the wolfling but then he saw that perhaps the invigorating shake was what it needed. A back leg jerked and Trog laid the animal down and began to lick her vigorously, ruffling the hair backwards. She needed warming. Pip struggled up the bank and ran towards them but, as he did, Trog grabbed the wolfling between his teeth, his eyes flitting anxiously upstream and began to run, the little cub's legs flapping as he went.

Pip stumbled on, despairing of catching the animal and cast over his shoulder, wondering what had so startled the dog. He thought at first that it must have been one of the shades in the undergrowth, but it wasn't. It was the trappers. The Ovissian held Brock and was beating him about the head with the handle of his whip. Ryder had his bow aimed at Trog. He loosed the arrow, nocked another and fired again. Trog dodged left and right.

Pip froze, uncertain what to do. "Run, Trog, run!" he shouted in desperation.

The trappers had cut the angle of the curving river to catch up with them. Trog was still within bowshot.

"Run," Pip yelled and, without any thought for his own safety, ran in front of Ryder.

"Pip, no!" Brock shouted. "You'll get yourself killed."

Pip didn't care. He needed that dog. Rescuing Trog would bring him glory; and glory was worth dying for. Besides, Ryder wasn't a good shot; he'd already proved that with the stag. But he was a better shot than Pip had credited him. The boy's desperation to save Trog meant that he barely noticed as the first arrow skinned his shoulder. The second, however, pierced his arm, the force of it spinning him round and he stumbled to the floor, the punching pain forcing a scream from his throat.

Ryder fumbled for another arrow and aimed at the

fleeing dog. Brock struggled with the Ovissian and had the chain from his manacles looped around the man's throat. Kobolds screamed and yelled in frenzied disarray.

"No! No!" Pip screamed, the pain in his arm suppressed by his fear for the dog. "Help us! Mother, Great Mother!" he pleaded as Ryder's arrow flew.

His prayer was answered with a high-pitched animal yell. He rolled over, clutching his arm, to see Trog in a ball on the ground, whimpering softly. He couldn't see the wolf.

Leaving Fingers to struggle with Brock, Ryder ran for Pip and dragged him up by the scruff of his neck. Fingers was getting the better of Brock and caught the end of Brock's chain and swung it. It cracked into the side of the old man's face, felling him to his knees.

Ryder flung Pip down beside Brock and yelled at the kobolds to guard them. The little tree men bristled around Pip and jabbed and brandished their little sharpened staves uncertainly at Brock though there was clearly no need. The man was out cold, lying face down amongst the pine needles.

Ryder returned with the dog and dropped him by the two prisoners. Trog still held the limp body of the little wolfling in his jaws. Ignoring his own pain, Pip pushed himself upright to tend to the animals. The barb of an arrow had skimmed Trog's shoulder, revealing the red muscle beneath. The arrow's path had sped on until it had embedded in the shoulder of the little white wolf cub held in the dog's jaws. Trog let the cub slowly down into Pip's lap, surrendering the animal to his care, before his head collapsed back to the ground in exhaustion.

Fortunately, most of the arrow's energy had been spent as it ripped through the dog's tough hide before it had come to rest on the wolfling's shoulder bone. Exhaustion slowed Pip's wits as he fought for what to do. His arm was one entire throb of pain and he was beginning to feel sick. The world about him was slowly spinning. He tried focusing on the wolfling cradled in his arms. She felt so cold and limp. He had to keep her warm, he told himself as his head reeled. Though weak and giddy, he tried to stroke her coat and, with immense effort, reached his arm forward to cradle her head. Dimly, as his head slumped back alongside Brock, he was aware of her sucking on his finger for comfort.

When he awoke his arm was too stiff to move. It felt painfully tight where a bandage now compressed his arm and the skin was shiny with swelling. Though faint with fever, he was aware of a foul smell.

"We should finish them off here," the Ceolothian growled. "The boy won't make the journey anyhow. The wound's gone bad."

"I told you, I'm not murdering any fellow countryman even if they are Torra Altans," Fingers snarled back at him. "You hear? Besides, we'll get good money for them if we sell them to the ruby mines. They always need more men. I could do with the money and we'll get nothing if we just leave them."

With stabs of pain ripping through his injured arm, Pip pulled his head up to see the little pup in his lap. Someone had removed the tip of the arrow and bandaged the shoulder.

He remembered little else of what passed that day other than being lashed to the back of a pony and being bruised and chafed by chains and raw-edged wolf traps. Trog had an iron collar clamped tightly around his neck, the edge cutting into the back of his ears. The kobolds were trudging along with increasing reluctance, hanging back and scowling at the trappers. Pip had the suspicion that their numbers were thinning.

He remembered even less of the night except that he thought he would die of pain. By then his entire left side and even his face were swollen. Exhaustion dragged him down into fitful sleep and he dreamt he heard the screams of the dead, "Ma! Ma, help me!" The yell jerked him awake and he realized it was his own cries.

But Ma was dead. The memory was like a choking cloud. Even now he never allowed himself to remember the dreadful day when she was lost to the Vaalakan axes. He coped only by not thinking about it. He was still certain it was his fault. There should have been something he could have done to save her. He had sworn that he would protect her with the vehemence and sincerity that only the innocence of a ten-year-old boy could; but still she had died.

Master Hal had later found her body but they wouldn't let him see her. He'd overheard hushed rumours that her head had been severed but nobody would answer his questions. He had failed her and would never be able to say he was sorry. Unable to raise his sickened head, he curled up and hugged the wolfling to him.

That night the pain kept him awake. The crescent moon seemed to slide so very slowly, scything through the pointed tops of the firs, that he thought he would never see daylight again. Amongst the trees, he fancied that silver shapes danced in the moonbeams, cackling wickedly. Some came running out to tease him, young girls, thin veils draped around naked bodies, pulling playfully at his arms, urging him to join in the dance.

"Come, we know how to ease your pain. Please, come," they entreated him with gleeful giggles. "Come, play with us." He rubbed at his eyes and when he looked again their hair was aflame and their beautiful white skin began to char and peel, bubbling as the layers of fat beneath sizzled and popped. Too weak and pained to be afraid, he looked at them with detachment.

"Great Mother, have mercy," he whispered as the images faded. He didn't know if he were hallucinating or whether he saw the fetches of Hobs Slack. Eventually the moon slipped away behind the trees but still Pip could not sleep for the deep sickening throb in his arm. Again, he could see shapes, horses and men moving through the trees, but dismissed them as the delirium caused by the poison in his blood.

As a glimmer of grey dawn seeped under the dark canopy of the evergreen trees, he saw that the men were real and not a part of his nightmares. Heads bowed close, they were talking intently.

"And the one on the forest road too. We've seen to the bridge on the Vaalakan trade road but he wants the one to the north down too. Then he wants them drawn off the road deeper into the woods where there'll be no chance of discovery. He wants a distraction."

"A distraction, eh? Well, I always threatened I'd burn the nursery woods."

Pip recognized Ryder's voice, dull and monotonous though the sound was like cold water splashing into Pip's face. He was suddenly alert.

Pip closed his eyes, wondering what it might all mean. He couldn't bear to wake Brock, whose face was black and swollen with bruises. The old man needed to sleep.

Eight men, their ponies laden with skins and traps, sat about the fire. Ryder left them to check on Pip and Brock's bonds, kicking at a kobold that got in his way. The creature shrieked and fled to the other kobolds that cowered away from the fire.

Pip eyed the kobolds. Poor wretched creatures, they seemed so confused and ill-equipped to deal with the devious nature of man. Though the boy had hated them for their part in his suffering, he was determined to thwart Ryder.

"They're going to burn the woods," he whispered to the kobolds when the trapper returned to the fireside. "You hear? I overheard them early this morning."

One kobold looked at him in that way that made Pip want to squint because their eyes were set so close together. Its beaky mouth dropped open and then it scampered off to the largest kobold in the middle of the pack.

Suddenly the chattering ceased. Through the entire journey Pip's ears had been buzzing with the constant prattle and chirrups of these simple creatures and now there was silence. Without him seeing how, the kobolds were gone, vanished into the woods. Pip felt strangely lonely without them.

CHAPTER TWENTY-FOUR

Fighting for breath, Caspar mustered all that was left of his strength. "Go with the others."

Catrik shook his head and stroked the youth's forehead, wiping back the blood-matted hair from his eyes. "Do you think I could leave you?" The old man grunted as he pushed himself to his feet and pulled at Caspar's arms. "The Baron would never forgive me."

"He'll never know," Caspar reasoned.

"You can't be sure. A pound to a pinch of snuff those fairy people will just as likely pop over and whisper it in his ear. I couldn't have the Baron thinking ill of me after my death. I died happy with nothing to fret for, pleased that I had served my master well. And now that I'm dead, I've no mind to change my habits. Now if you can just put yourself to helping me here so I can get you up on my shoulder—"

"No, Catrik, you must rejoin the column and save your own soul," Caspar insisted weakly but the old wellmaster was not listening and began dragging Caspar by his arms. The pain in the youth's ripped skin was terrible as he was heaved over the rough ground. He fought back his moans.

"Please, let me be: it hurts too much," he complained.

"I don't care how much it hurts you, lad. Cruel to be kind, as they say. I'm not leaving you to rot, especially not when you've no right to be here. You were always meddling with things you shouldn't, and now look where it's got you."

Catrik's short and stocky frame, though old and weakened by the last months of his life, still had power enough to lift him. Driven by his determination, he managed to heave the youth over his shoulder. The youth's limp arms thumped and bumped on his back at each hobbled stride that the old wellmaster took.

Blood trickled from Caspar's chest down his arms, coiling round his wrists and fingers to leave a snaking trace on the wet ground behind them. The scavenging dogs, still wary of the verderers ahead, that lapped at the trail.

Catrik was stumbling under his weight and again Caspar insisted that he saved himself but the wellmaster forbore even to reply. Away in the gorse to left and right, the commoners watched and waited. Caspar could snatch the occasional glimpse of a limb or tuft of hair amongst the spiny bushes on either side of the path but he hardly cared. His mind was elsewhere – on the shadow. Its image invaded his head and he sensed it was sniffing along behind them. The commoners' dogs seemed to sense it, too, because they looked behind them in alarm and fled with their tails between their legs back into the rough. Creeping low through the shadows as if shunning the light, it was there; he knew it.

"Hey!" Catrik shouted after the retreating column. "Hey you! Verderers, what about us?"

A silver arrow shot over their heads through the rain and landed in the gorse behind them. A verderer was quickly at their side, his song strong and commanding. He scooped the youth up into his arms. Though standing only shoulder high to the old man, he was obviously very much stronger and carried Caspar effortlessly and swiftly towards the rear of the column.

"I've got the last of them," he called to his fellow verderers with some relief.

One nodded, the green feather in his peaked cap bobbing with the movement. "The last of them! And what of those that went to the wind?" he asked dryly. "What will Talorcan say?"

The main body of souls was halted just within the boundaries of the wood and most of the verderers guarded the perimeter of the ragged column while the rest sifted through the souls, tending to their injuries.

Caspar lay heaped with the limp bodies of four men and women who smelt bloodily of death. "Brid!" he cried out, needing her comfort.

Her warm hand touched his. He forced his leaden eyelids open and looked up into the beauty of face, her striking green eyes welling concern. Her other arm was still wrapped around the small girl, who had cried out for her mother. Caspar looked at Brid and blinked. Already she was the Mother in temperament, he thought, and then prayed that didn't mean that the old Crone was dead.

"You're beyond my help," Brid explained sorrowfully. "I don't have such powers."

"Here, verderer!" Catrik's voice demanded gruffly. "Here! This one's alive and needs your attention. Haven't you learnt your jobs yet in all these millennia?"

Caspar couldn't think that anything could relieve his pain until he felt the touch of the magic in their song. Deep within his mind long low powerful notes swelled in counterpoint to hectic skeltering top notes that cascaded through the melody, like water running over rock. He felt strong like he'd never felt before, the healing powers of the immortals giving him substance in the hope that he could walk through Rye Errish and on into

Annwyn. The screaming pain in his chest was gone; the wounds to his shoulder and arms healed. All that remained was the stinging in his scalp where the tortured man had tore at his hair. Somehow that slight injury was untouched by the song.

As his strength returned and the verderers withdrew to heal others, he gathered his wits and looked at Brid. "Do you believe in the Devil?"

She looked at him in surprise. "No, of course not. Why?"

"Because I saw him! He was there in the heath, black as a bottomless well. I saw the Devil and his hooded wolf."

She shook her head. "No, Spar, you saw only the manifestation of your own fear; a commoner and his dog that your fear mutated into the Devil and his hellhound."

"It was a hooded wolf not a hell-hound and I wasn't afraid."

"There was never a man born that wasn't afraid of eternal oblivion," she contradicted.

Caspar knew he had been mortally afraid but he wasn't about to admit it and was certain his fearful imagination had not conjured the image. Brid raised her eyebrow at him as if asking why he bothered to deceive her and he pulled his gaze away and refocused on the little girl clutching possessively at Brid's hand. Her eyes were red with weeping and her mouth trembled but she kept stiffly quiet. Fern also hovered close to the Maiden and, as Caspar looked around, he realized that several others sought her comfort, notably the merchant's serving girl and a sprightly young man who, judging by his floury smock, looked like a miller. The shredded remains of his right arm hung uselessly at his side.

The man offered Caspar his good hand to pull him to his feet and gave his name. "My father owns the mill nearest the north gate of Bleham. I fell into the grinding mechanism – got my sleeve caught," he explained, waggling his mutilated arm. "Must have ruined an awful quantity of flour that day. Poor Pa, he wouldn't have known whether to ditch the stuff in reverence to me or have it baked up with some cinnamon and ginger to hide the colour."

"That's terrible," Caspar gasped.

"Oh, there's worse goes in the sack some days; he's got a good sense of humour. And he's needed one what with this latest corn blight. But as for me, he's plenty more sons to take my place." The man was turning his face away from Caspar even before he had finished speaking and focused on the glowing warm light that lay beyond the eastern horizon. "It feels good, doesn't it?" He drew in a deep breath. "It feels like going home at the end of a long hard day. At last, to be with my maker!" He moved off, transfixed by the glow in the east and Caspar envied him his sense of peace. Was that really what it felt like to die at the right moment? He hoped so.

The verderers soon had all their charges mended and on their feet. Caspar moved forward with an impassioned vigour that he had never before experienced. He breathed in; his lungs felt powerful and his heart strong. He would have guessed that he was at least six inches taller except he still couldn't see over the heads of those in front.

He wanted to march beside Brid, only that wasn't so easy now. He jostled for position with Abelard, who like Fern and the little girl, refused to leave her side. He looked at her with affectionate despair. Ever generous with her soul, she had taken responsibility for the welfare of all who touched on her life. "We must see that we get them to Annwyn. Every one," she insisted.

Waifishly thin and pale, the little girl was soon in Brid's arms, though she was smiling now and playing with the Maiden's long coppery brown hair, twining it through her fingers and watching it uncurl with fascination. After several miles, rocking to and fro in the comfort of Brid's arms, the girl was soundly asleep. She had entrusted herself to the young woman and Caspar could see how Brid could never break that trust.

As they broached another rise, Caspar noted the look of gladdened relief on the verderers' faces. The glow from the east was growing and Caspar guessed they must be nearing their destination.

"Worst journey to date," the nearest verderer complained to one of his comrades.

"Talorcan will be furious. He'll have us work in the dungeons – or worse the kitchens with the women."

The first verderer shuddered. "Best not think on it. We'll be at the lake soon enough now."

From the top of the rise, they could see out across the rolling heath to the sombre dark of the dense pine forest interspersed with lighter pockets of mixed woods on the horizon. Mud clogged their feet and made the going heavy and their clothes clung to them as the rain persistently wept from the dun grey sky. A fan of sunlight spread beneath a gap in the clouds and brightened a tract deep in the forest ahead. It glinted red on a lake, whose shallow borders were hazy with fluid mist stained warm like blood.

"It's good to be a Belbidian and not a Ceolothian," Abelard commented, which brought a hearty cheer from many of their companions.

"Yeah, but who would want to be a Torra Altan," another sneered. "Wretched highlanders! You'll see shortly how wrong you were about your Goddess when we cross through the gates to heaven. Bah! Pagans! You're the ones that have brought all this trouble to the rest of Belbidia, all this plague and disease. It's about time King Rewik took some control and forced that Baron Branwolf out of his castle and had him replaced by a decent soul. I lost twenty ewes and my best tup to the plague of seeping boils and failing ague last year and that's sure enough what weakened my heart. The sight of all those weeping boils sucking away their life! Then this year with the wolves harassing the flocks in lambing time my heart wouldn't take the shock. That Baron Branwolf has a lot to answer for."

It was neither Bríd's shouts for calm nor the sudden insistent notes of the verderers that stopped Caspar from flying to his father's defence but a sudden pain to his head. He slapped a hand to his scalp as if he had been stung and felt the strength seeping out of him as if someone were drawing on his life force. He stumbled and moaned, stricken with the pain. The verderers were distracted from their watch by his behaviour and turned in towards him, leaving the column exposed to attack from the forest. Too late he heard the snarls of attack. Without turning he knew they were hooded wolves.

"Stand together!" he yelled weakly as panic took hold around him. "The verderers will protect us." But the waves of fear that rippled through the throng washed away their self-control.

"No, Fern no," Brid was suddenly shouting but it was too late. He fled and disappeared under the low sweeping branches of a beech that rested its old boughs on the leafy ground amidst a bed of daffodils and primroses. The wolves gave chase.

"Fern, come back," Brid shouted but her voice was blasted by the piercing notes of a hunting horn rising above their baying. The whole forest seemed to stand still as if all recognized the clarion call of eternal death. The hunt had tracked them down. It was as if the wolves had led Talorcan to them.

Caspar grabbed Brid's arm. "We must run too," he yelled. "There's no hope for us here. We must behave as the others or they'll single us out."

As the other souls began to scatter in different directions, Brid and Caspar set off after Fern, Brid still clutching the young girl's hand while Abelard stumbled painfully at her side. Catrik came last, protecting their rear.

His vigour gone, Caspar breathlessly dodged beneath branches and fought through brambles, trying to force a way to the thicker cover where the hunt would have more difficulty following. They glimpsed Fern only as he crossed into a glade ahead, leaping impossibly high over the undergrowth and fallen trees. "Run!" he piped over his shoulder. "Run!"

Encumbered with the little girl, Brid was struggling to keep up until Caspar scooped the child up in his arms. His heart sank. They should have left the girl behind but then he knew she would only have followed.

"We're so near the gateway," Abelard panted. "We must head for the lake."

"Near, but how will we know when we are really there?" Catrik asked.

"Hurry, hurry!" Fern's urgent voice squeaked from close by as he circled back to them through the trees, urging them on faster.

"Yew trees," Brid said instinctively. "Somewhere by the lake there will be yew trees, a circle of them. Yew is the tree of reincarnation; it must mark the gateway. I'm sure of it."

"Hurry!" Fern yelled but his voice turned to a scream that was drowned out by snarling wolves.

Caspar thrust the girl back into Brid's arms and crashed through the undergrowth after the little woodwose. He didn't know what he could do but he had grown fond of this poor little soul who was so determined to get back and protect his offspring. Something else was running, coming from behind at great speed, hooves barely making a sound as they rushed through the undergrowth. It must be the hunt, Caspar thought in despair. They had finally caught up with them.

A flash of white sped past him, its star-bright brilliance at first convincing him that it was something belonging to the High Circle. Judging by the fearful speed, he thought it must be a unicorn but then he saw the beast; a white hart leaping with great strides through the forest, the twelve points of its antlers lowered as it charged towards a wolf whose jaws gnashed at Fern's heels.

The black wolf was caught beneath its hindlegs, shovelled onto the antlers and tossed into the air. It somersaulted once before the sharp points of the antlers tore through its flank, cleaving a slash of red from its hip to its chest. The white hart ran level alongside Fern with easy strides, lowering his armed head to keep the wolves at bay. He gradually slowed and turned in a wide circle with Fern on his inside so that the little woodwose bumped along his flank just as he would if he were running with the herd.

They were turning back towards Caspar and Brid who carried the little child between them. Abelard and Catrik had their knives drawn, though the wolves were wary, now that the great hart was circling back for them. As they ran, Abelard tripped repeatedly amongst the brambles, his ruined knees buckling beneath him.

"Hurry! Go on without me," he yelled as the sound of the horn screeched out through the forest. "You're nearly there."

Caspar was torn between staying at Brid's side and turning back for the archer. His step faltered and Brid swung round at him. "Help him, for pity's sake, Spar, while I take the girl. We're nearly there. I can see it now. There ahead, the lake and yew trees."

Caspar ran back for Abelard and grabbed him by his arm as the archer tripped over the exposed root of an old, twisted hazel that had struggled to grow amongst the taller birches.

"Go on, Spar, go on. Y' mustn't wait," the man begged. "Please get the Maiden there. She must get back. For everyone's sake, please get her back."

Brid had slowed too and it was quickly clear that none of them was prepared to leave the archer behind. Finally, the great white hart came to a trembling halt behind them, steam rising up from his sweating quarters. Fern stood by the stag's head, blowing and snuffling as if he were communicating with the beast.

"Father says he will carry you," the little horned woodwose said.

Caspar didn't stop to question the name Fern gave for the beast as he urged Abelard towards the huge stag. Hot breath snorting from its flaring nostrils, it stood to a good sixteen hands and, with such magnificent antlers, he was a kingly beast, fiercely intimidating.

Though the impressive stag stood waiting for them, he was clearly nervous, trembling as the humans approached and shy of letting them touch him. Caspar burnt with frustration as he tentatively held out a hand and the beast blew at it before retreating a step, seemingly torn between the desire to help and its fear of them. Brid nudged the youth aside.

"Here, let me," she murmured in the softest and mellowest of voices. "Old stag, we won't hurt you," she whispered.

"He's the same stag. Look, there's an arrow wound to his hock." Caspar pointed.

Brid didn't pause to answer but, inch by inch, she reached her hand towards the hart's withers. They twitched nervously but finally relaxed as she touched him. His stiffly held head lowered as the tension eased out of him.

"He's clearly happiest with you," Caspar said. "If you get up first, he might accept Abelard more easily behind you."

She nodded and with light athleticism placed one hand on the stag's withers before vaulting up onto his back. He snorted and threw up his head but, with Brid's soothing words, relaxed enough for Abelard to be helped up behind.

The raucous, blood-chilling whoops of the hunt had been veering away, distracted by other souls of the column, but now the sounds of baying and splintering wood wheeled towards them.

"The yews. Get to the yews," Caspar yelled at Brid and thumped the stag on the quarters so that the animal spurted ahead.

"Ma! I want my ma!" the young girl cried and Caspar scooped her up and ran after them, breathing heavily under her weight.

"Outlaws! Outlaws ahead! I see them," a huntsman's cry alarmed Caspar.

The fastest of the huntsmen burst through the trees behind Caspar, the hooves of his sleek golden horse pounding the leaf-mould. Unlike the verderers protecting the column, who were dressed in green jackets and hunting leathers, these golden-haired beings of Rye Errish were boldly resplendent in gold and red suits, their feathered caps flouncing with the gait of their horses.

They moved with astonishing speed and within seconds a hand was reaching down and brushed the collar of Caspar's jacket. He twisted and wriggled to break free and, with the girl in his arms, dived for the cover of the trees and their drooping boughs where the mounted hunter would find it harder to follow. A second rider ignored Catrik and made straight for Caspar. The youth ducked under a beech, forcing the rider to sweep round the far side of the tree into the path of the first huntsman.

In their enthusiasm to catch him, the two riders blocked each other's path and, swerving to avoid one another, were momentarily entangled in branches. Caspar ducked between them and, with his legs pumping beneath him and the girl bouncing on his shoulder, he burst forward towards the misty shores of the lake.

Ahead loomed the dark ring of yew trees. Brid and Abelard on the magnificent stag were nearly there and he was certain they would make it. He prayed the Pipe would work. With great relief he saw Brid and the archer duck beneath the lounging bows of the ancient yews and slither from the stag's back to stand in the centre of the yew circle. Brid had succeeded in getting Abelard to safety but foreboding chilled Caspar's heart as she turned and caught his gaze.

He struggled to run faster with the small girl who unbalanced his stride. His lungs rasped with the effort and he didn't know how much longer he could hold her weight in the crook of his left arm. His grip was slowly failing. A huntsmen sped up behind him and was quickly alongside. Caspar slashed out sideways with his knife but the huntsman didn't try to grab him, as he had anticipated. Instead, he urged his horse sideways, barging him into the thick of the undergrowth, which snared his ankles and Caspar fell heavily in a tangled heap with the small child beneath him. For a moment his world was a whirl of bramble shoots and horse's legs as he rolled over and over, bramble shoots tearing his skin as he struggled to get to his feet and avoid capture.

With only a hundred yards to go before the grove of yew trees, the second huntsman appeared with a net. It flashed through Caspar's mind that all they need do to stop him was to fill the air with their disconcerting song that shackled all free will. But one look at the huntsmen's faces beneath their peaked caps told Caspar why they did not: this was the hunt, this was sport. The fire of energy and exhilaration burnt brightly behind their eyes; rather than resorting to magic, they sought the thrill of pitting their skills against his.

The realization gave Caspar no more than fleeting hope. He could see no escape. They were stronger and faster on foot let alone mounted on the horses of Abalone, sleek golden beasts with silvery tails that galloped as if they floated on air and could turn on a sovereign. The huntsmen rode gracefully without saddles and with only light bitless bridles of silk rope even though the horses snorted and tore at the ground like the most fiery of destriers.

Caspar scrambled up, forcing his way through the brambles that were like claws hooking into his clothing, twisting through his hair and scratching at his face. The girl cried in alarm but still clung tightly to him. A bramble twisted around his arm, snatching it back, and he stumbled again. Putting his hand out to save himself and shredding the skin of his palm, he fell onto a jagged stump unseen beneath the dense spring growth.

The first huntsman had slid from his horse and was making fast progress on foot. Lighter and faster than Caspar and clearly more at home in the woods, he wove through the tangle of vegetation almost as if the brambles had pulled aside for him. He grabbed the girl and flung her aside. She screamed as the thorns wrapped round her. Caspar couldn't reach her and lunged deeper into the undergrowth. The brambles formed an impassable network of thorns and he knew he had made his own trap. He could go no further. He felt his face and hands were wet with blood as he tried to thrash through them but the more he struggled, the faster he became entangled.

The huntsman had him. A fierce grip locked around his ankle and dragged him backwards, face down, through the thorns. He clenched his fists over his face, trying to protect himself from the skin-tearing brambles but he had no strength left to fight against the huntsman's superior powers.

The hounds were coming. He could hear their avid baying as they caught his scent. The huntsman hauled him upright and screwed his fists behind his back and, though he could have used his knife at any time, he chose not to. Instead, he held him ready for the hounds.

Dear Mother, forgive me; I have failed, Caspar prayed. I have achieved little in my life and now I have failed you.

The dogs came, leaping over logs and weaving in and out of the trees. Spar focused on their pinned-back ears, their pared lips and their teeth that grew huge as they bounded towards him. The ignominy! To be shredded into a thousand pieces by the hounds of Rye Errish; he couldn't believe it. Rather than intense panic, he felt numb with the shock. The knife would have been better.

But his numbness was lashed by the cries from the little girl floundering in the brambles. "Ma!" she cried. "The woman promised she'd take me home to Ma. Ma!" she shrieked in panic.

Caspar felt unutterably sick as one hound swerved

towards her. Then the panic hit him just as it had hit the little girl.

His last soul-searching thoughts were for Hal. He had failed here but was grateful that at least his uncle would shoulder his responsibilities and look after Torra Alta for him when he failed to return home.

He would miss him. "Hal," he murmured and then yelled loudly, "Hal!" as he smelt the hound's breath in his face.

CHAPTER TWENTY-FIVE

"Ceowulf, see to the wagon," Hal ordered.

He was thinking only of the practicalities of rescuing their situation and any thought of protocol was swept from his mind as he broke the chain of command. The men were near panic and his one concern was to unify the column.

"Dismount," he thundered, fearing the horses were ready to bolt, "and draw swords."

Ceowulf was busy reversing up the wagon but was hindered by Hardwin's horse wildly plunging and kicking out at the men.

"Hardwin, get off your horse. All of you. Tupwell, Prince Renaud, unhorse," the big Caldean shouted sharply over the babbling mayhem of tormenting spirits that slid between the trees.

"How dare you? Remember to whom—" Renaud's words were cut short by a panicked shriek from his horse. The animal tossed its head, dipped its quarters and made as if it were about to rear.

Hal grabbed the prince's bridle. "Do it, sir. Please! It'll encourage the men." As Renaud complied, he looked to the other nobles. Tudwal could remain mounted for all he cared and, besides, his horse, like Secret, was as calm as a bishop at mass. "Prince Tudwal, take the fore," he shouted, surprised that the fierce Ceolothian prince hadn't already done so. "Prince Renaud, Hardwin, stand by the wagons." He knew they would be less fearful with the men around them. "Tupwell, the rear." Hal's voice boomed in deep throaty tones that carried purposefully through the men. He was greatly relieved when Ceowulf, applauded by a great cheer from the men, finally had the wagon rolling freely forward.

Though startled and white-faced, they responded to his commands. He needed them to march forward away from this place and, to achieve that, he needed them to believe they were safe from these apparitions – even if he wasn't himself entirely convinced of the fact.

He drew the runesword and held it aloft. "See the sword given to me by the Great Mother. See the spell-woven edge feared by all those of the devilish dark. Fear no longer and march with me, men!" he cried, riding up and down the length of the column. "Ceowulf, a song."

Following the booming voice of the Caldean knight, the men of Belbidia raised a stirring refrain. Refusing to admit to any fear, Hal stared full into the faces of the dread sights before him, whilst urging the column back into lines. With new-found courage they marched on. The forest grew darker and the wispy shapes of men and women and their piteous cries of grief became more substantive. A girl flung herself at his knees, sobbing and whimpering.

Hal gripped his sword tighter. "Great Mother," he murmured, "take this image of death from my mind. Go back to the Otherworld," he told the woman. "Look to the solace of the Great Mother. We are all her children; draw comfort."

Momentarily he wished for Brid's depth of faith as the eerie screams and cries pierced the forest gloom. Though the image of the girl dimmed until she was no more substantial than swirling specks of dust caught in a shaft of light. He raised the sword higher and sang louder, his voice tuneless but strong, the chanted words unifying the column.

To his left a line of shades trudged east along a deer track. Marching in ordered ranks, they seemed untroubled by the princess's entourage and somehow distinct from the other tormented souls of the forest. Hal found no trepidation at the sight of them; they seemed preoccupied and self-contained within their slow marching column.

Hal cantered forward to join Ogden, who gave him a lopsided smile, his eyes still betraying his fear. Hal grinned back in encouragement. White-faced, his eyes flitting around him, Cai fell in alongside. "Prince Tudwal wishes to inform you, Lord Hal, of a solid bridge used by loggers some way upriver. He's leading us to it. It'll be strong enough to take the wagons. The forest tracks aren't easy for wagons but at least we'll be getting away from the darkest parts of Hobs Slack."

Hal shared Cai's sense of relief and spread the word that, as they worked their way northward along the banks of Skins Gutter, they would gradually be leaving the ghost-ridden woods behind. The apparitions began to fade and he was just thinking that they had seen the last of them when he was disturbed by bitter and despairing cries for help coming from the far side of the river. Hal tried to close his mind to them, fearing that the pleas were designed to lure him back into the phantom-infested maze of the forest. He joined in Ceowulf's song to distract him further but the cries only sounded more real. He was tempted to investigate but was distracted by loud shouts from the head of the column.

"Fire! Fire! Through the trees to the right," Tudwal was shouting and pointing to black tree trunks silhouetted by flickering orange light. "Ceowulf, Hal, take a dozen men and see to it."

Hal hesitated. He didn't want to leave the wagons; his charge was to protect the princess. Besides, the fire looked small and was no threat to them. Surely it would burn itself out of its own accord quickly enough; after all it was the middle of Ceolothia's rainy season. He peered through the trees at the flickering glow but, as he did so, he heard screams.

Ceowulf was organizing the men but Hal couldn't wait for them. He could hear cries, inhuman high-pitched squeals, and the crackle of dry timber as it took flame. He had seen something, too; an old woman. Dressed in shabby green rags, her tangled hair like strands of frayed rope around her shoulders, she had beckoned him.

The sword in his grip tingled, compelling him towards the fire. There was something so earthy and natural about this old woman; he knew Brid would want him to help her. He had not heard the old woman's words but she had called to him. Something deep within his soul told him that she had recognized the power of his sword, the sword lent to him to honour the name of the Great Mother. He sensed the sword was answering the woman's cry. She needed his help and he could not deny it.

She clutched the sticklike hand of a small little upright being that waved its free arm frantically. It was quite the most absurd sight he had ever seen and he was about to dismiss the images as more phantoms, when he remembered what Brid had told him of the little creatures living in the woods. Kobolds, he remembered; small little men half akin to trees.

The woman called again. "Help us. In the name of the Great Mother!"

As she turned and hobbled towards the smoky glow

behind her, Tudwal's dogs broke past Hal and, with great looping bounds, raced after her.

Hal swung up onto Secret's back and pressed his spurs to her sides. "Call them off!" he yelled at Tudwal as he sped after the woman and towards the heat of the flames.

But the woman was gone. He had seen her just as clearly as he saw the trees around him. She had been clutching at an old willow for support; but he had blinked and she was gone. Hal galloped towards the willow in the hope of finding the old woman. The dogs reached the spot some moments before he did and were running round in frantic circles, snuffling excitedly as if they had caught the scent of a deer. Hal, however, didn't bother to look further for her; he was too distracted by high pitched screams and the sight before him.

A gang of men had forked up several piles of leaves, dried bracken and branches around the bases of a line of trees. They were putting torches to the kindling and wafting their jackets to encourage the flames. Through the smoke came desperate yells of fear.

The men froze as Hal burst into the clearing.

"Beat those flames out!" he ordered loudly but the arsonists fled into the forest. He flung himself from Secret's saddle and shouted back to Ceowulf to hurry with the men.

The heat was stifling and the air thick with smoke. Burying his mouth and nose in the crook of his elbow, he lowered his head and ran between two fires and into the thick wall of smoke towards the screams. Beyond the line of fires, the smoke thinned somewhat though the wind still wafted smuts forward that quickly took flame in the dead leaves of the forest floor.

He staggered in his stride. Strange shapes loomed before him. The noise came from small, distorted birch trees, their branches waving like panicked arms. He drew a choking breath, certain that his smarting eyes deceived him. He blinked and looked again. Yes, definitely, they were birches but standing amongst them were creatures, living beings with barky skin and hair like traveller's joy in winter – old man's beard as it was known in the mountains around Torra Alta. Amid the tangle of branches, narrow, warty faces with slitted nostrils screamed out of the trunks of the trees. Each had only two branches, and they were vaguely reminiscent of long-fingered arms. Like the birches, they had spreading roots anchoring them to the ground but, in addition, each of these rooted creatures had a brush of suckers growing up from the roots. The suckers were thin and spindly with branchlike arms that were wrapped fearfully around the trunks of the mother trees. Their high-pitched screaming was like that of any terrified child.

Scampering from the direction of the river came more kobolds, squealing and shrieking with dismay. Grabbing at dead branches or brush, they beat frenziedly at the fires, some getting so close that they were scorched and took flame like dry faggots. The others screamed and shrieked in horror but battled on to save their rooted offspring.

With one arm across his mouth to protect him, Hal beat and kicked at the flames. He hoped the others would hurry but what he wasn't expecting was the hobbling old woman to re-emerge from the forest. Despite her bowed age, she beat vigorously at the flames alongside him.

"Use your sword," she croaked with a voice of strange authority.

He didn't hesitate to obey and, in one sweeping movement, unsheathed the weapon. With scything sweeps at the undergrowth, he began to clear a fire-break that would protect the rooted creatures, and he was battling furiously as Ceowulf, Ogden and a dozen troops came rushing to aid him.

The crisp winter undergrowth gave easily to the sweep of his sword, allowing the men to drag aside the brambles, bracken and branches to form a break, which gave them enough space to stamp at any flames that sparked across the bare divide.

It was hot and Ceowulf was sweating heavily beside him as they fought back the fires. Hal's eyes stung and his skin itched with the heat. At last, they had the flames contained. They dragged at the fires, stamping out the charred sticks to beat out the last glow from the embers. Hal's breath rasped, his hands were cut, and red burns were already beginning to swell on his cheeks. Sweat dripped from his brow. The kobolds, however, gave him no time to recover as they swarmed over him, shrieking with joy. Leaving him gasping for breath, they quickly abandoned him to embrace the little saplings and their mothers who chirruped in delight.

But it was not all joy. Many kobolds had lost limbs, their hair smouldering, and some lay like black mummified objects, every ounce of barky flesh peeled away by the flames.

Ceowulf stared at the creatures in disbelief. "So, the stories are true. I thought Keridwen was making it up when she told us how mother kobolds root into the ground to give birth, drawing on the life force of the Great Mother until their koblings are fully grown." Sweat ran from his forehead, forming white runnels in his soot-blackened skin.

Hal swept his eyes around the scene. Seeing that all the fires were out, he thought to pursue the gang of men that had caused this atrocity but he was stopped by shouts of alarm coming from the road.

All thought of the kobolds was gone from his mind as he leapt to Secret's back. Yelping dogs, the clash of metal and the cries of women filled the air. He crashed through the last of the trees before Skins Gutter and found himself two hundred paces to the rear of the escort. A large band of men clad in shabby skins, like the smaller gang he had seen starting the fire, were attacking the wagons. Princess Cymbeline was well defended by Ceolothian troops but Tudwal was still right at the front of the column and a long way from her.

Hardwin was fighting with a remarkable gusto that Hal had not expected but he was not skilled with a sword and was quickly unbalancing himself in the saddle. It was only seconds before the bandits dragged him from his horse by a billhook. With the knight down, the robbers were savagely cutting a direct path towards the princess.

"Cymbeline!" Hal cried. "Tudwal, Tudwal! Your sister! Look to your sister!" he yelled as he dipped and weaved through the trees. But the Ceolothian Prince was unable to disengage from the three men that set upon him with cudgels and knives.

With sword drawn, Hal thundered into the midst of the column, and, with one slash, cut the arm from the rogue nearest Cymbeline. He fell to the ground to be trampled underfoot by the wagon horses. With a clean thrust, Hal pierced the shoulder of another, deliberately trying only to disable him so that he had someone left to question later.

Tupwell, like Hardwin, was close to the princess, thrashing about with his short, ornately decorated sword. The men scattered away from him for fear of being inadvertently maimed by the lavish sweeps of his weapon. Renaud, as Hal expected, held reticently back behind two lines of troops.

Ceowulf burst through the trees, his great heavy charger running down one of the ruffians. His javelin spat from his hand, piercing the neck of a second and in the next moment he had his sword drawn and was slashing it downwards to cleave through the skull of a third. With both Hal and Ceowulf in the fight, the remaining bandits fled for the woods. Hal leapt from his horse to grab the man he had wounded in the shoulder.

"Cymbeline!" Tudwal shouted. "Are you unharmed? Cymbeline!"

The prince dropped from his horse and barged his way through the troops, flinging even wounded men aside in his efforts to reach her. Cymbeline was gasping, her shoulders shuddering, though she made an effort to stiffen her pose and toss back her head, defiantly throwing off her fear. She spoke sharply in Ceolothian to her brother and shoved him away when he tried to embrace her.

"But you're hurt, sister," he declared loudly in Belbidian. "Look, your cheek's bleeding." His face blackened in anger and his entire body stiffened like a panther crouched to spring. Hal had a sense of imminent doom. Tudwal spun round. With great force and skill, he sprang at the prisoner and buried his sword deep in the man's chest, making a clean and expert kill.

Hal couldn't believe it. "He was our prisoner! And we could have questioned him!"

"He injured my sister!" Tudwal, was shaking with rage and kicked at the dead body with his boot so that it rolled onto its side. Hal winced as he heard the ribs crack beneath the impact and watched with disgust as the prince planted his foot on the man's face and withdrew his sword.

"Steady on! The ladies . . ." Renaud reminded Tudwal.

Hal wiped his own sword clean and returned it to its

scabbard. "You didn't have to kill him. We needed him for questioning."

"Questioning. What's the point in that? They were opportunists. The sight of the wagons—"

"They went straight for the princess," Hal interrupted.

"So? A lady so well guarded is bound to be worth a high ransom. Merely opportunists. On my return I shall cleanse this area of them and see them all punished but, at the moment, my sister's safety is my priority. We haven't got time to scour the woods. The fire is out and I'm sure we are all agreed that the best thing to do is proceed as quickly as possible."

There was a general murmur of assent amongst the troops, who were still breathing heavily after the assault. Hardwin was helped to a wagon, fortunately suffering more from shock and bruises than any serious injury.

Crawling along the track that hugged Skins Gutter, the wagons rolled north for the loggers' bridge that Cai had mentioned. Tudwal's dogs were sniffing ahead excitedly and the Ceolothian prince moodily pushed his way to the fore to see what had caught their attention. He halted suddenly as the road swung round the bend.

"What the—"

"Kobolds," Ceowulf told him. Evidently, they had scampered ahead to intercept the wagons.

"Devil's spawn," Tudwal snarled.

As Hal approached, the kobolds began leaping up and down in excitement. Though they chirruped and cooed like birds, Hal realized they were cheering. One rushed up and bravely patted his leg, nodding his head up and down in an attempt to thank him. Despite himself, Hal found he was blushing. Then he saw the old woman again, her skin dark with forest mud and her hair a moss-matted tangle.

She bowed towards the two princes, though with a lack of reverence, and, with one eyebrow slightly raised, nodded at Hal and Ceowulf. It was almost as if she knew who they all were. When she spoke, it was not with the dull monotonous accent of a Ceolothian but with the singing lilt of the old tongue of the Caballan.

"Thank you for saving the little kobolds."

The little tree men chattered and tugged at her arms. One or two of the smaller ones had clambered up onto her stooped shoulders and were dragging at her hair. She patted them affectionately, showing no irritation as they scampered around her, pawing her with their dark scratchy hands.

The kobolds rushed forward, bobbing and bowing enough to make Hal feel quite giddy. They then began pointing excitedly towards the river and tugged at the soldiers' horses to encourage them forward, their scratchy voices rising in excitement.

Evidently the old woman understood their tongue. She crouched to listen to one of the calmer, larger kobolds and seemed instantly alarmed. "They say there's some people who need help."

The kobolds leapt up and down in agitation.

The woman continued, "They're held captive by some men."

"We should send a party on ahead to help," Prince Renaud volunteered.

Tudwal nodded. "Lord Hal, Lord Ceowulf, take some men right away."

"But the princess . . ." Hal was reluctant to leave. "There might be another ambush."

Ceowulf nodded. "You're right." He turned to the kobolds. "How many men hold this man and boy?"

The kobolds argued and squabbled and gesticulated

wildly. Many of them dropped to all fours and made strange panting and strangled noises. At last, the scraggy-haired woman said, "Two, I think and lots of dogs."

The kobolds continued to scamper around on the ground in mimicry of the dogs and some were pointing at Tudwal's hounds who had been leashed by the men to prevent them from attacking the creatures. The dogs evidently found kobolds as tantalizing as rats but they seemed even more excited by the old woman, sniffing and straining forward, half-throttling themselves in their efforts to get to her.

Hal laughed. "Two men! Well, in that case Ogden and I shall go alone. If Ceowulf remains with the princess, I am happy." He bowed a polite farewell and was pleased to see Cymbeline's approving smile at his gallant behaviour. He stroked the yellow scarf at his neck.

"Be careful," she murmured and shot him an anxious look. Hal was persuaded by that one glance of concern that he had won her. A smile of satisfaction spread across his face and, feeling entirely pleased with himself, he rode forward after the strange old woman who refused any offer of a horse. The kobolds carefully arranged themselves in his wake, cowering behind his sword as he rode forward. Ogden was silent as they rode on but was smiling to himself.

Hal looked at him curiously. "What is it?"

"I was just thinking how dull it'll be when I return to Farona after all this excitement." Clearly Ogden, like himself, held no trepidation at the thought of confronting two men and their dogs. They rode on, more curious of their companions than wary of any oncoming battle. "I mean, when was the last time anyone saw such peculiar creatures in Farona?"

"You don't want to go back to the king's service then?"

Hal asked, steering Secret around the bowl of a tree. He frowned at the old woman immediately in front of them. Although she was bent and hobbling, she seemed to have no trouble in keeping ahead.

"Well, I have no choice now, do I, sir? There's few of us born that get the say-so of what we do and don't do during our lives." He flashed Hal a sudden grin. "But I'd like it more if the king appointed a man such as yourself to head part of his army. There's rumours that Prince Renaud is to be made his chief general and I don't think it'll work out too well. With all due respect, sir, he don't have the way with men. They listen to you though. You see, you listen to them and they respect that." He laid out his opinion without any hint of obsequiousness.

Hal smiled at the simple approval.

"And I dare say you'd be quite keen to join the king's troops in Farona now," Ogden continued.

Hal's pride was not so swollen as to miss Ogden's quick sideways glance nor the sudden quietness in his voice as if he were probing for a reaction. "Dare say that I might. But what exactly are you driving at, sergeant?" Hal's voice was suddenly stiff.

Ogden flushed. "I'm not saying anything. I was just wondering now . . . well, now that Princess Cymbeline . . . well I thought Farona might appeal to you but—"

"Lord Ceowulf's been talking to you." Hal cut him dead.

The man nodded, obviously relieved that his task was done. "Well, indeed, sir. Your friend is troubled by you and persuaded me to say something in warning." His round face flushed a deeper red. "But as I say, sir, it ain't my place. And besides, sir, what really concerns me right now is what these creatures are fretful about." He hastily changed the subject, evidently wishing he had never said anything in the first place.

"What?" Hal asked distractedly, still thinking that Ceowulf had a great deal of nerve putting Ogden up to this. His scowl was quickly lifted by a laugh, however, as he considered poor Ogden. The man was blustering through his apologizes, saying once again that it wasn't his place and how he remembered being young once too.

Hal squinted into the gloom of the forest, looking for the old woman. She had a way of suddenly being swallowed into the shadow of a tree or vanishing into a hollow. He didn't like it and liked it less when the woman suddenly appeared just in front of them, frowning sternly almost as if chastising him for taking the situation so lightly. Feeling uncomfortable under the woman's reproachful glare, he hurried forward with the kobolds chattering wildly behind.

Hal stopped in his tracks. He could hear barking, a booming bellow of canine fury interspersed with ridiculous high-pitched squeals that could only come from one particular dog. His mouth sagged open in astonishment and, though his mind was stunned, his body reacted fast. He pressed his spurs to Secret's sides, rose up in the saddle and drew his sword.

"Trog!" he shouted. "Trog! Trog!"

Without any thought for his own safety, he charged through the undergrowth and burst out into a small clearing by the water's edge. A team of shaggy ponies trudged beneath a heavy burden of wolf pelts. Dogs, large trapper dogs by their rangy build and liver-coloured coats, snarled and snapped around their feet. Hal would recognize trapper dogs anywhere; he had seen them often enough, accompanying their masters to Torra Alta. Two sinister-looking men, one blond and one dark, both garbed in wolf skins, were wrestling with a man and a boy. One was dragging the screaming boy by the ankles and the other yanked on a chain that was fastened about the man's neck.

A short squat terrier, white except for the streaks of blood around his shoulders, was cruelly shackled by a circular iron plate clamped around his neck. A chain was welded to the collar and the far end secured to a horse. The terrier had the chain between his teeth and was squirming and shaking to get free.

Hal had no thought to halt and assess the situation. He charged forward in mad rage, bursting through the cover of the forest. These men had Brid's dog!

The blond man with a grubby beard looked up in alarm just as Hal raised his heel and raked his spur into his startled face. Hal wheeled Secret and reached for a throwing knife as the second man dropped the boy and fumbled for a bow. One flick of Hal's wrist and the knife spun through the air and sliced into the man's shoulder. Hal ruefully thought he needed to practise more diligently with his knives; it hadn't been an expert job.

Ogden engaged the bearded man who had struggled to his feet, blood pouring over the teeth of his exposed jaw where his cheek had been ripped away. The trapper didn't have the fighting skills of the sergeant who cut him obliquely across the chest and, with the next pass of his sword, hacked into the thick muscle of his thigh.

Seeing that neither man was likely to have any fight left, Hal relaxed and slid from Secret's back. The dark trapper was clutching at the knife embedded in his shoulder, his hands clawing at it in agony. Before Hal could reach him, Trog launched himself at the writhing man and it took all Hal's strength to pull the terrier off. The man's face was scarlet and shredded. His hands sprang to where the dog's curving teeth had incised away a chunk of his cheek down to the bone.

Hal thought at first that the dog had also eaten the man's fingers but quickly realized it was an old wound. He saw no need to secure this ruffian and turned towards the chained man and boy.

To Hal's amazement the man saluted him.

"Master Hal, sir! I knew the Baron would send someone for us. I knew you'd come, sir," he cried, beaming from ear to ear. Down one side, his face was black with bruises, his neck and wrists were raw from rusted chains and he looked thin and tired. Hal knew this man but couldn't believe it.

"Brock?"

"Aye, sir."

Hal looked back to the ragged-looking boy, whose thick dark brown hair fell across his face as he cradled something in his arms. He jerked his head up at the sound of Hal's name and in utter disbelief Hal looked into Pip's eyes.

"You found us, Master Hal! You found us. Look, she's hurt. She needs food." Pip stumbled forward, holding up a little white bundle in his arms.

Hal looked at it incredulously and then at Pip who, he feared, had lost his mind. "Pip, it's a wolfling. Why are you crying over a wolfling?"

"They shot it with an arrow. The bastards shot it and she's an orphan like me and she's mine and they shot it!" the young boy blurted in confusion.

"Never mind the wolf, you're badly hurt. Your arm. Now take a few deep breaths, Pip, and steady yourself," Hal said calmly. "It's only a wolfling and, if its hurt and without a mother, it would be kinder to put it out of her misery."

The look of fear in Pip's wide eyes was like those of an unearthed fox.

"He's been through a lot, sir," Brock explained, slumping to the ground in exhaustion. "The wolfling means everything to him. He nearly drowned to save the pup. Poor lad, he's lost his reason over it."

Hal took a deep breath. Rather than worry about Pip's reasoning, he turned to practicalities. First, he needed to cut Brock's and Pip's chains. "Ogden, search amongst the horses and find some tools that will loosen these shackles," he said. "Trappers carry all manner of ironmongery."

He then turned to the wounded men on the ground. The shorter, blond one that bled heavily from the deep wound across his thigh was out cold but the one with the fingers missing was groaning pitifully. Hal yanked him roughly to his feet. "What were you doing kidnapping Baron Branwolf's men?"

"Sir, my lord, I'm just a trapper, an Ovissian trapper. I don't know what's going on here. It was Ryder there that said we should take them. I was only trying to do an honest job of killing wolves." His hurried words slurred wetly through the blood that seeped from his ragged lips.

Hal wasn't listening to this blurted string of excuses. He only heard that this obnoxious man was an Ovissian.

"Well, you're in luck, man," he said savagely, not caring that the trapper bled heavily and was shaking with pain, "Lord Tupwell of Ovissia is with my party. He will deal with you." Hal doubted that the man would live long anyway, and he was weary and concerned to return to the princess. Too many dreadful things had happened in this forest.

"Right, let's see you up onto a pony each," he told Brock and Pip. "We'll get you fed and seen to the moment we get back to the main party."

While Ogden heaved Brock onto the back of a sturdy pony, Hal helped Pip who obsessively clung to the wolfling.

He then secured the prisoners onto a further two pack ponies before mounting Secret and leading the string back towards the royal party.

They had gone some distance when Hal suddenly stood high in the saddle and scanned the area around him. He had heard someone cry his name. Automatically he reached for his sword. Someone had shouted out his name. Then came the screech of a merlin followed by Tudwal's urgent cry, "Cymbeline! Cymbeline!"

The princess's cries wailing through the trees and the fearful shriek of the merlin cut through Hal's mind, heightening his senses and pumping adrenaline through his veins. The screech was mixed with a distant bellow of fury. He drew Secret in and listened, trying to orientate himself in the confusion of the forest. She was heading away from the river and back into Hobs Slack, surely. He dropped the lead rein into Ogden's hand and spurred his liver-chestnut mare forward. After plunging through undergrowth, he was grateful when he broke out onto a track and could make better speed.

What was Cymbeline doing mounted? Her fool brother must have ordered everyone back up onto their horses. The sounds of panicked animals alarmed the forest. Birds shrieked in fright. The princess's cries rang through the trees; she was to his right but the undergrowth and closely woven thatch of blackthorn and hawthorns were too thick to break through. He could do nothing but follow the track he was on until the forest thinned.

"Hold on, Cymbeline!" he shouted encouragement, spurring Secret to a furious pace. He was acutely aware of her yellow scarf about his neck and knew that to prove himself as her champion he must save her. "I'm getting to you." He pressed on faster and swallowed hard as he saw a line of men, women and children ahead. They blocked the track.

"Get out of the way! Clear the road!" he shouted but when not one of them so much as raised a head he knew he was already back in the depths of Hobs Slack. They weren't real, he told himself, gritting his teeth and charging on. Secret threw up her head in alarm as he drove her on, her stride shortening fractionally as if she doubted his request.

"Go on, girl," he told her firmly, trying to convince himself that these shadows couldn't harm them.

The highly schooled mare responded with confidence and didn't break her stride as they swept into the line. The cold ran through his body. For a second, as he shared the same single space with the fetches, he saw them fully. The sweep of their emotions raked through him. In the flash of an instant, he smelt blood and vomit, embalming unctions and incense. He heard moans and screams, laughter and promises; lived their lives and witnessed their deaths. From some he experienced their contentment; from some a slow sap of strength, every breath a torment of effort; from others violent stabs of pain. But the worst was the agony of disease and stench of burst pustules from bodies overpowered by agues. Hal's flesh crept with the sense of contamination and he urged his horse faster to clear the column. Cymbeline's cries were closing on him from the right and the thorns gave way to spindly silver birches.

He forced his way through the branches, twigs lashing his face until he broke through onto her track. The princess was just ahead now, her merlin a tossing swirl of thrashing wings about her wrist. Hal saw in horror that its tresses were caught in her gauntlet. Tudwal was at her heels, shouting, and vigorously whipping his horse to a faster and faster pace, gradually gaining on her. Hal thumped his heels into Secret's sides.

The squarely built Ceolothian lunged across to grab Cymbeline's reins, hauling her mare to a halt with sheer brute force. It took all his efforts to hold her panicked, plunging palfrey as the merlin flapped in terror. It was still pinned by its tresses, spinning upside down and shrieking horribly.

"Let go of it!" Hal yelled at the princess as he hauled Secret to a halt alongside.

"I can't. She's twisted through my fingers," Cymbeline shrieked back, tears streaking down her panicked face. "Help me! Help!" Her arm was being yanked back and forth by the bird.

Secret thankfully remained calm despite the merlin's panic. Squinting against the beating wings, he grabbed Cymbeline's falconry gauntlet in one hand and the bird's legs in the other. He strained to hold the creature still so that the princess could use her other hand to free the tresses.

While Hal struggled against the alarming strength of the terrified bird, Cymbeline, though her fumbling fingers trembled, summoned the composure to unwind the knotted leathers. The merlin was free and, with relief, he released his grip. It flapped off, circling away to gain height, peeling out a thin arrow-sharp cry that split the heavens.

Hal followed the bird's flight and sucked in his lower lip, hiding his expression of pain. His hand had been deeply cut by the curving talons. Princess Cymbeline was close to sobbing and looked down at his hand in horror and then up at his face. "Oh Hal!" Evidently, she couldn't express herself but her eyes were bursting with gratitude and admiration and the young raven-haired man felt like a hero. "Oh, Hal, your hand!"

He smiled stoically. "It's nothing." He dismissed the injury in a deep well-rounded voice, trying hard not to wince as he wiped away some of the blood with a handkerchief and then bound the cut. "Are you hurt?" he asked anxiously but saw with relief that her gauntlet had protected her arm. To disguise his own pain, he squinted into the sky and followed the flight of the shrieking merlin.

"What frightened it?" he asked, sucking at the smaller cuts higher up his wrist, but he never heard an answer.

"No!" Cymbeline shouted as her palfrey half reared and Tudwal fought to hold her. The princess finally lost her composure, dropped her reins and flung her arms around the palfrey's neck in defeat.

The horse was wild-eyed and Tudwal was having an impossible task of holding her as his own stallion bucked and screamed.

"Stand," he commanded in Ceolothian and cuffed the animal across the back of the neck, only making matters worse. A dribble of blood trickled from the war-horse's mouth where the bit dug cruelly into its lip. Hal tried to snatch at Cymbeline's reins but he couldn't get to them and, instead, manoeuvred Secret to block her path.

"Get off. Throw yourself to the ground," he shouted.

Cymbeline's jaw sagged in bloodless fright. "I can't! Hal, help me, help me! It's coming again."

She buried her head in her horse's mane and wailed. A thin roar, close but strangely muffled, cried out from the trees.

Though trembling, Secret turned to face the veiled shadow of a creature that loped towards them. It was like seeing something through a mist. He saw the outline of a face, the face of a vast cat with fore claws slashing at the air, but it was being powered by the quarters of a brutish horse. A vast red span of leathery wings snagged in the branches around it. The sight of the winged lequus sent Cymbeline's panicked mount into a frenzy and the palfrey finally broke free of Tudwal's fierce grip and bolted. The prince charged after his sister, leaving Hal to face the ghostly beast alone.

He snatched up his throwing knives as the immaterial creature charged. He hurled one, then another and then his last but each cut clean through the translucent being. He drew his sword and braced himself, ready to pierce its chest but there was no need. As the great blade swept into the air, the lequus retreated into the cover of the forest, its haunting shriek trembling the air. Whether it had feared him as a knight or had recognized the power of the Great Mother in the sword, Hal cared not. Without further ado he turned Secret and sped after the princess.

Hunched over Secret's outstretched neck, his spirits sank as he realized they were charging away from the river and deeper into Hobs Slack. The hair at the back of his neck was tingling and a shudder ran the length of his spine. Others were riding with him. He couldn't see them, but he could feel the air being buffeted around him. Secret was fired up with excitement, though strangely not with the fear of a bolting horse but the glee of an animal joining the hunt.

He was being overtaken. They were sweeping past him. He blinked, dazzled by a flash of gold and the glint of silver as the sun filtering through the trees was caught on a polished blade. The atmosphere stank of the sweat of bloodlust and the fear of driven animals. Silvery shadows dived this way and that into the cover of the trees. He blinked again and they were gone.

He was left daunted by the sense of great power in the riders that had swept past. No smell of death or decay had surrounded these apparitions. But he had little time to dwell on them as he dodged and weaved between tree-trunks and overhanging branches. Cymbeline was shrieking ahead and he must rescue her.

The track was widening as it cut through an area of glades. He could see her galloping towards a ring of yews at the shores of a lake. Her horse was bucking and kicking out wildly with its heels though the movement was hampered. Again, he caught sight of a flash of red and the raking swipe of a lion's claw. The lequus had outrun him.

There was blood, a great stream of blood gushing from the quarters of Cymbeline's horse. The princess was screaming for help and faintly, as if hearing life from a dream, Hal could hear snarls and growls and the unmistakable yelling of hounds on the scent. The world seemed suddenly strange and he felt sick with disorientation. Inexplicably, some preternatural sense compelled him to slow. Other members of the escort party were shortly overtaking him.

"Help!" Cymbeline screamed, turning her beautiful face in panic towards him as he drew Secret to a halt. "Help me, Hal!"

Black-eyed with fear, her face a picture of distress, the princess was in dire need of him. This was his chance to make her forever indebted to him.

Cymbeline's voice cried out, "Hal!" time and time again in utter panic.

Her palfrey was dragged to its knees. Troops were moving to her rescue, as the princess's escort caught up with her. Even Ogden with Pip and Brock and the squealing, gibbering kobolds were stumbling into the scene. But Hal didn't care.

"Hal!" they were shouting, trying to stir him into action but he couldn't respond.

"Master Hal!" Pip's high voice cut through the deeper

shouts of the men but even that wasn't enough to rouse him.

There was another voice calling to him and, though he couldn't place it, he knew it was infinitely more urgent. It seemed to be calling from within himself, from deep down in his soul. The voice? He couldn't place it. His conscience? No, it wasn't that; it was a lost voice, a lost part of himself. He felt confused and dizzy, the others around him distant, incorporeal. It was like looking at a ship sliding silently into the stillness of a sea mist. The despairing voice cried out to him as if from across a vast wilderness.

"Hal!"

CHAPTER TWENTY-SIX

The defiant yell stuck in Caspar's throat. The gnashing hound before him had dropped to its knees, a silver arrow embedded in its shoulder. The arrows fell thickly about him and instinctively Caspar knew that only a skilled Torra Altan bowman could fire with such speed – though he could not explain the silver arrows.

Abelard, he thought. He looked to the grove and saw him standing before Brid, drawing back his bow to loose another silver arrow. It dawned on Caspar that the ancient archer must have been collecting the verderers' fallen arrows along their journey.

The silver arrow skimmed Caspar's head. He flinched but, with gritted teeth, stood stock still to enable Abelard to maintain his mark. Closing fast behind him, he could hear the rustling of the huntsman's quick light feet through the crisp undergrowth. He knew he could not outrun him and that his best chance was to stand firm and trust to the archer's skill. He prayed his courage would hold and bit his lip, steeling his nerve and fixing his eyes on Abelard. The tension screamed through him. Abelard paused for a moment, taking a vital, steadying breath to ensure his aim. Caspar could hear the huntsman at his back, singing triumphantly. A hand jerked his shoulder back and, cringing, he waited for the punch of steel but it never came. A silver arrow whistled past Caspar's ear and then came silence.

He spun round. The huntsman was gone but there beside the flattened bracken lay his knife and peaked feathered cap. Sparkling dust, like condensed moonbeams and fragments of starlight, stirred briefly above the two objects before being dissipated by the breeze.

A hound was poised to spring on the helpless child as she screamed in the brambles and he snatched the moment to save her. He stooped for the huntsman's knife and flung it. The blade cartwheeled through the air and, though Caspar was no expert with a knife, it seemed to take on his will. With startling accuracy, it sliced into the dog's neck, bursting open the jugular. A fairy knife, he thought; deadly accurate.

All around him souls were running to escape the hunt, red-jacketed riders hollering and whooping ecstatically in the glee of the chase.

"Run, Spar, run!" Catrik shouted from the yew circle.

Huntsmen swerved towards him. He roughly grabbed the little girl, wrenched out the knife from the dog's neck and slashed his way through the brambles. The vegetation sprang aside from the blade and he now understood how the huntsmen had made such easy progress.

"Ma," the girl wailed, her fingernails digging into his skin. The huntsmen were closing swiftly.

The horse! The huntsman's horse was there ahead of him, rearing in the dappled golden sunlight that pierced the beech trees. A beautiful glistening mare, with a floating mane and tail, reared and slashed the air with cream hooves. Caspar almost stopped in his tracks and caught his breath at the sight of her.

"Great Mother, help me," he pleaded, holding out his hand towards the animal. Whickering, she swished her head from side to side and shifted her weight uncertainly from one foreleg to the other. He clicked his tongue, encouraging her to stand still for him. Turning his head slightly away from her, he took up a non-predatory stance and waited. She would come to him, he was confident.

The mare eyed him warily for only a few more moments before advancing purposefully towards him with a whinny of greeting. He knew he had a way with horses and he had not met one yet that wouldn't come to him. Her velveteen muzzle brushed his outstretched hand. He slid his hand up and soothed her neck. Seconds later he had his hand on her withers and threw the child up onto the mare's muscled back before vaulting up behind her. Like the knife, she responded to his will. She sped away like light glinting off a sword, racing towards the circle where Abelard, Catrik, Brid and Fern stood yelling for them to hurry. Brid clutched the Pipe of Abalone.

Caspar could hear the hooves of another horse close on his heels and kicked on towards the circle. With dismay he saw Catrik abandon the safety of the yew circle, yelling and running towards him. "Get away from him, you fiend," the old wellmaster howled at the huntsman closing on Caspar. "Master Spar, quick!"

"Catrik no," Brid shouted, thrusting the Pipe into Fern's grasp and running after Catrik. "Come back."

"No!" Caspar yelled, his eyes focusing beyond Brid on the woodwose who, trembling in fear, held the Pipe poised to his lips.

He prayed to the Great Mother that Fern's nerve would hold as Catrik ran towards him followed by Brid and now Abelard. Caspar's heart sank at the chaos.

"Get back," Spar yelled, galloping towards them.

"Look out! To your left," Brid shouted in return.

A red-capped huntsman hacked his way through the undergrowth, but Caspar was less worried by him than his dogs that were already bursting forward into the open ground right before Catrik and Brid. Caspar stabbed his heels into the mare's golden flanks and raced forward onto the close-cropped sward of open ground before the circle of yew trees. The white stag bellowed and danced around Brid, keeping the hounds at bay, but Catrik was unprotected. With a savage howl the dogs rounded on him, dashing and snatching at him as he fought them off with broad sweeps of his knife.

Hunched forward with the girl clutched to his chest, Caspar sped across the ground, the wind lifting his hair. Catrik yelled with pain as one of the salivating dogs tore at his arm. For a moment Caspar saw the gossamer, ghostly outlines of people swirling across his path. He jerked at the startled expression on a grandly dressed man. He squeezed his eyes shut, his mind reeling in panicked confusion. He could have sworn it was King Rewik's brother.

The great stag lowered his heavy antlered head at the dogs and they fled to a cowering distance. Abelard and Brid wasted no time dragging Catrik towards the yews. As Caspar drew level, he slid from his horse to take Brid's place and together he and Abelard bore Catrik's weight across their shoulders. The old wellmaster was barely able to walk, his lacerated arms and legs streaming with blood. The blood was warm and sticky, oozing between Caspar's fingers where he gripped the man's arm. Still bearing the child, the golden horses followed them into the circle of yews.

Fern held the Pipe up to Brid. "Brid, let it sing," he cried.

She took it but didn't look at it, merely toying with it in her hands.

"Brid, Brid!" he cried. "Make it sing. Play the notes and make it sing."

Her fingers moved wistfully over the Pipe's pearlescent finish but her eyes stared beyond the yews into the forest. Caspar knew what had stopped her as a single rider on a dazzling horse blazed towards them.

"Brid!" he yelled, dropping Abelard and sprinting towards her. He tried to grab her and turn her gaze away from the rider but she twisted out of his grip.

His shouts did nothing to distract her from Talorcan's elegant form as the verderer swooped into the midst of the milling huntsmen halted on the perimeter of the circle, his voice beautiful and compelling. All birdsong ceased and time seemed to stand still as if the verderer's song broke all laws of nature.

Over his huntsman's red suit, resplendent on his sleek golden horse, Talorcan wore a shimmering cloak of black velvet edged with ermine. A plume of eyed peacock feathers flounced above the horse's head and turquoise feathers were woven into its black mane and tail along with silver threads and satin ribbons glimmering like starlight in a midnight sky. Talorcan's huge yellow eyes, glowing like fireflies, reached across the glade to trap Brid in the web of his spell.

"The Pipe, Brid, the Pipe!" Fern shrieked, dancing up and down in agitation. "Play the tune."

Abelard grasped and squeezed her hand. "My lady, I've waited near half a millennium to ensure the safety of the Trinity. Play the Pipe, I beg you."

Brid's arms dropped down by her sides in defeat as she looked towards Talorcan.

"It's only a spell," Caspar told her quietly, trying to reach the hidden depths of her mind. "Just a spell. He doesn't love you. He wants to use your powers to enhance his own. He doesn't want you; he wants power."

Brid didn't seem to notice him. She brushed her hand

across her cheek, wiping away a stray hair that irritated her face, almost as if sweeping him from her mind. Seeing her reluctance to play the Pipe, the hunt closed in threat around the yews.

"Brid, I love you," Caspar cried out in desperation. But as the words slipped from his mouth, his thoughts were filled with May's hazel eyes and coiling chestnut hair. He knew in that one instant that he loved May. She needed him and they could be equals: when he looked at Brid he saw not only her but the image of his mother and Morrigwen too. She was One of the Three, surrounded by the awesome aura of the Goddess. It had taken the entire journey through the forest for him to recognize the truth of his emotions. He loved her, yes, but not with the basic, instinctive love of a man for his woman.

His cry must have cut through the intense web of Talorcan's song to reach Brid because, with a flicker of hope, she turned her deep dragon-green eyes on him. Then contempt curled her lips. Caspar's heart stuck in his throat as he realized he had disappointed her. He had failed her by loving her as a priestess and not as a woman. She blinked and her expression dulled as she was sucked into the verderer's song.

Fern leapt up and down in distress. "The hunt, Brid, the hunt!"

The huntsmen tilted eagerly forward in their saddles while the hounds pared back their lips and crouched ready to spring.

Brid's hands raised the Pipe and for a brief moment she looked at it as if simply admiring the grain of the wood and the pearly inlays that outlined the holes. The stark grooved runes of her spell were deeply defined in shadow while the rest of the Pipe glistened. The sunlight caught it, dancing on the polished surface of the metal and caressing the swirling patina that glossed the ancient oak surface.

Talorcan's song grew louder and more insistent. Holding the Pipe in one hand, she reached for her sickle with the other. Sparks scorched the atmosphere as she struck at the Pipe to score the runes of unbinding into the wood. At last, she would play its song. Caspar stiffened in anticipation of their journey.

"Hurry! Hurry! Hurry!" Fern squealed while leaping up and down and snorting in unrestrained frustration. "Brid, come on, come on! I must return to my fawn."

Abelard, his hands and face smeared with Catrik's blood, cradled the old man and looked on in expectant but patient silence. Good, honest men, true to the last; Caspar thought. At last, he would take them home.

The little girl tugged at his hand. "The lady promised she'd take me back to Ma," she murmured.

"And so you will go," Brid told her without dragging her enthralled eyes from Talorcan.

More huntsmen gathered around the yews, waiting in confusion at the sound of the chief verderer's song. His voice was not filled with the triumph of the hunt but poured out his enslaving song of love. They circled uneasily, their gold and red suits glistening in the brilliant spring sunshine. The white stag retreated into the centre of the circle, antlers lowered in threat as Talorcan pushed his way through the hunt and slid from his horse to stand before Brid.

"Fern," Brid murmured and the little creature looked up. She pressed the Pipe into his hand.

Caspar couldn't think what she was doing and he stared blankly at the movement, unaware of its importance. "Save your child," the priestess murmured.

The woodwose snatched up the Pipe and, without hesitation, pressed his pursed lips to the mouthpiece. A screech like an owl, a tuneless peal of clashing notes, blasted their senses.

"No, don't!" Abelard shouted. "Fern, stop!"

But the little horned creature could not be drawn from his one intent of getting home to save his young fawn. Even as Brid fled the circle, he played on. Abelard tried to catch her but he was too late: the Pipe of Abalone had cast its spell. Caspar felt it penetrate the elements, drawing them in, intensifying the air about them, the physical laws of nature shredded by the magic.

He blinked in dismay and bewilderment as everything beyond the perimeter of the yews blurred as if veiled by tears. Helplessly, he watched as Talorcan clutched Brid by the wrist, his head thrown back in triumph.

She raised her hand in a wave of farewell. Caspar's eyes reached towards her but he knew as he looked into her fading eyes that he didn't reach her soul. Her lips moved but he heard no sound. I'm sorry, he thought she was saying but he would never be sure.

Then everything became confusing. He could see a sword, a brilliant golden sword marked with blood red runes. It seemed to hover in mid-air. Caspar recognized it at once; it could only be the runesword; it could only be Hal's. The runesword had no equal in their world and surely not in this. Through the dimming light beyond the circle of trees he saw that the hunt had seen it and that Talorcan had seen it too.

"Hal!" she shouted, her voice cracking in agonized despair. Talorcan drew her close. "Hal! Help me."

Caspar's heartstrings tightened. Looking towards her fading image, he saw her jolt awake from the spell. Sudden desperation swept across her face. But it was too late. He tried to claw his way towards the edge of the circle only to find Catrik's bloodied hand holding him back.

"I'm sorry, Master Spar, but I have to save you. I must protect you. You must get home to Lord Branwolf."

"Let go!" Caspar tried to shake him off but Catrik was determined and it was already too late. Caspar saw her for a moment of vivid colour that dulled to mauves and greys like the early morning mist over marshes. Everything but the yew trees and the lake had vanished. He felt drawn towards the water. The mists feathering its edges swelled to absorb all around them. Soon everything beyond the circle of trees was nothing but a darkening mist and then blackness; pure empty infinity, too big, too vast to contemplate. Caspar feared the everlasting emptiness.

His mind could not begin to comprehend what he saw. It was like standing alone on a bleak craggy peak in the black of a silent, moonless night. He knew as he looked into that one blackness that its immeasurable unending nothing would drive him mad if he tried to define it.

And then there, like the evening star alone in the heavens, was a tiny point of light. Gradually it began to swell. Caspar looked towards it and felt his heart warm with hope and was overwhelmed by the certain knowledge of forthcoming bliss. The light began to swell towards him. All life, all desire, the communion of the single consciousness, he knew it was there. For a second his heart lurched towards it as did the hearts of all of those caught within the circle. Even the wild golden horse whickered its awareness.

"Ma," the little girl murmured in utter happiness. "Ma, I'm coming home."

"Heaven!" Catrik sighed.

Abelard fell to his knees. "Great Mother," he murmured. "I have failed again."

Caspar knew what was important to him. Though the

bliss of Annwyn beckoned it was not yet time. He could wait. He had not yet fulfilled the purpose of his present life; it was not yet time to go home. He looked longingly at that light but knew he could not take the final step towards it.

He withdrew from the beckoning glow as did Abelard and Fern. The white stag bellowed a kingly roar, thrashing his antlers and raking the ground with his cloven hooves, eagerly greeting the light but he, too, did not pace forward. Caspar put his hand on the golden mare's bridle to steady her as she snorted in agitation, shying away from Annwyn, which was not for her. She belonged to the Otherworld, to the stuff of starlight and heavens.

It was happening so quickly, so fast and yet seemed to take forever. Caspar re-lived every thought he had ever had, saw every face that he had ever seen within the space of one timeless breath. He even had time to realize that if it hadn't been for the hunt they could have stayed with the column and played the Pipe with all hundred souls within the confines of the circle. The Pipe did not prevent those who wished to reach Annwyn from passing across but rather allowed them a choice.

A narrow beam of light swelled towards them from the glowing star. A ghostly pathway of light stretched out towards them until, at last, it reached down and cupped the grove in its caring grasp. The little girl scrabbled towards the light and Catrik strode eagerly forward without hesitation. With one foot on the beam and the other still in the grove, he turned to salute Caspar.

"I have done my duty, Master Spar, and pass on gladly."

Tenderly the light flowed around the young girl, wrapping her in the energy of life. Her eyes brightened and her wan skin flushed with vigour as, in wonder, she spread her fingers and watched the light flow through them.

Caspar smiled. Brid had promised her and had kept true to her word. The girl was going home.

A look of uncertainty, however, slowly dawned on the girl's innocent face and she slithered from the light and clutched Caspar's hand. "Not yet," she murmured.

Caspar could not move towards the wondrous pathway of welcoming light though his heart longed for the succour and freedom from the responsibilities of life. His task was still unfinished. The light curled so tenderly around Catrik who beamed with utter satisfaction, pawing the glow around him so lovingly like a kitten kneading its mother. The flow of light poised for just a moment in anticipation, beckoning those that held back but, when none moved forward, it retreated and swept away, back to the distant point of light.

Caspar knew his chance had gone and he had to face the realities and the harshness of life once more. The light faded and a growing smell of warm earth mould filled his nostrils. Leafless trees rattled their branches in a crisp breeze that played upon his face. Beyond the circle of yew trees, he could see holly, beech, birch, oaks and blackthorn. And horses and soldiers. And . . .

He stared in complete disbelief. And Hal! His kinsman's great runesword swirled round his head, as he called, "Brid, my Brid, where are you?"

CHAPTER TWENTY-SEVEN

"Brid! Brid!" Hal knew it was her voice.

"Master Hal, what's the matter, sir?" Ogden let go of the pack ponies bearing Pip and Brock to grab Secret's bridle.

"Get off me, you fool," Hal snarled angrily, driven to the point of madness by the sound of Brid's voice. "Can't you hear her?"

Though weak with injuries, old Brock snatched at Hal's leg and held on with stolid determination. Trog, who at first had leapt in frenzied attack after the lequus, now froze in his tracks, his pointed ears flattened to his bulbous skull. He galloped towards the grove of yews.

Restricted by Ogden and Brock's efforts to save him from his apparent madness, Hal turned coldly to the men and drew the white steel of the runesword. He held the point of his sword at the old man's throat. "Stand aside, Brock."

"Sir, you're ailing," Brock protested.

The sound of baying hounds was gone and so too was the lequus as if frightened away by whatever had swept past. Tudwal held Cymbeline in his arms and was doing his best to keep her from seeing the torn carcass of her horse.

"She could have been killed and you did nothing to protect her." The prince's lower lip trembled with rage though Hal barely noticed the man was there.

His mind was elsewhere and these fools, these madmen were in his way. Ceowulf was trying to stop him but he barged past and ran after Trog towards the circle of yews. He knew he had heard Brid and he knew that a yew grove would be sacred to her. She had taught him that a yew was one of the most sacred trees, the tree of everlasting life, the tree of rebirth. And here was an entire ring of them. His mind raced through these facts but still he could make no sense of anything. How could he have heard Brid here in Ceolothia? Had the trappers taken her as well as Brock and Pip? Uncharacteristically bemused, he felt unaccountably afraid and irritated by the others buzzing like flies around him.

Suddenly they ceased to pester him and a deathly silence fell upon the wood. Only Trog moved ahead of him. The rest hung back as the gory smell of bloody slaughter filled the air. Again, he glimpsed flashes of silver and ephemeral figures. Around the edges of the yew grove, shadowy bodies ducked and weaved through the branches. A ghostly mob of men, women and children were running in panic. Now Hal could see bright flashes of glorious, golden horses and the glint of weaponry. As the figures raced towards the yews, their feathery outlines took on more solid forms. Black hounds snarled and snapped at the fleeing spectres. Silver spears flew from huntsmen's hands and men and women shrieked in pain. As the huntsmen rode into the thick of the mob, the dogs began to attack with frenzy. Those maimed by the hounds still crawled on towards the grove.

A woman was screaming hysterically.

Hal registered the sound sharply though it did not distract him. It was only the princess, he thought dismissively, screaming in horror at the sight of the mangled bodies around him. What did it matter? She wasn't Brid.

Nothing else mattered. Nothing else in the world mattered but Brid and, deep within his soul, he knew she needed him.

He filled his lungs and called her name. Holding his sword out before him, he stepped slowly round. Trog was barking with frightened angry yelps at the air before him.

Hal closed his eyes, summoning his courage. "Great Mother, guide me through this hell," he murmured. "Forgive me, I've sinned – sinned against you and the woman I love. Cymbeline meant nothing. She was just the hopes of vanity, a stab at riches and power, things that tempt in fantasy but are nothing in reality. Great Mother, help me find Brid."

He looked beyond Trog, who howled piteously, towards the yew grove, hoping beyond hope that she would be there. Ceowulf was running to catch up with him and, swords drawn, they advanced towards the circle. Ogden panted behind them, side-stepping a squirming body and grimacing in disgust. Hal barely noticed his companions as he marched on, never once taking his eyes from the grove.

She must be there.

"The power of Necrönd has been released. Someone is playing with it and summoning the creatures of legend. Spar is a fool," Ceowulf accused.

"'Tis the heart of Hobs Slack," Ogden murmured brightly as if covering his fear.

They halted.

The world seemed to rock as if it had paused and begun to spin the other way. The sweet smell of daffodils and fresh damp dew on spring leaves filled their nostrils. For a fleeting moment the rustling leaves underfoot turned to lush grass. A dazzling flash of brilliant light burnt into his eyes and he threw his arm across his face. Then it dimmed and, as he pulled his fingers away from his eyes, he saw it as a light full of hope and promise like a guiding lantern in the dark of the storm, showing his way home. Then everything was back to normal . . . only it wasn't.

He blinked, took a few stumbling steps forward and blinked again. For a fleeting moment he thought he saw the old wellmaster Catrik. But that was absurd! Catrik had died three years ago now, murdered by Spar's uncle that treacherous priest Gwion. But the sight had been so convincing that he couldn't help himself for calling out, "Catrik," as he ran into the grove.

"Catrik," a voice echoed with great sorrow.

Hal feared he was going mad. He knew that voice almost as well as he knew his own. He spun round and staggered on his feet, unable to believe his eyes. His arms went limp, letting the weight of the great runesword sag to the ground, as he stared at Caspar. In disbelief he reached out slowly towards his kinsman but, when he touched solid flesh, he grabbed Caspar's arm and pulled him towards him. With just one look at his kinsman, Hal knew something was terribly wrong. There was no need for his nephew to explain the dire tragedy of the situation; the perplexed despair was written across his face.

"Hal, she . . . Brid—," the auburn youth stuttered in hopeless explanation.

Caspar was not alone. Hal looked past his shoulder, searching for Brid. A small frail-looking girl clutched the hand of a man dressed in the garb of an ancient peasant as if he had come from a time of the great plagues. A little beyond him was something that Hal thought could only be a grotesque dwarf. He gapped at the trotters and the short horns sprouting from the creature's head. The little dwarf looked utterly relieved though he shied away from the rest of them. A stag, an enormous white stag, stood trembling in the middle of the grove beside a dazzling golden mare. There was no sign of Brid.

"Where's Brid?" Hal demanded coldly. "Where is she?!"

Caspar was speechless, his eyes brimming with tears. The oddly dressed peasant looked utterly beyond despair and caught the youth's arm. "The Maiden . . . after all these years and I've failed her, again." His dialect was strangely Torra Altan.

"Where, in the name of the Mother, is Brid?" Hal bellowed.

"Y' bloody selfish, spineless little creature," the strangely dressed peasant rounded on the dwarf. "Y' played the Pipe without her."

"I had to get back."

"I'll kill y'!" the man threatened.

Caspar put his hand on his shoulder to restrain him. "It wasn't Fern's fault. She made her choice. Talorcan—"

Caspar glanced hesitantly towards Hal and the raven-haired man knew that his nephew had news he didn't want to hear. He stared at him, his anger and fear willing the words from the youth's throat as if hauling a murdered body from a well.

"She's on the other side, Hal."

"The other side of what?" Hal's voice was like ice.

"She's in the Otherworld. She's beyond this life."

"She didn't want to come back," the little dwarf, whom Caspar had called Fern, blurted, as if defending his actions. "She didn't want to come. She wanted Talorcan."

Hal grabbed Caspar by the collar and yanked his face close up towards his. "Where in hell is she?"

Caspar's cerulean blue eyes fixed him clearly as he sadly explained, "The Otherworld, Hal. Rye Errish, the land of fairy. We slipped through a gateway, a portal between the dimensions. We should have been killed by wolves but we weren't and we slipped through a gateway and found ourselves in the Otherworld instead. She nearly got back, just like we did, only, at the last second, she wouldn't come. One of the beings there, a verderer, cast a fairy spell over her. She's trapped in the land of spirit. Her soul has been captured by him and she will reside there forever. We can't get her back!"

As he told this tale, Caspar's eyes flitted around the edge of the grove. Hal slowly let his kinsman down from his grasp and followed his nephew's gaze, taking in the thirteen people . . . Or were they people? They appeared first as gossamer phantoms and then solidified into sparkling creatures that floated above the ground. Though quite small, standing at least a head shorter than Caspar, they emanated an air of strength. All had outlandish yellow eyes, fantastically beautiful as if shot through with sunlight.

"The ealdormen of the High Circle," Caspar muttered.

One stepped forward. Though short by human terms he had a strong body and was taller than the other twelve beings. He wore a crown decorated with acorns. Though the sight should have been strangely ridiculous, Hal saw only majesty in the being.

"You have earned the right to return to your lives," the ealdorman said solemnly. "You outran the hunt. You must honour the Maiden's promise and give me back my Pipe."

Caspar looked towards the little creature with short horns jutting through the curls of its head and nodded. Shaking timorously, Fern held out the Pipe to the ealdorman and he eagerly took it, examining it with great care.

"But what of Brid!" Caspar begged. "Lord Duir, return her to us. We cannot lose her."

"I am sorry, truly I am. The Earth needs her," Duir

rumbled, without taking his eyes from his precious Pipe. "We understand that the unending chain of knowledge passed from high priestess to high priestess will die. It is sad but it is her own choice. You all chose at the end and she has chosen to remain."

"No! Lord Duir, no, you must not allow it," Caspar pleaded, his voice cracking with sobs.

Hal raised his sword. "Give her to me!" He advanced on the crescent of thirteen ealdormen only to be repelled by a shrieking noise. He staggered backwards as if butted in the face by a shield. All thirteen of the encircling figures were in song, focusing on him, forcing him to the ground. His sword was flung from his reach.

"You cannot have her." A woman with flowing hair and white robes stepped forward from the thirteen while the rest sang on. "There are laws."

"I will have her," Hal screamed, not caring what the creature was talking about. "Brid! Brid! I must have her. I cannot live without her. Brid!" he screamed in agony, the pain of his loss ripping at his heart.

"There is nothing you can do, nothing. Give in to your grief."

Hal couldn't move. His body felt encased in lead. He could only blink and stare helplessly into the face of this beautiful being whose yellow sun-shot eyes looked piteously on him. He wanted to cry with his pain but instead yelled out in anger, refusing to accept their words. "How dare you take Brid from me?"

One of the ealdormen, who, unlike the others, held a book rather than a staff, tapped at the tome in his hand. "We have done nothing, mortal. We merely uphold the law."

"What law allows you to steal Brid from me?" Hal bellowed. "I need her! I love her!"

The ealdormen with the book continued, "You cannot have her. She has passed on into Rye Errish and is now outside the cycle. She will remain there forever." The words were solemn, matter of fact, but there was a hint of regret and the yellow eyes seemed to search into Hal's desperate soul. He joined the others in chorus and Hal found his body locked rigid against his will.

He tried to reach for the runesword, fighting to will all of his energy through his fingers but they seemed set in ice. The pain was unbelievable as he was driven by the desire to move and yet could not. But he must to save Brid.

"Brid, Brid please no," he wailed. "I cannot lose you."

If he had the sword he could kill them, kill all of them. They had taken his Brid. He would kill them even if he had to kill every last one to get her back. He couldn't live without her. His soul was a chill void and the beat of his heart like a dagger stabbing at him from within.

Caspar was crying. Pip and the oddly dressed peasant were crying and he was certain they all cried with the terribly grief of losing the Maiden. He knew so many people loved her; but not in the way he did. He would not cry as they cried. The pain was too deep. Though his soul was being ripped from him, gouged out by grief, he would not cry.

He would kill them. If only he could reach the sword . . .

He focused on his hand and then, as if plunging his arm into burning oil, he inched his fingers across the earth.

Utter blackness swallowed his will as the song grew louder and the disabling pain more intense. The pain rampaged, a shrieking beast within his head, a rage of red savaging his mind. He forced himself to gather what was left of his will and drew it into a deep part of himself. Somehow, he had to grow beyond his senses and above the pain. He must detach his will from his physical being. He must find that last inner refuge within his head that could not be reached from without. He must transcend the flesh.

He was weakening rapidly with the excruciating pain but the blackness was building. He closed his eyes and looked in on himself until he saw the pain as a frantic wild bull, blood dripping from its horns as it gouged and trampled. Then he imagined building a corral around the beast to contain it. And though it raged on, he shut it into one small part of his mind, freeing his will so that he could act.

The second the gate closed on that steaming bull, his hand jerked forward. He gritted his teeth, straining to keep the raging pain contained and, shuddering with the effort, he clawed his way towards the sword. Suddenly the familiar grip of the hilt was in his hand. The energy of the Goddess thrilled through his fingers. The tremendous rage that he felt within him was now swept aside by an abrupt and inexplicable peace as if he were cradled in his mother's arms. It was as if he had been in the black of a storm-tossed sea and then flung upon the still of a warm beach. The world stood still for him.

"Great Mother, thank you," he murmured as a sudden lightness overwhelmed his being. But the moment was transitory. He was flung to the ground, the hard, cold, loveless ground.

He knew at once this was not the soil of the Great Mother and that he had crossed to the Otherworld. The shock made him lose control of his restrained mind and the pain returned with a vengeance. This time it stabbed into his stomach and he folded around it.

The others were gone. Caspar, Ceowulf, the troops, all

gone though the High Circle of thirteen still surrounded him. Their song, however, had ceased. One dressed in black and carrying a staff thick with thorns grinned broadly. The rest looked aghast.

The ealdorman with the book worriedly thumped it into his hand. "The law has been broken. He had no right to will himself here, no right at all."

"A law is not a law if it cannot be broken," the ealdorman with vengeful thorns on his staff replied with satisfaction.

"You are a fool, Straif. He has not broken it," the lady in white spoke calmly. "His soul was dying without her. He has passed through the barrier between worlds because he is no longer complete without her."

Hal could hardly focus on these strange beings for the growing warmth within him. She was here, he knew she was here. He could feel the pulse of her heart.

"Hal!" her voice cried out in relief, in hope, in love. "Hal, you came for me. You heard me."

The youth stepped slowly round. She was gripped in the clutches of a lithe man of fine features, barely taller than herself. He was dressed in clothes of glittering scarlet except for his green peaked cap decorated with an eyed peacock feather and a shimmering black cape.

"An elf," he spat. "A creepy elf. Let go of her!"

The being shook his head. "No, she is mine. She came freely to me."

"Brid!" Hal felt sick to his soul. "How— how could you?" he stuttered lamely. He felt cheated, betrayed. "I crossed worlds for you."

"He trapped me with his song," Brid defended herself, "and bound me with enchantment."

"Don't judge her so harshly. Were you not just similarly caught in a similar spell of enthralment? Cymbeline's riches?" One of the thirteen, the extraordinarily beautiful ealdorwoman dressed in white with ash keys hung around her neck, was standing by his shoulder.

"But that was different."

"How so? We see all. We know all. We are not bound by the same laws but can pass between the worlds. Occasionally you see us, usually you don't. If you do, you see us like a mirage caught in dewdrops on the flowers; tiny little creatures like butterflies as the water reflects the happenings across the divide. We see and we know all and you cannot hope to lie to us," the lady warned.

"But I didn't love Cymbeline," Hal started to protest, suddenly appalled by the touch of the yellow silk scarf on his neck.

"No, of course not, but some part of you wanted something of her that Brid did not offer. Wealth, land, position . . . ? Brid brought you only love. But you cannot pass between worlds for material goods or position. Only for love. It is the only thing that is soul deep."

The sturdiest member of the High Circle, who possessively clutched the Pipe, turned towards the elf-like creature. "Give her up, Talorcan. He has crossed worlds for her. Their souls cannot be parted."

Hal looked in disgust towards the elf-like being and a chill spread across his heart as he noticed the dark shadowy figure at his back. About him were gathered a host of snarling hooded wolves and behind him squatted the winged lequus, its head bowed submissively.

"Keep her, Talorcan," the man in the shadows ominously ordered. "I have need of her and I wish to see her suffer. She must suffer! I will bring you a far greater power than the Pipe of Abalone if you keep her here."

"You must give her up," Lord Duir boomed. "You have no choice."

"Then kill her, Talorcan," The figure stepped forward from the shadows. He was cloaked in a wolf's pelt, the long snout of a bare wolf's skull masking his face. "Kill her," he yelled. "Or lose this power I promised you. Use your knife and she will be gone forever."

"Hal, help me!" Brid begged, thrashing to get free of Talorcan's grip.

"Step closer and I cut her throat," Talorcan threatened. "She will go to the sun to be the stuff of the universe, all consciousness lost, her soul burned away."

Hal turned to the circle of thirteen beings for mercy. "You must stop him."

"They can't," the man beneath the wolf pelt gloated. "They can't stop him. Their song has no power over verderers and they need the consent of twelve others of his kind, which they know they will not get, before they can pass judgement over him."

The ealdorman with the book pulled a beech nut from his beard and studied it thoughtfully. "We cannot stop him but we can make an exchange." He looked at Hal. "By rights you should not be here and we would be within the law to send you back. But would you give up your soul for hers? The law is all about bargains."

"No!" Brid cried.

"Better me than you," Hal replied solemnly. "The world needs you and no one could ever say that of me." A flicker of a smile spread across his face.

"No!" Brid sobbed.

"I have to." He turned to the Circle. "I give myself freely. Send the Maiden home." Numbly, he knew that he was saying farewell to everything and everybody forever but, worse, he was losing Brid.

CHAPTER TWENTY-EIGHT

"No," Talorcan refused. "I want the girl and I will not give her up."

"Make the exchange!" Lord Duir thundered. "His love gives him the right to sacrifice himself for her."

"Ha! But what love? They have proved it themselves that they have no such love," Talorcan retorted triumphantly. "She succumbed to my song and he to the riches of a princess. How then can they have true love?"

A member of the High Circle that had not spoken before thrust her staff of hazel at the scarlet-robed verderer. "Fool, they are human; they have needs and wants beyond your soulless imagination. Look at them. She is little more than a girl yet she carries the woes of the world on her back. He has ambition, great courage, direction of purpose and awareness – skills that would make him a great leader of men – yet he does not possess the position to use these skills and nor is he ever likely to if he marries the Maiden. True love does not bind them into utter contentment and peace with one another; it simply means they cannot live without each other. There is nothing righteous or pure about true love; it is merely the love that blends souls. It does not prevent them from being human."

"But I need her," Talorcan raged.

Brid struggled against the clutch of the verderer. Brandishing his sword high, Hal rushed him only to have his path blocked by the man in the wolf pelt cloak who sprang forward, a pack of hooded wolves baying at his side. As Hal tensed his grip ready to strike at him, the light shone full into the mask of his wolf skull and Hal saw through the staring eye sockets to the man behind. He saw no eyes, only oozing tissue. He recoiled at the sight. His sword was aimed at the neck but as he faltered, the swing of his sword lowered, skimming before the man's chest.

A wolf leapt forward to protect him. Hal looked beyond its curving fangs and its ribbed palate down into the depths of its dark red throat. He heard the vicious snarls but he was not afraid: he had the runesword. The great blade cut the air and bit deep through the wolf's chest and on into the head of another. He hacked viciously. Brid was screaming for him.

He slashed back and forth, cutting through a jawbone then severing a leg until the remaining wolves retreated and nothing stood between him and the elf-like being that held Brid.

"I will kill her rather than lose her, do you hear?" Talorcan threatened. "I have seen millions upon millions of souls pass through this world on their way to the one consciousness and none have been as beautiful as her. She is mine. I claim her."

The verderer's dagger jerked closer to Brid's pulsing jugular and Hal dared not take a step closer. The blade was like nothing he had ever seen. Shimmering like moonlight, the spike of the blade forged from a white glossy metal with a turquoise patina that swirled in the sunlight, it was the stuff of the heavens.

Not knowing how he could save Brid, Hal despaired. He had reached a deadlock with the verderer, their eyes battling while their bodies remained in tense stillness.

He was sickened by the whirling yellow irises rimmed with black. Looking into a human's eyes was like looking into their soul, gaining insight into the real person within; but looking into the verderer's eyes was like glimpsing into the unimaginable power of the sun. Talorcan rocked backwards and the knife pressed deeper into Brid's skin. The colour drained from her cheeks and her lips moved in prayer.

Hal tightened his grip on the runesword. He could not stand by and do nothing. He knew he must attack.

The verderer's mouth stretched into an oval and he produced a piercing note that sliced into Hal's belly like a hunter's gralloching knife. Stabs of lightning jabbed up his spine into his brain and his eyes swam. The sound grew louder and the pain swelled to envelop his entire body. He tried to focus only on his hands that were shaking before him. The sword, he must hold the sword: it was his only hope.

"Great Mother," he prayed, but felt strangely detached from Her. There was none of the usual sense of strength welling up from the earth, no surging sense of courage nor invincibility. This soil was without warmth, without life. This was after all the Otherworld and not the earth of the Great Mother. Here the usual imbuing surge of courage from the sword failed him.

He clenched his fists tighter around the hilt, but Talorcan's voice grew higher and more insistent. The agony throughout Hal's body was focused like a thousand stinging wasps onto his hands.

He gasped from the raw pain. Struggling to find the wherewithal to endure it, he reminded himself of how the brave heroes had withstood brutal torture during the Ceolothian war, their arms plunged into boiling oil and limbs broken one by one. He had always wondered how they had endured it and now he would learn; he had to learn because all that mattered was saving Brid. He needed focus. The sword, focus only on the sword, he willed himself; the cool hard metal, the razor-sharp blade that he had so loving polished and deburred with his whetstone every night. He concentrated on the runes, the runes of hope, the runes of victory, the runes of courage.

Strength seeped back into his fingers and his clutch tightened. As it did, the magic in the sword fed back into him. With the howl of anger raging in his throat, he raised the blade, swinging it above his head. Knowing that he could not rush the yellow-eyed verderer, he trusted all to one last, brave hope and fixed his eyes on Brid, willing her to understand his intention and ready herself. He prayed his aim would be better than it was with his throwing knives. He had to have faith. With a yell of effort, he hurled the runesword. It flew like a javelin towards Talorcan's heart, missing Brid by the barest of inches.

She didn't flinch.

He had seen the courage in her eyes willing him on. There was no sobbing, no cry of relief, nothing so simple. She looked somehow satisfied as if she had always known he would succeed, had known the measure of his courage and strength, and had known that he was man enough to endure the pain. For the first time he felt her equal. She had needed him to win through, to endure all to reclaim her and he had not failed.

Hal was aware of nothing else around him and marched forward to claim her. She might be the Maiden, she might be one of the Three, but she was his, a part of him.

She stepped into his embrace and softly kissed his lips. "I cried out for you, and you came," she said simply. "You came across the great divide, across the barriers between life and death."

A flickering movement above them caught his eye and Hal looked up. The sun was brilliant in the sky. He squinted against the dazzling light and fancied he saw Talorcan's body born aloft on the vast turquoise and silver wings of the High Circle. The sun hurt his eyes. Brid clasped her arms about his waist and pressed her head against his chest, hugging him tightly. He lowered his gaze and looked down at her through a haze of spangled lights burnt into his vision by the great fireball. He blinked up at the trees around him, trying to clear his vision. For just a second, he thought he saw the black shape of a wolf stalking towards them but the image twisted in his sun-dazzled eyes and he saw, not a wolf, but Caspar yelling his name, "Hal! Hal!"

Hal could barely believe his eyes and merely hugged Brid tightly, so tightly.

Someone beyond the circle of trees was shouting, "A wolf! A wolf! What the hell is this boy doing with a wolf? I don't want to know about these peasants; I want to know about a wolf, here in my lands." It was Tudwal's voice, loud, domineering and insistent. Pip stood weakly by a pony and was backing anxiously away from a raging Prince Tudwal. "There are stiff penalties in Ceolothia for harbouring wolves. Little imp, speak up! What are you doing with it?"

Hal was too exhausted and shocked to act. He merely groaned inwardly at the thought of Pip causing trouble already. He would have thought the boy was too weak and sick to create such a nuisance.

"Give the beast to a soldier," Tudwal ordered. "Someone wring its neck."

"You'll die first." There was an acidity in Pip's voice. Fierce like a wolf cub himself, he had snatched a knife from the pony's pack and held it up in threat. "I've been through hell for this wolf and I'm not giving her up."

There was a gasp from all around.

Brid stiffened in Hal's arms. "A wolf cub!" she exclaimed and pushed away from him. Hal knew the moment had passed when she belonged only to him. She was a priestess again. He sighed and let her go.

He had no need to intercede on Pip's behalf; for once Caspar had responded more quickly. "Leave the lad alone," he snarled in warning at Prince Tudwal whose stature entirely overshadowed the small seventeen-year-old. "He is under my command and you will not chastise him."

Prince Tudwal blustered for a moment and then, seeing the way in which the Belbidians gathered around the boy, threw his hands in the air in resignation. "I have better things to occupy my time than you mad, squabbling Torra Altans." He spun on his heel and paced away, back to his sister. Hal was surprised. The prince must truly have been distracted to allow Pip to go unpunished.

"Pip, you're safe!" Caspar exclaimed. While he tried to extract some explanation from the boy as to how he got here, Brid was concentrating on prizing the wriggling bundle of white fur from his hands.

"Be careful, my lady," Pip said quickly. "She's wild and will bite if she's not used to you."

Once in Brid's arms, the wolfling showed no such malice but rather licked and nuzzled against her cheek as if the Maiden were an old friend. Once he had released the wolfling, Pip clutched at his injured arm and began to sway groggily. Ogden eased him to the ground.

A frail, wan-looking little girl, who had been clinging to Caspar's hand, rushed to Brid's side and wrapped herself around her legs. The Maiden stroked her hair. "It appears we all have much to tell, though out tales must surely be linked for we cannot all have come together at this place without there being some divine design." She smiled in satisfaction as she spread apart the wolf's hide to reveal a red scar where the arrow had pierced its shoulder. "And here is a sign."

"What sign," Pip demanded, struggling to rise. "I've checked her all over."

Brid pointed at the dry clean scar.

"My lady, it's just an arrow wound. The poor creature would have died without Pip's nursing," old Brock said, looking at the clean dry scar on her shoulder.

Caspar stared in wonder at the scar, which had healed into the shape of the rune: ᛒ. "But it's your rune! One of the runes Morrigwen cast before we left: Beorc, the signature rune of the Maiden."

Brid smiled. "You found her, Pip. You found the wolfling. Let us pray that this can make some amends for the murder of the sacred mother wolf. You found her wolfling and she has brought us all together. You're a hero, Pip." She dropped to her knees and hugged the boy, who blushed and grinned with pride.

Hal smiled to himself. Pip a hero for rescuing a cub! The idea was preposterous yet he felt generous towards the boy. He was back with Brid and nothing could displease him now. He looked around him. Cymbeline was busy brushing kobolds off her as if they were fleas whilst clutching tightly to her brother's hand. He wondered how he had ever thought she could bring him happiness. Guiltily, he remembered her tiara glittering with sunburst rubies.

Despite his happiness at saving Brid, Hal felt strangely detached from the other Torra Altans. Pip, old Brock, Brid, Caspar and apparently Trog all shared something with this wolf that he didn't yet understand. Still, they would explain when all their silly over-excited exclamations were finished and they had stopped fussing Pip, who looked all too pleased with himself. Hal groaned. His fool nephew was already offering him promotion to the position of sergeant. Sergeant Pip! It sounded terrible.

"Where did you find the wolfling?" Brid asked Pip as she gently examined his arm.

"The trappers had her, only they weren't trappers," Pip started to explain.

Hal suddenly swung round at Pip's words. It was too much of a coincidence that these men, who had been trapping wolves in the Torra Altan Boarchase, had come to the very depths of Trows Forest. They had to be all part of the same band that had attacked the princess and her escort.

Pip tugged at Hal's leg, gesturing that he wanted to whisper something. Hal dropped down beside him. The boy's peppercorn-dark eyes flitted past the soldiers, who were dragging away the trappers, and rested on one who sat on his horse, watching intently. He wore Belbidian livery. "Master Hal, I saw him in the wilderness. That soldier, the one with the very long legs that's too big for his horse. I saw him in the wilderness of Vaalaka, talking with the trappers."

Hal noted the soldier, imprinting his face in his mind. He knew he could do nothing about the man until they crossed safely back over the borders of Belbidia. He could not safely accuse his own countryman in front of the Ceolothians for fear of repercussions to the rest of the Belbidian troops. He turned to Pip and merely said soothingly, "You're tired and sick. Don't trouble yourself with anything."

Brid bound Pip's arm with fresh bandages, administered the juice from some crushed herbs and stroked his brow. Sleep quickly overcame him.

Hal was relieved by Brid's presence, aware that she had lifted much of the responsibility from his shoulders.

Together they watched as the two trappers were bound and placed on the backs of their own horses and led away.

"We can't risk another ambush. We shall have to be more vigilant over the princess," Hal began then wished he hadn't spoken.

"The princess! Your precious princess!" Brid flashed him a look full of anger and resentment and glowered at the yellow scarf around his neck.

Hastily he pulled it off. "And Talorcan?" he returned. Their moment of peaceful reunion was over.

Ceowulf tapped him on the shoulder and nodded towards Caspar. The youth was standing over Princess Cymbeline's horse, examining the hide that had been ploughed into red furrows by the lequus. He was prodding at his crooked nose and then searching the shadows anxiously. Withdrawn into himself, Caspar looked lost and alone.

He looked up at them, his deep blue eyes almost black with fear. "Have I caused this? What Keridwen warned has come true. I visited Necrönd and let the creatures from the Otherworld slip across the divide." He stroked his hand over the unmoving flank of Cymbeline's horse, raising a cloud of buzzing flies. "Even the Great Mother cannot forgive me."

Hal patted him affectionately on the shoulder. "We shall be home soon; Morrigwen, Keridwen and Brid will find a solution."

Brid smiled down at the wolfling cradled in her arms. It squeaked and gave her a slurpy wet lick with its long pink tongue. "All will be well, Spar. We have found the wolfling as Morrigwen wished and the Trinity will hold strong. Whatever magic the Great Mother has blessed it with must lead us now to my successor." She kissed the soft white head of the orphaned cub and then turned her gaze on the wan little girl who clutched at her leg.

Fern was hopping about in agitation. "All this fuss over a wolf. A wolf! It's wrong. It's bad. I must get home to Sorrel. When is this herd moving homewards? Why won't they hurry? We must go."

The strangely garbed archer strode over to the little man and took his hand. "We're going home right now," he said comfortingly in his heavily burred Torra Altan accent. "So stop making a fool of y'rself."

Hal nodded towards the archer. "Who's that?" he asked Caspar as his kinsmen extracted himself from his gloom and held out his hand to the golden horse.

Caspar gave a wry smile. "Abelard the archer—"

"Bowman to the baron," Hal finished the line of the well-known ballad and laughed, thinking that his kinsman was joking.

"I want to go home," Fern wailed again.

Hal looked towards Brid. "And so do I."

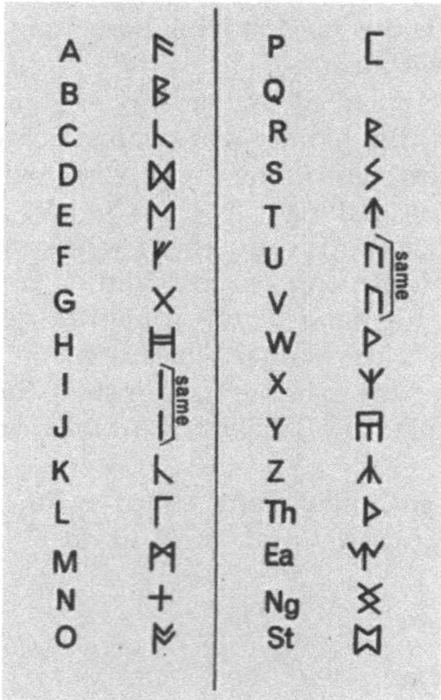
A
B
C
D
E
F
G
H
I
J
K
L
M
N
O
same
P
Q
R
S
T
U
V
W
X
Y
Z
Th
Ea
Ng
St
same